SEEDS OF GREATNESS

Jon Canter grew up in Golders Green. He studied law at Cambridge before becoming a TV and radio scriptwriter. Among the comedians he's worked with are Clive Anderson, Rowan Atkinson, Dawn French, Stephen Fry and Hugh Laurie, Lenny Henry, Mel Smith and Griff Rhys Jones, and Arabella Weir. He lives in Suffolk with his wife, the painter Helen Napper, and their daughter Nancy. *Seeds of Greatness* is his first novel.

JON CANTER

Seeds of Greatness

VINTAGE BOOKS
London

Published by Vintage 2007

2 4 6 8 10 9 7 5 3

First published in Great Britain in 2006 by
Jonathan Cape
Random House, 20 Vauxhall Bridge Road,
London SWIV 2SA

www.vintage-books.co.uk

Addresses for companies within The Random House Group Limited
can be found at: www.randomhouse.co.uk/offices.htm

The Random House Group Limited Reg: No. 954009

A CIP catalogue record for this book
is available from the British Library

ISBN 9780099492849

The Random House Group Limited makes every effort to ensure
that the papers used in its books are made from trees that have been
legally sourced from well-managed and credibly certified forests.
Our paper procurement policy can be found at:
www.randomhouse.co.uk/paper.htm

Mixed Sources
Product group from well-managed
forests and other controlled sources
www.fsc.org Cert no. TT-COC-2139
© 1996 Forest Stewardship Council
FSC

Printed in the UK by CPI Bookmarque, Croydon, CR0 4TD

For my mother-in-law
Barbara Napper

1

That's All We Have Time For

I've got a life but it's not my own. It belongs to Jack Harris.

How did it come to this? I'll try to answer the Big Questions, the ones we all ask at the end of the story when we look back to the beginning:

A) What happened?

B) Why me?

C) Who am I anyway?

We're pupils at Golders Hill Primary School. I'm eight. Jack is eight and a half. At the end of the day, we walk to the bus stop and get a number 2, 13 or 28 to the stop at the top of Hodford Road. Jack takes the short walk home up the hill while I, because my father isn't as rich, take the short walk home down the hill.

One day, two stops early, Jack says, 'Let's get off here'. No explanation is given or asked for. Eight-year-old boys don't explain.

Jack jumps off and I follow. He leads me down an alley to the side of Golders Green Station. Through a window, we see a moustachioed man washing up in the kitchen of a restaurant.

Jack taps on the window. The moustachioed man opens it. Jack says, 'Got any chips, mate?' The moustachioed man is not surprised. He must have met Jack before.

He disappears and returns with a hillock of chips on a square of greaseproof paper. 'Thanks, mate,' says Jack. He makes the 'mate' sound matey.

I watch Jack eat the chips. He doesn't take his eyes off them. He eats the long thin crispy chips and their short thin brothers, till all that's left are the black-eyed chips and the ones shaped like capsized boats.

'Go on,' he says, thrusting these runt-chips at me.

I eat them. I never expected chips at all. They're a bonus. Then we walk home. We don't have enough money to take another bus.

We get home late. Every day for the next three months, we stop off at the window and get home late. Eventually, our late arrival becomes the norm. It's no longer considered late.

That first day, I tell my mother we had to wait a long time for the bus. She believes me. She knows I wouldn't do anything to upset her. And Jack's mother believes him, because Jack is with me and I'm a good boy who does nothing wrong.

But I know how wrong all this is. Jack's demanding something for nothing. And he's getting it. This can't go on.

After three weeks, Jack asks the moustachioed man his name. It's George. A week later, he asks George where he lives. Finsbury Park. Six weeks later, a joke: 'That's a big moustache, George. What do you keep in there? Haven't got any chips in there, have you?' George laughs.

Here we see the nascent chat show host (though Jack will come to abhor the term and insist on 'talk show'). He's made George laugh. He's made George feel like a guest.

Jack smiles at the cleverness of his joke. I say nothing. On the way to the window, not two minutes earlier, I'd wondered out loud if George had any chips in his moustache.

2

I'm not asking you to feel sorry for me. I'm just saying. I understand that I made my remark to Jack off camera, as it were. I didn't say it to George, under the lights, where fame is won.

I'm not bitter. Jack earned that laughter. Look how he treated my comic conceit. He didn't just say 'Have you got any chips in your moustache, George?' No. He worked up to it. First stage: 'That's a big moustache, George.' Second stage: 'What do you keep in there?' Fractional pause before the leap to the punch line – 'Haven't got any chips in there, have you?'

The hop, the step and the jump. The comic triplet. Jack, at eight, understands.

Then he says, 'Listen, George, if you ever need any furniture, you talk to me, OK?'

George nods. He's an immigrant from Cyprus. He has four daughters. He has a budgie. (This much we've learned, over the months, thanks to Jack's precocious hosting.) There is every evidence that George's life is hard. But now it's easier. If he needs any furniture, he has an eight-year-old to talk to.

George turns his head to talk to someone behind him. We walk off with our chips.

Next day, as we walk to the window, we see that George isn't there. We wonder if it's his day off, though George hasn't had a day off since we met him.

There's an angry man at the window, a bald man. He opens the window before Jack can speak. 'It's finished, all right? No more chips. Just piss off out of it.'

Jack walks away, without demur, then turns to me and says, 'I can't do business with *him*'. It's a phrase he's learned from his father, Danny Harris, a pioneer of flat-packed furniture in the United Kingdom.

Jack is not a loser. The bald man's the loser, deprived of the chance to supply Jack with chips, in exchange for nothing.

I don't contradict Jack or question his conclusion. No, Jack can't do business with the bald man. Now George, him you could do business with. Those were the days.

I can't sleep that night, not for hours. I hear my parents' footsteps on the stairs, their bedtime tooth-brushing, the slam of their door. I think about George and the wrong that we did him.

I know the bald man is – was! – his boss. For three months, George dispensed the chips with impunity. Then yesterday, I know, I'm sure of it, the bald man entered the kitchen at just the right (wrong) moment. He saw George at the window dispensing free chips and fired him.

Now, nearly forty years later, I think of George in his Finsbury Park house. The four daughters weep downstairs. What will become of them? I see the foodless budgie, belly-up. I see George, staring at his eyes in the mirror, illuminated by the bathroom's bare light bulb.

He shaves off his moustache and puts it in a brown manila envelope. He licks and seals the envelope and writes his wife's name on it. He stands on the edge of the bath and ties the light flex round his neck. He jumps. The light goes out.

Years later, his widow watches *The Jack Harris Show*. 'That's him!' she hisses at Sting. 'Don't talk to him! He killed my husband!'

Next day, as we pass the restaurant on the bus journey home, I wonder out loud where George is now. Jack shrugs. It's over. He doesn't care.

That's why Jack grew up to be Jack and I grew up to be me.

That's why I'm his biographer and he's my biographee.

Two weeks ago, I left the bookshop in Yoxford, Suffolk, in order to write the biography. Everyone was there: Tim the owner, my co-workers Rose and Lydia, suppliers, printers, wholesalers, favourite customers, local authors. (Am I a 'local author' now? It sounds inferior to the real thing, as 'local wife' does to 'wife'.) I'd worked in the bookshop for fourteen years.

In my leaving speech, I remarked on the changes I'd seen. The coffee was better. The quality of the books was much the same. But their posture was different. When I started, they were all vertically aligned on shelves, side by side, like sentries. Now half of them were piled horizontally on tables, face up, like stacks of sunbathers.

It didn't go well. The whole thing was too written, too literary. When you say it out loud, on a Friday evening, to people who don't mind you but want to go home, nothing happens. What would Jack have said, had he worked in this bookshop instead of being on televison? Something like: 'I love reading. Reading's my life. My wife's had SHAKESPEARE tattooed on her back so I can read Shakespeare in bed.'

It's just not me. That's all I can say. But it is me, isn't it? It's me imagining what Jack would have said. If I can put those words in his mouth, why can't I put them in my own?

I can't remember what I said after 'sunbathers'. I wasn't listening to myself. I was thinking that my 'stacks of sunbathers' simile didn't really work. Sunbathers are never in stacks. It's a nonsense. You can't sunbathe with a sunbather on top of you.

At the end of the party, I stood by the door. One by one, the suppliers said 'All the best, Dave!' and I replied 'Thanks!' and hoped they'd supply their own name.

Then Rose and Lydia approached. I dreaded this because I wasn't sure if I was meant to kiss them. In their different ways, they're unkissable. Rose is an unmarried woman in her fifties. She's had breast cancer. She plays the violin and writes letters for Amnesty International. She gardens at the local hospice. It's stated clearly on her face that she doesn't need the kisses of men to give her life meaning and value.

Lydia, by contrast, is so kissable that a man like me daren't even shake her hand, for fear he'll end up as footage on regional TV news. *David Lewin, 48.* That's what the reporter's voice will say as you watch me walk to the Crown Court building.

In the year we've worked together, I've done everything in my power to avoid her. If she's in Fiction, I'm in War. This is absurd, of course. The Yoxford Bookshop is the size of a 'living room full of books', in Tim (its founder's) loving phrase. Everyone in the shop is unavoidable.

Just a few weeks earlier, I see Lydia table-stacking Jack's charity *Crack-A-Joke* book (of unfunny jokes he'd neither written nor read but charitably lent his name to). 'God, it's Jack!' I say. Wouldn't you? Of course you would. When you see an old friend's photo on the cover of a book, you shout out his name, as I did.

'Oh, it's "Jack", is it?' says Lydia.

'He's been a friend of mine since I was six. I didn't say it to impress you.'

'Well, you succeeded.'

And here she is now, with Rose, come to say her goodbyes, which are redundant since we live in a small town, a town of hellos and more hellos, till you die or leave – and why would you leave, since the landscape is beautiful, the sea is close, and the property prices are mercifully lower than London's?

'I can't imagine you making any money,' says Rose.

Uncannily, that's what Jack said to me when I left school. But Jack said it as a compliment. To me and to himself. He was telling himself he'd make a packet, unlike me.

I say nothing. What can I say? I'm in my late forties and I've risen to no rank. My contemporaries run multinationals; they invade countries.

6

I look at Lydia, across the abyss that divides us. I study her like an archaeologist admiring a Roman coin. *The naked midriff dates this girl as early twenty-first century.*

'What exactly will you be writing?' she says, with more contempt than curiosity. I swear her belly turns up its button at me.

'I don't know,' I reply, though I know exactly. I can't say I'm writing the authorised biography of Jack-is-it Jack. It's too boastful and too unlikely.

All I've said is, I'm going off to write a book. No wonder they're contemptuous. We work in a bookshop. There's no need for my book. There are plenty already and more on the way. It's like working in an undertakers and saying that you're going off to die.

Lydia, gorgeously cruel, cruelly gorgeous, hands me the last two undrunk bottles of sparkling Australian wine. 'Here, take them. You might need them.'

These aren't a leaving present. These are provisions. One day, she's implying, they'll be all I have.

I learnt how to barrack the television from my grandmother, Ida. We watched films together when I was a boy, afternoon films from the Thirties and Forties. Even before the film started, Ida started, tut-tutting loudly at certain names in the opening credits.

Then, when these names came to onscreen life, in the form of Leslie Howard, perhaps, or Jean Harlow, she'd tut-tut even louder. 'Dead now,' she'd say.

Dead now, dead now. As a four-year-old, I used to wonder if that 'now' meant Leslie and Jean might come back to life later, like Jesus, the Jewish man in the stories that weren't meant for Jewish boys like me.

7

Jack is dead now, so he's ripe for biography. But what qualifies me to be his biographer, apart from my being alive?

Caroline Bliss, as so often, has the answer.

Caroline Bliss wanted Tim because he was the coolest guy in his year, with his black curls and his eloquent silences. For Caroline Bliss, at that point, cool was cool. Ten years later, when rich was cool, Caroline Bliss married a rich man. Then she divorced him. She craved wealth and power. There's no going back.

We're students at Cambridge. It's 1974. Tim speaks once or twice a week, only on cool subjects. He never mentions washing-up, acne, socks, work. We sit around, me and Caroline Bliss and Tim, in the terraced house Tim and I share in The Kite, the coolest district in Cambridge, with rugs on the windows in lieu of curtains. We're listening to a double live album by the Grateful Dead, with Sally Jakes (dead now) and Alan Mitchell (Minister Of Transport).

Tim remarks that Dead albums don't have sides or, if they do, the sides don't matter. You can't prefer one side of a Dead album to the other, because the joy of their music is its sidelessness.

Caroline Bliss nods. She's meticulously careful not to express her own opinions, since she knows her function is to be Tim's chick, which involves making Earl Grey tea and being beautiful and never saying anything heavy.

Then Tim, who is a joint ahead of us, makes his second remark of the week, observing that he doesn't know anyone who believes in God. I nod. Sally and Alan nod. But Caroline Bliss just can't bear it any longer. She's repressed them too long – her ambition, her intelligence, her aggression, her Head Girlishness, and now they burst out of her like the alien in *Alien*.

'You can't become Prime Minister if you don't believe in God.'

I look at Tim who looks away. Embarrassment, that least cool emotion, makes him study the back of the double live album, assuming he accepts that Dead albums have backs and fronts.

'It's true,' says Caroline Bliss. 'One day we're going to leave here and make our way in the world. We're not going to be sitting around listening to music when we're thirty.'

Thirty! Caroline Bliss wants to be Prime Minister by *thirty*.

That night, Tim and Caroline Bliss don't sleep together. They never sleep together again; though she does, eventually, marry Alan Mitchell.

Alan, as befits a Minister of Transport, runs several miles a day. He plays squash with the Prime Minister and wins. He tried losing, apparently, but the Prime Minister shouted, 'Don't you patronise me, Alan! I patronise you!'

The day after Jack's funeral, Caroline Bliss rings me at the bookshop to invite me to her office to talk about 'a project'. She's the editorial director of Maypole Books, A Division of Something Nasty.

I've worked for Hackney Council and in language schools and lately, as we know, in a bookshop. But I've never had a 'project'. I've taken the idea of the gap year, that interval between school and university when you don't have to do anything or be anyone, when your function is to wait and hope and enjoy and earn a bit of money, go to New Zealand, work for Oxfam, make friends, read, gaze, love music, reflect – I've got drunk on that notion and absorbed it into my bloodstream. I've had a gap life. That is why I'm free to meet Caroline Bliss the following afternoon. I only work half a day on Wednesday. Even my week has a gap.

I sit in Caroline Bliss's office with her assistant, Sarah, waiting for Caroline Bliss. Sarah and I exchange pleasantries. After half an hour, I fear I've no blandness left in my body. I ache for an unpleasantry. But it won't come from me. I'm still the nice person I was by the restaurant kitchen window, as will shortly be confirmed.

In she comes, the opposite of me, a powerful, successful, perfumed woman. She signals that she has little time by not sitting down. She starts: 'You're the man for this, David. You're nice and you'll keep it light.'

Already, I'm struggling to keep up. She's missed out the beginning. She's not defined the 'it' that must be kept light. This conversation? This office? The light?

Caroline Bliss looks me in the eye and tells me all about myself. I've written articles, I've written radio plays, I've worked in the book business, I was a friend of Jack for forty years, I was the last person to see him alive. I'm the man to write his authorised biography. She and his widow, Rita, have decided. That is the 'it'.

'Jack was a much loved man. Let's not knock him. There's been too much knocking of celebrities lately. If we carry on knocking celebrities all the time, people won't want to be celebrities any more. Just keep it light and funny and touching and we'll all have a big success. Can you do it?'

Sarah writes down everything Caroline says, nodding muppetly. She's a sarah in the Young Publishing Army. Many of her fellows will fall along the way. In this building alone, in the next twelve months, they'll probably lose two sarahs, a poppy, various kates. But Sarah will survive. She knows what has to be done: agree with Caroline Bliss.

Do I agree, though? I didn't come here seeking authorised biography. I've had authorised biography thrust upon me. I'm only an approximation of the writer she describes. *I've written articles.* I've written four articles for the Nottingham-based Bob Dylan fanzine, *Clothes Line*. Maybe two hundred people have read them. And that makes me happy. I only want them read by the few who love Dylan as much as me. Success would be a failure. *I've written radio plays.* Ten years ago, Helen William, who works in BBC Radio and knows Caroline Bliss, asked if I was interested in writing a radio play. I said I'd love to write a play about Matisse and Picasso. She said she'd love to see it when I wrote it. I didn't write it and didn't write it. On the first anniversary of our meeting, she sent me a cake to celebrate the non-play's first birthday. That, of course, was it. A play can be bad or good; it's a matter of opinion. But a cake is a cake. I only had to not-write for one more year and I'd get another cake.

'Yes. Thank you. I'll do it,' I say.

'Great,' says Caroline Bliss. She opens the door of her office and shouts at a faraway lucy: 'Lucy! Can we have some coffee in here? You're a star.'

And, yes, Sarah writes that down. I swear I see her hand move across the notebook. She's wise. One day, she might ascend to Caroline Bliss's position. It is good she knows well in advance how to order coffee successfully. She should note that Caroline Bliss doesn't say please. Instead she gives praise. She says *you're a star.* But of course the words boomerang back to her. She's saying, in effect: *I'm a star.*

She gives me nine months to write it. I'll earn twice as much in that nine months as I would working in the bookshop.

Emerging from sleep, I feel Jess's hand on my back. Her thrillingly chilly thirty-four-year-old hand. Fourteen years younger than my hand. You mightn't think Jess young. But I do. I can't believe my luck, even now, even after we've been together three years, including that mercifully brief separation after she abandoned me on the road.

11

We don't live together. Jess is a painter. Her studio is in the garden of her parents' house, about ten miles away in Great Glemham. She stays there two or three nights a week. But the rest she spends in my two-up, two-down cottage in Yoxford. We are the two who go up and down.

'You're making progress.' That was the last thing she said to me, before she fell asleep. I thought her remark might be a cue for sex. It does, after all, suggest movement. But she chose sleep. We've not had sex since Jack died. It will return, though. It always does.

If you're a man over forty-five, unmarried, childless, not quite living with your girlfriend in your low-ceilinged cottage, you're gay. Aren't you? Admit it. Gayness, sometimes considered a problem, is in your case a solution. It solves the problem of who you are.

I'm not gay, though, and even if I were, I don't think I'd have the courage to be so. I think I'd repress it, deny it, withhold the information. Especially from my mother. I don't care how clichéd that sounds. My mother is depressed. She's in a psychiatric hospital. I can't tell her I'm gay (which I'm not, incidentally). I don't want to tell her anything she'll have to 'cope with'.

In my half-awake dream state, I picture the scene. It's four years hence. Jess has abandoned me for good. I've become gay, out of disappointment. I know that's not politically or psychologically correct. But there you are. And there we are, by my mother's hospital bedside: me and Magnus, house manager at the Theatre Royal, Norwich. (This is a dream, remember.)

Magnus doesn't want to be a secret. I understand his point of view. So here I am, introducing him to her as Magnus, the man I love and live with. I say it loudly and proudly and immediately, so there's no confusion; so she doesn't think, here's my son and some man who's going to give me pills.

Her brow furrows. She shakes her head. She speaks falteringly. 'You love a man,' she says. It's not a question, just a re-statement of something she doesn't understand. 'No, I love Magnus,' I reply. I'm trying to make a point here. It's not Magnus's manliness I love but his Magnus-ness. Just as, if I'd brought her a black woman (which is far more likely, of course, what with my not being gay) and she'd said, 'You love a black', I'd say, 'No, I love Susan'. (Note how that name doesn't suggest a skin colour, by the way.)

My mother cries. And Magnus, poor man, cries too. He doesn't cry because he's hysterical or over-sensitive. That's a fundamental misunderstanding of the house manager's job. If there's a fire in the theatre, or an audience member drops dead, Magnus wouldn't go into immediate action and burst into tears. He's unflappable.

No, the reason Magnus is crying now is exhaustion. He knows what's coming. An hour and a half of explanations, recriminations, repetitions, black-as-night tea which no milk can weaken, hospital biscuits, old and tired and sad: mad people's biscuits.

Last week, when we visited Mummy, I introduced Magnus as the man I loved and lived with. The week before that, I introduced him as the man I loved and lived with. The week before that, I introduced him as the man I loved and lived with.

Mummy – and this is not her fault – has developed senile dementia. Every week, she forgets she's met Magnus before. Every week, I have to come out to my mother.

By this time, Jess's hand has warmed up. The dream's over. I'm awake.

'How you going to start the book?'

'With the title,' I say. That sounds sarcastic, so I soften it. 'I'm going to spend the day on the title. Not the day maybe. The morning.'

What's my testicular cup-size? 4B? I feel as if I've never found a 4B ball-bra that lifts and separates, supports and warms, so comfortably as Jess's palm.

That morning, I decide to call the book *Jack Harris*, which has a simplicity and directness I like. Then I decide to call it *A Life of Jack Harris*.

I can't define the distinction between *Jack Harris* and *A Life of Jack Harris*. But if I were a bookbuyer – which of course I am – I'd more happily part with my money for *A Life of Jack Harris* than *Jack Harris*. I'd assume that *A Life of Jack Harris* would be deeper, broader and draw more conclusions about life and Jack Harris. Some Puritan gene would tell me it was more deserving of my money.

Now my creative juices are flowing, they can't be easily staunched. I decide to go for a title that doesn't mention Jack by name. That shows confidence. What about a phrase that sums up our shared knowledge of Jack? Jack was on television. We all know that. So: *That's All We Have Time For*. Yes, I like that. It says something, I think, about the transience of the medium and the permanence of death.

But, sooner or later, I find it trite and arch.

Since Jack's appeal was his chutzpah, I think of *Jack The Lad: A Life of Jack Harris*. But the repetition of *Jack* is irksome. I revert to the simple *A Life of Jack Harris*.

After two or three hours, though, I come to hate its false modesty, so very un-Caroline Bliss. This is not *A Life* I'm writing. This is *The Life*. This is the only life of Jack Harris you'll ever need.

The Life of Jack Harris, then. That maddens me too. Like *A Life*, it says nothing about its subject, other than that he's dead.

The Life and Death of Jack Harris. Yes! Something urgent has entered the title. Reportage, a hint of conspiracy theory, the whiff of the grassy knoll. But that's exactly what she doesn't want. It's not light or funny or touching.

I call Sarah and tell her the book's called *That's All We Have Time For*. Sarah rings back to say that Caroline Bliss loves it and she loves it and everyone loves it in the office, which is open-plan to make love spread faster.

All I have to do now is write it.

I begin my research by visiting Jack's brother Marcus at his home in Leicester.

On the train – I still haven't passed my driving test, which is one of the reasons Jess abandoned me that day, on the road to Westleton – I feel nervous as a kitten. It is, after all, my first day in my new job. I'm now a biographer. No – a Biographer. That's better.

If a woman drops dead at the end of the compartment, and the other passengers crowd round, uncertain what to do, I can say, 'Let me through, I'm a Biographer,' and write about her life.

Jack's with me, in spirit. Today, he's giving me professional advice, since I'm travelling to interview his brother and Jack was an Interviewer, famous for it.

The first rule, he told me, is Always Pretend To Be Interested. The second is Never Ask a Question To Which the Answer Can Be Yes or No. The third is Ask Something They've Never Been Asked. ('How much do your breasts weigh?' – a question he put to both Cher and Peter Ustinov.)

I start to feel sick about four hours short of Leicester, which is to say, the moment I leave my cottage. The sick feeling never goes away, Jack said, no matter how many times you say *hellogoodeveningandwelcometotheshowwe'vegotagreatshowlinedupforyoutonight*. Always, an hour before, you're overwhelmed by the need to vomit, defecate and masturbate. Your best hellos, your best fantastic shows, are achieved by going out on stage in a state of hyper-need. Then the show itself becomes your unstoppable satisfaction, your uber-splat, your vom-def-gasm.

I haven't seen Marcus since his father's funeral. I ask him to tell me about himself. This is not Biography, you understand. This is small talk, designed to put him at his ease. Then I'll go in with some questions. All Biographers do it like this. It's standard practice.

Marcus lives in a detached house in Bushby, which he bought two years ago for six but is now worth seven-five. He's an Independent Financial Adviser, married to Anita, who does garden design. They're members of the local synagogue and keep a kosher kitchen. They have two children, Harry and Michael. Harry is doing Business Studies at Leicester University. Michael is studying Information Technology at the University of Leicester.

(Apparently, the University of Leicester is what they used to call Leicester University; Leicester University is what they used to call Leicester Technical College. On the other hand, because I'm staring at a painting of Three Sad Clowns on the wall above Marcus's head, because I feel closer and closer to puking and shitting, but curiously far from orgasm, it could be that the University of Leicester is what they used to call the University of Leicester.)

I put my portable digital recorder on the table.

'Shall we start?' I say.

'Yes,' he says.

It's the last time I'll ask him a question to which the answer can be yes.

'What's your first memory of Jack?'

There's a long pause. But I can edit that. (You don't even need to know about it.) Marcus sinks into the sofa, as if regressing.

'I don't think I have one.'

'Course you have!' I reply, encouragingly.

'Maybe I've forgotten it.'

I try harder.

'No! You can't forget your first memory of your brother. You can suppress it, you can lie about it, you can recoil from it' – I'm on a roll now, a vom-def-gasmic roll – 'but the one thing you can't do is forget it. By definition, you can't forget the first thing you remember.'

I've tried too hard. I've gone too far. I sound like the sharp, investigative author of *The Life and Death of Jack Harris*.

'Why don't I give you my second memory?'

I lower my voice, look into his eyes and pretend to be interested.

'OK then.'

'He fell out of his high chair trying to steal my teddy.'

'Right,' I say. 'That's good. Thank you.' I don't know what to say. I could ask him his third memory. I could ask him how much his breasts weigh.

'Do you have any memories that are light and funny?'

'Falling out of his high chair was funny.'

An hour later, after carefully saying nothing very much, he concludes our discussion with an observation fit to end a Biographer's career: 'He was my brother. What can you say?'

I know that his dullness has been hard-won. He's had to distance himself from his famous brother, through contentment, through conventionality. There was only room for one teddy-stealer in their parents' house.

Don't confuse his dullness with inoffensiveness, though. He said that to me, he really said it, that stuff about buying it for six a couple of years ago and it now being worth seven-five. Did he not stop to think that my cottage might be worth no more than his garage?

I buy ten raffle tickets for his favourite charity, LJEC – Leicester Jewish Elderly Care. It's the price of getting out of his house before it rises further in value.

The following day, I visit Sylvia, Jack's mother. I go via my own mother's psychiatric hospital in Middlesex, which is hardly en route. I can never think of it as en route anywhere. It's too terminal for that.

I want to give her my *naches*. If Jack was defined as a boy by his *chutzpah*, I was defined by my *naches* – the word for the joy a boy brings his mother by being appointed an Authorised Biographer.

'Good journey?'

'Yes thank you, Mum.' In my forties, I'm still polite to my mother. It's a way of avoiding anything impolite, like the facts. Or, rather, the fact – her presence in this place is the only fact.

The consultant, who's prescribed lithium and a course of ECT, has decreed she's too old and vulnerable to undergo psychotherapy. The dredging up of memories might cause her pain. And to what purpose?

The purpose would be autobiography. He's denying my mother the chance to work out her true story.

It may go something like this: 'I married my husband because he was a decent, clever man who asked. I had a daughter then,

18

much later, a son. For the last forty years of our marriage, my husband didn't want me. And I didn't have the things I wanted, because he never became as rich as I would have liked.

'I was profoundly unhappy. But I enjoyed going to Wigmore Hall concerts and Bergman films at the Everyman Cinema, Hampstead. I was delighted by my children's academic achievements. I repressed my unhappiness till now, when it's too late to do anything about it.'

It would relieve both of us if she said some if not all of this stuff. But instead we have tea. Then more tea. Then it's time for tea. After tea, tea arrives. In this place, even the tea is incontinent.

And here come the mad people's biscuits on a milky-green plate, of the milky-green plateness unique to jumble sales, charity shops and hospitals. The plate alone makes me want to cry. I pick up a shortbread, limp as an old man's cock. I put it back.

My mother's voice is soft and tremulous. She's still pretty, in her sadder than sad way, and she still wants everything to be poetic, to chime with her sensitivity.

'It must be beautiful in Suffolk now,' she says. She says it every time. 'Yes,' I say, as I always do. To what purpose would I disagree? If a serial killer ran amok in the farm shop, I wouldn't change my story.

'Listen,' I say. 'I've been appointed the authorised biographer of Jack.'

It's *appointed*. That's where the *naches* is. Distinguished men and women, with grey hair and half-moon glasses, have appointed me. They've unanimously agreed I'm 'tremendously able'. They've granted and bestowed. They've entitled me to wear an Authorised Biographer's gown.

The concept, I'm afraid, eludes her.

'What?'

'I'm going to write a book about Jack.'

My mother tut-tuts, as her mother did.

'Oh dear. That's a lot of words.'

Sylvia's old people's home is a converted rectory in Elstree, Hertfordshire. All rectories are converted in Hertfordshire. This is footballer countryside, rector-free. What is a rector, anyway?

In the windows are silk flowers in huge Greek-style vases. What else do you put in the windows of an old people's home? Skeletons? I'm energised by the vases' kitsch, an antidote to my mother's fading radio of a life.

I enter and sign in. They ring her room and let her know I'm coming. I walk up the stairs. The smell of concealment is everywhere. Flowers, air fresheners, bleach and ammonia conspire against the odours of the old.

Jack, who of course will never be old, said the place his mother would most like to live was a lavatory in Florida.

Jack paid for his mother and a friend (usually a Mrs Pearl) to holiday all over the widow-friendly world. But wherever Jack's mother went, Miami or Madrid, it was of the lavatories she spoke. 'This is a wonderful hotel, Jack,' she'd say. 'The lavatory's as big as the room.' He once told me he was flying his mother to Rome to 'visit the Sistine lavatory'.

I walk down the corridor. Each room has a TV with the sound turned up and up and UP! It would be deafening, if you could deafen the deaf.

'Sheena May' blasts from the room on my left. 'BBC News' from the right. Finally – boom! – 'Washington'.

Sheena May. BBC News. Washington. This was what did for Jack, at the end. The rhythms were predictable, the guests interchangeable. Sheena News. BBC Wash. Mayington. Sheena Wash. Beingbee News. Mayceeton.

I rehearse my smile and fix it on my face.

I knock on the open door of Sylvia's room. (All the doors are wedged open, for emergency's sake.) Mercifully, the television is off and her ensuite bathroom door is shut, sequestering all odours.

And there she is, slumped in a chair by the window, old-person style. Sylvia Harris. It's over twenty years since I've seen her. Though it's unmistakeably her, I'm shocked by the lavender wisp of her hair, the concave cheeks, her shrunken frame.

I pull up a chair very close to her. I take her right hand in both of mine. I say, 'How are you?' (This is what I do with my mother.) Then, because of that association, 'My mother sends you her best regards.'

Though not, technically, true, it could be. They were never friends. But they're over eighty. They have a bond. Being eighty is like being eight, when your parents say, 'Go and play with Jonathan. He's eight too.'

Sylvia smiles. The eyes remain, while everything else falls away. Filmy, yes, but the vibrancy shines through. I feel tearful. This is my friend's mother. The worst thing that can happen to a person has happened to her. She's alive and her child is dead.

I'm not sure she recognises me. I say, 'I'm here to talk about your son.'

'That's nice,' says Sylvia. 'Is he coming to see me?' For a moment, I fear the worst. Then I remember she has a living son too. Marcus.

'No, I meant your other son.' (I can't bring myself to say her dead son's name to her.) 'I'm writing a book about him.'

'Oh,' says Sylvia. 'Why are you doing that?'

I want to laugh. The question is so direct and unexpected and so redolent of the Sylvia I remember, fighting her way through life, not frightened (unlike my mother) to say the obvious, earthy thing.

'So many people love him.'

'Really?' she says.

'Yes,' I say. 'Of course. He always had something special, didn't he, right from the beginning.'

Sylvia smiles. She blooms. I feel my confidence growing. For the first time, I believe I can do it. I can write a light, funny, touching book about my much-loved dead friend.

'Tell me what it was like at home, when he was growing up. Do you remember lots of laughter?'

'Oh yes.'

Damn! I've asked a question to which the answer can be yes.

'But he struggled to please his father, didn't he?'

'We all struggled to please his father.'

In a soft voice: 'Why do you think that was?'

I feel her soften in return.

'You know what men are like. They want it all their own way. They don't want to listen to your troubles.'

That's perfect. It's touching and insightful but not dark. It makes you smile. It's very *That's All We Have Time For*.

'Did you know when he was growing up that he'd make his mark on the world?'

She considers this.

'Shall we have some tea?'

I'm not fazed by this. In fact, I turn it to my advantage.

'If you answer my questions, you'll get your tea, I promise.' (Firm but fair, I've acquired, already, a professionalism of which I thought myself incapable.) 'Did you know when he was growing up that he'd make his mark on the world?'

'He always had a head for business.'

Yes. Just as she, his mother, always had a vulgarity my mother disdained, drawn as my mother is to Higher Things.

Who else but Sylvia would describe television stardom as a business? Jack, were he here, would agree with her. A business whose product was himself.

I hear her lavatory flush. She has a friend in the lavatory. Of course she does. It's the only place to be.

I have to seize the time before the friend emerges to distract us. I have to ask the dead son question.

I think of Sheena May, whose face I don't even know. Sheena May in a war zone. Sheena May with the parents of the rail crash victim. She does her job.

Sylvia needs to tell her story, just as my mother does. Unlike my mother, Sylvia has the chance. She wants to, I'm sure. It's a sign of health. Sylvia needs and wants to tell me how she felt. As a mother. As an elder of the tribe. There's touching-funny and touching-sad. The book needs both.

'How did you feel when your son died.'

'My son died?'

I hear the tap running in the bathroom.

'How can he have died? I spoke to him this morning.'

I have to hurry now.

'No. Your younger son. He died two weeks ago.'

'No!'

She emits a sound that's neither a cry nor a scream. A high, keening sound.

Her friend rushes out of the bathroom.

'What's the matter? Tell me!'

Sylvia covers her face with her hands. Tears ooze through the gaps between her arthritic fingers.

A nurse enters, alarmed by the noise.

'I'm so sorry', I say to the nurse. 'I was talking about her son. I thought she knew he was dead. She's forgotten.'

'What are you talking about?' asks the bathroom-friend, sharply.

I look at her. The bathroom-friend is, unmistakeably, Sylvia Harris. More unmistakeably, it must be said, than the crying woman I've been talking to.

The nurse gives the crying woman a tissue.

'Calm yourself, Mrs Pearl.'

'Oh for fuck's sake!' I say, unhelpfully. I don't intend to say it, just to think it. It's a moment of Tourette's.

'It's all right, Miriam,' says Sylvia. 'Your boys are fine. He thought you were me.'

'I thought you were Sylvia, Mrs Pearl,' I add, redundantly. Then I make it worse by adding: 'Your sons are alive.' As if I have the power to a) end their lives and b) bring them back again, in a dead-now-but-not-later fashion.

'He told me my son was dead,' says Mrs Pearl.

'You're all right now, Miriam,' says the nurse.

'I'm so sorry,' I say to Sylvia. 'How are you?'

'How am I? What are you talking about, how am I? Look what you did to her.'

'I'll get her some tea,' I say.

'She doesn't want tea. You want tea, Miriam?'

Mrs Miriam Pearl shakes her head. Of course not. She doesn't want tea. Not now. Now, for the first time since she moved into the home, she doesn't want tea.

I know, as I leave Sylvia's room, that I can't write *That's All We Have Time For*, the authorised biography of Jack Harris. I can't write the book I've been paid to write. Not writing it will have terrible consequences. Jess will leave me. But Caroline Bliss won't have me killed. She's far too proactive for that. Whatever she wants done to me she'll do herself. I can't think about that. I'll think about it in seven months, when *That's All We Have Time For* is due.

What matters now is the truth. 'Tell me the truth, Dave,' Jack said, the night he died. (I didn't, of course.) Rita, the widow, and Caroline Bliss would not want me to tell you the truth. That, I suspect, is why they hired me. Yes, I know my subject. And, yes, they believe I can write. But mostly they believe they're powerful and I'm malleable and discreet. They believe I'm a nice man. But what kind of man in his forties is nice? He can only be nice if he's weak-willed or blind to his nature. Or an authorised biographer, paid to dissemble.

And what about you? Would you buy the authorised biography of Jack Harris? That 'authorised' guarantees you won't get what you want. You want the truth. You want the truth because it's noble and enlightening and brave and true. And filthy. It's got everything.

There's no biography without filthy truth. Bring on the prostitutes. Shower me in cocaine. The only exceptions are biographies of foods, currently in vogue. Sugar, say, or salt. Fish. You're not looking for sexual tittle-tattle when you buy *The John Dory Story*.

But you won't be buying this book at all. It can't be published, not while anyone named is alive. People have feelings and lawyers to express them.

What is it then? It's our dirty little secret. It's a long postcard to be sent to people I know and trust to keep it to themselves: Tim, the ever-present; Geoff and Ruth Bergman; Sol Kleinmann; Helga and Steffi Schreiber of Munich (? address); Janet the cook; Helen William, in lieu of the radio play; Lloydie, who told me

I'd never get anywhere till I wrote about my mother; Charlotte, Michael, Michaela, Sue, Rhys, Sarah the Princess of Darkness, Rob, Matthew, Hugh, the three Jos, Clever Trevor, Spanish Angela, Murray (loving friend and loyal under-achiever), Crag and Cindy.

This is a wonderful feeling. How many writers start a book, knowing the names of their readers?

I dedicate this book to my mother, who'll die without telling her story. That won't be my fate. For this book, as is already plain, is as much about me as Jack. This is the story of Jack and me. There'll be bits about me but all those bits will lead to bits about him. I'm not a fool. I know his famous life is more interesting than mine.

A first novel, they say, is always autobiographical. Why can't a first biography be autobiographical too?

2

The Early Years

Jack was born in 1954 but so were a lot of people. (No one would pay me to write that. I can get away with anything now.)

Danny and Sylvia named him John, English as you like. As a little boy, he changed it when he heard people refer to John F. Kennedy as Jack. That's the first thing Jack ever said to me – he had the same name as 'the King of America'.

Danny, who fled Nazi Germany in 1936, was born Emmanuel Wachsler. He became Daniel Harris in 1940, not to sound less Jewish but, with vicious irony, to sound less German.

Danny was famous, like his son, but only for a day. The day was Sunday August 4th, 1968, when Polly Nicholls's interview with him was published in the *Sunday Times* colour supplement.

As research, Polly had bought a 'Baker Street' flat-packed Dining Chair from the DHF – Danny Harris Furniture – range.

'Danny Harris looks at me with a wary, watchful eye. He is very attractive for, frankly, a rather ugly man. When I tell him it took me over an hour to assemble the chair, his reply is typical: "So sit on the pack". I pursue him – does it not say ASSEMBLES IN MINUTES? Mr Harris is un-fazed. "What's an hour but a lot of minutes?"'

Danny understood that his customers weren't readers of the *Sunday Times* colour supplement.

Danny Harris was a loyal husband to Sylvia for twenty-five years, except when he wasn't. 'No one knows your father like I do,' Sylvia told Jack, often. Was that why Danny never left her? Or was that why he didn't always want to be with her?

When Danny Harris died, Polly came to the funeral at Golders Green Crematorium. She still had a perfect, Quant-style, black pageboy bob, which she told me she maintained with daily ironing. She went on to tell me everything, without my asking. Even at nineteen, I was discreet and malleable. She could unburden herself to me while I, in return, would not unburden myself to her.

He sent her flowers on her birthday, long after their affair was over. He was a gentleman. After you, no, after you, my dear. Champagne and roses. Would the lady care for some dessert? Breakfast in bed in the Hilton, Oslo, where Danny is meeting his timber wholesaler.

'He put me on a pedestal, it was wonderful,' said Polly. 'I suppose it was so he could look up my skirt.'

Danny's face, in my memory, is more sad than ugly. He wanted bad news, unlike my parents, who only wanted good. In fact, he greeted me with 'Hello, David, what's the bad news?' It was a pleasure to give it him.

'I failed my driving test, Mr Harris.'

'You failed your driving test?' – this repetition not an ethnic verbal tic but a ploy to give him time to work out his response.

'You failed your driving test? Your mother will be thrilled. Less crashing.'

Danny was a successful man, haunted by melancholy, self-loathing, secretiveness and rage. Maybe that was why he and Jack fought so viciously. Danny was trying to prevent his son turning into him. He knew the pain of being him and didn't want his son to suffer it.

Danny Harris didn't know what 'condiments' were.

We're thirteen, freshly barmitzvah'd, in our first year at Highgate Senior School. Jack and his parents have come to dinner at our house, for the first and last time.

My father, Philip Lewin (born Philip Levinsky) offers Danny a pre-prandial glass of sherry, though he himself doesn't drink.

The youngest of nine, the first in his family to go to university, my father is a barrister. His father was a draper. His mother took in washing. He grew up with nothing and now he puts on a bowler hat and goes to his chambers in Lincoln's Inn, where he drafts opinions on arcane aspects of shipping law, which is all of them. He reads political biographies and works of military history, eschewing fiction, which he dismisses as 'whodunnits and who-slept-with whom'.

Despite Danny's wealth – no, because of Danny's wealth – my father regards himself as Danny's intellectual and moral superior. At my father's funeral, there will be no mistresses; only QCs with arrogant eyes and ferocious eyebrows, looking like elderly eagles. They'll shake my hand and tell me my father had 'a first-class mind'. Only now do I realise this is barristers' code for: 'He could have been as successful as me. But he lacked my charm.'

I prefer to think of my dad not as charmless but shy. He forces himself to be extrovert, adopting chummy golf club mannerisms, such as calling men of his age 'Old Man': 'Can I offer you a glass of sherry, Old Man?'

Danny takes the glass and says, 'Not so much of the old!' My

29

father chortles unconvincingly. Danny's obvious remark confirms his oft-repeated verdict: Danny's a 'rough diamond'.

My mother, Leah, is more ambivalent. Proud as she is to have married a Professional Man, she struggles hard to contain her jealousy of Sylvia's fur coats, which my dad could never afford to buy her. She takes refuge in what she calls 'the higher things in life'.

Danny and my dad, having nothing to say to each other, listen to the women talking. Leah tells Sylvia she recently saw 'the most marvellous *Traviata*'. She knows that Sylvia knows nothing about opera. She's finding things they don't have in common and expounding on them.

Sylvia, a big woman (bigger than her husband), loves show tunes. My mother considers this embarrassing.

Here they are then, my parents, lording and ladying it over Jack's.

Jack and I, trapped in an adult lounge, wonder how long it's going to be before the meal is over and we're released to go to my room and listen to records. Soup. Chicken. Fruit salad. Surely that can't take more than an hour. The less our parents talk, the faster they'll eat. Their awkwardness is painful – things are going well.

We sit down to our meal, which Leah wheels in on a golden trolley.

'Don't slouch, Jack,' says Danny. Jack sits bolt upright. He unslouches to an absurd extent, like a kangaroo in headlights.

Sylvia says to my mother, to cover the soup-slurps, 'You must be thrilled David got a scholarship.'

'Oh yes,' says my mother, 'we are. He's such a good boy.' She ruffles my hair. To be called a 'good boy' in front of Jack is a butcher's knife to my still-growing penis. And the ruffling of the hair, what's that? It's a flourish. It's the butcher tossing the penis-stump to his dog.

Jack looks deep into his soup. Any moment now, his parents will say something about him. Something jovially hurtful: 'The day Jack gets a scholarship, there'll be a national holiday!' Something unfunny like that. Then the adults will laugh, in that adult way, where they all laugh though they know it's not funny.

Jack's parents say nothing. I feel sorry for Jack, who always seems older, more worldly than me but now looks childlike and vulnerable.

Then I understand why his parents are quiet. Jack's mother is waiting for my mother to say something nice about Jack. Jack's mother, after all, has just said something nice about me. That's what adults do. They trade insincerities.

But my mother doesn't say anything about Jack. 'It's an excellent school, marvellous facilities for theatre and music,' she says. She pronounces theatre 'thar-ar-tar'.

She says nothing about Jack because she thinks Sylvia's insulted her. (I discover all this later, when I hear my parents fighting in the bathroom while I'm 'asleep'.)

According to my mother, 'You must be thrilled David got a scholarship' means 'You must be grateful because, unlike us, you're poor.' My father brushes his teeth far longer than necessary, so he doesn't have to respond. He married my mother for her prettiness and style. She looked up to him, this scholarly suitor a dozen years her senior. He wasn't prepared for her disappointment.

At the dinner table, Sylvia gives up waiting for my mother to talk about Jack. Instead, she does it herself.

'Jack, after dinner, why don't you show Mr and Mrs Lewin your card tricks?'

Jack can't look at his mother. He can't tell her why he can't show my parents his card tricks. There's no beginning to his reasons and no end.

'If he's not doing card tricks, he's climbing trees,' she continues.

No. Please. No. Don't suggest that, after dinner, Jack shows my parents his tree-climbing.

No one speaks for longer than is socially acceptable.

'Delicious soup,' says Danny, finally.

'Isn't it! Pass the condiments, Old Man,' says my father.

'Pardon me?'

'The condiments, Old Man.'

Danny looks blank.

'The condiments!' urges Sylvia, who's never heard the word either. For all she knows, the condiments are next to the traviata.

Danny scours his end of the table for something that might be condiments. His face pinkens. He puts his hand on the handle of the water jug. 'This?'

'The condiments!' My father's voice is loud now. He's exerting his authority over the younger, richer, less educated man.

Sylvia stares at the flowers for some time. Condiments? But why would my father need flowers?

Then she sees the what-must-be-condiments, so close to Danny's plate that, in his panic, he hasn't seen them. She passes them to my dad.

Danny is as angry as I've ever seen him. He struggles to maintain that secretive, melancholic expression the ladies find so intriguing.

'You couldn't say "salt and pepper"?'

The condiments sit in a tripartite silver container, consisting of three pods and a central stem. One pod for the salt, one for the pepper, one for the mustard. So it's entirely in character for my father to point out: 'There's more to "condiments" than salt and pepper, Old Man. "Condiments" includes mustard.'

'"Condiments" includes mustard.' It's a stunner. Note the

singular verb-ending. It's not condiments plural that 'include' mustard. It's the singular collective noun – 'condiments' – that singularly includes the mustard.

'You're going to put mustard in your soup?' says Danny, his face so red it seems to be on fire.

My father says nothing. His lips pucker in a form of silent amusement. He's signalling to my mother and me that he can't debate with Danny Harris, because a rough diamond can't pursue a line of argument as a barrister can. The rough diamond resorts to emotion. He grandstands. Judges don't like that.

I can't look at Jack and Jack can't look at me.

'Keep your elbows in,' says Sylvia to Jack, creating a diversion. Adults are clever like that.

On Yom Kippur, the Day of Atonement, our families meet in the foyer of the synagogue. Not meet exactly – coincide. Danny gives my father a nod that's not even cursory. It's several degrees short of cursory, just stronger than non-existent.

But me Danny smiles at. 'Hello, David. What's the bad news?' I know what he's thinking. The bad news is, I'm the son of my father.

Jack takes me to one side: 'What you doing later, Dondiments? Wanna go to the park?'

Every year, on Yom Kippur, at the end of the morning service, we go to Golders Hill Park, to kill the achingly long hours between the morning and afternoon Service. Yom Kippur is a day-long fast, the holiest day in the Jewish year, which is like your year but more painful.

Without meals to look forward to, eat, recall, expel, 'fast' is a misnomer. I reply: 'Yeah. I don't know why they call it a fast. It's more like a fucking slow.'

Jack laughs. We're thirteen, we laugh at this. It's not my job to make the joke funnier than it was. And, yes, I did say 'fucking'. I want to sound older. Jack's voice has broken and he's felt a girl's breast. I know, because he gave me his hand to smell and I didn't know what sort of thing to say, or what sort of thing to smell. (When I'm a student, I'll say 'fucking' not to sound older but to sound more working-class. Alan Mitchell will laugh out loud when I say to the barman in the Baron Of Beef: 'And some fucking cheese and onion crisps, mate.')

We go in for the morning service.

This story, this bio-autobiography, this protest . . . it's going to get less Jewish as Jack and I get older. Let's deal with the Jewish issue now, as we'll never feel more Jewish than we do on this Yom Kippur, 1968.

Jack and I don't confuse our religion with God. In fact, though we've been to Hebrew classes every Sunday for five years, we couldn't tell you anything about Him.

He's Jewish, of course. Who else but an immigrant would dream a dream like His? The *chutzpah*, the *meshugene* braggadocio, the manic over-achievement: in six days, He creates Heaven and Earth. And then He rests. He spends time with His family. Family's what counts, you can hear Him saying, in that immigrant pioneer tone, manly-sentimental.

He's a Jew and an American, God (born Godnick), which explains everything. But He's not on our radar, as a deity, not like Barbra Streisand.

To boys like us, Judaism is a Godless belief in scholarship (me), business (Jack), *chutzpah* (Jack), anxiety (me), Rosh Hashanah, Yom Kippur, the Marx Brothers, arguments, hard work, jokes (you're not telling it right), Frankie Vaughan, Helen Shapiro, the

34

Shabbos prayer for bread, the Shabbos prayer for wine, Arthur and Jonathan Miller, Brian Epstein (dead now), chopped liver, remembering the Holocaust but giving young Germans a chance, handbags, Miriam Karlin, uncles, *mishpocheh* (distant family – uncles-in-law, say), David Kossoff, Sydney Tafler, the State of Israel, fear, fur, gloves, our parents, smoked salmon.

The belief in our parents can't be overstated. It's their nature and nurture that have made us Jewish. I'd never have been Jewish if I'd been brought up by wolves.

In the park, Jack scuffs his shoes kicking leaves, earth and conkers. He gets bored. He always gets bored, which is one of the reasons he's no good at lessons. Nowadays, he'd be diagnosed with Attention Deficit Disorder; whereas, in 1968, he's 'thick'.

Jack decides to climb a tree. I'm reluctant. I don't want to dirty the turn-ups of my suit. As a compromise, I climb to the lowest branch. Jack stops several rungs above me. He's a jungle boy, Jack, quick and decisive with his foot and hand-holds. He doesn't look down.

Don't think I don't know what you're thinking. 'Oh, I get it, the tree-climbing stuff is a metaphor. One boy climbs up to the sky. The other is almost grounded. How deep. How symbolic. Thank you, Mr First-Time Biographer.'

I'm sorry but you can piss off. Seriously. Every moment of your life, your actions express your character and destiny with brutal directness. Do you think we don't know all about you from the way you say hello, the way you walk, your answer-phone message? It's all there, always.

Yes, the tree stuff is pure *Reader's Digest*, nauseating in its folksy simplicity. But don't blame me. Just because a thing is simple doesn't mean it's not true.

Jack suggests we walk to the Golders Green Road. He wants to buy the Jim Reeves single, *Distant Drums*, which is number one.

I tell him we can't do this. Work is forbidden on Yom Kippur and shopping is classified as work. Jack says that shopping can't be work or people would get paid for it.

If eating on Yom Kippur is murder, buying a record is more like not paying your fare on the Underground. It's the kind of bad thing a good boy does.

On our way, we pass the restaurant from which Jack procured our free chips. It's changed hands. It's Italian now.

I tell him I can't pass it without thinking about chips.

'Come on then,' says Jack. 'I'll buy you some chips'. He enters the restaurant. I remain outside. He comes out and asks me if I'm coming in or not. Then he goes back in.

I don't want Jewish passers-by to see me loitering outside a restaurant. Would I not be less conspicuous if I were inside?

I walk a few paces and loiter outside a shoe shop. Look, Jewish passers-by, this is me outside a shoe shop, with my back to the window. Not only am I not shopping, I'm not even looking in the window.

I go into the restaurant, because Jack is in there and I want to be with him. Otherwise I have no excitement in my life and, ultimately, no book. Otherwise I have no story.

At first, I don't see Jack. Then I hear him calling from a table in the window. I sit down. I turn my head swiftly as my parents' friends the Lightstones stroll past, outside. Did they see the back of my head? Could they be sure it was me? Would they pick out the back of my head in a wrong-way-round identity parade?

I ask Jack if we can sit at a different table, as it's cold by the window. He's gracious.

He calls the waiter over and asks if we can move. The waiter says, 'Of course, young man!' He indicates an empty table at the back. (All the tables are empty. It's twelve o' clock on a Tuesday. And it's Yom Kippur.) Jack gives him a ten shilling note. Jack gives the waiter a ten shilling note. For indicating.

I read the menu. I say nothing about the ten shilling note. Eventually, Jack can't stand it. 'It's a good idea to tip heavily. You get better service.' I nod.

'Have what you like. It's on me.'

Only then does it occur to me I have no money. Why has Jack got so much money? He doesn't even do a paper round. It must be because his father gives it to him. Danny wants his son to learn how to handle money just as, when Jack's fifteen, his parents will go to Brighton for the weekend, leaving Jack alone in the house to lose his virginity to a girl called Erika, whereas my mother would have stood on our doorstep with a broom to scare Erika off.

The confusion in Jack is palpable. He wants to shock his father but be like him. 'It's a good idea to tip heavily' aren't the words of a thirteen-year-old. This is a father speaking through his son. This is ventriloquism.

The waiter returns. 'Slow day,' says Jack.

The waiter grins, professionally. 'It's nice when it's quiet!'

His voice is loud and full of false cheer. 'So, gentlemen, what can I get you?'

Why was the waiter gone so long? Was he phoning the Chief Rabbi? Jack orders the kidneys. The waiter looks at me. I think about saying 'Nothing for me.' I order a salad because, as everyone knows, a salad isn't food.

'You want chips!' says Jack. Then, to the waiter, 'Bring him some chips!'

The food arrives. Jack complains to the waiter that his kidneys are 'overcooked'. He bisects one with his knife, exposing a pinkish tinge. 'Look, it's bloody.'

'You mean "undercooked", sir.'

Jack, the little big man, stares at the waiter with the full force of his ignorance.

'What am I, a chef? Take them away and bring them back when they're different.'

Half an hour later, coming out of the record shop, I burst into tears. It's what my mother would want, this proof that I'm a sensitive boy who appreciates the Higher Things in life, who knows when he's done a Lower Thing.

'They'll smell the food on my breath!'

Jack, touchingly, doesn't mock me. He takes me into the chemist shop next door.

Back in the park, at the water fountain, he hands me the toothbrush and toothpaste. Like salad, like kidneys, they've been criminalised.

I brush ferociously, to obliterate the lettuce and potato blood. Then I offer the brush and toothpaste to Jack. He makes a face. 'I'll be OK,' he says. He leans forward and, with delicacy, sniffs the air around my face.

'I can't smell chips,' he says.

'Can you smell toothpaste?'

'Definitely,' Jack replies. 'Your mouth smells clean as a whistle.'

'That's no good then, is it!' I say, with my superior intelligence. 'Why would my mouth smell of toothpaste unless I'd been brushing my teeth?'

'You have been brushing your teeth.'

'Yes. So my parents will know I've been eating!'

Jack feels belittled. 'I'll see you in synagogue,' he says and walks away. Then he turns round and punishes me with his generosity, as he'll do much later, when he's much richer and can hurt me more.

'You don't say thank you? I bought you lunch!'

I kick a heap of leaves, in anger. It's unconvincing, as my anger often is. (Even now, Jess says I mistime my anger, fatefully delaying it till it's no longer relevant. As a consequence, it seems self-dramatising and ineffectual.)

The leaves fly up. I bend down, pick up a leaf and chew, till my breath smells leafy. It feels biblical, this punishment that's also a cure. Someone, surely, somewhere in the Bible, spake unto someone and bade them eat the dead leaves of the tree.

In the synagogue, my father and I chat amiably. If he does smell leaf, so what? A leaf isn't food. I'm a Jew, not a caterpillar.

A dozen rows away, Danny Harris sits with his dull son Marcus and Kidney-Breath Jack. Jack doesn't say a word to them. He breathes through his nose. He immerses himself in his prayer book, rocking back and forth like a mega-Jew at the Wailing Wall.

In the synagogue foyer, at the end of the service, Danny Harris takes me aside and asks, without humour:

'Is Jack all right? I'm worried he's got religion.'

'No, Mr Harris. I'm sure he hasn't.' He nods. I am a good boy, a parent-pleaser. I would not tell a lie.

Jack is with me and I can use him, as I did an hour ago, when the phone rang and a voice sing-songed: 'Hi, it's Sarah, how's everything going, just thought I'd check in, see how you're doing.'

I hunt for the meaning of this. Sarah, Sarah. Damn. It's Sarah of the sarahs.

'I'm doing great,' I lie. 'I'm excited,' I say, thinking of Jack with his head in that prayer book displaying, ironically, a supreme belief in himself. He knew he'd get away with it. He had faith. He's the boy on the cover of the self-help bestseller *You Are Your Own Religion: Believe!*

'We're excited too,' Sarah says.

'You're not as excited as I am,' I say. Sarah folds.

'Caroline Bliss is very concerned we get lots of celebrities in the book.'

'Of course she is. Me too.'

Sarah gives me a list of the celebrities Caroline Bliss wants in the book. I don't recognise one of the names and ask Sarah to repeat it. 'You know,' she says. 'The model with the tits'. And so, when she says the next name, Nelson Mandela, I think, 'The man with the prison'.

The model has tits. Nelson has prison. Huge prison. Are her huge tits real? Was his prison? Were his twenty-five years in prison inflated, the better to draw attention to himself? In any event, Jack interviewed them both. They have a right to be in *That's All We Have Time For*.

Caroline Bliss, I'm sure, can't wait for the launch party. It will be all the excuse she needs to write a note to Nelson, requesting his presence for sparkling white wine and canapés. The poor man had no canapés for twenty-five years.

At Jack's house, a few weeks after Yom Kippur, my leaf-sucking career gathers pace.

At the end of Sunday lunch, we retire to the black leather Chesterfield sofa which dominates the Harris living room. (The house is devoid of the flat-packed furniture that financed its purchase.) The deep pile carpet is the colour of milky coffee. There's a coal-effect fire so big it makes you want to ring 999. A marble table with gold legs displays Sylvia's collection of marble, teak and ivory lions and tigers, fashioned by craftsmen for people with terrible taste.

My mother has good taste, which isn't the opposite of Sylvia's terrible. It's more like no taste at all. The creams, browns, beiges and apricots of our living room are designed to be classily neutral. The statement they make is inaudible. But that's better than saying the wrong thing, like Sylvia.

Danny gives me and Jack cigars. 'A good cigar's better than a woman,' he says. I've never heard of 'a woman' before. Instinctively I know my mother and sister and cousin Judith aren't 'women'.

Along with the cigar, he hands me an implement. Jack sees me holding it gingerly, takes it from me and, in senior partner style, shows me what it's for. It's a cigar-circumciser.

Sylvia comes in with a tray of coffee. 'You're spoiling them,' she says. 'They should learn,' says Danny.

Nothing like this happens in my family. My father's ill-at-ease with displays of sensual pleasure. He's teetotal, not out of moral conviction, just fearful that alcohol will cloud his first-class mind. He's a bastard for bitter lemon, though, my dad, a fool for it.

The previous Sunday, on a cultural day trip to Canterbury, he leads us nervously into a pub for a 'drink' before lunch, since this is appropriate day trip behaviour. We're a Jewish family assimilated enough to admire a cathedral, inside and out, before repairing to a hostelry. Maybe the landlord will call my dad 'squire'.

He marches us to a table by the window. We sit there, drinkless, as he remarks on the antiquity of the beams and fittings. He tries to seem relaxed. I've never seen my father in a pub before. Finally my mother says, 'Well? We're thirsty.'

He raises his hand, as if hailing a taxi, and calls to the girl behind the bar: 'Miss! May we order some drinks?' Does he not know how a pub works? Or does he think he belongs to an elite for whom it works differently?

Not wanting to be unworldly or superior, like him, I inhale the cigar. 'Don't inhale!' says Jack. Danny laughs. 'He won't do that again, will you, David!'

'No,' I splutter, as Sylvia rushes out and rushes back in with a glass of water. 'Stupid,' she says to Danny. 'They're thirteen years old.'

'It's a nice smoke,' says Jack. 'Not too hard.'

I've no idea what he means. I suspect he doesn't either. But Danny nods, approvingly.

'Where d'you get them then, Dad?'

Danny turns to Sylvia. 'We bought them at Oslo airport, didn't we, at the duty free, remember?'

This is Danny as Sunday God-husband and father, dispensing largesse, resting, wallowing in his own well-being. 'We got this there too, didn't we?' he adds, pouring Sylvia and himself glasses of brandy. 'I'll spare the boys the cognac. They got to have something to look forward to!'

'I've never been to Oslo,' says Sylvia. She knocks the brandy glass off the table with the back of her hand and leaves the room, slamming the door.

Danny, clearly, shouldn't have forgotten that Sylvia wasn't in Oslo. I don't know why that's made her so angry.

The men (us) puff on their good cigars, saying, as is traditional, nothing. Danny looks mournful. Then he says, 'You can do what you like. But you mustn't get caught.' I don't know if he's talking to himself or us.

Sylvia returns, with carpet shampoo. Silently, vigorously, passive-aggressively, big Sylvia attacks the stain.

'Don't worry about it,' says Danny, suing for peace.

'You're going to worry about it, are you?' says Sylvia, from her kneeling position, with fury.

He should have taken her to Oslo, no question.

'How are your parents, David?'

'They're fine thank you, Mrs Harris.'

'Still going on their archaeological trips?'

'Yes,' I say. Then, sensing more is needed from me, to change the mood for the better: 'Next month they're going to St Albans. The former Verulamium.'

This is good stuff. It must be, because Sylvia smiles: 'That's nice.'

'Why don't you go upstairs and play records?' says Danny. We go upstairs and play records, leaving Sylvia and Danny to their silence.

Peace will break out when Sylvia decides. Not before. Then they'll carry on and on and on. Marriages are characterised by a dogged determination to see the thing through. This is a society of survivors. Danny and Sylvia Harris have escaped from Nazi Germany. Marriage, schmarriage. They've survived worse things than marriage.

A week later, on the 210 bus that takes us from Golders Green Station to Highgate School, Jack shouts down the aisle to Galton-White, a boy in my class who's sitting on his own. Galton-White always sits on his own.

'Hey, Galton-White!' Shouted, Galton-White's name sounds even more unlikely.

He turns and looks sternly at Jack, thick Jack Harris, who doubtless has something thick to say. Jack indicates the cleft between Galton-White's eyebrows. 'I see you've got a new spot, Galt.' It's true. Cyclops-style, Galton-White has developed a custard-and-pink third eye between his official ones.

'Don't point it at me when you squeeze it, Galt. Splat-kerpow!'

Galton-White stares at me before turning wordlessly away. I try to look as pained as he does. I certainly don't snigger, though Jack accompanies the splat-kerpow! with a not unfunny mime of his face imploding as he's zapped by a soft bullet of Galton-White pus.

For Galton-White's sake, I'm trying to distance myself from Jack. It's a disingenuous project. I sit next to Jack on the bus every morning. I'm Jack's friend and audience. If anything, my presence makes him worse.

What does his presence do to me? It makes me seek out Galton-White later that day. It makes me nice to him.

I'm nice. Jack's not so nice. That's clear. Everyone at school knows that. But what does niceness mean and where does it end?

I ask Galton-White if he's going on the Hendon and District Archaeological Society trip to St Albans. (Professor Galton-White, his father, is the chairman.) He isn't but he's pleased I've asked. I tell him I'm not going either and give him my reasons. This not-going to St Albans is what we have in common. I try to make it last.

Years later, as a first-year student at Cambridge, I make an unsolicited call on Galton-White in his room at Queens' College. He is, of course, working.

I remark amusingly that he has a 'very solid view'. (His room looks out on a brick wall.) I add that, as a mathematician, it must inspire him to be in the same seat of learning that spawned Isaac Newton and Wittgenstein. (Since when does a 'seat of learning' 'spawn'? Why am I there, seeming so interested?)

He nods. The top button of his shirt is done up. That infuriates me. Is he going to be like this for the rest his life? The answer is, yes, but that's only a matter of weeks. He takes an overdose at the end of his first term.

A month afterwards, I get a letter from his mother, thanking me for all the kindness I showed James at school and Cambridge. James! I never called him that in his life.

Nastiness like Jack's didn't do for James Galton-White. It was all in the letter: 'In our last phone call, James told me he felt himself an unworthy successor to Newton and Wittgenstein'.

So, it was me then. Me with my unsolicited visit, my 'interest', my concern for his intellectual welfare. Thick Jack's nastiness he could dismiss, he could rise above, but the kindness of David Lewin, fellow undergraduate, academic high-achiever – that hurt. I compared him with giants and made him feel like a pygmy.

Jack wasn't pretending with Galton-White. He genuinely didn't give a shit. I was trying, very hard, to be nice. Anyone who tries that fails. It's just being kind to be cruel.

Next morning, as the bus goes up the hill to Highgate, Jack unwraps a piece of chewing gum from its silver wrapper. It looks like a strip of cream-coloured lino from a doll's house corridor. He offers the gum to me and I say no. This is our ritual. Jack always gets out chewing gum at this point in the journey, just so he can walk into school in breach of the rules: 'Chewing, Harris!'

We get off the bus. As we pass Galton-White (dead now), he turns and sees us. Jack covers his face and ducks manically, in putative fear of spot explosions.

We cross the road. Jack says: 'My dad screws around.'

Why now? Where's this come from? What's the link with Galton's spots?

The school buildings loom. There isn't much time. We don't see much of each other inside those buildings.

'How do you know?'

'He was in Oslo with his bit on the side.'

I want to be part of this. I want to be as grown-up as Jack.

'Does he still think a good cigar's better than a woman?'

'What?'

'He said a good cigar was better than a woman.'

'What you talking about?'

Jack's not impressed with my man-talk. It sounds lightweight after his. I throw myself on his mercy.

'Why's a good cigar better than a woman, then?'

'It's not.'

'Oh.'

'Nothing's better than a woman.'

He says this with such authority that I clam up. We're a few yards from the gates now.

'It's OK if you don't get caught.'

'I remember.'

'What d'you remember?'

'I remember your dad saying that. When we had the cigars.'

Jack warms to his theme.

'You got to be careful out East, though. Oriental fanny can knock your middle stump out the ground.'

'Does that mean your parents will get divorced?'

'No. He's a man. It's what men do. Mum knows that. See you.'

'See you, Jack.'

People think of Jack as shallow because he was a television personality. He asked shallow questions of his smiling, laughing, self-promoting, two-dimensional guests.

But Jack wasn't a television personality. He had a television personality, certainly, he couldn't have survived without one. But the more this television personality thrived, the more awards it won, the more money it made, the more it was in the papers, the more Jack clung to the secrets that gave him, in his view, the depth that makes for a personality that can't be switched on and off.

Jack, the day of the dad-screws-around revelation, seen from afar at lunch, spooning his unwanted plum crumble into his neighbour's jacket pocket – Jack, even then, has a depth and maturity to which I can only aspire.

At thirteen, I don't have secrets, proper secrets, involving sex and betrayal. I have no revelations about my parents' private lives.

Do my parents, in fact, have private lives? It hasn't occurred to me to wonder.

That night, I study their faces for private-life potential. My father, this intellectual snob, this cerebral man is, if nothing else, my father. I'm evidence, no, proof of his sexual prowess. Esther, my sister, is too.

Esther's nine years older than me. I feel like an only child with a sister. What does the gap signify? Have my father and mother had sex only twice, with an eight-and-a-quarter year gap? That's how it looks to a thirteen-year-old.

From my midlife vantage, I can picture those intervening years: my father retreating to his study, night after night, to work on his next erection, assuring my mother that something of this kind, a magnum opus, cannot be hurried. He leafs through his bound copies of *Shipping Law Review*, looking for an article, a letter, a Ship of the Month, that might fire his erotic imagination.

As for my mother, there's no chance. That Oslo night, she reads Daphne du Maurier by the gas-effect fire, listening to the pre-war Schumann recordings of Dame Myra Hess. Is it sexual disappointment that's propelled her to Higher Things?

Within my earshot, she's talked about sex once. A few days earlier, Esther, home from Essex University, all frizzy left-wing hair, has tried to convince her that women are entitled to orgasm. (My father is safely out of the room. And my young presence, far from inhibiting Esther, spurs her on.)

My mother's wary. 'If a woman enjoys sex, she gets a taste for it. That's the problem.'

'For godsake, Mum, it's your only life! Sheila and I have orgasms all the time.' I tomato. I beetroot.

'Pas devant l'enfant,' says Mum, as if I'm not second in French behind (of course) Galton-White, le garçon qui va mourir.

Now, at last, I have a secret. On the bus, in the morning, I could tell Jack that my sister Esther's what I, in my ignorance, call a 'queer lesbian'. But Jack won't care. That has nothing like the power and weight of his father Danny's heterosexual, adulterous Euro-screw.

When Jack finally meets my sister's partner Sheila, at my father's funeral, he asks me why she has to be so ugly. I find this offensive. But offensively true. It's only what I've always and offensively thought.

Why has my sister lived for thirty years with an ugly woman? It upsets me to think there was a political component in Esther's object choice. The heart's not theoretical or correct. You can't say, 'In theory I love you'.

It's not as if Sheila has pretty feet or nice ears; nothing. And the worst of it is, her ugliness encourages my mother, from her psychiatric hospital bed, to continue believing that her only daughter Esther 'hasn't met the right man'.

As Jack said, when he saw Sheila: 'Your mother needn't worry. She *is* the right man'.

We're fifteen now. Jack looks more and more like a Jewish gypsy. He has a hook nose, an absolute you-got-a-problem-with-that kosher conk which, when he's got lots of money, he'll do absolutely nothing about. You have to salute him for that.

He's six inches taller than his father, who's told him to stop growing as they can't afford bigger beds. Jack sleeps in the foetal position. He can never be sure when his father is joking.

His mouth and eyes are playful, ready for laughs, pronounced. They look like they're on the point of leaving his face. I have a photo of us, taken at Marilyn Joel's fifteenth birthday party. It looks as if our features are going in opposite directions; his, out into the world, and mine, in on myself.

This is not to say he's always extrovert. Jack can out-introvert anyone. He can be in a room and absent himself at the same time.

He sits with his head perfectly still. He fixates on a point on the wall. Then he raises his right thumb and forefinger and, in the manner of a crane, lowers them precisely onto the roots of a few strands of hair growing out the crown of his head. He twirls these strands round and round, round and round, round and round, round and round. Always the same strands. The same clockwise corkscrew.

During these round-and-round interludes, Jack can't be contacted. His personality's hibernating. Yet he still dominates the room.

Here's one of me, dancing with Marilyn. But it's Jack in the background, alone on the sofa, you look at. What's going on in his mind?

Yes, that's the question. What goes on in Jack's mind?

I have to be more American. When confronted by that vast enclosed space – the inside of a person's head – American biographers do what Americans do so well. They invade.

What is Elvis thinking on the morning of August 4th, 1962, when he wakes at 6.48 in Suite 891 of the Las Vegas Hilton?

That's how it starts.

As he gets out of bed and walks toward the bathroom, he probably allows himself a smile of satisfaction at the reception afforded his most recent movie, Follow That Dream, *which has reached number five on the box office charts. As Elvis deposits a four-ounce, three-and-three quarter-inch nutbrown stool in the aqua green twenty-four inch deep American Standard Toilet at 6.51, he may well cast his mind, wistfully, in the direction of Marilyn Monroe. It's destined to be Marilyn's last twenty-four hours on earth. Is Marilyn, just 249 miles away in her Brentwood home at 12305 Fifth Helena Drive, thinking about Elvis too? Is she thinking, you're the only man in America who can understand what it's like to be me?*

You turn the page, hoping it's over. But the page-turn's just a lull between bombardments:

At 9.53 Eastern Time, which is 6.53 for Elvis and Marilyn, John F. Kennedy arrives at his desk in the Oval Office at the White House, 1600 Pennsylvania Avenue, NW Washington, DC 20500. Is the six-feet two inch 35th President longing for Marilyn? At 6.54, as Elvis opens his three-and-a-quarter inch by two-inch mouth to eat the first of the day's fourteen cheeseburgers, is he thinking that JFK's the only man in America who can understand what it's like to be him? At this moment in history, are Elvis, Marilyn and JFK thinking about each other? Can it be true? It can. We are the witnesses.

Let me try.

Jack is in the school changing room, before the Heathgate House v Southgate House football match. He's in a crowd of boys, alone.

He doesn't know I'm watching him. He takes off his jacket, shirt, tie, vest, trousers, socks and pants. (Is this a bit gay? No matter. Let's keep going.) He hangs them on his peg. He side-foots his shoes under the bench.

He puts on his shirt and shorts and socks. He sits on the bench and ties the laces of his boots.

He stands, turns and stares at his peg. He ruffles his hair with his right hand, as if the peg is an imaginary mirror. Then something troubles him. He plucks at his shirt with his thumbs and forefingers, loosening it. Then he un-tucks it completely and lets it hang outside his shorts.

Is Jack thinking about football? No. Is he thinking about girls? No. Is he thinking about himself? Yes. Jack believes that if he thinks about himself enough, the girls and the football will follow. They'll arrive at his feet.

Jack thinks all the time about getting attention. He can't do it by being outstanding at Latin or English or History or Woodwork, traditionally the subject at which thick pupils excel.

Jack's subject is himself. He gets attention by being outstanding at being himself.

He's thinking that the shirt-outside-the-shorts works for him in many ways. It marks him out from the other players. It makes a particular footballing statement: I am talented, I am elegant and I do not get my due. (Shirt-outsider Glenn Hoddle, born October 27th, 1957, capped only 53 times for England, is the exemplar here.)

Best of all, it's against regulations.

As Jack walks out of the changing room and approaches the pitch, he's thinking he will shortly have an altercation with Mr Blakeley, the housemaster.

Jack thinks a lot about petty regulations: how to contravene them and get away with it, how to sail close to the wind of them and, as here, how to expose their fatuous nature.

Jack is thinking that a shirt altercation with Mr Blakeley, in front of his fellow players, will make him look heroic and Mr Blakeley small-minded and foolish.

Sure enough, from the touchline, Mr Blakeley shouts 'Harris! Shirt!' Jack thinks, yes, this will happen just as I hoped. It does.

JACK: (faux-naif) What about it, sir?

BLAKELEY: Tuck it into your shorts, boy.

JACK: Will that help me play better, sir?

BLAKELEY: Just tuck your shirt in!

JACK: Can I take it out if I score the winning goal?

BLAKELEY: Do you want to put me you in detention, Harris?

JACK: I just want to score the winning goal, sir.

There's a pause, which is all Jack needs. Jack's thinking: I've won. For the sake of the team, the House, the ethos of the school, nay, the Empire, Mr Blakeley must be seen to support his scoring the winning goal.

BLAKELEY: (reluctantly) Yes. Now tuck your shirt in!

JACK: Yes, sir.

Jack thinks how many are the ways to say 'sir' without conveying respect.

JACK: (tucking his shirt in) I feel a better player now, sir.

BLAKELEY: What did you say?

JACK: I said I feel a better player because I look neater now, sir.

A mass snigger spreads through the team. No one can do sarcasm better than Jack. He underplays it so skilfully. Jack's not an actor, you understand. He thinks acting's not for him. It involves learning lines and understanding Shakespeare.

What is he then, if he's not an actor? A comedian? No, he's the teenage forerunner of 'a popular TV and radio personality'. He's a popular classroom and changing room personality.

We take our positions on the pitch. Jack is centre-forward, I'm centre-half. I say, 'You better score the winning goal, then,' one of those eager, can-I-join-in-too things I say to be part of his life. Jack shrugs. The shirt moment's passed.

Jack doesn't think about scoring winning goals. Ahead of his time, Jack believes in service.

In the twenty-first century, strikers (as centre-forwards are now known) talk about getting service from their team-mates. A striker needs his team-mates to serve him with passes, headers, free kicks, corners and knock-downs. If they serve him well, he'll flourish. If they don't, he can't be blamed for not scoring.

Jack embraces this. He believes in strolling around looking languid and waiting to be served. He would no more run to get the ball than, in his forties, he would run to the kitchen of The Ivy to get his monkfish.

Genuinely talented, studiedly lazy, he's our top scorer, with two goals in six matches, so Mr Blakeley's obliged to play him. (I should explain that Heathgate House always loses. This is because where you live determines what House you're in. If you live in Golders Green or Hampstead Garden Suburb, you're in Heathgate. And if you live there, you're probably Jewish and have no tradition of footballing excellence. You just don't. You can buy a football club and they still won't give you a game. Sorry.)

The match begins. Mr Blakeley, hating laziness, screams at Jack to 'Run, boy, run!'

Jack does nothing in the first half. Mr Blakeley singles him out as we suck our half-time orange segments: 'This is a team game, Harris. You've done nothing for your team. Work for your team or you won't play again.' Jack nods and shows his teeth, obscured by peel.

But Jack does nothing in the second half, either, except put his hands on his hips and shake his head at the poverty of the service.

With five minutes to go, however, I boot the ball in the general direction of Geoff Bergman on the left wing. Geoff, without looking up – 'Look up, Bergman!' – squares the ball into the middle.

It speeds towards Jack, who's hanging about, trying not to get his legs dirty. Jack swivels as the ball approaches and strikes it, still-moving, with his left foot, into the top-left hand corner of the net, some thirty yards away. With his left knee bent and his right elbow perpendicularly above it, Jack looks like an award-winning photo.

'Goal!' shouts Mr Blakeley, as if it's something to do with him.

Jack raises one hand in the air, with not enough force to hail a taxi. He thinks it's right to look jaded. He thinks he's telling the world how bored he is of scoring goals like this.

You'll always remember where you were when you saw it. It's a goal of era-defining vintage. Galton-White, forced to watch the match to support his House, utterly immune to all things sporting – even Galton-White claps his gloved hands. Mr Blakeley shouts 'YES!' and does a little gallop up the touchline.

When he looks back towards the pitch, he sees Jack take his shirt out of his shorts.

He waits for the applause to subside. He gives our goalkeeper time to resume his position after ruffling Jack's hair.

Then he shouts, once more, 'Harris! Shirt!'

Jack, re-adjusting his hair, shouts back, 'Winning goal, sir.'

Mr Blakeley is outraged by this arrogance. 'There's five minutes left, boy! Shirt!' Jack puts up his hand as if to say, I'd love to carry on this conversation but I have work to do. Southgate House kick off.

Now, of course, everyone knows what Jack's thinking. The very birds in the trees know. He's thinking he'll do anything and everything to keep the score as it is.

Jack's everywhere. Interceptions, hair-threatening headers,

tackles, sliding tackles. Look, there he goes – Jack runs fifty yards to dispossess the Southgate House left-winger, inches from Mr Blakeley's feet.

This is everything Mr Blakeley's ever asked of Jack. Tireless devotion to the team's cause. And Mr Blakeley hates it. He knows Jack's only doing it for his shirt-outsiding self. It's insolent. It's hypocritical. It's virtually cheating.

Everything in Blakeley's moral universe has been perverted. He wants the opposition to score. When I tackle the Southgate inside-right, inches from our goal, Blakeley can't help himself. 'Penalty!' he screams.

Then Jack makes a mistake. He forgets that it's not just a matter of preventing the other side from scoring. No one on our side (except for Jack) must score again either. For then the winning goal would not be his.

With moments to go, he forgets to be negative. He hits a sweet pass into the path of Nigel Hoffman.

Nigel runs towards their goal. Blakeley screams: 'Go on, Mr Hoffman!' ('Mr Hoffman'?) A Nigel goal will make everything right. Blakeley's precious House will win. And, much more important, the winning goal won't be Jack's.

Jack, Mr Blakeley, Nigel Hoffman. They're the Elvis, the Marilyn, the JFK. Each is thinking about the other. I'm the witness.

Jack waits till Nigel has only the goalkeeper to beat. Nigel rounds the goalkeeper. He's just about to shoot.

Jack shouts: 'You can't fail!'

Nigel looks down at the ball. He's absorbed the word 'fail'.

Mr Blakeley puts Jack in detention anyway. Of course he does. 'Disobedience.' Mr Blakeley thinks Jack's a bad influence.

Jack thinks about ways to prove Mr Blakeley right. It's the beginning of the end of his school career.

* * *

55

One evening at home, the phone rings. The phone is on a table in a hall. It has a chair beside it. This is the era of immobile phones in positions of domestic status.

'Meadway 2183', my mother answers, irritating my father. 'They know what number they've rung. State your name!'

'Yes, this is Leah speaking,' says my mother into the receiver.

'They shouldn't have to ask who's speaking. It prolongs the call!'

'Hello, Mr Harris. Yes he is. I'll get him.'

My father shakes his head, to indicate he's not available. But it's not my father Danny's ringing. It's me.

Danny has a proposition. He wants me to coach Jack in Latin. Of all Jack's bad subjects, it's the worst.

Danny says, 'You could do it Sunday morning, before the football. I'll pay you, of course. How much would you charge?'

'I don't know, Mr Harris. I'll ask.' I put my hand over the receiver and explain the situation to my father. My father says that ten shillings would be appropriate.

'Ten shillings, Mr Harris.'

'Ten shillings? Don't insult me, David. I want you to take this seriously. Say, "a pound".'

'A pound.'

'A pound! What am I, made of money?'

My parents hover, anxious, suspicious.

'You got a table there?' asks Danny.

'Yes.'

'Bang the table and shout "Fifteen shillings".'

'Fifteen shillings!' I shout, banging the table with my fist.

'Don't be crude,' says my mother.

'It's a deal,' says Danny. 'See you Sunday.'

'He's agreed fifteen shillings,' I tell my father, as my mother's considered too delicate to discuss financial matters.

'You fool! If he agreed fifteen shillings, you're worth a pound!'

'But you told him to ask for ten shillings,' says my mother.

'Nonsense,' says my father, though we all know it's true, then walks briskly up the stairs to his study.

'You did well,' my mother says to me. 'It's hard to argue with a man like that. He's virile.'

'*Vivamus, mea Lesbia, atque amemus.* Take it word by word.'

Jack puts his finger under the word '*vivamus*'. Latin, like all written language, makes him dizzy. His finger is a little reading-stick he uses to steady himself.

'*Mea Lesbia.* That's "my lesbian", presumably. How long's this lesson meant to be?'

'Your father's paying me fifteen shillings. I think I'm duty bound to teach you for an hour. Latin's just a matter of learning the rules and following them.'

'That sounds terrible.'

'No, it's intellectually satisfying. It's like maths. *Vivamus* – let us live. There you are. You carry on.'

Jack goes to the bottom drawer of his bedroom desk. He gets out a mahogany box decorated with an elephant, so crudely carved you'd think the elephant did it.

From this he takes a joint and a cigar. He lights them both then hands me the cigar. 'Go on. That'll kill the smell.'

While I smoke the cigar, he smokes the joint, not offering it to me on the grounds that I'm teaching.

Nowadays, dope's a non-drugtaker's drug. A man like me smokes dope twice a week with his friend Tim. (How sad it is to know how often I do it. Moderate usage – the mark of a non-drugtaker.)

If you walk past Tim's front room, at 10 pm on a Thursday or Friday – it's the pink house opposite the pub in Yoxford – and, through a chink in the curtains, you catch sight of me 'toking' on my 'Suffolk parsnip', what will you think? You'll probably think – bless! – there's a middle-aged man trying to cure his multiple sclerosis.

In the housing estates of Leiston, of course, a few Suffolk miles away, there's smack and crack and something new-fangled the fanglers will christen *kack* or *fack* or *pack*. I know nothing of these hard-hitting drugs, the ones that turn you into a shaky-voiced mugger on a TV documentary, in silhouette only, your whole self literally blackened.

'What happens if your dad comes in?' I ask Jack.

'We'll hear him come up the stairs,' he replies. 'Or you will. I'll be too out of it.'

This is a lie. Dope has no effect on Jack. He doesn't aspire to and can't achieve the condition of mellow.

For Jack, it's the buying of the dope that matters.

Jack buys his dope outside the Roundhouse, London's grooviest rock venue. He buys it from Ned the Big-Nosed Freak, while I hang back in my familiar I'm-with-him-I'm-not-with-him way.

Ned, whose hair conspires with his nose to give him the appearance of a gonk, is a roadie for the Edgar Broughton Band who, in my opinion, are only mildly seminal. But no matter.

The first time he sells to us – by which I mean Jack – Ned asks us if we're schoolboys.

'No,' says Jack, 'We're firemen.'

'Cool. What station?'

This answer, free from human intelligence, is a more potent argument against drugs than any of our headmaster's Victorian-style homilies. (The man is obsessed. In assembly, he reads out articles from the Sunday supplements, in his best prophet-ofdoom voice. To hear our headmaster sonorously intone 'when a kid drops a tab' is heaven.)

I, of course, with my commitment to the truth, feel obliged to put Ned right. I tell him we are in fact schoolboys.

'Cool,' he says, as he would if we told him we were about to chop off his head. 'My old man's in a school. Don't let school fuck with your minds. Schools are run by straights. They don't know which way the wind blows.'

I don't have the heart to explain that this is what our parents pay for. They want fully qualified straights, with tweed jackets and pipes, unconcerned with the wind's direction, to fuck with our minds. And they expect to see results.

Back in his so-called study, Jack takes a drag. '*Vivamus*. Let us live.' (You see? His short-term memory's utterly unimpaired.) He coughs. 'Christ, it really burns your throat. If they made this stuff legal, no one would touch it.'

Here in my study, in the twenty-first century, I have six box files of press cuttings to help me write *That's All We Have Time For*. There are probably five hundred profiles of Jack, each one a snack version of his life. Almost all speak of a 'misspent youth' or 'wild years' or 'juvenile delinquency'. It's nonsense.

Look at this piece from 1994 by Amy McCracken in the *Brisbane Courier-Mail*. When Jack was sixteen, writes Amy, he 'jumped off a tree on to his teacher'. Amy, you've got a brazen, outdoorsy, Oz sort of name – find yourself a teacher and a tree and try it.

Jack, in the course of his life, didn't even have a police record (except for motoring offences, which we all agree don't count). He wasn't a rebel. Nothing he did was designed to be destructive, only to build himself up. Jack bought dope to show he was A Man who could and would do what he liked.

There's a knock at the door and, with no more warning, Danny enters.

'You seen the Latin dictionary, Dad?' says Jack, opening and closing the drawers of his desk, ostensibly searching for it as he palms the joint into the top drawer.

Danny looks at me and my cigar. 'What are you celebrating? Has he learned something?'

I, of course, feel far more guilty than Jack. I instinctively abase myself. 'I'm not sure I'm a natural teacher, Mr Harris.'

'I'm sure you're terrific. I'm paying you to be terrific.'

Jack gets up from his chair. 'I think it's in Marcus's room.' He leaves.

'Is it hopeless?' Danny asks me, man-to-man.

'I don't know,' I say. Looking to reassure him, I add: 'You've gone a long way without Latin, Mr Harris.'

Danny goes quiet. He's just been flattered, in a back-handed way, by the teacher. Then he turns to me and says, intimately, tearfully, as if I were his brother or something: 'I want him to be smarter than me'.

Does he? 'Your parents are very lucky,' he tells me, turning me from his brother into the son he never had.

Jack marches back in. 'I found it.' He slams the dictionary down on the desk. It is, in fact, Jacqueline Susann's *Valley of the Dolls*, the hardback edition with the jacket taken off.

'D'you mind, Dad? We're working.' A little plume of dope smoke squirms through the keyhole of the desk's top drawer.

Danny withdraws.

'So come on,' Jack says. 'What about Melinda Spears.'

'I can't stop thinking about her,' I reply.

'Yeah? She's too clever for me.'

'Too clever for me': those words will sustain me for weeks. Melinda Spears is too clever for Jack. But she's not too clever for me.

* * *

At this point, Jack and I have known Melinda Spears for less than eighteen hours.

The way it works is this: every Saturday night, the teenage population of Golders Green, plus handbags, gathers in the forecourt of Golders Green Station to giggle and shout and exchange information.

The prized information – the currency to be traded – is party data. Who, where, is giving a party? When you ring the bell and the front door opens, who should you say you know?

The answer to that is simple: 'Phil Cohen'. Jack and I have gatecrashed countless parties claiming to be friends of 'Phil Cohen'. At first, we were friends of 'Dave Cohen'. But, as it turns out, 'Phil Cohen' is more popular. He goes to more parties than his putative brother Dave.

And, yes, sometimes the host or hostess keeps us on the doorstep while she fetches Phil Cohen to come and vouch for us; at which point, of course, we have to leave. But then again, on one such doorstep, in Wildwood Road, Jack actually befriends the Phil Cohen who's come to deny he knows us. And, happily, this particular Phil Cohen is sometimes at parties we gatecrash claiming to be friends of 'Phil Cohen'.

All we need is an address.

The Melinda Spears night, though, we draw a blank. Jack works the forecourt, pumping Rebeccas and Ruths and Michaels for information. There's nothing, or nothing they're willing to pass on to him.

So. Plan B: we walk. We walk the streets of Hampstead Garden Suburb in search of parties, starting at Hoop Lane Crematorium, which is dead. (This is no joke, as we'll see later. Jack can find a party in a crematorium, all right.)

For a mile, nothing happens.

This is why people buy houses in Hampstead Garden Suburb.

They are paying to have nothing happen. To ensure nothing happens, there's no place in the Suburb for youths. (*Youth* is splendid, *young people* are nice but *youths* are bad.) The Suburb has no shops, with windows that youths can smash. No buses, for youths to fight on the top of. No streets, where youths can buy drugs with a street value. Drugs, the Suburb believes, have no drive or crescent value.

Even the burglaries, of which there are many, are not carried out by youths. We pass the just-burgled house of my mother's best friend, Bea Goldman. She was a concert pianist before she married Arnold. (Arnold is the Goldman of Mangold Petfoods.)

Last Monday morning, removal men arrive at Bea's house. Mrs Sheinwald, who lives opposite, draws her curtains at five-thirty – why do middle-aged women wake so early? – to see them carrying Bea's dust sheet-covered grand piano into their van.

Mrs Sheinwald is surprised. She didn't know Bea and Arnold were moving. Bea and Arnold, on holiday in Cannes, are surprised too.

My mother, who worships Bea, has spent most of the week phoning her friends to recount the story. It gives her such pleasure to swill the key words round her mouth: dust sheet, grand piano, Cannes, professionals.

The professionals are, of course, the burglars. They didn't even damage the banister when they took Bea's wardrobe downstairs. My mother is essentially telling her friends: 'My best friend Bea has only the finest burglars. Every man jack of them is a connoisseur. Why, one of them looks like David Niven. They only stole Bea's grand piano because they wanted to play it.'

My poor mother. Twenty years later, my flat in Hackney is burgled by a youth so whacked on smack, so cracked on shakatak, that he shits on my living room floor before (or after – forensics don't relate) grabbing my video cassette recorder, which was probably stolen goods already. I bought it in a market in Dalston; it had one of those almost-brand names, like Hoshida or Panatachi. It must have been worth virtually nothing. Perhaps he left the turds in part-exchange.

When I recount this burglary, my mother calls it 'another nail in my coffin'. That's her coffin, you understand.

She grew up in Hackney. She thought she'd left its poverty and hardships and youths behind. Why am I living and working in Hackney, as a clerk for the council? From the East End to the suburbs – that's the journey of her life. How is it I've gone back to where she started? Why can't I afford somewhere better? Like Jack. For Jack, who at fifteen is little better than a *youth*, has become a rich and, let's face it, virile man.

A week after my burglary, she sends me a press cutting from the *Daily Telegraph*. The residents of a Buckinghamshire village are 'up in arms'. Their new neighbour, TV star Jack Harris, has erected twenty foot high black gates at the entrance to his estate, destroying, they claim, the character of the village.

And there it is: a photo of the gates.

I know what my mother is telling me, through the medium of this photo. My Hackney flat attracts the worst kind of burglar. Jack's Buckinghamshire gates attract the best. Bea Goldman's burglars, twenty years on, are combing their silver hair and donning their cufflinks. It will be an honour for them to clean out Jack's estate.

After a mile and a half, something happens. We turn a corner and see and hear journey's end. A crammed-with-bodies lounge, from which the standard light bulb has been removed, to be replaced by a red one. The red light that says 'brothel' in Soho says 'party' in Hampstead Garden Suburb.

'Hold on, Phil, we're coming!' shouts Jack.

We have to ring the bell four or five times, as *Honky Tonk Women* is playing, loud to the point of distortion.

In my nervousness, I observe that the Stones are, above all, fans. Their love for other people's music is what makes theirs so great. In their sublime amateurism, they sound like the greatest school band in the world.

Jack is slightly bored. He isn't interested in the burgeoning art of rock criticism. He wants to get inside the house.

Finally, finally, the door opens.

'Hi, we're friends of Phil Cohen,' says Jack.

'No you're not. You're gatecrashers,' says Melinda Spears. She smiles. 'Come in.'

You open the door and what do you see? Jack and me. You know instantly I'm more sensitive and clever than Jack. I don't have to say anything. And I don't.

As Melinda leads us into the kitchen, Jack bombards her with his personality: 'It's a terrible thing Phil's not here. He's got our bottle of wine.'

I, meanwhile, learn about Melinda Spears by looking. I realise she's not like Jack or me. She's Jewish but not as we know it.

There's a pine dresser in the kitchen – the least kosher of all woods. There's mess, too, the kind of mess that in Jack's or my house would indicate an unprofessional burglary. Look at the dresser. Piles of papers where the 'best plates' should be; books on psychiatry and psychology and sociology, novels by Richard Brautigan and Iris Murdoch and Saul Bellow, yellowing journals, glass mugs filled with interesting stones from beaches. These people go to beaches that *don't have sand*.

And there, in front of the dresser, maturely luscious, is a woman who can only be Melinda Spears's pine-loving mother, laughing with some girls who can only be her daughter's friends.

This is beyond compare: Melinda Spears's mother goes to Melinda Spears's parties. And she laughs. And the guests laugh with her.

A laughing girl lights a joint. Melinda Spears's mother's eyelids remain un-batted. Sure as a circle is round, the joint arrives in her thumb and forefinger. She lifts it to her lips without missing a beat, as if this were normal, which, here in this house so near yet so far from my own, it palpably is.

I turn to see Jack doing card tricks for Melinda.

Card tricks for Susan Sarandon. Card tricks for Sir Anthony Hopkins. We remember the thunderous applause, from Susan and Tony and the studio audience. It's not the trick they're applauding. In illusionary terms, the trick is no more than quite good. They're simply amazed a talk/chat show host can do something more than talk or chat.

But this is a kitchen, not a TV studio where you're meant to show off. This is a teenage boy who's packed his cards in his jacket before going out on Saturday night. This is embarrassing.

Melinda, lovely Melinda, pretends to be amused as Jack asks her to pick a card. But I know what she's thinking. I look at her and she looks back. She knows I know.

Melinda applauds, as Jack reveals her chosen card underneath a bowl of crisps. They have a further, brief exchange, then Jack gives me a nod to say he's going upstairs. I decline.

He goes upstairs. I study the bookcase. Melinda pours a drink for a friend. Then she comes over to me and says, 'What the fuck are you doing reading?'

'What the fuck are you doing reading?' Those are the first words she says to me, me on my own, me without Jack. I'm smitten. The humorous needling. The lovely use of *fuck* to add piquancy, to be – dare I say it – a condiment. And the irony. Anyone can see she was born to read and is mocking the thing she loves.

'It's the books,' I reply. 'They're provoking me.'

I'm so happy. This is a moment the like of which Jack never experiences. He's never talked books to a girl in his life.

Melinda and I talk about Bellow and Brautigan and Murdoch and Plath. I tell her I find Plath terrifying. She understands. We talk about everything and nothing. Talk pours out of us. She's more clever than me, more unconventional. Our minds marry and there's no impediment.

Then Mark Leboff walks in. Mark is a rich kid who gets what he wants. He travels to school by chauffeur.

Mark puts his arm round Melinda. I feel sick. He says 'hi' to me, investing the word with all the she's-mine he can muster.

Mark Leboff will grow up to be chairman of Tottenham Hotspur plc or Tottcorp or Globaltott, whatever the money-stinking hell they call it now. When the Spurs manager's pictured with his latest purchase, some stubbled Cameroonian defender busting out of his suit, that's Mark in the background, grinning like the natural flesh-trader he is.

I look Melinda in the eyes and I say, 'Nice to meet you. I have to go now.' I say 'nice to meet you' to remind her that we've only just met. I am that romantic figure, the stranger who turns up on your doorstep. 'I have to go now' tells her I'm sad beyond sad that she's with Mark Leboff, who isn't good enough for her.

I know she understands all this.

I fight my way upstairs, to the ever-increasing sound of *Spoonful* by Cream. I step over a boy and a girl on the stairs. He's asking her if she likes the Cream. I'm so angry and upset I correct him: 'It's not the Cream. It's Cream. You wouldn't say the Free or the Jethro Tull. You wouldn't say the Simon and the Garfunkel.'

I wish Melinda Spears were on the stairs to witness this. I want her to know how passionate I can be.

Outside the red-lit dancing room, Jack is wedged between two giggling girls. He's shouting at one of them that the card she chose can be found down her T-shirt. She's shouting back that she doesn't believe him. I interrupt them to tell Jack I feel tired and have to go home.

He tells me I can't go home, I've only just arrived. I tell him I'm going. He says if I have to go, I have to go. Then he and the girls get back to their giggling business.

Walking home, I feel certain I'll see Melinda Spears again. Something happened between us. I know it and she does too.

But she's got a boyfriend. I can't ring her up when she's got a boyfriend. That would be crass.

Back in Jack's study, for the Latin tuition which begins (and ends) with *vivamus*, Jack's telling me Melinda Spears is too clever for him.

'So what d'you think of the girl with the card down her T-shirt?'

'I don't know. I only saw her for a –'

Jack's heard enough. He doesn't want an essay.

'I screwed her under the coats. She wasn't bad, actually.'

I don't know what I'm supposed to say. In fact, I'm not supposed to say anything. Jack merely leaves what's known as a decent interval. Then he cracks on.

'You never know, do you?'

I shake my head, sagely. No, I never know. I never know because I've never slept with anyone. Jack's aware of this, yet he includes me in his Never Knowing Club. Why do we pretend?

'She was better than Marilyn actually.'

I have to say something now or Jack will never stop.

'Shall we get back to the Latin?'

'Is there any point?'

It's supposedly a Jewish trope, to answer a question with a question. Why does Jack do it? Why does anyone do it? He's trying not to answer my question.

Including the T-Shirt Card Girl, Jack has notched up three so-what-d'you-think-ofs. Throughout his life, he uses this phrase to indicate a conquest. In the early Eighties, for example, he'll say to me, 'So what d'you think of the weather girl on Thames TV?' Later that night, he'll even allude to it. 'So what d'you think of Margaret Thatcher?' he asks. Then adds: 'Not that I've had her.'

His first conquest is Mark Leboff's au pair, Erika. This is when his parents go away for the weekend, so Jack can lose his virginity.

That's right. She's an au pair. It's an early Seventies soft-core porn film fantasy. Surely, you're thinking, this cannot have happened. (From behind, we see 'Erika' unclasp her bra, its washing-instruction tag un-sexily visible. 'Jack' sits on the bed, in his white Y-fronts and grey socks, grinning beneath his Zapata moustache.)

Wait, there's worse: Erika's Swedish. Now you really don't believe me. But Erika's real, I can prove it. Her father's Norwegian. She has a Swedish passport but she's half-Norwegian. There are soft-core films about Swedish au pairs, but none about half-Swedish, half-Norwegian. Half-Norwegian au pairs are real.

Then he gets hold of Marilyn Joel. Marilyn, whose parents are divorced, who's slept with a junkie who lives in a squat – she's a girl boys dismiss as 'easy'. But, given that most boys haven't slept with anyone, 'difficult' would be more accurate.

Jack has sex with Marilyn twice. But he talks about 'a couple of times' as that makes it sound more like three.

Jack has a genius for this kind of verbal inflation. Two weeks after the Latin lesson, he celebrates his sixteenth birthday with a lunch at the Angus Steak House in Highgate.

He buys the lunch and orders the wine, which he sends back because it's 'corked'. I suspect the waiter brings back the same bottle. Jack sniffs again: 'Yeah. That's what we want. Nose like Streisand.'

When the subject gets on to sex, well before the steaks arrive with their watercress and mushroom companions, Jack asks all of us how many of the girls we've slept with have been on the pill.

Nigel Hoffman says he's never asked, which is an excellent lie as it's true. He's never asked, of course, because he's never had to. Nigel's a virgin like me, as is Geoff Bergman. We're partners in no-crime.

It's Geoff's turn. In the great tradition, he answers Jack's question with another: 'How many of the girls you've slept with have been on the pill then, Jack?'

Jack says: 'Fifty per cent.'

Everyone goes quiet. But I go quieter than most. T-Shirt Card Girl. . . Erika . . . Marilyn. For Christ's sake, Jack, I want to shout, how do you get fifty per cent of three?

After the Latin lesson and the football kickabout on the Hampstead Heath extension, I get home to a miracle.

There's a note on the phone table, in my father's hand: SUNDAY 11.30am DAVID LEWIN – MELINDA SPEARS RANG. PLEASE RING HER THIS EVENING. SPEEDWELL 6555.

I ring Jack immediately.

'Did you give Melinda Spears my number?'

69

'No.'

'She rang me.'

'That's great, Dave. Well done.'

Sunday lunch is roast chicken, roast potatoes, carrots and frozen peas. My father, eyebrows furrowed, carving knife and fork in hand, peers at the chicken as my mother puts it in front of him. He spears it with the fork, to check the juices are colourless. At times like this, which is every Sunday lunch, my father has the air of a forensic pathologist. I expect him to turn to my mother and ask: 'Time of death?' She, as always, says she's too tired to eat after so much cooking.

I quiz my father about the note. Why did he write 'David Lewin' when I'm his son? He tells me that was whom (sic) Melinda asked for. She provided the appellation, not him.

Does he know what it's about?

'It's about her wishing to speak to you.'

My mother looks concerned. 'I hope she's nice.'

I don't see much of Jack in the next few weeks. This is my Melinda Period, which no one can take away from me.

Melinda is my first love, which begs the question: did Jack have a first love? After all, there's nothing compulsory about it. You can live and die without one.

In 'Ask A Celebrity' (*Northampton Echo*, March 21st 1998), reader Peta Collins of Ashmount Drive gets straight to it: 'Who was your first love?' Jack's reply is interesting, to say the least: 'I never knew what love was till I first saw my son. So I'd have to say it's him'.

Of course, we can't be sure if this is Jack speaking. It may have been written for him by a PR person who knew just what Peta would expect. 'I never knew what love was till I first saw my son' – it could be a line from a country and western standard. Perhaps a song becomes a standard precisely because its sentiments are standard.

Certainly, my-baby-taught-me-to-love is a standard celebrity heart-outpouring. In fact, now everyone talks like a celebrity, it's standard for non-celebrities too. Peta might have got the same answer if she'd Asked A Taxi Driver.

Jack's definitely never mentioned love in the context of Erika, Marilyn and Card Girl. It's not what he's after. He's after numbers, experience, volume, percentages.

That's the difference between us. I'm actively pursuing first love. The reading, the school prizes for English, the introversion, my whole not-Jackness, they've made me crave that dizzying cocktail. I want sex. But I don't want it without love.

I pick up the phone to call Melinda at six that day, then put it down, unsure whether six is 'this evening' or still late afternoon. I pick up the phone again at six thirty but clock up another refusal. I'm fearful my voice will come out too high.

When I call at seven, Melinda doesn't recognise me. She tells me I should speak in my normal voice. I lapse into it and everything's all right.

It turns out she got my number by ringing the five Lewins in the phone book who live in London NW11, the Golders Green area.

We arrange to meet at Kenwood the next Saturday night, for an open-air concert. She brings a picnic. I bring a rug and wine. We lie on the grass and look up at the heavens. On the other side of the lake, two hundred yards away, an orchestra plays Beethoven's *Pastoral*. Apparently. There's audible music in the air. That's as much as you can tell. But it's enough. The grass and the stars do the rest.

What makes Melinda wonderful is how unpredictable she is.

Her mother's a sculptor, her father's a theatre critic. She's grown up in a house without standard conversations. She goes, fearlessly, where her mind leads her, talking to me throughout the concert, ignoring the stares of the woman to her right and the bald-headed man in front of me.

Is Mark Leboff her boyfriend, though? She rang five Lewins to find me. Would she have done that if Mark were still her boyfriend?

Jack would just ask. I've stood next to him many times when he's asked a girl in words of one and two syllables if she's got a boyfriend.

I'd never say that. I'm interested in the potency of the unsaid. Melinda and I, with our mysteries, meet. We explore each other. Why did she flick her hair behind her ear when she saw I'd seen her, across the lawn?

Though I tell her a hundred things, I know she's deducing the hundred and first, the thing I don't say, which is, of course, that I'm falling in love with her.

At the end of the night, I walk back with her to her house, although she keeps telling me it's out of my way. What I don't say, which is potent, is that I want to go out of my way for her. I don't have to say it. I'm doing it.

When we reach her gate – or rather, when we turn the corner and see her gate and are tense from wondering what will happen when we reach it – Melinda's radiant confidence dims. She stops. She tugs at the ends of her hair. I want to hold her and tell her that everything will be all right. But I don't. Not yet.

She lets me know that she and Mark broke up after the party. He took her for granted. He didn't respond to her as a person, only as an idea: His Girlfriend. She was his to take to places, to show off, buy things for. I wonder how anyone could ever take Melinda for granted.

She tells me, the words all bunched up, that I'm much more sensitive and clever and nice than Mark. Then she's gone. I never reach the gate.

Jack never asks me about Melinda Spears though he knows I'm seeing her, as I go out of my way to mention her name. For example, during one of our Latin lessons, when Jack asks me the time, I say: 'I think I left my watch at Melinda's house.' To which Jack replies, not unreasonably: 'It's on your wrist.' Consciously or not, I'm trying to provoke him into asking me about my relationship; while, at the same time, revelling in its secrecy. I mean, I don't think I'd tell him if he asked me about it. It's my private life.

Melinda and I go to the Everyman Cinema and the National Portrait Gallery. We drink beer at the Freemason's Arms in Hampstead and coffee in the Coffee Cup in Hampstead. We see the Doors at The Roundhouse. I introduce her to – no, I point at, and she introduces herself to – Ned the Big-Nosed Freak. We smoke dope in Regent's Park then commune with the animals in London Zoo. Guy the Gorilla, heavy-set, self-centred, reminds her of Mark Leboff.

All the time, I hold back and hold back, giving her the freedom to be herself, not burdening her with my desire, as Mark the Gorilla did from the first time he looked at her.

When the moment's right, nothing will stop us. Everything unsaid will be said. There'll be a volcano.

Melinda loves to argue and I love to argue back. Out of the blue, she'll say she can't listen to the Beatles now she's heard the Velvet Underground. The Beatles seek to please their audience, whereas the Velvets, true artists, seek only to please themselves. That's an hour on the phone in itself.

We've never kissed. This is deliberate policy on my part. Once, when we were parting, she tried to kiss me on the cheek and I withdrew, alarming her. She asked me if I didn't like her anymore. I shook my head, I smiled, I walked away. Then I turned back and smiled again. I knew she'd understand what I meant by that: when I did kiss her, that would be it. Everything would follow.

For the fifth successive Saturday night we turn the corner and see the gate. Two things happen, simultaneously. Raphael, Melinda's elder brother, a student at Hornsey art school, pulls up on his motorbike; Mark Leboff gets out of a parked car. The driver is Mark's elder brother, which gives the whole thing an odd symmetry.

Mark shouts at Melinda. Melinda tells him to fuck off. Mark says she's a lying bitch. I tell Mark to leave her alone. Mark doesn't look at me, which makes me angry. It's as if I'm nothing.

Mark carries on abusing Melinda. I go into a strange state, a dream state where I can't stop events unfolding as they will, even though I'm the one apparently making them happen.

I tell Raphael to give me his helmet and the keys to his bike. He tells me I'm not insured. (It's amazing how dull bohemians can be.) I tell him it's an emergency and grab the helmet from his hand.

Now I'm on the bike. The ignition's on. I'm revving. I'm sexy. I shout: 'Melinda! Come on!'

She's surprised to see me like this. So's Mark. Distracted, he loses his momentum. He stops shouting at her and can't start again.

Melinda runs towards me. Mark shouts after her: 'Don't be fucking stupid! He doesn't know what he's doing!'

Melinda gets on the bike and puts her arms round my waist.

We go a short way, at frightening speed, then we fall off the bike.

* * *

74

Three Saturday nights later, Melinda sits up in bed, in her night-dress. Her left leg's in plaster.

I sit on the edge of the bed. Side One of Miles Davis's *In A Silent Way* comes to an end. I turn it over then head back to the edge of the bed.

'Hold me,' she says, then with arms akimbo, left thumb and forefinger on right seam, right thumb and forefinger on left, Melinda volcanoes her orange nightdress high over her head.

I know not to look at her nipples. That would be insulting. Equally, I know not to look in her eyes. That would be insulting too. So I fix on a midway point.

'Take your clothes off then,' she says. 'Of course,' I say, staring at her collarbone.

Instinctively, I turn round, presenting my back to her, as I would to a stranger in the changing room, before sport.

'You don't have to turn round,' she says. I say: 'It's what I always do.' I'm thinking of the changing room but, accidentally, it sounds as if I'm drawing on my sexual experience. It's an Angus Steak House remark – I've undressed with my back to a hundred per cent of the girls I've been to bed with.

When I'm down to my pants, I turn round, wanting her to see the purple bruising on my left leg and the bandage on my knee. We're survivors.

'It's OK. You can keep your pants on,' says Melinda Spears. I keep them on. Had she said it was OK to take them off, I'd have taken them off instead.

When we're under the covers, she lies on her back and I angle myself towards her, resting on my left side. I put my right hand on her thigh. I'm shocked by the unforgiving hardness of the plaster.

'You're lovely,' she says.

'You're lovely,' I counter.

'No, I'm not,' she says.

It's the start of my sexual career. I don't yet know that girls will never admit to being lovely. They'll admit to looking lovely or cooking a lovely risotto but never to being a lovely person. They know themselves too well.

'I could never do to you what I did to Mark,' she says.

'I'm completely in love with you,' I reply, though it's not a reply to what she's just said.

'I couldn't go out with you for six months then dump you. I could never hurt you like that.'

I don't say anything. I try to work out what she means.

'I love spending time with you. You're so funny and nice. You're like half a perfect man. Shit, sorry, does that sound like an insult?'

'No,' I say.

We lie there. She twists her upper body and puts her left palm on my back, stroking it tenderly, as Jess will thirty years later. I feel safe. I feel we're strong together.

'I'm really sorry I hurt you,' I say.

'You didn't. It was an accident,' she says.

'When I saw you on the pavement, I thought you were dead. But I knew I could bring you back to life. Because of the power of my feelings.'

This is all true. But she doesn't like it. She doesn't want to hear about the power of my feelings.

'Don't say anymore, OK? Let's just lie here.'

We lie there. Then she says, 'I'm so sorry I can't give you what you want, David. I know you'll find someone who will.'

She kisses me on the lips, with tenderness. She slips her hand down the back of my pants and strokes my coccyx. I can feel tears welling up. But then they're stopped in their tracks, as I ejaculate.

Melinda Spears removes her hand. She waits patiently as I judder and shudder my way to completion.

'You have to understand, David. That won't happen again.'

On my way home, I write in my head the poem that appears in *Mantra*, the Highgate School Literary Society Magazine, October 1971 edition.

The poem ends as follows:

> *I remember*
> *When I left*
> *I was older*

When I wake up in my bedroom on the Sunday morning, churned up and feverish from the night before, a nightmare is being played out on the floor beside my bed.

My mother is picking up my underpants to check if they're clean enough to wear.

'What's this in your underpants?' she asks me.

Surely it can only be one thing in my underpants. My mother must know about that thing. It's the secret of life, the secret of my life, which can't be a secret to her. And yet there's nothing disingenuous in her question. It's possible she's never seen the thing. She's heard it, maybe. A long time ago, my father might have made a sound as the thing rushed out of its little penile tunnel at the start of its brave journey.

At a time like this, thank God for Jack. People believe the worst of him.

'Jack stuck glue in them.'

'I knew it. Why's it always Jack? Why don't you ask the Galton-White boy over to play?'

'It was only a joke.'

'Well, it's not very funny, is it?

'No.'

I say that 'no' with full priggish gusto, as if I'm as appalled as she is at Jack's poor taste in jokes.

'I'll put them in the wash. I've a good mind to send them to his mother. I'm sure her washing machine's bigger and better than mine.'

Told of his selection for the Heathgate cross-country team, Jack asks Mr Blakeley if Jews haven't suffered enough. Why a sport where you run all the time? Jack loves soccer and tennis, with their half-times and changeovers. Jack likes sports with inbuilt commercial breaks.

I shouldn't really be running at all. My leg is still sore. I'm running because Mr Blakeley has told me he's relying on me.

My soreness and Jack's reluctance make us run at the same speed. After a mile, we're at the back among the losing pack.

Galton-White shambles along beside us with his tragic pre-suicidal gait. Mr Blakeley has decided he needs his character formed, but it's his body, built for maths, that's against him.

I'm listening to my breathing and trying not to think about Melinda. I'm thinking about her less now, maybe two thousand times a day. As I go over and over it, I try to reduce it to its essence. I was intimate with her, that's what counts. I've never felt closer to anyone.

Who was playing, though, when we kissed? That's what I'm thinking about now. Was it Miles Davis? Or one of his sidemen? John McLaughlin on guitar? Herbie Hancock on –

Jack's talking to me. This is a surprise. He's making an effort. It's harder to talk and run than to run.

'There's something I've got to tell you,' says Jack.

My legs feel heavier. I tense. This is the moment, after the car comes off the road and before it hits the ditch, when your whole life doesn't flash before your eyes, oh no. The ditch flashes before your eyes. You only see the ditch.

Here it comes.

'I never slept with Melinda. Mark Leboff thinks I did but I didn't. She's too clever for me. She's your kind of girl. Girls who ask what you're thinking.'

I stop running. Jack follows suit.

'She thinks you're the perfect man. She told me. You're the perfect man. You and me. We make the perfect man. So don't get upset, all right? Nothing happened. We got naked two or three times. But I couldn't do it.'

Jack shakes his head. 'I just couldn't do it. Never happened to me before.'

'I'm sorry,' I say.

That's right. I offer my condolence for his failure to have sex with the girl I love. They got naked two or three times. But there was no sex.

Usually, Jack says 'two or three times' to make you to think it was four when in fact it was two. In this case, the converse applies. He wants me to think he was naked with Melinda *fewer* times than he was; so, when he says 'two or three times', I know it was four.

Jack walks off the cross-country course into a thicket of trees. I carry on walking the course.

'Come on,' he says. 'We'll catch up.' He sits against a tree. 'Come on, Dave.'

'I can't,' I say. 'It's against the rules.'

'No one'll find us. What about this?' He climbs the tree. 'Who's going to look for us here?'

He's right. No one looks for runners up trees.

I follow him up the tree, though my leg makes it difficult. I've done it before, after all. I did it that Yom Kippur when we broke our fast. The precedent comforts me. I'm a lawyer's son.

Jack has got naked with Melinda four times. To him, that's nothing. *'Nothing happened.'* Yet my single naked encounter with her is everything to me.

I cling to the tree. The tree is what stops me from falling. In a few moments, I tell myself, I'll leave Jack behind and catch up with Galton-White. Mr Blakeley knows my leg is bad. He'll know I tried my best.

When Leboff turned up at Melinda's gate, he was jealous of Jack not me. He knew. He knew about the naked. Who else knew? Yes. I see. I don't want to but I do.

Melinda knew. All the time we were together, from the concert in Kenwood to the jazz in her bedroom, she knew about herself and Jack. Does that mean all the happiness I had with her is cancelled? I was happy then, I'm unhappy now. Is it that simple? Or can you be unhappy retrospectively?

'You didn't make a move, Dave,' says Jack, from his higher perch. 'I know you got close. She told me. You have to show girls you want them.

'When the moment's right, you put your hands on their tits, really gently. You turn one clockwise. And the other anti-clockwise. That gets them every time.'

'For fucksake, Jack! She's not a safe!'

A bird flies out of the tree, scared.

'This'll make you feel better.'

Jack takes a little ivory box from the pocket of his running shorts, opens it and produces a ready-made joint and a lighter.

I feel scared and excited and uncertain and lonely. I feel so many things I feel nothing, as when you mix twenty five colours together and get a kind of khaki-grey.

I take the joint and smoke it. I feel I need to be bad.

'No hard feelings, Dave.'

'No hard feelings, Jack.'

The bird flies back into the tree. I smile at it.

We can fly out of the tree, though. We're unauthorised. We can say anything and go anywhere, in space and time.

It's the day after I've mistaken Mrs Pearl for Jack's mother. I've arranged to visit Melinda Spears. I can't cancel it. I'm too curious. I go.

I sit in Melinda Spears's Brighton kitchen, with her sixteen-year-old daughter Natasha, and Emilio, a sweet Brazilian man in his twenties. Professor Spears, like Caroline Bliss, is running late. Since when does a powerful person call to say they're 'running early'?

You may know Professor Spears. She teaches American Literature at Sussex. She writes books and articles. If you listen to intelligent radio in the morning, or watch intelligent TV at night, you'll have seen or heard her introduced as a 'cultural commentator'.

The woman is a real Jewish beauty, with those soulful animated eyes and the long grey hair. I'm not sure about the earrings, though. Always the hoop earrings. I suppose they're a kind of logo, as in, 'Get me that woman who knows about things, you know . . . hoop earrings.'

She bursts into the kitchen, loudly apologetic. She kisses Natasha, then Emilio, who I thought was a lodger but kisses like a lover. He may of course be both.

'Hello, I'm so sorry to keep you waiting. Faculty meetings go on interminably. Did you know that people text during meetings now? You're speaking to them and they're texting each other about your hair.'

I tell her I didn't know.

'How are you? It's lovely to see you. So you're writing a biography of Jack. That's marvellous.'

Natasha sniggers. Natasha's not fat, because people aren't fat now. But she's big with issues. Stuffed full of issues. She's an issue whale.

Her principal issue, her Ben and Jerry's Chunky Lard with Lumps issue, is her relentlessly charismatic mother, who finds things marvellous.

'Jack represents a strain in English culture that fascinates me,' says Melinda, though I haven't asked her a question and never imagined the interview would take place here, with others present. 'He appears to be a rebel but in fact he's in hock to celebrity culture, as we all are. He's an insider-outsider.'

'Get that?' says Natasha to me. 'I'm going to my room to cut myself, Mum, call me when it's supper, OK?'

This is better than anything Melinda says in the next ninety minutes of *as it weres* and *in a senses* and *what's extraordinarys*. Sarcastic it may be. But heartfelt.

Melinda, with her polished and interesting opinions, wears me down. Just say something uninteresting, I want to shout. Say 'pass the sugar' or 'it's nice out'.

This is a woman who, at fifteen, talks throughout a concert. You can't love a woman like that, can you? They only want to know what you're thinking so they can tell you what they're thinking and why their thought is better than yours.

But, at fifteen, up that tree, I can't see beyond my heart. I'm love's fool.

I want to get out of the tree and back to the race. I stay because Jack is the closest thing to Melinda I know. I stay because I have faith in Jack. Jack and I get away with things.

We smoke. After a minute which could be an hour, or an hour

which could be a minute, I pass him the joint and say: 'She's an incredible girl, though, isn't she? You know that, don't you?'

'Don't say a word.'

Why does he say this? I don't understand. Then I hear the foot-steps. I see Mr Blakeley marching along the cross-country course, looking ahead and behind and right and left, like a fool. What's he going to see there? We're up here.

Mr Blakeley is thirty feet away. I can't describe him in any Elvis-ite biographical way. I can't say *five-foot-nine-inch Martin Blakeley crunched the horse chestnut and birch tree leaves with his size eight tan shoes, bought the previous Saturday in the Freeman, Hardy & Willis Sale for just* – sorry. He was then, and is now, unmemorable. He was a disciplinarian, not so tall, not so short. That's the best I can do.

'Harris?' he calls, more in despair than hope.

On the branch above me, Jack makes no sound.

Mr Blakeley shouts the name this time, as if he's reading the register. 'Harris!'

But still there's no response.

Mr Blakeley is reading the Heathland Register, I think, as the dope takes hold. He's called Harris twice, to no avail. Now he'll move on. 'Hawthorn?' 'Jackdaw?' 'Larch?' 'Magpie?' I smile at these thoughts. Dope makes me easily pleased.

'Lewin!'

Lewin. That's my name. A teacher has spoken my name in the wood. It cuts through everything.

My voice, when it comes, surprises me with its loudness, as if it emanates from an alien creature within. But it's me who's speaking, it's the essence of me, the boy who follows rules and pleases adults and wins school prizes.

'Here, sir!' I say.

* * *

Mr Blakeley makes us run back. It's a nice touch. He runs alongside us, to make it worse. And, exquisitely, he times us.

There it is, on the school notice board next day. The winner of the House Cross-Country Race is J. Hancock (Eastgate House) in a time of 19 minutes 28 seconds.

D.J. Lewin (Heathgate House) and J.F. Harris (Heathgate House) tie for 89th place, in a time of 67 minutes 45 seconds.

The key thing to notice is the tie. That was Jack's idea. He thought it would look more absurd if we recorded the same time.

We're on the bus back home, after the race. Galton-White isn't on it, of course. He caught a much earlier bus.

We haven't discussed it. I haven't known what to say.

'I'm really sorry, Jack. I didn't think. I heard my name and I answered.'

'You did what you had to do,' says Jack.

That makes feel less of a fool and more of a hero. A hero's always true to himself, no?

'Why didn't you keep your mouth shut, Dave? You're too bloody honest. They'll expel me. My dad'll go mad.'

'I'm so sorry, Jack.' Then, as a comfort: 'I'll be expelled with you, you know.'

Jack says nothing.

That evening, my mother asks how the run went. I tell her I finished last. She assumes this was because of my bad leg. She tells me it was sensible of me not to hurt it by running faster.

My parents know nothing about me. I'm growing up. I have

a secret life. I take drugs. Soon, everything they thought they knew about me will be disproved.

The morning after the race, I walk into school with Jack.

Boys shout. They point and laugh. But they don't approach. Jack and I have an aura. We're protected from these other boys by invisible twenty-foot gates.

They know we've done something. But they're not sure what. We hear that we went to a pub. We hear we screwed two girls in the wood. We smoked in a pub with two girls. We ran the course backwards.

'You're in trouble!' shouts a squitty little third form boy, no more than thirteen years old.

I can't look at him. I look straight ahead, at the door of the headmaster's office.

Jack turns to the boy and waves.

Cecil Crompton, our headmaster, is a figure out of his time. A classical scholar, a Victorian-style pedagogue, The Cromp has deep-set, beady eyes set in a huge-nosed face. He looks like the child of cartoon parents.

He sweeps down corridors in his black gown, exuding the pomposity and jolliness of Empire. When delighted, his eyes blaze into yours, and he booms 'Indeed!' When angry, his gown flaps and his head shakes, like a discombobulated penguin.

He turns his unhappy thoughts into chunks of Latinate prose, to be pondered, construed and translated. This is how The Cromp tells Form 5A to shut up: 'There's an element of unrest in this form which displeases me greatly.'

Jack displeases him greatly. I please him greatly. Amen.

I love school because I'm good at it. I've won the Ernest Hawthorn Prize for Classics and the George Crabtree Prize for English Literature. Who were they, Ernest and George? Nineteenth-century worthies. They probably had slaves. They might want the prizes back if they knew I was 'of the Hebrew persuasion'. I don't care. I have their imprimatur.

I love school because there's certainty. The future is laid out before you, in rooms. I can go into a room like Lower Six Mod – never mind what that means, it doesn't matter – I can go into Lower Six Mod and know that I'll spend the next year there, the one after this, the one before the one I'll spend in Upper Six Mod, in the room opposite.

Jack would never go into a classroom, voluntarily.

'You have brought shame on the school,' says The Cromp.

'You have brought shame on the school, which cannot be tolerated,' he adds, with his genius for saying things twice, then adding.

'I shall address you first together. Then I will ask you, Lewin, to remain and you, Harris, to wait in my secretary's office. Then after I've addressed you on your own, Lewin, I will address you, Harris, on your own. Is that understood?'

We nod, having understood for some time. Jack fidgets.

The Cromp delivers his oft-quoted sermon about drugs. It's always he who oft-quotes it. We hear about the menace to society, the soft drugs leading to hard drugs, the Pusher at the Gates. (All Pushers were at Gates, in those innocent days. Nowadays they do deals from carphones as they drive to their house in the country. Pushers have their own Gates now.)

'Yesterday's incident showed a fundamental contempt for the values of this school. The values of this school are the values of society. The values of this school, as the values of society –'

At three that morning, eyes open, I've imagined that expulsion will make Melinda want me, just as, when we were falling off the bike, I imagined she'd want me when she woke from her coma and saw me gazing down at her.

She'll want me because I'm an outlaw.

But I'm not an outlaw. Here I am now, in the headmaster's office. There's a rivulet of sweat snaking between my buttocks, as if Jack had trickled oil down the back of my pants.

I don't want to be expelled.

Jack, who always saves me, can't save me now. He's gone.

'I do not have words to express my disappointment.'

Jack's in the secretary's office. He's left me alone with the headmaster.

'I am so terribly disappointed in you. You, an intelligent boy, have let yourself down.'

My parents will kill me. No. They'll kill themselves and let me live to know it.

'You have let yourself down. Grievously. Can you essay one good reason why I should not expel you?'

I can't of course. I said 'here, sir' from up that tree. I knew I'd done wrong and I wanted to be expelled.

'One good reason why I should not expel you from this school, forthwith? Is this the Lewin that won the Ernest Hawthorn Prize and the George Crabtree Prize? The Lewin of whom we all had such high hopes?'

He stares at me with his firing-squad eyes. He asks me to sit. He remains standing.

'I'm going to ask you some questions now. Consider your answers very carefully. Very carefully indeed.'

'Did you or Harris or a third party purchase the drugs consumed that afternoon?'

What answer does he want? That's all that matters.

He doesn't want the answer 'me'. He wants but doesn't expect the answer 'Harris'. That's why he's included the 'third party'.

'A third party, sir.'

'Would you be prepared to elucidate the name of that third party?'

He expects me to refuse.

'I'm afraid not, sir.'

He nods. This is good. I'm honourably refusing to incriminate the third party. Of course, he and I know the third party doesn't exist. The third party is in fact the second party, Jack. I'm refusing to snitch on Jack.

Technically, my answer's true. I didn't purchase the drugs consumed that afternoon. I gave Jack money which Jack gave to Ned the Big-Nosed Freak. But that's different. That's investing, not purchasing.

'Whose idea was it to take the drugs?'

I wait to be offered the standard options: A) Me. B) Harris. C) A third party, codenamed The Phantom. But no options are forthcoming.

It was not my idea to take the drugs. I cannot tell a lie.

'It was not my idea, sir.'

I'm still not snitching. I'm still not a snitching self-serving collaborator. Let others work out whose idea it was, of the two of us in that tree. My lips are (virtually) sealed.

'I thought not,' says the headmaster. He's all a-quiver now. Everything is falling into place. He struts up and down, excited, past a painting of a whiskery, saturnine predecessor: George Crabtree, headmaster (1887–1911).

The late George Crabtree wants me to stay. The Cromp wants me to stay. They want me to bring glory to the school. They want me to win a place at Oxford or Cambridge.

'Then we can safely deduce it was Harris's idea,' says The Cromp, with booming smugness.

I feel loathing for him and myself. So I do what my father has told me a witness should never do: I offer up unasked-for information.

'I went along with it, sir.'

'Ah well. The good are often led astray by the bad.'

No. I can't have that. I start talking, unsure where my talk will go.

'I'm not sure the dichotomy's that simple, sir.'

He's nonplussed. But he doesn't interrupt. I've used the word 'dichotomy', which is to be encouraged. It's to be encouraged greatly.

'There's a great tradition in Western civilisation of artistic experimentation with pharmacological substances.'

Yes. I know where I'm going now. It's fine if I smoke dope. I don't do it to cock a snook at authority. I certainly don't do it for fun. Unlike that snook-cocking funster Jack, I smoke dope to uphold the traditions of Western civilisation

'One thinks of Thomas de Quincey and *Confessions of an Opium-Eater*, sir. One thinks of Aldous Huxley and his experiments with mescaline, as chronicled in *The Doors Of Perception*.'

'You've made a mistake. Do you regret it, wholeheartedly?'

I can't look him in the eye, anymore than I could look at Melinda Spears's nipples. 'Yes, sir,' I say to his nose.

'I'm prepared to look upon your indiscretion with leniency. Not that I will allow it, in any sense, to go unpunished. But in the light of what you've told me, I must regard Harris as the primary wrongdoer.'

This is long enough looking at anyone's nose to know where you've seen it before. It's the nose of Ned the Big-Nosed Freak. They say The Cromp's son went to America and was never heard of again. But they're wrong. I'm sure of it. This is the school where his old man fucks with minds.

'I know your son Ned, sir,' I say.

The Cromp goes deathly quiet. The grandiose authority drains from his face. I could push him over with my finger.

'Harris and I both know him, sir. Your son's just like Harris, sir. They're not evil. They're young men going through a phase. They should be kept within society, sir. Not, with respect, sir, expelled. I won't say any more, sir.'

No. To say more would be indiscreet. There's no doubt, though, from The Cromp's expression that he's understood exactly what I've not said. I'm offering discretion as to the source of the drugs. In return, all I seek is the non-expulsion of Jack and me.

If it's blackmail, so be it. I've reached the limit of my badness. Blackmail is the crime that suits a boy like me. A non-violent crime, the components of which are knowledge and discretion.

'Stand up, please.'

The Cromp has a look I've seen elsewhere. It's the one I saw in Melinda Spears's eyes, when I signed her cast with my jism. It's the look that signals the termination of intimacy.

The headmaster, back to his best, booms: 'When Mr Blakeley apprehended you and Harris in the tree, Harris was in possession of the drugs. Not you. Do you understand?'

'Yes sir.'

'Cannabis, as is well-documented, impairs short-term memory. Did you smoke cannabis in that tree?'

'I can't remember, sir.'

He nods his assent.

'None of what has passed between us today will ever leave this room. Do you understand?'

'Yes sir.'

'Failure to run continuously in a cross-country race is a very serious matter. Do you understand that, David?'

David. Oh yes. David understands.

The Cromp suspends me from school for a week. For stopping.

Eileen, The Cromp's secretary, is a female, a gender rare in our school. She's Irish, with long brown hair and a mellifluous voice. Nobody isn't in love with her. Even Magnus Thornton, who claims he's gay. (He is – he's now the house manager at the Theatre Royal, Norwich, the dream boyfriend I out to my mother.) Magnus says he wants to hold Eileen and plait her hair, like a doll.

Eileen's wearing an orange dress.

I come out of The Cromp's office. Jack stands, ready to go in. I'm not sure what to do with my face. But it doesn't matter. He's not looking at it.

'You should wear more orange,' he says to Eileen. 'You can get away with it.'

Jack goes into the office. Eileen waits till he shuts the door behind him, then smiles.

I wasn't there. I don't know what happened, only what Jack told me.

The Cromp accused Jack of 'corrupting a silver riddle' by taking drugs in a tree. It has taken me more than thirty years to work this out. I'm sad Jack died before I could explain. He corrupted a *sylvan idyll*.

The Cromp told Jack he'd be writing to his parents to tell them he was expelled from the school with immediate effect.

Jack told The Cromp that one day he'd make him sniff his Jag.

The whole thing's a fix, a blatant injustice. That night, at home, the injustice continues. My mother screams at Sylvia Harris down the phone: 'Your son forced my David up a tree!'

An hour later, my father knocks on my door. I'm listening to John Coltrane playing *Summertime*. He stands there, uncharacteristically perky. He recognises the tune and unwisely whistles along to it. Jazz is precisely what you can't whistle.

'We all do it, you know,' he says. 'I committed indiscretions when I was young.'

I wonder what he means. Is he referring to the night he didn't brush his teeth? A self-absorbed man, not by nature parental material, he talks as if he were in a play, acting someone called 'Father'. Or even 'Second Father'.

'You'll make further mistakes, I've no doubt. It's the obvious people who do best. They know what they want and pursue it in an obvious way, which means that they have an infinite capacity to negotiate and renegotiate. The essence of negotiation is to make the other party feel lesser.'

I don't see Jack for a month. His father makes him take his O-levels anyway. Uniquely, Jack sits his exams at a table in his parents' lounge. Danny's obliged to hire an invigilator to sit there with him, day after day. It's a punishment, yes, but it's also a kind of spoiling. Like Mark Leboff's chauffeur, Jack's invigilator is a rich kid's appendage. Jack, who never learns his name, calls him 'my invigilator'.

In answer to all the Latin questions, Jack writes '*Vivamus vivamus vivamus vivamus*'.

He proves the old adage: write what you know.

BOY EXPELLED FOR SMOKING POT IN TREE

John Harris, 15, of Woodfield Avenue, Golders Green, a fifth-form pupil at Highgate School, has been expelled for smoking cannabis during a cross-country race. Harris left the course to take the drug in a tree, where he was apprehended by his Housemaster, Martin Blakeley, 46.

Headmaster Cecil Crompton, 56, said: 'We cannot tolerate this evil cancer at the heart of our society.'

I'm sitting in Jack's bedroom. I've come to say sorry. I want to tell him exactly what I said to The Cromp, which I never have, not in detail. I want to confess that I collaborated with the enemy. I want to explain why.

But he's ahead of me. He's always ahead of me.

'Forget it. You gave me the push I needed.' He takes back the cutting from the *Hampstead & Highgate Express* and reads it, yet again.

'Typical, isn't it? They say I'm fifteen but I'm sixteen. The press distorts everything.'

'What are you going to do now?' I ask.

3

Into The Wilderness

Every showbiz biography starts with a dream. You root for the dreamer as he follows his dream and fights for it. You fear for him as a host of dream-crushers slam the door in his big-eyed, hopeful face.

At some point, you find yourself thinking that the dreamer will fall by the wayside, even though you know that can't be true. You've bought the book precisely because the man lived out his dream. You haven't bought a book about a man on the wayside, of whom you've never heard.

Nevertheless, that wayside-jeopardy is compulsory. A life story's not a life but a story. There's no story without the overcoming of odds.

Let's say our man's English. He's a singer or comedian, dreaming he'll be a star of stage and screen.

There's a scene, just before the dream-door opens and fame rushes in, when our dreamer's alone in a car or motel or café. It's raining. It's Sunday night. It's Cleethorpes. It's Accrington. It could be Widnes. It is, to be sure, a Northern town that evokes the death of dreams. I apologise if you live in any of those towns. (Or Batley.) I don't make the rules.

Nobody came to his Cleethorpes gig. Nobody laughed in

Accrington. Nobody hired him after his audition for *Cats* at the Lloyd Webber Theatre, Widnes. (Or Batley.)

Our dreamer, at this low point in his life, loses faith in his dream. All his dream has ever brought him is hurt. He never wants to think about his dream again. (NB – he reaches for bottle?)

Then he sees something he never forgets. It could be a lame dog. Or a bird with a broken wing. Maybe it's a bird with a broken wing on the back of a lame dog.

The lame dog shuffles down the street on its three good legs. The bird with the broken wing struggles to be airborne.

He looks at this scene through the Sunday night Northern rain on the window (or windscreen). And he says to himself: 'No! I'll never give up on my dream!' (NB – radio plays *My Way*?)

But here we are. Jack is sixteen. And still there's no dream. How can this be?

The dream should be around page one. That's what Caroline Bliss would say. On page one of the manuscript of *That's All We Have Time For*, she'll write 'Dream?' (Not that I'll ever give her that manuscript. It's too late now. I've gone too far with this.) And she'll underline it, as she underlines everything in her life.

First, you state the dream, as bald and unmistakeable as an egg. Then you give evidence that your subject dreamt the dream from an early age.

For a singer, you write: 'He always dreamt of being a singer. Before he was old enough to walk, he sang along to songs on the radio.' For a comedian: 'He always dreamt of being a comedian. Before he was old enough to walk, he made funny faces.' For a sprinter: 'He always dreamt of being a sprinter. Before he was old enough to walk, he sprinted.'

This isn't *That's All We Have Time For*. This is the truth. Jack had no dream. Who dreams of hosting a chat show? This is what I'll never write:

Sylvia, now a sprightly, twinkling eighty-two-year-old, vividly remembers the first time she knew Jack had a gift that would one day make him a household name.

'He always dreamt of being a host. Before he was old enough to walk, he hosted,' she recalls.

'I remember one evening when my husband came home from work. I was in the kitchen, putting flowers in a vase. Jack was in his high chair, bashing his fried egg with a spoon.

My husband walked in and put his briefcase down. He kissed me then he smiled and said: "Hello, little Jack!"

Jack put his spoon down calmly on the side of his plate. Then he looked up at his Daddy and said: "Hello. Good evening. And welcome."'

A year after his expulsion, Jack waits outside the school for me and Geoff Bergman and Nigel Hoffman.

Jack is a shelf-filler in a delicatessen in the Golders Green Road. Thursday is early closing.

Geoff, Nigel and I walk to a café on Highgate Hill with Jack and his moustache. There we listen, awed, to Jack's despatches from The World.

'I've been looking for a flat. It's not easy. You want somewhere you can take someone back to, don't you?'

We agree, from the depths of our ignorance.

Agitated, he tugs at the left-hand end of his moustache. He knows it won't come off.

'You're leaving home, then,' I say.

There's someone like me in every drama, someone who plod-dingly summarises what needs no summarising. In a drama about the Abdication of Edward VIII, for example, there's always a Royal Plodder who says, 'You're giving up the throne for the woman you love, then, sir.' Sir nods, too polite to add that he knows this already. Everybody knows it. The woman who cleans the throne knows it. And yet there's a certain plodding pleasure in hearing it put into words.

Jack reaches into his pocket and takes out a packet of Benson & Hedges.

'Excuse me,' he says.

Jack leaves the table to ask for a light. There are only two other customers, neither of whom has a light, so Jack asks the waitress. The waitress goes behind the counter and finds a box of matches. Jack thanks her. They talk and laugh.

During this, none of us says anything. We're thinking about the waitress. Each of us knows he's too inhibited to do what Jack is doing.

Jack returns to the table. 'It's good not to carry a light,' he says. 'You meet people.'

Jack smokes, though he's no good at it, no good at it at all. He kisses the tip, then blows before the smoke can do its work and its damage. We of course, in our school uniforms, aren't offered the packet.

Nigel glances at me then Geoff. It's the glance of a man who can't believe the quality of the smoking he's witnessing. Nigel, a short, wiry, intense boy with an abrasively sharp mind, has never really liked Jack.

'Yeah, my dad's thrown me out the house so I need somewhere to live.'

'How can you afford it?' asks Nigel.

'He'll pay. On condition I work in the business.'

We're silenced again, absorbing the complexities. It seems that Danny's disowned his son in order to own him better.

'You don't want to work for him, though,' I plod.

Jack shrugs. 'I get a place.'

He finishes his coffee, kisses his cigarette, screws up his face. 'I hate these things.' He stubs it out. 'Makes your moustache taste of tobacco. I'm giving up.' He picks up the pack. 'Coffee's on me.'

He goes to the till and pays the bill. We watch as he persuades the waitress to take the cigarettes, even though she's embarrassed and is not a smoker herself.

The waitress is a thalidomide victim. We've admired her dexterity. We've inwardly saluted the management of the café for giving her a job. We've hoped our faces registered nothing when we saw her for the first and second and third and fourth times. But we've not chatted to her and made her remember us, not like Jack.

Jack sits back down, with the air of a man who's taught us a lesson in manhood. This is what men do in the world. They find flats. Pay bills. Give fags to thalidomide waitresses.

'My dad wants to open a store in every town in England. Well, not in. On the edge of. That's the future.'

We nod. We don't know anything about the future of flat-pack furniture.

'None of you will ever sell anything.'

Is this prediction, contempt or envy? Whatever it is, it's accurate. Geoff Bergman will be a dentist. Nigel Hoffman will be an economist. And I, of course, will work in a bookshop for fourteen years.

I know, I know. But working in a bookshop, in a small Suffolk town, is not selling. Mostly, you're dispensing information. Of my fourteen years, a year was spent explaining that we didn't stock pens. Six months were devoted to telling people where was good for lunch.

'Do you think I should keep my moustache?' This is not to us but to the waitress, as she leans to put our cups on the tray with her pincer-like half-limbs.

'No. You should shave it off. It hides your face.'

Eighteen months after that, in the Freemason's Arms in Hampstead, Jack and I are celebrating the greatest triumph of my life.

I've been awarded an exhibition to read English at Cambridge. My mother has never looked and will never look happier. She's dizzy from watching her dialling finger. Her telephone voice, through constant performance, is as metronomic as the Speaking Clock. My mother is the Speaking Mother. This is what she says: 'Hello (WOMAN'S NAME), it's Leah. How are you? Good. I thought you'd like to know – David's been awarded an exhibition at Corpus Christi College Cambridge.'

Her mother was born in Poland. She was born in the East End. And now here's her son, speeding towards Corpus Christi College Cambridge, an arrow in the heart of the centre of society. What could be better? What could be higher? What could be more more?

I'm opening the bowling for England with Winston Churchill (capt). As we saunter on to the pitch at Lord's, Noel Coward (wkt) sings my song, in all its insouciant alliteration: 'He's the Boy from Corpus Christi College Cambridge'.

Jack arrives in the pub and hands me a carrier bag. Inside, I find a bicycle pump and a mortar board. I'm touched. I ask what he wants to drink. He tells me to stay right where I am, goes to the bar and returns with a bottle of champagne.

'That's fantastic!' I say. 'I didn't know you could get champagne in a pub.'

'You can't,' he says, not explaining, as if I wouldn't understand. (I still don't.)

He tosses a packet of cigarettes on the table.

'I thought you'd given up.'

He shrugs. I notice he buys packets of ten now, in an attempt to reduce the number he smokes. He pours the champagne.

'Here's to Professor Ondiments.'

I drink. I swell with confidence and pride.

'I don't know if I want to be a professor. That requires a supreme critical intelligence. Maybe it's better to be a creative force than a critical one. You could argue that a fifth-rate novelist gives more to the world than a first-rate critic.'

Jack nods but says nothing. I expand on my theme. My voice loudens. The nearby drinkers, all denim and beards and roll-ups, or gypsy dresses and centrally-parted Joni Mitchell hair . . . they can tell. Here's a boy with a first-class mind. He's forceful. He's reflective. He's subtle. He's the boy from Corpus Christi College Cambridge.

As I drink more and more, Jack drinks less and less. He doesn't smoke at all.

'It's like my dad. He's a barrister. He's essentially a critic of the law. He spends his time interpreting and giving opinions. Wouldn't he better off enforcing it?'

Jack looks puzzled. 'I don't understand. You want your dad to be a policeman?'

I take another sip. An idea fizzes and bubbles.

'No. In a sense, I wish my dad were a criminal. I mean, one's father constructs an ethical fence which one can climb over or not. But maybe one finds out who one is quicker if one's dad's the wrong side of that fence.'

Around me, they can't help listening. They've never heard this idea so brilliantly expressed. They've never heard it expressed at all. It's that priceless thing, a new idea.

'You've always been clever, Dave.'

I wave the compliment away. 'There's clever and clever, Jack. Excuse me.'

I go to the toilet. My head spins. I'm sick.

When I return, Jack's no longer in his seat. He's in the other bar, offering his unopened packet of cigarettes to a blonde girl who's sitting with a group of friends. She looks unsure. Jack insists. They talk. Her friends laugh. Finally, she takes the packet. Jack walks away. Her friends tell her, go on, go on! She gets up and pursues him. She asks him something. He nods. She goes to the bar to buy him a drink.

What am I meant to do? Return to the toilet? I've no more sick to give.

Jack, who hasn't drunk all evening, takes a pint of beer from the girl. Then he sees me and tells her he must rejoin his friend. She quickly borrows a pen from the barman and writes her name and number on the back of his hand. He reciprocates.

I'm an intellectually pretentious boy, drunk with self-regard. (Please. Allow me to be hard on myself. It will give me greater licence to be hard on Jack.) But I believe in something. I believe in scholarship.

What does Jack believe in? I thought he believed in giving up smoking. I thought he believed in giving away his terminal packet of cigarettes to someone less fortunate than himself. In that Highgate café, he did these things sincerely. But he's taken that sincerity and turned it into a technique.

He buys cigarettes to not-smoke. He buys them as currency, to give to girls, bogusly claiming he's giving up.

He turns himself into a conman and the girls into prostitutes. Is that too strong a word?

He's trying to buy sexual favours with packets of cigarettes. And, to add insult to insult, he's using packets of ten.

What sort of man is Jack, at eighteen, that he can walk into a tobacconist's and think to himself, it's cheaper to give up smoking packets of ten than packets of twenty?

He's a businessman, that's what, who calculates he can halve his investment and get the same return.

He's a businessman who works for his father. I'm an intellectual and a prig. This was what was always going to happen.

'You OK, Dave?'

'Yeah, I'm fine.'

'You smell of sick.'

'Yeah. I was sick. But I'm fine now.'

'Would you like this beer?'

As he proffers the beer, I see the back of his hand. She's written 'Christi' on it.

'Why's she written my college?'

'What?'

'That girl wrote Christi.'

He puts the beer down. We study the back of his hand together.

Yes. Of course. Chrissi. I see that now. Jack is welcome to her. I could never love a girl like Chrissi. She puts hearts above her 'i's.

At university, there are no parents. They're absent, along with the insights they give you into the nature of their sons and daughters, who are now your new best friends.

Into this parental vacuum, you can pour anything. You can say, as the guy who lives next to me in college does, 'Hi, I'm Switch.'

There's no mother or father to scold him and tell you his name has always been Rupert. It's Rupert's first term in Year Zero. He can be whoever he wants.

Tim, of the Dylan-curls and the long-held silences, has a father who's an admiral. But it's not something he talks about. There's no something he talks about. It will take me more than a year to discover that not only is his father an admiral but his mother played tennis for Hampshire. Tim, like me, like everyone, is a university orphan.

This is why I dread the arrival of Jack. Jack's a representative of my past. He may not be a parent but he knows who I am and what I was.

I don't want Jack to ask me, in front of Tim, why I'm walking in that newly-minted way. Jack won't understand that I've outgrown my old walk, along with my boyhood clothes and hair. I lope now, in a round-shouldered way, weighed down by my greatcoat, which makes me feel I'm wearing a backpack *and* a frontpack.

This is me now. This is New Me, with my lope and the bush of hair. It's not long but what it lacks in length it makes up in width. This is Year Zero Dave, demotic Dave, never known as David.

Jack tells me he'll arrive around eleven on Saturday morning. I tell him I'll meet him at the station. I wait on the platform. But he doesn't get off the train that arrives at 10.56, nor the one after. At half-past eleven, I leave the platform to ring his parents. They're the only people I can think of who might know where he is.

But he's there, in the station foyer. He's driven to Cambridge station. It hadn't occurred to me he'd come by car. And it hadn't occurred to him to question my meeting him at the station when he was intending to drive.

We look at each other as if we're unsure who the other one is. As we get in the car, he says: 'I've got a present for you.' The present covers both back seats. Jack won't tell me what it is.

'So what d'you think of my car?' Jack asks. This tells me, as we've established, that he's having a sexual relationship with his car. But cars, like parents, are something nobody in Cambridge has. Jack's on my territory now. There are ten thousand of us without a car and, more tellingly, maybe half of this pedestrian population (my half) are left-ish and piously indifferent to material things, unless they're books or records. We just don't care about cars.

'It gets you from A to B,' I say. This is not even true. We're in a traffic jam. It would be too cruel to say it gets him from A to A.

Eventually, we find a parking space, a ten-minute lope from the centre. It takes two of us to carry the package. With my lope and his walk, we fail to find a good rhythm.

We drop off the package in my room. He tells me to open it later. I ask him what he thinks of my room.

'Yeah,' he says, paying me back for the car.

I take him on my Saturday tour of Cambridge, which, though I've been in residence just a few weeks, is rigidly ordered. We start at Andy's Records in Cambridge Market. I suggest he buys Mike Oldfield's *Tubular Bells* for a mere ninety-nine pee. 'Is that good?' asks Jack, ill at ease, reluctant to risk the money.

'It's far out,' I reply, which tells him nothing. My people, my new people, don't ask if *Tubular Bells* is good. Everyone owns a copy. Like King's College Chapel or the River Cam, *Tubular Bells* is a feature of the landscape. Is the River Cam 'good'?

At the Castle pub on Castle Hill, we meet Tim and Helen William. We drink pints of Greene King. We eat New Dave pork pies. (Dave was one of the Chosen People; New Dave is a man of the People.)

Helen likes clever men, Jack can tell, so he doesn't talk to Helen. Tim doesn't talk to anyone, basically, so Jack doesn't talk to Tim. Then in walks Charlotte Crouch, in her fur jerkin, eyes blazing. He talks to her all right.

'Hi, I'm Jack. I love your fur. What is it?'

'It's fake,' says Charlotte.

'Yeah? They're killing fake animals now?'

Charlotte looks at him and looks away, which is worse than not looking at him in the first place.

The personality drains from Jack's face as Charlotte, without warning, lambasts Kissinger's bombing of Cambodia. Jack leans lower on the bar, cowering near Tim, who can be relied on not to lecture him or demand his opinion.

It's not just that Jack knows nothing of Kissinger except that he sounds Jewish. Jack's never met a sexy girl with political opinions. Melinda Spears had political opinions but Jack didn't find her sexy.

He's probably thinking – forgive me, I should be more Elvis-biographer – he's *definitely* thinking a sexy girl shouldn't have political opinions. They'll make her less sexy.

And, let's not forget, Jack's a retailer now. He can't afford political opinions, which are bound to alienate someone. A retailer needs all the someones he can get. If this Kissinger wants to buy a teak-style veneer bedside cabinet from the DHF flat-pack range, well . . . who he bombs when he's not buying it is not Jack's concern.

'Has anyone got a fag? I'm out,' says Charlotte. I leap in. 'Jack's just given up. I'm sure he's got one.'

'If he's given up, he won't have one,' says Charlotte.

'That's right,' agrees Jack, aching to be somewhere else.

'Oh well.' Charlotte raises her pint glass. 'Here's to your next poem, Tim.'

Jack steps away from the bar, as if distancing himself from a vomiting customer. He's terrified to be too close to what he now learns is a poet. The politico was bad enough. Just how inadequate can one town make him feel?

'I've given up that cigarette thing,' says Jack bad-temperedly, as we walk from the pub to the betting shop, where I have an assignation with Switch.

'You've given up giving up, eh?'

He nods, too defensive to be teased.

The smoking motif continues in the betting shop, whose air could be bottled and exhibited in the Victoria and Albert Museum: a Woodbines and Player's No 6 fug that's gone now, wafted into history.

I introduce Jack to Rupert/Switch and his pals, Alex and Johnny. Alex and Johnny ooze old money and blond self-confidence. Switch, as his name no longer suggests, was at Eton with them. He's the most richly charming of them all.

'You a bastard for the gee-gees too?' he asks Jack, offering him a roll-up. Jack looks at the impeccably tubular roll-up as if it were a turd. Alex and Johnny give Switch a red pen and ask him to circle horses' names in *Sporting Life*.

'Why's he smoke roll-ups?' Jack asks me. 'He's rich, isn't he?'

Jack no more understands Switch than Charlotte. He can't cope with the student mind. Yes, Switch could buy cigars for everyone present. But he smokes roll-ups out of kinship with his fellow patrons, the snaggle-toothed pensioners and stunned Irishmen. By rolling his own, he spends even less than they do on their Woodies. Switch wants to know how it feels to be poorer than the poor. His cheap suit is every bit as cheap as theirs. I happen to know it belonged to his Nanny's dead husband.

Jack refuses to bet. Switch and I lose two quid after two quid. Before the 4.05 Novices' Hurdle at Chepstow, Switch tries to goad him into action. 'Come on, Jack, you can afford to lose a couple of quid, can't you?'

Jack tells Switch he can afford to lose far more than that. He gives Switch twenty pounds and tells him to put it on Farmer's Boy. Then he heads for the door.

'Hold on, matey!' calls Switch. 'There's no Farmer's Boy in the race.'

'I lost already then. Come on, Dave.'

Why's Jack trying to show up my new friends?

'Look! There's a couple of you!' says Jack, hugely amused, as we walk from the betting shop back to my college. And, yes, there are two guys on the other side of the road loping along in greatcoats, each with an Andy's Records carrier bag. Let Jack mock. I'm happy to see two people like me. I'm happy to see two thousand. I don't find their cloneship belittling. On the contrary. I feel reassured.

Everything I do, I do because my fellow students do it. Everywhere we've been today – the market, the pub, the betting shop – my presence has been validated by the presence of three or more of my peers.

Jack doesn't need the kind of reinforcement an institution can bring. He'd never study furniture retailing, never wear a T-shirt saying Flatpack U. He's peerless.

We reach the porter's lodge of Corpus Christi College Cambridge.

'What are we going to do now?' asks Jack, expecting an answer he won't like.

'It's Massed Bells at six-thirty.'

'What's that? Your life's so weird.'

In my small, privileged cave of a room, Jack's present occupies half the space between the bed and the window.

At half-past five, we finally get it open, with the help of a Stanley knife borrowed from an engineering student, who can be trusted to own that kind of thing.

'Happy Birthday, Dave.'

'It's not my birthday.'

'It will be.'

'What is it, Jack?'

It's a drawer, but not as we know it. It's a new product, intended for what Jack calls 'young people who live on their own' – his curious, detached term for the group to which he belongs.

DHF have identified a gap in the market. The gap is under the bed. I am, Jack tells me, the first person in England to have an Underbed Storage Unit.

I don't have it yet, of course. It has to be assembled. Here it all is, inside the package: pieces of wood, metal runners, an instruction leaflet, a polythene bag with screws and two handles, a kind of key thing. The prospect is terrifying, especially to me, who's grown up in a house where doing it yourself means making your own phone call to plead with a gentile to come and do it for you.

There's a knock at the door: Tim, Helen and Charlotte, wondering what we're up to. Jack, who's kneeling on the floor, springs to his feet.

'Come in, you can give us a hand, it's going to be great!'

Next door, Switch hears the noise and comes to find out what's happening, Jack greets him like an old friend: 'Switch! You any good with an Allen key, matey?'

For the next three quarters of an hour, we're all in Jack's business. Yes, the Unit is mine. But his is the business we're in.

For the first time in Cambridge, Jack is himself. He's jokey, he's excited, he cajoles and manipulates – literally so, as he manoeuvres Helen into the position of the stick man in Figure G. We're nearly there. Figure H is the endgame.

Helen slides the top of the unit into place and we all applaud. It's the biggest storage unit we've ever seen. Wide as my bed, and tall as the gap beneath it.

'Come on then, Dave. Do the honours.' I kneel and prepare for Figure H: the placing of the unit under the bed. Jack has saved Figure H for me because it calls for no skills, beyond placing.

'Hold on,' says Jack. 'We've forgotten something. The prayer for launching a product!'

'Fire away,' I say. Jack rocks back and forth and intones: '*Baruch utoh adunoy elohainu melech haolom boray paree ha storage unit!*'

'God, you're so Jewish!' says Charlotte to Jack, excited by the Hebrew. 'When did your family come to this country? Were they fleeing a pogrom?'

She manages, somehow, to make this sexy. Jack gives her his family history but keeps it brief. He's keen to see the unit in place.

(What Charlotte says to me, after Jack's gone, is: 'Your friend's so sexy. I'd love to give him some head.' It sounds, now, more dated than erotic. Does it even make sense? Yes, you can give a person 'some' crisps. But surely with 'head', it's the packet or nothing. She's trying too hard. But, then again, we're all trying too hard. I'm trying too hard to be so many things. I'm trying to be left-wing, I'm trying to be cool, I'm trying to be hippy, I'm trying to be myself.)

I clear my Underbed of shoes and the Barclay James Harvest

LPs I keep meaning to sell. Then I slide the prayed-for unit towards the gap.

It won't fit. The Underbed Storage Unit won't fit under my bed. The height's not a problem but the width is. The legs are in the way. It would be fine if the bed didn't have legs.

Jack pales.

'Sorry, Jack,' I summarise, 'it won't fit between the legs. I suppose I could, you know . . . remove the legs and rest the bed on the unit.'

He can't speak.

'It's not made to support the weight of a bed,' says Helen, with the calm clarity that will take her to the top of the BBC Radio Drama Department. We all stare at the unit and wonder what it's made of. Plywood? With some kind of plastic veneer? It's certainly very flimsy. Tim, later, ventures the opinion that it's made of 'pappadom'.

Switch draws on centuries of savoir faire and masterfulness. 'Come on,' he says, 'let's put it under the window.'

'Yeah. An underwindow storage unit,' says Tim.

Switch and I swivel the unit round and place it under the window. 'All's cool,' say Tim and Switch, in unison. Everyone nods, except Jack. The event, for Switch and Tim and Helen and Charlotte, is over. We're getting ready for the next event. Massed Bells starts in ten minutes.

'I better skin up a sausage,' says Switch, exiting and returning with a lump of hash and the necessaries.

Tim and Switch and Charlotte and I suck on the hash teat. Helen abstains, as she always does, because she was a head girl and knows her limitations. Jack abstains because he's brooding on the failure of the Unit.

It seems to me that, far from expanding, Jack's mind has contracted. He used to fight against his father's expectations. He sought out ways to rile him. (I'm the parent-pleaser, not Jack.) Now here he is, deeply concerned about the future of the Unit. Corporate Man, in his father's corporation. Why does he care if his dad's forgotten that beds have legs?

Compare and contrast dope and coke, the joint and the line. 'Joint' suggests something shared, a joint activity. Whereas 'line' is cold, geometric, singular.

Switch lets his mouth fall open. He looks like an upper-class cod. I move my face close to his. I blow my smoke into his mouth and – mlop! – he clamps his lips around it.

Go on. Try sharing your coke with a friend. Move your face close to theirs. Blow your coke out of your nose and – fnaah! – up their nostril.

Jack will be a coke man, before the end. Or should I say The End.

The next thing I know, I'm alone with Jack. I turn on my hi-fi. I get my record out of the carrier bag. I open the windows wide.

I put the record on the turntable and stand with the stylus ready and waiting above the already-spinning disc.

Outside, from the main gate to New Court, I hear Alex's booming, moneyed voice counting down from ten to one.

He blows his whistle.

I lower my stylus.

Massed Bells begins.

It's the happiest moment of my life and the unhappiest of Jack's. And of course I'll write more about his moment than mine, because writing about happiness, like the thing itself, can't last.

Massed Bells is the synchronised playing of *Tubular Bells* on two hundred hi-fis in two hundred rooms in Cambridge. Fifty in Corpus and fifty each in St Catharine's, Pembroke and King's.

Yes. Two hundred. In a student population of ten thousand, it's not that many. Tim and I, who conceived it, meant to extend it to every college in Cambridge. But we failed to get it together.

Of course we did. This isn't a project about success. We're not aiming for a world record. We don't want to be on TV. We're not even after a photo in the *Cambridge Evening News*. What would they photograph? Grooves?

That is not to say we've been casual. We didn't arrive at *Tubular Bells* without effort. So many seminal LPs were rejected: Lou Reed's *Transformer* (too vicious), the first Roxy Music (too cerebral), John Martyn's *Solid Air* (too ethereal), Pink Floyd's *Dark Side Of The Moon* (too bleak), Rod Stewart's *Every Picture Tells A Story* (too Rod Stewart). That's Tim's opinion. Rod can't be Rod Stewart enough for me, not in his early, brilliant period.

Neither of us can remember who suggested *Tubular Bells*. We think it has something for everyone: it's progressive, it's rocky, it's folky, it's pastoral, it's whimsical in a very English way. The whole thing smacks of the teenage prodigy in his boarding-school bedroom, which is not far off the mark – Oldfield recorded it, aged nineteen, in Richard Branson's studio in Oxfordshire, playing almost all the instruments himself.

You could say, as Caroline Bliss does, why not assemble an orchestra and get them to play it? Then it would be a proper activity.

She misses the point and substitutes a more successful point of her own. We don't want a high-achieving thing like an 'activity'. We simply want to listen, en masse.

Jack sits on my bed, twirling his hair. 'This is such a waste of time,' says Jack. 'How long's it going to go on for?'

Does Jack love music? We know he loved Neil Diamond. But what does 'love' mean? For New Year's Eve, 2002, Jack flew his mother and himself to the Pepsi Center in Denver, Colorado to hear Neil Diamond in concert. Or did he? Was the concert not the pretext for a multiple non-musical quest? Jack and Sylvia were really in search of the perfect airline seats, limousine transfer, hotel rooms, pre-concert supper, concert seats, hotel and, of course, the perfect bathroom/comfort station/powder room/can.

That, of course, is only the half of it. There are his mother's cousin Ruby and her husband Sid to be catered for and over-whelmed. There are the negotiations with Neil's management for a dressing room schmooze to culminate in *Auld Lang Syne* and a kiss for Sylvia from Neil.

In the event, all Sylvia gets is a signed photo; presumably, it's signed by Neil. Jack feels rejected. Yet his mother pronounces herself thrilled with the visit. The hotel was beautiful, with plates so clean you could eat your dinner off them. And the pillows! The pillows were the biggest she'd ever seen. They alone were worth sitting through all those songs for.

There's silence in my college room. Outside, Alex is counting down from ten to one. Then he'll cue Side Two.

I get to my feet. Jack's disappeared. Side Two starts without him.

An hour later, by dint of a telephone message left at the Porter's Lodge, I join Jack for supper at the Garden House Hotel. This isn't right, this isn't right at all. This is the Cambridge of parents. Your parents, your ghostly parents, buy you meals in hotels.

'It's a good Chicken Kiev,' says Jack. 'I've done a lot of trav-elling in the last eighteen months. I know what I'm talking about. What do you think of the wine?'

'Not much,' I say, though I've no views at all. I just want to rebel against Jack's authority. By buying my supper, he's turned himself from my guest into my host.

My rebellion backfires, though. He agrees. He studies the bottle and discovers that the wine is Australian. He asks the waiter to explain himself.

'Australia's a great wine-producing country,' says the waiter, which is news to Jack. 'Would you like me to bring you a superior example, sir?' Jack, rebuilding his ego after the Unit fiasco, has no doubts.

'Yeah, bring me the best you have.'

'Certainly, sir.'

The wine arrives. We agree it's better, though we can't say how.

Jack gestures at the river and beyond, to my greatcoated and Afghan-coated and fur-jerkined peers, as they fight the November chill. The wind, they say, comes straight from the Urals to Cambridge with one aim in mind: hurt the students.

'This whole place is so unreal, Dave. I don't know how you stand it. What are you going to do when you leave? Books don't teach you anything about the world.'

We hack our way through our Black Forest gateaux, saying very little. The coffee arrives, in thimble-sized cups to advertise its strength and authenticity. This coffee, says the coffee, with utter self-importance, must not be drunk. It must only be sipped.

I feel lonely. What have I got in common with this man, with his university of life talk, that makes him sound so old and Northern?

Then something happens and he's no longer a man.

What happens is this: the bill. I see it, upside down but no less deadly. I know what he's thinking. I don't expect him to say it out loud. It's the saying out loud that tells me the bravado's gone.

'Christ, Dave, the good wine was seventy quid.'

'Shit. That's heavy.'

'What's going to happen to me?'

'Can't you afford it? I mean, if you can't afford it . . .' I trail off. I've no idea what will happen if he can't afford it. I certainly don't want to pay it.

'It was really good, though, wasn't it?' says Jack.

'It was really tasty,' he adds, sounding younger with every remark.

'It was great, Jack. I really enjoyed it. I wish I could drink my own urine.'

He smiles. I've helped. I've definitely helped.

Jack writes a cheque for a hundred and nine pounds, which includes a ten per cent tip. I argue against this. Seven quid of that tip relates to one bottle of wine. Does a seventy pound bottle require more delicate or difficult handling? Does it weigh, for example, ten times as much as a seven pound bottle?

Jack takes this in but overrules me. He doesn't want to lose face. 'Let's get out of here,' he says.

He leads the way out of the restaurant. Then, confusingly, he walks up the stairs.

'Cancel it,' I say, referring to the hotel room we're in, the one Jack checked into during Side Two. 'I'm sure they'd give you your money back or something. I thought you were going to sleep on my floor.'

'Don't make me sleep next to that thing.'

'The thing's not your fault. It's your dad's fault. You just work for him.'

I couldn't be more wrong. His dad knows nothing about 'that thing'.

After eighteen months of being the boss's son, learning the

116

business, taking criticism, knuckling under in return for the salary and the rent on his flat, suppressing and suppressing and suppressing his ego, Jack struck out on his own. He had an idea. It was Jack's Big Idea: the Underbed Storage Unit. Jack had to bring it to fruition on his own, without any help from his father. Every prince is a king-in-waiting.

Prince Jack got on to the 'new product Swedes' (sic) and told them what he wanted. The first thing he wanted was secrecy. They were to deal with him, only him. What were they to think, those Bjorns and Monikas? They didn't think, we're not taking orders from a nineteen-year-old. They took in his surname and got on with it.

The more Jack tells me, the more excited I get. I enjoy Jack's disaster, as any friend would. All friends, surely, are *schadenfreunds*. But there's admiration too. I'm remembering why I like him. There's no one else in my life who operates on this scale. What's the worst thing that can happen to a student? An essay crisis? A broken heart? A denim shortage? Jack's out there, in the world, getting it wrong with consequences as far away as Sweden.

Jack specifies the dimensions of the unit, based on his researches. (Basically, he measures his own bed.) The Swedes agree, down the phone. They don't question it. Jack's the boss.

They submit their designs. Jack approves them, with minor changes. He knows he has to be unhappy with something and decides to dislike the handles.

The Swedes change the handles, then send him their invoice. Jack hadn't foreseen an invoice; he'd assumed they were salaried employees who worked for his father, not people who charge by the hour. And, of course, there are many more hours in Sweden. At midnight, the Swedes had their sleeves rolled up, designing storage units in the sun.

Jack questions the hours and they reduce them, reluctantly. They submit a replacement invoice.

Two people can sign company cheques – his father and his father's business partner, Sol Kleinmann.

'What could I do?' asks Jack. 'I couldn't forge Sol's signature.' No. Of course not. Jack and his father are blood. If you can't forge your father's signature, whose can you forge?

And then what? Jack's created his own world. He's free to make up the rules, down in that black hole under the bed where he's prince of all he surveys.

He gets on to the factory where the furniture's made, just outside Stockton-on-Tees. Heir to the throne . . . secret project . . . he knows how his system works. Jack orders them to make up five thousand units. A cautious figure. Jack's intending to test the market, in towns with a high proportion of single people. Like Cambridge.

This caution is evidence of his maturity; when his father finds out what he's done, as he surely will, Jack wants him to recognise that his son has a business brain as well as creative flair.

I don't know what to say. By now, it's nearly one in the morning. Jack's been talking for three or four hours.

'I have go to bed, Jack.'

'Yeah. You're right. Listen, thanks for the guided tour. It's been a great day. Only cost me about fifteen thousand quid.'

He leaves for London in the morning. He misses Sunday morning frisbee on Jesus Green. He misses lunch in Grantchester. He misses everything, never to return.

Every day, when I wake up, my eye, which used to be drawn to the Klimt and Schiele posters, goes straight to Jack's Unit. Those handles really do seem to follow you round the room.

I put my shoes in it, along with the Barclay James Harvest LPs. Within a week, it's stuffed full of stuff. I can no longer open it. Such is the stuff's volume and weight, it takes two of us to open the thing, each one tugging on a handle. Who wants a drawer six feet wide and three feet deep? The Swedes have been bad. The bloody thing has the opposite of rarity value. It has rarity worthlessness.

But I have to admit, it's an attraction. The thing becomes known as Dave's Drawer. People come to my room to see it.

Jack, to me, was always famous, even when he was obscure. For me, there's no Before He Was Famous. In Cambridge that day, in a literal way, he did what celebrities always do: change the room. When I enter a room, the room stays the same; whereas, when a celebrity enters a room, people speak differently, re-choreograph themselves, feel more alive. Some make a big show of ignoring the celebrity, to prove that this puffed-up new arrival won't affect them at all. But that big show is new behaviour. They've changed.

Ten days after Jack's visit, a foreman at the factory rings Danny Harris to check if he really wants a drawer six feet wide and three feet deep. Danny puts the phone down and shouts 'JACK!' – so loudly that his secretary vacates his outer office, to allow him to kill his son in peace.

Danny, I learn, doesn't do that. He just says: 'How could you do this?' He says it over and over, every which way: accusingly, disbelievingly, more in sorrow than anger, more in anger than sorrow. He stops at every stop on the how-could-you-do-this line, from '*How* could you do this?' to 'How could you do THIS!' To all of them, Jack says: 'One mistake!' The more he says it, the less it convinces his father. It's not that convincing to begin with. The First World War, in a sense, is one mistake. (I know all this from Sol Kleinmann, who was in the next office. He seems to have relished every moment.)

Finally, Jack cracks. If his father doesn't respect him, he's going and he's not coming back. Jack storms out the office. Unfortunately, he leaves his jacket on the back of a chair. So he has to storm back in to get it.

'Take it,' says his father, 'like you take everything. That's my jacket, I paid for that jacket. Go on, take it. Order five thousand more and make me pay for them too!'

'You paid for it, you have it!' says Jack, throwing the jacket on the floor. 'I hope it chokes you!'

He re-storms out, then realises the jacket has his money in it. So he goes into Sol's office and borrows five pounds. (Sol's very amused at the notion that a jacket could choke Jack's father. 'If it had buttoned at the collar, maybe.')

For the next two days, Jack doesn't speak to his father.

On the Thursday morning, his mother intervenes. She rings Jack at his flat and tells him he should write his father a letter. He's young, he's made mistakes – 'One mistake, Mum!' – he should let his father know he's sorry. Then he can get back to work.

Sylvia Harris is no fool. She has two sons, one of whom, Marcus, is hardworking, sensible and reliable. The other son, Jack, was expelled from school, attracts women and forges cheques. She knows which son's going to make his mark on the world. That's the son who should be running the business, while his brother trains to be an accountant, with the long-term aim of working for, but not supplanting, his father. If Jack's the Prince, his brother Marcus is the Duke Of Somewhere, a professional sibling, famous for being a brother; the one of whom it's always said, if his brother gets run over by a bus, he's King. But the Prince always travels by car.

'Sorry, Mum. I can't do it. I'm not talking to him ever again.'

He's right. Next morning, his father dies.

Jack's nineteen when his father dies. I could have written: 'Danny Harris dies when he's forty-seven'. But Jack's the priority. As Zoe Taylor says (*Independent On Sunday*, June 11th, 1995): 'You lost your father when you were nineteen. Was that the worst thing that ever happened to you?' She doesn't ask 'Was that the worst thing that ever happened to him?'

Jack replies simply:

'He was my father.'

In its gravity, its dignity, even its metre – the three monosyllables, the duosyllable, the dying fall of the *er* – Jack's answer achieves a marvellous grace, without saying anything at all.

'Ondiments, it's Jack, my dad's dead. Luckily it was quick. He didn't know what hit him.'

I'm too young to know that every death comes with its own phrase. It's as if this phrase is billeted on the death by the authorities. The Phrase is accepted gratefully. It gives everyone something to say. For Jack's dad, The Phrase is *luckily it was quick*.

Sixteen years later, when my dad dies of cancer, The Phrase is *luckily he had time to say goodbye*. He was told he had six months to live and, with lawyerly pedantry, he died after six months. But had he dropped dead without warning, like Jack's dad, it would have been *luckily it was quick*.

Then there is The Term. With Danny Harris, it was Ischaemic Heart Disease. What is 'ischaemic'? Can you catch ischaemia? Can you get ischaemia by worrying about what the hell it is? I don't know. I don't even want to know. But I know that, armed with The Term and The Phrase, I can cope.

Sitting in my bedroom in my parents' house, a schoolboy's bedroom that no longer feels like mine, I brood on the death while listening to Dylan's *I Pity the Poor Immigrant*. Then I ring Geoff Bergman, who says: 'I know. He just called me. Ischaemic Heart Disease. But luckily it was quick.'

Danny had a heart attack in his office. The last thing he did was ask his secretary, Margaret, to make him a cup of coffee. Margaret, an unmarried woman who'd worked for him for nineteen years, brought the coffee into his office, put it on his desk and stirred it, like she always did.

Then she saw Danny lying on the floor. She cried out. Sol Kleinmann ran in and gave Danny the kiss of life. (Danny was, according to Sol, 'a very good kisser'.)

Sol rang for an ambulance. He and Margaret sat in the office. Margaret wept. Sol put his arm round her. They knew Danny was dead.

Later that day, Margaret resigned. Not because Danny had died but because, while she and Sol were waiting for the ambulance, Sol drank Danny's coffee.

When I hear this, I too am appalled. It's an act of grotesque opportunism. Your friend and partner lies dead on the carpet. You can't drink his coffee. You just can't. It shows disrespect, not just to him but to Death. You have to respect Death and behave well in Its presence.

When I commiserate with Jack about Sol's behaviour, he doesn't agree. He's with Sol.

First, why waste coffee? Second, his father took two sugars in his coffee and Sol takes one. So Sol knew, as he reached for the coffee, that it wouldn't taste good. But he drank it anyway, so as not to waste it. If anything, Sol's was an act of self-sacrifice.

Jack gets angry when I reply that 'why waste coffee?' is the kind of remark that provokes anti-semitism. He accuses me of living my life in fear. I should do what I have to do and not worry what people think. He tells me if he dies with a coffee in his hand, I should go ahead and drink it.

It's December 27th 1973. No one's away on holiday. Christmas, back then, runs from Christmas Day to Boxing Day then stops. We're in the East Chapel at Golders Green Crematorium. 'We' means everyone: the Lightstones, the Goldmans, the Dunstan Road Cohens, the Kreitmans, the Leboffs, the Sheinwalds, the Hoffmans, the Feigenbaums, the Sterns, the Golds, the West Heath Drive Cohens, the Birneys, the Vetchinskys, the Goldenbergs and the Cronins, with their daughters Rebecca and Rebecca. Forgive me, it's thirty years ago. Rebecca and Rebecca are not twins. It's just that I can't remember the one who's not Rebecca's name. Worse, I'm becoming convinced as I write this that the one I think was not Rebecca, was, in fact, Rebecca. It's Rebecca who was not Rebecca.

It's my first funeral. My parents didn't take me to my grandparents' funerals, fearing it would upset me.

I want the funeral to be spiritual and profound, not superficial. To me, it doesn't matter what people wear. Respect for Death is not a question of clothing. My parents insist I wear a dark suit and black tie. When we're safely seated, I loosen the tie. I stare at the Rebeccas. I know for sure I won't marry either. I'm too unconventional.

Then the Bergmans walk in. Geoff doesn't even have a tie. He wears a suit but it's a denim suit. Mrs Bergman has the look of a woman who regrets she has a womb. Two shoulder-length black skirts of hair hang from Geoff's centre-parting.

Mrs Lightstone tut-tut-tuts. 'It's a scarecrow,' says Mr Lightstone. My mother squeezes my wrist and nods at my loose tie knot. I wince and look away.

Geoff takes his seat. He won't forget what he's about to see. He, of all people, will be the one who propels Jack to television fame.

Fifteen minutes later, Marcus stands before us, clutching his speech as if, were he to drop it, it would smash.

Marcus begins: 'My father was born on May the 11th, 1926. He died on December the 20th, 1973.'

Sol Kleinmann makes a face. Marcus, he fears, is going to account for all the days in between.

'His beloved younger brother Stanley was born on June the 8th, 1931.' There. Sol's wrong. Already, five years of Danny's life have passed.

Were I Marcus, I would do exactly what he's doing. I'd mention everyone and everything. I'd pay my father's death the respect it deserves, equating respect with detailed research into my father's life.

Marcus pauses briefly, waiting for his hands to stop shaking. But they don't. The words must be blurred from their animation. Not once does Marcus look up from his precious piece of paper. He's written on both sides, so his whole speech can fit on a single sheet. He's thought, no, I won't have two sheets of paper. I don't want to run the risk of the second sheet getting detached. He's pictured it in advance, as I would. The second sheet flying away, the Rabbi bending down to retrieve it at the same time as him, the awkward after-you-no-after-you.

Marcus pays tribute to his father's outstanding energy and business drive. He calls him a devoted father and a loving husband.

How many sons have stood where he's standing and spoken those words? The next devoted father is probably on his way, in his hearse. That doesn't diminish what Marcus says. We can place ourselves on the continuum of grieving humanity.

Marcus stops, thanks us and, still avoiding our gaze, sits back down in the front row, next to his mother.

Jack walks on, looks at us and says: 'Who's going to drive me mad now?'

The room changes. It reddens. I can feel the collective blush. My mother tut-tuts.

The only person who laughs is Geoff Bergman.

'My dad was short . . . my dad was powerful . . . my dad had secrets . . . typical of my dad to go and die without telling anyone first.'

What's he on about? It's *devoted* father, not *short* father.

Jack has no piece of paper and appears to be making it up.

As he talks, he walks from side to side. Nobody moves at a funeral service. The widow doesn't move, the Rabbi doesn't move, the congregation doesn't move, the dead person doesn't move. A funeral, surely, is a hymn to stillness.

I distract myself by staring at the coffin. I know I'm not a religious believer. I'm a Jew with no faith, an atheist Jew. What do I think is in that coffin? Does it contain a soul?

It's no good. Jack's changed me. I no longer feel profound. The coffin, inevitably, reminds me of the Underbed Storage Unit.

Jack, still walking, takes a pink silk handkerchief out of his pocket. 'My dad and I fought all the time. But I still got him this Christmas present. He died before I could give it to him. I don't know what to do with it now. I suppose I could blow my nose on it.'

He smiles at the Rebeccas, who giggle with nervous excitement.

'Thank you,' he says.

Now I understand. Jack's doing a stand-up routine, in the American-Jewish style. Hence the wandering. He's a wandering Jewish stand-up. When he ends, I expect him to say: 'My name's Jack Harris. I'm here every Wednesday at eleven. You've been a great audience. Good morning!'

We're at his parents' house, in the kitchen.

'Amazing speech,' says Geoff. Jack nods. Then he pauses, as any proto-celebrity would; he's giving me time to add my compliment. I thrust my spoon into the potato salad. The moment passes.

'A lot of it was wasted on this crowd,' says Jack. Sol waves at Jack and Jack moves off to join him.

What will Jack do now? Working in his father's business was his destiny, as going to university was mine. If you'd seen us, at eight, at that restaurant kitchen window, you'd have pointed at him and said *furniture* and at me and said *Cambridge*.

Sol's business partner Danny is dead. Today is the first day of the rest of his death. Sol must act.

Sol doesn't invite Jack to come back and work in the business. Instead, he tells Jack he's a smart boy with an 'unusual mind'. He's sure an opportunity will present itself to Jack. When it does, Jack will seize it with both hands.

After a decent interval – as the caterers are emptying the ashtrays – Sol has a talk with Sylvia. He persuades her Jack's talents lie outside the business. He also persuades her to sell him Danny's stake, to secure her own future.

The business, he explains, with a heavy heart, has been in a slump since the Seventies began, what with poor sales figures, the oil crisis, property prices and inflation. (He probably adds the break-up of the Beatles.) Sylvia should get out while the going's good.

Sylvia duly sells Sol Danny's stake. But when Sol himself sells out to some Finns, two years later, hey presto, the business is thriving. Sol gets enough money to keep him in Florida, in coffee, for the rest of his life.

When that happens, Sylvia tells Jack that Sol is and always was a crook. But Jack can't help admiring him. He even visits him in Miami when Sol's an old man, living with his fifth wife. Each of Sol's wives is younger than the one before. The fifth is about nineteen. Basically, after her, it's death or prison.

The business goes out of the family. Jack goes out of the business. He's in the wilderness now.

4

The Road To Fame

The Garden of Rest at Golders Green Crematorium is twelve acres. (You see? *Research*.) Danny Harris (1926–1973) is memorialised by an azalea at the southern end, the Golders Green Station end. If you visit the garden, you'll surely feel the healing power of Nature. Of course, a small voice inside you will keep on saying, *boy, what a prime piece of real estate – you could build a lot of flats on these azaleas!* Don't worry. That's your dark side. We all have one. Just ask Sol Kleinmann.

Jack drives me there in the spring of 1974. He talks about his sex life. Since his dad died, he's been very active. He claims to be 'worried' about the number of girls he's had. There's a new thing in America called 'sex addiction' and he's concerned it might be coming over here.

Keen to change the subject, I ask him what else he's been doing. He tells me he's been spending a lot of time in the Garden of Rest.

He has nothing to do, no job to go to. His mother, spoiling him as he'll later spoil her, makes sure he doesn't lack for funds. (Under the terms of his father's will, he won't receive his inheritance till he's twenty-one.) Bizarrely, the garden has become Jack's wilderness.

He goes there to reflect on his role in his father's death. His role, he believes, is central. He thought that when his father found out about the unit, his father would kill him. But the opposite happened.

'I gave my dad a heart attack, Dave.'

As he drives into the crematorium car park, I tell him not to blame himself. His father's father died of a heart attack too, so genetics must have played a part. Jack almost snaps the handbrake: 'You don't understand!' He's turned his father's death into a drama written by and starring Jack. There's only one part and it's his.

He smiles at a woman as we get out the car. 'That's Carol. The cleaner.' Jack knows the cleaner. He truly is Mr Crematorium.

He knows her because the first time he came (post-funeral), he asked Carol where he could get a cup of coffee. She directed him to the café.

Adjacent to the café is a private room where mourners are gathered for drinks and sandwiches. Jack looks at them and feels excluded. The next time he comes, he wears a dark suit and black tie.

It's not like gatecrashing teenage parties. There's no front door to be shut in your face. He walks in. No one, at first, even notices him, as he tucks into the smoked salmon sandwiches.

Eventually, he finds, some kind woman will come up and say hello; by which time, from some cursory eavesdrops, he's worked out who's dead.

It's no hardship to shake her hand and express his sorrow. On the contrary, he's happy to do it. He feels a kinship for all mourners. He's happy, too, to tell her who he is. He's Phil Cohen. He works for the firm of accountants of which the deceased was a client.

This, he's glad to say, always kills the conversation. It's ischaemic in its potency. He's then free to get back to the chopped liver. (Fact: I've never learned to drive. As a consequence, I have a highly developed sense of who I should be nice to, in a room, in order to get a lift. Jack, who never learned to cook, had a similar sense of how to get people to give him food.)

On his fourth or fifth mourners' lunch, Jack marches up to the buffet and says: 'Not smoked salmon sandwiches again!' Luckily for him, this tactless outburst works in his favour.

'It's so predictable, isn't it?' Jack turns. 'I told Mum to make them serve something else. We don't have to have what everyone else has. Oh well.' She introduces herself as Nicky. Jack introduces himself as Phil.

Their relationship, you might think, is therefore based on a lie. But no. Nicky has lost her father. When Jack/Phil says he lost his father six weeks before, when he says it's the worst thing that's happened to him because he feels responsible, when they console each other in Jack/Phil's flat that night, it's all true.

'What happened after that?' We're crossing a bridge over an ornamental pond.

'That was it. I didn't see her again,' replies Jack.

'Why not?'

'I can't stand being an accountant.'

I laugh. He looks askance. It's not a joke. Jack, in his wilderness years, uncertain what he's meant to be doing, wants me to believe that when he throws himself into something – say, imaginary accountancy – he does it with complete authenticity and intensity. He's discovered that imaginary accountancy isn't for him. The imaginary hours are too long; the imaginary numbers make his head spin. So he can't carry on seeing Nicky. He's living a lie that's wrong for him.

Jack stops. 'I know you don't think much of me.' He says this in a soft voice, looking down, avoiding my gaze.

These are the times when I feel we're reproducing our fathers' relationship. I'm the scholar to his rough diamond. I'm the one who patronises and feels himself to be of greater worth, intellectually and morally. I want him to know it's not like that.

'You shouldn't –'

Jack holds up his palm to shut me up.

'I'll prove to you I'm worth something.'

Jack's not talking to me. He's talking to the azalea, his father.

'You'll never know but I'll prove it to you anyway.'

A woman stops at the neighbouring rhododendron. She's in her mid-twenties. Jack can't keep his eyes on the azalea.

'Who did you lose?' he asks her.

'Pardon?'

The question surprises her, with its odd, Americanised wording.

'Who died?'

'My mother,' she replies. 'Long time ago.'

'I'm sorry,' says Jack. He observes a few moments' silence, out of respect.

Then, with a heavy heart, he says: 'My dad died.'

'I'm sorry,' she says.

They stand quietly, side by side, brought together by loss. Then she smiles and waves at a man of her age who's walking towards her, across the bridge.

'Come on,' Jack says to me. 'It's lunchtime.'

Let's deal with the night I lost my virginity. Jack was there, of course he was, though not in person. It wouldn't have happened without him.

I was so much in love with Anna I could hardly speak. What use was speaking anyway? I don't speak Italian. Yes, Anna was in Cambridge for an English language course. But by the evening, when she saw me, she'd had enough English-speaking for the day.

We spent most of the time in my room listening to *Blood On The Tracks*. Dylan devotees believe it's one of the great works of art of the twentieth century. You can disagree. You're entitled to your opinion. But I think you should know you're wrong.

Anna loved it. She could see that I loved it so she loved it too. That was evidence of her feelings for me.

In my experience, or inexperience, there can be no sex without love. There can certainly be love without sex, though. On this crucial night in May 1975, there's a great deal of love without sex. There's a river of love without a drop of sex.

I'm desperate for *Blood On The Tracks* to end. We need one of those silences that can only be filled with sex.

But you never get to the end of a great work of art. I mean that metaphorically, of course. In a literal sense, we'll get there. But we can't stop before then. We can't cut it off. This is *Blood On The Tracks*. It demands to be heard, in its entirety. In that sense, we'd be better off listening to *Chirpy Chirpy Cheep Cheep*.

Would we really fill the silence with sex? I can't bring the moment to its crisis. What if she rejects me? What if it goes wrong?

Then the absent Jack makes his presence felt. Anna, who's as frustrated as me, gets up from her chair. She's not sure where to go next. She tries standing at the window but that doesn't work. She can't sit next to me on the bed. What if I reject her? What if it goes wrong?

Anna sits on the Underbed Storage Unit. The top gives way. She shrieks with laughter. I make the short journey from the bed to the unit. I lean down to pull her up and, within fifteen minutes, I'm a man.

Two nights later, I'm a man again. Then her course ends and Anna returns to Pisa.

* * *

133

In the summer vacation, I fly to Pisa. Jack gives me a lift to Heathrow, which is generous of him. Later, his generosity will threaten to destroy me. Not now.

'Sometimes, sex is fantastic and sometimes it feels like nothing.' This is me talking. This is David Lewin talking in the manner men talk, which I've learned from Jack. After two sexual acts, I know.

'You've got your foot on the ladder, Dave.'

'I love her,' I reply. When I talk of love, I sidestep competition. There's no measure for love, no calibration, no ladder. Dave 'Two Rungs' Lewin wants to talk about love.

As he drives me down the M40 to Heathrow, I talk about nothing but Anna. Or is it the M4 or the A40? As the passenger, happily, I don't need to know. Anna drives, I tell him. Anna's going to drive me around Tuscany. She's going to borrow her brother's car. Anna's brother's called Gilberto. Gilberto, at twenty-two, is already bald. Anna likes my hair long. Anna's hair is brown and short and hangs over her right eye. Sometimes, to see things at a certain angle, she has to toss her head. I love the way Anna tosses her head.

Jack says only that he's happy for me.

'Good luck!' he shouts, as I walk from his car towards Departures. I thank him, of course, but a lover doesn't need luck.

Anna works in the day in her brother Gilberto's leather goods shop. She's saving up. She wants to go and live in Rome and work in a travel agency. So I spend the days alone, wandering around Pisa, looking at the sights. There's far more to Pisa than just the Leaning Tower. If I sound like a brochure, you understand – I love Anna and she wants to be a travel agent.

Her parents are very nice. We smile a lot and they're impressed I know the names of so many kinds of pasta.

I sleep in the spare room. Late at night, I sneak into Anna's bedroom. But we just cuddle. We know this isn't the time or place. We both sense the all-seeing gaze of the Pope and her parents. She's arranged to borrow Gilberto's car on Friday night. We'll go somewhere then and I'll be her *uomo*.

On the Wednesday night, as we lie there side by side, heads on the pillows, Anna says: 'You're a very nice man but we don't have nothing in common.'

When Jack picks me up from Heathrow, it's my turn to say little.

When he asks me how it went, I tell him I don't want to talk about it. He says how sorry he is. I don't mind that. I'm not someone who minds people being sorry for him. I'm sorry for me myself. I'm partial to all the singer-songwriter emotions: self-pity, yearning, wistfulness, rage at love's injustice, unshakeable belief in your own uniqueness. Is this last an emotion? It feels like one.

What I mind is Jack's wisdom. Here it comes now, as we stop at a roundabout:

'That's the thing about foreign girls. It's great to begin with. They're on holiday so they're on for it. And you look, you know, what's the word, not "different", what's the word?'

I shake my head. I don't want to help.

'Come on. What's that word?'

'Exotic?'

'That's the one! Galton-White would be alive if he'd met a foreign girl. English girl sees a virgin in a mac. Foreign girl goes, oh, that's an interesting mac. Never seen one like that before. Must be English.'

We exit the roundabout on to some really big road.

'Foreign girls are great for a while. Then you find you've got nothing in common.'

My experience is not unique, insists Jack, with his reductive wisdom, so unsinger-unsongwriter.

'I think you're right, though. It's not about numbers any more. I've done that. I'm ready for love. Can you put on Capital Radio? Ninety-five point eight.'

That summer, Jack's working in telephone sales, for a company that makes and installs windows, doors and conservatories. Jack still has a way to go before he becomes TV Jack, the reason we're all here.

By contrast, that summer I stop developing. Though heavier and greyer now, I'm the person I was then, full stop. I think the same, vote the same and wear bigger versions of the same jeans and shirts. I still listen to *Blood On The Tracks*, which I own on vinyl, cassette and CD. When technology permits, I'll download it into the hot water tank, so I can play it through the taps.

'You're a very nice man but we don't have nothing in common.' A man can argue with that, passionately, convincing the woman that if they have love in common, they don't need anything else. Or he can agree with it and suggest they have sex.

After all, Anna's remark is a lurch into truth. It says, let's stop pretending, let's say what we think. The gloves are off and when the gloves are off then surely the knickers will follow. Let's climb the third rung. It's late. The Pope and your parents are sleeping.

I neither argue nor go for the sex. I just say, softly: 'We don't have anything in common.' Then I'm quiet. I leave Anna's bedroom a minute or so later, never to return.

This ironic detachment, this refusal to compete, took hold of me that summer. They've never let go.

* * *

It was Jack's mother who suggested the telephone sales job, given Jack's retail background and gift of the gab. Jack deferred to her, happily, as he never did to his father. He knew that when it went wrong, as it surely would, his mother would forgive him.

It certainly went well to begin with. Jack won Salesman of the Month for February 1975. He told me I shouldn't take that too seriously, as February's a short month. But he kept his award for the next nearly-thirty years.

I've got in it front of me: a framed certificate from Jupiter Home Improvements – Adding Quality To Your Home. A true Seventies artefact, it smacks of slatted vertical off-white blinds, heavy manual typewriters – ting! – hole punchers, pot plants, secretaries called June, big tie knots, printers' calendars, Artex ceilings, magnolia walls, Tupperware boxes of crustless white sandwiches puking sandwich spread. It's signed by Area Sales Manager Alison White and UK Sales Manager Derek Huuuluuuy (?).

March to July go fine, too. It goes wrong in August. An angry man from Hertford rings Alison White to complain of Jupiter's aggressive sales techniques. He claims a Jupiter telephone salesman has been pestering his wife with calls. He's forced her into buying things she doesn't want, which he's had to pay for. Alison consults the telephone log and discovers the salesman is Jack.

Jack points out that the wife's calls to him exceed his calls to her. If anything, she's been pestering him. Alison, suspicious, asks if he and this wife have been having an affair. Jack denies it, explaining that she's not very attractive. Alison asks how he knows she's not very attractive. Jack claims she told him. Alison asks why she'd tell Jack a thing like that. Jack, showing off his under-standing of female psychology, explains that a woman says she's not very attractive so you won't be disappointed when you meet her. Alison asks: 'And were you?' Jack, making his one mistake, answers: 'Yes.'

Alison fires him for impropriety and 'deviating from the script'. Jupiter telephone salesmen have strict guidelines as to what they can and can't say.

Jack can't argue with the deviation, but claims the impropriety took place in his own time. He also points out that she bought over two hundred pounds' worth of Jupiter products. Alison shouldn't be firing him. She should be giving him August Salesman of the Month. Who else could sell two patio doors to a woman who has one patio?

Jack tells me the story as we walk round a West Hampstead supermarket, one Saturday lunchtime at the end of August. He's buying 'food' to 'make' for our lunch in his flat round the corner. I'm carrying the basket.

On the phone, the Hertford wife has a gentle, understanding voice. He wants her to know he's not just a salesman but a man. He tells her about the death of his father. She tells him she's lonely but not very attractive. She certainly *sounds* attractive. After a week of conversations, he gets in his car to drive to Hertford.

Jack goes to her house. She has an angry face, so at odds with her voice on the phone. She tells him her husband is down the pub and won't be back till closing time. She puts her hand down his trousers without undoing his belt. She tells him to do it to her in front of the fire.

She takes off her clothes and lies down on the carpet. Jack turns off the lights and takes off his clothes. He lies on top of her. She smells of cheese.

'What kind of cheese?' I ask. I have to ask something. I have to show Jack I'm man enough to engage with the detail. I can't ask if he loves her, can I?

'I don't know. What's it matter? Cheddar.'

The husband returns – as she knew he would – and finds Jack on the rug with his wife, about to have sex. The story becomes

Chaucerian now. It turns into *The Wife of Hertford*. She screams at the husband that she's paying him back for Maureen, whoever that is.

The husband looks at Jack and says: 'Bloody hell, you're a good-looking bloke. What are you doing with her?'

That remark is the trauma for Jack. Not the sacking, not the exploitation, not the waste of petrol. He hates the husband's remark. He fears it's true.

'Honest to God, Dave.' Jack says to me. 'She wasn't that bad. I *like* Cheddar.'

We proceed to the back of the queue at the till. Jack says: 'So what you going to do when you leave Cambridge? Professor or something?'

I can't answer. I look for a distraction. There's a small boy in front of me, pulling on his mother's arm, trying to drag her back to the sweets and chocolate aisle. She keeps saying: 'Enough, Little Jeremy! I've told you. Enough!' She has an Irish lilt that makes 'Jeremy' sound like a beautiful name.

'Hi,' I say. 'You worked at our school.' She smiles, without knowing who I am. 'I'm Dave Lewin.'

Jack goes into action immediately. He puts up his palm, inviting Little Jeremy to punch it, which he does, reluctantly. Then Jack invites him to punch it again, this time moving it out the way as his tiny fist's about to connect. Little Jeremy laughs.

Eileen looks at Jack, with gratitude and curiosity. She hasn't seen Jack since he was sixteen. But Jack is special. How many boys get expelled?

'You were expelled, weren't you? Sorry. I don't remember your name.'

I know what's going to happen. I'm not jealous. In fact, I want to help.

'This is Jack Harris,' I say. 'His dad's dead.'

He looks at me, shocked. Why would I say a thing like that? How could I be so heartless?

Minutes later, outside the supermarket, as Little Jeremy hits my palm with his fist, Eileen puts a comforting hand on Jack's shoulder. They're talking too quietly for me to hear. He's not looking at her. He's staring at a point just above the kerb, wearing his azalea expression.

It's time to answer Jack's question. What am I going to do when I leave Cambridge, in less than a year's time?

I'm not as casual as I'd like to appear. I study like an immigrant for my Part One exams. I work into the night. I miss meals. I lie awake. I dream exam answers. I must – must must – do well, to please my parents and their parents and their parents' parents. My great-grandparents came here from Lithuania for a reason. I must advance the tribe.

I look for my result on the notice-board in the English faculty. There's a long list of names, a skyscraper. On the top floor are the Firsts. Then there are a few floors of Two-Ones; several floors of Two-Twos, those humdrum time-servers who know their place; finally, a basement of hedonists and nervous breakdowns – the Thirds.

I look for my name in the Two-One level, where I expect to find it. It's there. I'm delighted. I know I can better it next year. I'll work harder and get a First. Then I can be a 'Professor or something'.

I look skyward, to the Firsts, and there is her name.

A First acknowledges depth of understanding, sensitivity to nuance, encyclopaedic knowledge, an appreciation of the inter-connectedness of all things. Caroline Bliss, that nuance-free zone, can't have got a First. How is it possible? She used ambition. She used determination. She worked more nights than me, missed more meals, had more and better exam dreams in which, instead of arriving at the faculty in her nightclothes, to be given the Serbo-Croat exam papers by mistake, she got a First. She made lists:

1) Nuance
2) Interconnectedness
3) Buy more box files

I can't compete if it means competing with Caroline Bliss. We don't have nothing in common.

I leave Cambridge with a Two-Two. I squat in a house in Hackney with Tim and Charlotte Crouch. I work for a local homeless charity, as it's low-paid and has no career structure. Tim writes poetry and articles for literary magazines and lives off the dole. Charlotte works for the Transport and General Workers' Union.

We take it in turns to cook. At the butcher's in Ridley Road, I seek out ever-cheaper cuts. Shoulder of lamb gives way to neck then scrag end. Finally I just ask for 'stewing lamb' and he gives me brown cubes from the nameless and shameless parts of the baa-baa's body. We call it Dog Bowl of Lamb. It's excellent if stewed for two or three hours then thrown away.

Every Thursday I make cheese, bacon, onion and potato hotpot. It is, basically, Wednesday's cheese, bacon and potato hotpot, onionised – what Charlotte, when she's New Labour, will call *modernised*. (She's a backbench MP now, so bland and predictable she could represent Stepford. But I bet, when she loses her seat, she'll be exciting again.)

Charlotte talks through all our meals. The woman's verbal stamina is admirable, as is her appetite, for onion, for bacon, for Dog's Bowl, for sex. She eats and stays thin, burning off the calories with righteous anger.

Charlotte sets the tone for the house. She identifies and fights oppression wherever she finds it, which is everywhere, since she seeks it out, day and night. Frequently she finds it in her own bed. 'You sit on a man's cock and he thinks he owns you.' I shake my head at this outrage. A cause like this calls for a banner. Pass me my big black felt-tip. What to write, though? No Man, No You. No Cock, No Think. No Woman, No Own.

I'm a problem to Charlotte, as I don't fight oppression. I believe it's enough to be near her. I'm happy cooking and reading and going to the Screen on the Green to watch every film or punk gig they want to project at me. I'm happy answering the door and telling whatever oppressor I find there that Charlotte's not in.

Men, it turns out, are the lovelorn ones. They love Charlotte and want to marry her, or they want out of their marriage so they can be with her – but they can't leave their wives for they love their children too much. It's pathetic to find them loitering on our borrowed doorstep: Brian (our MP), Peter (deputy head of the local primary school), Gladstone the First (hi-fi salesman) and Gladstone the Second (Yardie). Gladstone the Second's the worst. He slouches and mumbles. I can't understand a word he says. Stand up straight, Gladstone! Shoulders back! You're representing your country's drug dealers!

I never invite Jack. He wouldn't understand why we've chosen this life, with its leaks and its mice and the rotten banister we use for firewood. (To stave off cold, I shave in my greatcoat. One Christmas, for a laugh which isn't funny, I bathe in it.) And, of course, if Jack came, Charlotte might put some of her head near him, which would upset the emotional balance. I don't want her myself, though, not even when she offers me a 'pity fuck' to bring in the New Year of 1977. She gets angry when I tell her I don't love her. What about her sexual needs?

My parents despair. One day, when I'm out at work, my mother comes round. Tim lets her in. She's carrying two large John Lewis bags. He watches, helpless, as she enters my room and removes the rug from my bedroom window. It's a burglary, in reverse: *Mother, 54, Breaks into Son's Room and Hangs Curtains*.

To make her less unhappy, I apply for a job as a clerical worker in the housing department of Hackney Council. At the interview, Mrs Caesar from Personnel asks what qualities I would bring to the post.

'I can withstand tedium,' I reply. It's my attempt not to get the job. At least I can tell my mother I tried. But Mrs Caesar, an ample West Indian woman, throws her head back and laughs so hard, you'd think she's alerting God to my remark. I get the job. My mother can tell Bea Goldman that I'm working in local government.

I'm in a great tradition, that of sensitive literary young men who get a dull job in a big city, to save their talent and energy for writing their novel at night. This is what I do, apart from the writing the novel.

Jack feels vindicated. He was right, aged eight, to abandon the pursuit of knowledge in favour of procuring chips. Books don't prepare you – didn't prepare me – for life. Look where they got me. Nowhere. It's no use telling him I've chosen nowhere. That just strengthens his case.

Jack is advancing all the time. The first boy I knew who had sex, was expelled, lived in a flat, is now the first man I know who lives with an older woman. Eileen, who's thirty-five, calls the twenty-two-year-old Jack 'Lovely Boy'. They live in her small terraced house off the Kilburn High Road.

Eileen's allure is considerable. She left the employ of the man who expelled him, dismissing The Cromp as 'that bloody dinosaur'. (Her Belfast accent makes the *aur* of dinosaur as thrilling as a lion's roar.) She's a vegetarian and Irish Republican, which makes Jack, her English carnivore, feel exotic. He's the only man she's ever 'been with', apart from her childhood sweetheart, Vince, who's now her ex-husband.

Jack tells me this in the Kilburn pub where we're to spend the evening, as Eileen goes to the bar to get in the Guinness.

Vince is in prison. A wages clerk in a factory, he got sexually involved with his boss, an older woman called Margaret. Together, they invented a phantom employee. For two years, thanks to negligent auditing, they were able to pay him a week's wage for a phantom week's work and squander the lot on what the Judge calls 'the wages of sin or, rather, the sins of wages'. (My dad still dreams of my being a barrister, when *that* is the humour of judges.)

Eileen tells me the phantom's name was 'John Harrison', which is virtually Jack's name. She believes it's a sign. They were destined to be together.

Jack, who once forged a cheque, feels he knows what it's like for Eileen to discover her husband was a criminal. He finds it exciting to be in a criminal's bed; especially a criminal of the white-collar, non-machete-bearing type.

Jack tells me it's love. And so it seems. Eileen's passionate, demanding and generous. She blots out the past and the future. What else but love would bring Jack to a cavernous pub, not five miles from where he was barmitzvah'd, to sing *Danny Boy* with Eileen and her two hundred closest Irish friends?

Jack claims he's only miming. He assures me that, last thing at night, he goes into Little Jeremy's bedroom and sings him a Jewish lullaby, by Streisand or Diamond, usually *People* or *Beautiful Noise*. Little Jeremy loves these lullabies. At the end, he sits upright and claps.

It's midnight. We're locked in a Kilburn pub. I'm wondering if I can ask Jack to drive me back to Hackney.

Eileen's brother Brendan stands on a table and sings *The Patriot Game*. Eileen joins in. At the end, she shouts: 'Kill the English!'

Jack turns to me. 'It's all right,' he says. 'She doesn't mean me.'

Alone in her house in Golders Green, Jack's mother is doubt-less reassuring herself. Jack is sowing his wild oats. If he's sowing them, they will one day be sown.

Eileen thinks it's a marvellous idea. She will bring all her friends.

Jack, spending most of his legacy from his father, takes a lease on a restaurant in Golders Green, the very one where we broke our fast on Yom Kippur. This allows Eileen to say it's destiny.

The restaurant is to be called KV. KV stands for its cuisine, which is to be Kosher Vegetarian.

Jack writes to Sol Kleinmann to ask him if he wants to invest. I've got Sol's reply, dated June 23rd, 1978. It reads:

Dear Jack,

Jews eat meat.

Kind regards,

Sol

Eileen tells me she knows from his handwriting that Sol's a crook. And heartless. He doesn't even send his regards to Jack's mother and brother. Doesn't he know that family is everything?

This is true. Jack's brother Marcus helps him draw up the busi-ness plan and volunteers to do the books. His mother pays for an ad in the *Jewish Chronicle*. She buys a dress for the opening.

I tell Charlotte and Tim about the idea, as we chomp our way through our stewed meat-alike in a street in Hackney that was once as Jewish as it's now black. Their reaction is the same as everyone's. They don't know what to say.

As the opening night approaches, I admire Jack more and more. He has faith. It's not religious faith, obviously, despite the kosher. He has faith in the muscularity of his idea, in himself. Kosher will appeal to the older crowd, he tells me, while vegetarian will appeal to the younger crowd, keen to try something different. And I mustn't forget that overheads are lower for a vegetarian restaurant. I nod my head. I don't forget it. Presumably, you save on carving knives.

Eileen, who works as the receptionist for a graphics and design company, gets the menu designed and printed at a bargain rate. Eileen, Jack, Geoff Bergman and I leaflet every house in Golders Green, which takes us a weekend. It's important to state that, in blocks of flats, we don't dump a bunch of leaflets in the hall but place them under the door of each individual flat.

On the opening night, Jack moves round the tables at high speed, working them like a president, making strangers his friends. Geoff Bergman, now a suited dentist, hair shorn to keep it from falling in patients' mouths, tells me he's sure Jack will 'make it', on the strength of his performance at his father's funeral and here.

Eileen, as promised, brings all her friends who – and why wouldn't they? – eat a lot of potatoes. Then they leave, as the restaurant isn't licensed. Eileen doesn't tell them they're supposed to pay. They shout: 'You're a good man, Jack!'

KV, a name you can't remember, lasts three months. Jews think it's only for vegetarians and vegetarians think it's only for Jews. Jack can't face telling the staff it's over. Eileen has to do it. Before he leaves his restaurant for the last time, Jack puts up a sign in the window: Recommended by the IRA.

Jack still has a few grand left. He takes Eileen to America to 'look for business opportunities'. Little Jeremy stays with Granny

Deirdre in Harlesden. They visit Jack's mother's cousin Ruby in Denver, then drive to Santa Fe, New Mexico, where Eileen's best friend from school lives with a Native American man who makes jewellery.

That is why I appear in the squat one night wearing, on my little finger, a silver ring inlaid with turquoise, made by a Navajo. Charlotte asks if, by any chance, the Navajo's name is Two-Men-Kissing.

There's only one way I can explain. Jack's a cause. He was an educational failure, unlike us. His dad died. He's got energy and talent but has had, so far, no luck. As I tell her this, I realise it's what I believe.

In 1979, Glenn Masters is one of the most famous people in the TV-watching world. Don't take my word for it, though, because I'm not sure that's her name. It's a name that applies to an actress in America and a footballer/plasterer in England. It may have been Bobbi Masters. Darryl Masters? Anyway, I'm sure of her fame, which is what matters.

That summer, she comes to London to publicise the new, bigger-haired series of *Dallas* or *Dynasty* or *Houston* or *Family*. (We don't have a TV in the squat.)

Jack's read all about her in an article, the kind they'll write about him one day. Her Favourite London Sight is Brown's Hotel in Mayfair. Her One Indispensable Human is her manager, Roger Steinman.

This is all the information Jack needs. He tells me to wear a suit and meet him at Brown's Hotel at eight on Saturday morning. He's going to give Glenn a present. He wants a photo of Glenn with one of his rings on one of her famous fingers. For Jack, that will be priceless.

Jack tells the receptionist we have a meeting with Roger Steinman. But she's not to disturb him. We'll wait.

We take a seat, near the door, and we wait for Roger Steinman. We don't have a meeting with him, of course, so there's no chance he'll be late. Equally, he won't be early or on time. Also, he and his precious charge may already have left the hotel. They may have gone out for the whole day. But they'll return. They have to sleep.

Why does Jack want me there? He's a cause for me but I'm not a cause for him. He wants me because I'm company and audience, because I validate him still, with my academic excellence, even though I've done nothing with it. He wants me because I'm a fan.

At half-past ten, Glenn Masters emerges from the lift with Roger, a bald man with a sharp black beard which slavishly follows his jawbone. Glenn has a tiny frame but a huge head, with big blue unblinking eyes, built for crying on camera.

They walk towards the door. Jack stands and shoots his cuffs. Roger stops at reception. He looks like the kind of man who can't walk past reception. He needs messages! action! information! in his World of Now.

Roger orders a cab to 'Kew Flower Gardens'. He asks the receptionist how long the journey will take. He doesn't like her answer. Thirty minutes? Is she serious?

Glenn waits for the problem to be solved. Roger stands there, wanting Kew to realise who it's dealing with, and move its leafy ass closer to him.

Jack steps in, discreetly asking Roger if he may speak to Glenn. It's a masterstroke. Roger's not used to being sweet-talked. Who sweet-talks Beast when Beauty is near? He nods his head, then remembers himself and asks Jack to keep it brief.

Jack welcomes Glenn to London. His manner and looks put her at her ease. He seems so mature.

'I'm Jack. I'm President of your Kilburn fan club,' says Jack. 'Thank you, kind sir.'

This, then, is Jack's first *chat*. Everything's in place: Jack, a star, an audience. It's not a conversation, which implies an exchange. It's an extraction, an extortion. Jack chats because he wants a photo. On television, he'll chat because he wants laughter and embarrassment and anecdotes and Pain Exclusives that reveal the star's 'true self'. But, more than anything, he chats to get attention.

'I'd like to present you with a ring on behalf of all your English fans. May I?'

By now, a few seconds into their relationship, there's physical contact. Jack slips the ring onto the fourth finger of Glenn's right hand. Glenn tosses her mane and pronounces it beautiful. She looks more and more like a tall puppet.

Roger isn't fooled. Roger knows a fan when he sees one. Fans are either overwhelmed or overwhelming. Jack is confident and self-contained. He's an operator like Roger. A rival. A merchant of some kind.

'Did you make that?' asks Roger.

'No, sir,' says Jack. I haven't heard him say 'sir' since school. He must have picked up the term on his trip to the States. It still carries the insolent false humility it did when he said it to Mr Blakeley.

'So what are you, a jewellery salesman?'

Jack falters. Glenn, enjoying Jack's admiration, chides Roger.

'It's OK. He's a charming young Englishman.'

Roger puts his hands up. The expression says: you're the client, you have your way, but I'm right. You're the show but I'm the business. I know when someone's trying to exploit you.

'Is it OK if I take a few photos of you?'

This is too much for Roger. The photos have a commercial purpose. He can smell it.

'Leave your name and address at reception, you'll get a signed photo in the post.'

'No, no, I'm happy to do it,' says Glenn.

'Is our cab here yet?' Roger asks the receptionist, who sends the bellboy scurrying out to check.

'I'm really sorry to bother you,' says Jack to Glenn. 'I know you don't have time for me.' Jack turns away, hurt. It's a confident strategy. Glenn responds.

'That's OK, Jack. The cab can wait.'

'Kilburn Fan Club? Come on!' says Roger. 'You ever heard of Kilburn? I never heard of Kilburn. You heard of Kilburn?'

He barks this last to the receptionist. The poor girl looks pained. She wants to please. How can she unlearn the fact of Kilburn?

'It's near West Hampstead, sir,' says her male colleague, a fearless man-kisser who clearly sides with Glenn.

Roger turns on Jack.

'There's no Kilburn Fan Club, right?'

'I'm the president,' says Jack. It's another term he's picked up in America. Americans, he knows, stand by a president.

The bellboy re-enters. 'Cab's here, sir.' Jack's desperate now. He looks at Roger. 'Please. I hired a photographer.'

It's another masterstroke, I think, till I realise the photographer is me.

Jack walks over and hands me the camera from his Sainsbury's carrier bag. It's as bad as being in a theatre and having an actor take you onstage. You are real and the actor is false. I am real and Jack is false. It makes me feel sick.

'OK. One photo,' says Roger.

I look through the viewfinder. Glenn smiles at the camera. Glenn's eyeballs are not like yours or mine. They are shinier, harder, more protuberant. They scare me. It's as if she's had her eyeballs lifted.

Roger walks to the revolving door. Jack gives me a little wave of the hand. Faster, faster! He's standing a few feet from Glenn, on the verge of a famous victory.

Jack is a gifted bullshitter, though. I'm not. I deal in truth.

I lower the camera and tell him, truly, that I don't know which button to press.

Jack blames me. He gets angry, which is unusual, as I never expect to affect him.

The encounter with Glenn is terminal. Jack's confidence collapses. He takes it as proof that the world doesn't want him.

A few weeks later, he starts work in Eileen's brother Brendan's electrical shop in the Kilburn High Road.

Brendan wears a Navajo ring, which Jack has sold him at cost price. He wears it on the fourth finger of his right hand, two along from his nicotine finger. In Kilburn, Jack's jewellery is fashionable.

In 1980, nothing happened. I know. I was there. Jack worked in the shop. I worked for the council. Then we went home.

This would be unacceptable in *That's All We Have Time For*. C.B. would write in the margin of this page: <u>Hits and headlines.</u> Hits and headlines place the reader in the tide of history. It's exciting. Something's happening all the time.

While the papers were full of Prince Charles's friendship with a nursery nurse named Diana, Rubik's Cubes swept a Thatcher-led Sheena Easton-loving nation blissfully unaware that the murders of John Lennon and JR were just around the corner. It was the year British Leyland launched the Mini Metro. But it wasn't the year Jack launched his career. His dream of fame was further away than ever, though this was the year Fame *was released.*

Unlike the two million unemployed, Jack had a job. He worked in an electrical shop on the Kilburn High Road, its till shorn of the sixpences that ceased to be legal tender in that Moscow Olympics year when Ronald Reagan was elected President just as Barbara Streisand's Bee Gees-penned Woman In Love *was enjoying its second week at Number One.*

Forget it. Jack was a self-centred person. If nothing happened to him, nothing happened.

Sometime in early 1981, I go round to see him. Eileen is out, in the pub with her friends. Little Jeremy, now seven, is upstairs. Jack recites numbers down the phone to a take-away Indian restaurant then calls up to Little Jeremy to tell him to go to bed.

'Fuck off, gobshite!' shouts Jeremy.

Jack shrugs. 'Kids. What can you do?'

Jack tells me he's come to realise something about life. Money and ambition aren't important. That's exactly what I believe, of course, but there's no suggestion he's saying it to ingratiate himself with me. After four years of living with Eileen and Jeremy, he's concluded that family's what matters. He tells me I should get a woman and a child and a job working with family.

He goes out and brings back the numbers. We check them against the menu to work out what we're eating. After supper, I watch as he puts up a set of shelves in the kitchen. He drills holes, puts Rawlplugs in them, screws uprights into place, checks them with a spirit level. Nothing goes wrong. Look: no anecdote.

The shelves are intended as a surprise for Eileen. Satisfied, he joins me at the table to admire his handiwork. I congratulate him.

I've never seen him work with his hands before.

And now, with the meal over, he even smells grown-up. He smells like a family man who puts up shelves. Is the pipe for my benefit or his? How can Jack smoke a pipe? No one we know has ever smoked a pipe. He can't like it. Or can he? Is it something he's grown to like, with maturity? I never know with Jack. Is this pipe the thing itself – maturity – or an advert for the thing?

The door slams. He calls Eileen's name. She doesn't answer. She enters.

'Is the boy asleep?'

Jack nods.

'What d'you call these then?' she asks.

'Shelves.'

'What d'you call those then?'

This time he doesn't answer. 'Those' are also shelves, also empty, on the opposite wall.

I want to be anywhere else but here. But it doesn't seem to matter if I'm here or not. Eileen doesn't acknowledge me.

She grabs a hammer and attacks the most recent shelves. Jack tries to disarm her but she screams. 'Fuck off, gobshite!' A hammer, you would rightly think, has no chance against shelves. They're screwed in place. She should really be attacking them with a screwdriver. But Eileen's too passionate for a precision instrument. She hammers and screams abuse.

Jeremy walks in, still in his school uniform. He helps himself silently to a glass of water, then goes back upstairs. All the while, his mouth hangs slightly ajar. Perhaps he has trouble breathing through his nose.

To paraphrase Eileen's abuse: Jack used to be young and exciting but is now a boring gobshite parasite. Jack keeps saying: 'Put the hammer down, Eileen,' as if he were an old policeman. He's become older than his older woman and it maddens her.

She leans against the wall and bursts into tears. Jack approaches. She looks up and sees him heading for her, all calmness, all shush-shush-shush. She grabs the hammer and hits the pipe out of his mouth.

'I'd better go,' I say. I walk briskly towards the door. This has the effect I want. I provide a distraction. I save his life. Jack follows me out of the house. I save his life and get a lift home.

I save his life in the short term, that is. Eileen saves it in the long term. She kicks him out.

Eileen's kitchen is the Wayside-Jeopardy. If she'd allowed him to stay in it any longer, with his shelves and his pipe, he might never have become a Hit and a Headline. He might have grown old in that house.

Jack goes home to his mother. What kind of man, at twenty-seven, can live in the same house as his mother and retain his heterosexuality? I find it hard to have sex when my mother's in the same country.

Sylvia cooks for him and launders for him and all he has to do is eat and wear and be heterosexual. Jack is her Jewish Prince Charles. He's sown his wild oats and is ready to settle down. Like Charles, Jack's desirable and eligible and no one's quite sure what he does.

Sylvia decides to invite two candidates for dinner: Rebecca and Rebecca. (As I wrote that, I downloaded it at last. Rebecca and *Naomi*.) The sisters are still unmarried and share a flat in Hendon. A second bachelor must be found.

I go there, via the North London Line from Dalston Junction to Finchley Road & Frognal, then a bus, with the intention of not enjoying it. I'm way beyond marriage to a safe girl from my background.

Jack opens the door and tells me I can't wear jeans. The right knee, it's true, is worn away from reading. (I read with my left leg crossed over my right.) But I'm tired and hungry and I've come a long way. I protest. Take me as I am.

Jack says he'll give me twenty pounds if I put on one of his suits.

'I don't want your bloody money, Jack.'

'Fair enough. So wear it for nothing.'

Rebecca is a dental nurse who works for Geoff Bergman. (Geoff can't come because he's married.) Naomi is a buyer for Marks & Spencer. She compliments me on my suit but tells me it doesn't fit.

Naomi asks Jack what he wants to do with his life. Jack says he wants to work for himself. Naomi tells him he should work in a big company first. He can't be self-employed till he's been employed for at least ten years.

Jack, in a Wayside torpor, says nothing. It's left to Sylvia to defend him, by recounting his years of experience. He's worked in his father's business. He's worked in telephone sales. He's run a restaurant. He's been a jewellery importer. Her fierce, blind pride is magnificent. 'He's worked in the electricity business,' she says, not *he's sold toasters to terrorists*.

Naomi is right. Jack should apply for a job as a buyer for Marks & Spencer and – this is unspoken – ask her sister out. It's obvious we're not good enough for Naomi. But Naomi believes we're good enough for her less ambitious sister.

Jack and I look at Rebecca. Rebecca would look after you. She's a nurse, after all. It's not as if a dental nurse would only look after your teeth.

Jack should marry her. One of us should marry her. (It never occurs to Sylvia that either of the girls might prefer me.)

Rebecca's tall and slim and kind, with beautiful eyes. I'd learn to love her. She has a car. My mother would be happy and I'd be happy. It's simply a question of letting it happen.

I make her sound like a stereotype. Home-making Rebecca, as opposed to her stereotype sister, ball-breaking Naomi. But that's how it looks, I promise you. And this is a time when men like us need a stereotype. We've strayed too far. Jack with his Eileen, me with my squat. It's time for us to come home.

Rebecca asks how I'd feel if people squatted in my parents' house.

'I wouldn't like it,' I say. Rebecca looks disappointed. She was hoping for more, a confrontation that would test my mettle as a suitor.

Home-making Rebecca has broken my balls. She's not stayed true to her stereotype. Who does? Only Hits and Headlines Diana. Sweet Diana wouldn't ask awkward questions.

Diana (dead now) wouldn't ask Prince Charles how he'd feel if people squatted in his parents' house.

Geoff Bergman always knew he'd grow up to be a dentist. Before he had teeth, he dreamt of being a dentist. His father is a dentist, as is his uncle. Unlike Jack and me, Geoff's never struggled to prove he's worth more than his fate.

At school, Geoff always believed he was too short to have sex. For his fifteenth birthday, along with James Taylor's *Sweet Baby James*, I gave him a photo of a tribe of pygmies, to show him how wrong he was. He gave it to Ruth Lightstone, the first girl kind enough to have sex with him. Geoff told this story at their wedding. Geoff and Ruth will love each other till the day they die.

Please don't be nauseated. It's not all sweetness. Geoff, in 1981, smokes incessantly, which we now know to be the sign of a bad person. (From the sixteenth to the twenty-first century, of course, this wasn't so. Men smoked and wore hats. Amen.) Geoff's breath is noxious, even through a face mask. Then there's the leaning tower of his dental nurse Rebecca. I smile at her but my mouth, of course, is open in a silent scream.

Geoff's practice is located in the Golders Green Road. When I arrive in the waiting room, the clientele's unfamiliar – a group of sweaty, sleep-deprived men, the kind who drum their knees and nod to music that plays only in their heads. They know each other but say little, in a rough inauthentic working-class twang.

Why are they here, simultaneously? They can't have a joint appointment, so some will be waiting for hours. One, a gravelly Scotsman, tells his neighbour that he lives in Brixton. Why's he travelled across the river, all the way to Golders Green, to see Geoff Bergman? He must be at least two hundred dentists from Brixton.

Tired of these questions, I look for a copy of *Punch*, the so-called humorous magazine. There aren't any. Geoff's removed all the *Punches* and replaced them with copies of *New Musical Express*.

The explanation's simple. The sweaty men are stand-up comedians. They hate *Punch*, regarding it as a flatulent vessel for the kind of smug middle-class comedy they've come to destroy.

Geoff is a devotee of the Comedy Store, the Comic Strip and other alternative comedy venues. London is suddenly a funny place. All the funny people have never had it so good. All the unfunny people are 'being funny'. Their time has come.

Geoff's always there at the bar, after the gig, to congratulate the acts and offer them a cigarette. (Cheers, mate!) Word gets round, among the unshaven men and failed teachers, the former social workers, the token funny fat girls. Geoff, the short friendly guy, is good for a cig. And he's a dentist. (Yeah! A dentist!)

Comedians, at this infant stage of their careers, have to make everything funny. They must take every opportunity to prove themselves to themselves and others. So Geoff gets used to their comical ripostes when he says what he does for a living. (Fuckin' 'ell! Tell me to open wide, mate. Then I can drink my beer!) Over the years, Geoff's heard many dentist jokes. But he's a generous soul, who appreciates what these people go through. He always laughs. The comedians like that.

Within months, Geoff becomes the Comedy Dentist, the one you cross the river to see. But it works both ways. Tam Vietnam, the Scotsman, rings Geoff in the middle of the night, complaining of a violent toothache. Tam is pissed. Tam is ringing from a strange girl's flat. Tam's not sure where she lives. Geoff jumps in a fast car to Somewhere with his needle and bag.

Two nights later, prompted by the fat but genuinely funny Judy the Fish, Tam asks Geoff how much he owes him for the call-out. Geoff says he owes him nothing.

As a student at Bristol, Geoff became a Marxist. Geoff believes in from-each-according-to-his-ability and to-each-according-to-his-needs. I believe in these things too. But I don't act on them, unlike Geoff. Geoff refuses to exploit his dental ability. He believes that's what he has to give, and he willingly gives it to Tam, who needs it, in the middle of the night. Ruth, who's not a Marxist, often despairs. At least the National Health insists on paying him for the patients he sees at his surgery.

Geoff is a great man, in my opinion. I'd do anything for Geoff. When he tells me he's promoting Comedy Nights at a pub called the Holloway Tavern, I promise I'll be in the front row. He tells me to bring Jack.

I ask him what he's been doing. Nothing, he says. He's been sitting in his mother's lounge. Unlike Jack, I'm trained to sit in a room. University hones your room skills – reading, listening, smoking, thinking, talking, not talking, looking at posters. I feel sorry for Jack, who says his room is 'like prison'. I would be perfectly at home in prison. The food and toilet facilities would be an advance on the squat.

We're upstairs in the Holloway Tavern, waiting for the Comedy Night to start. Geoff, standing at the side of the stage, keeps looking in our direction.

'I hate earwigs!' shouts Tam Vietnam, the opening act, whose 'set' is a rant against random things that supposedly displease him. Jack doesn't move a facial muscle. Already, just a few seconds into Comedy Night, Jack is drawing attention to himself, through exaggerated stillness.

He's stony too, through Tony Mason, who mocks his own sexual inadequacies. Jack can't understand why any man would do that, even for money. Why make yourself unattractive to women?

But it's the compere who upsets Jack most. Jack's embarrassed by the gauche enthusiasm and painful banalities: all the 'marvellouses' and 'hilariouses' and 'big hands' and 'great big Holloway Tavern-style welcomes'.

'Come on,' I say. 'He's doing his best.'

'He should get someone else to do it,' says Jack.

At the end of the night, Geoff finds us at the bar and asks us what we thought. I say how much I loved Tony Mason. Jack says how much he liked Ivor Problem, who plays the xylophone with mallets attached to his head, like antennae.

'What d'you think of the compere?' asks Geoff, the compere, looking at Jack.

'Come on. I can take it.'

Jack appreciates Geoff, as we all do. He doesn't want to say anything hurtful.

'You're a brave man. I couldn't do it.'

This is the moment. Here we are. *I couldn't do it*, in this context, means that he wants to do it and knows he can, which is exactly what Geoff intended. Geoff knows Jack will do it better.

'Course you could do it,' says Geoff.

'Absolutely,' I say.

'Seriously? You think so?' asks Jack. He wants more affirmation, more praise. This is what makes him right for fame, even in its lowly public-house form.

'Definitely. You start next week,' says Geoff.

From this, everything follows. Geoff has released the monster, the Jack monster, the one that will be famous and die. Geoff is Dentist Frankenstein.

Simon Glazebrook (*Radio Times*, 25th–31st May, 1996): 'What was your first big break in showbiz?'

Jack: 'A friend of mine used to compere these stand-up nights in a pub. One night he got ill and I took over.'

How weirdly mis-remembered. Perhaps, in some monstrous way, Jack couldn't acknowledge Geoff's generosity, couldn't admit that Geoff had done him a favour. Or maybe generosity is, in fact, an illness.

'OK then,' Jack says to Geoff. 'But Dave's got to help me. You'll help me, Dave?'

'Yeah,' I say. As so often, I turn up at the end of the scene for, to me, no good reason.

That Sunday, I spend the afternoon writing jokes with Jack at his mother's house, in the room where I tried to teach him Latin. The choreography's instinctive. I sit at the typewriter, Jack walks from side to side, as he did at the funeral and will at the Holloway Tavern.

Jack can't sit at a typewriter. That's the good reason I'm here.

Sitting at a typewriter, writing: that's a literary exercise which calls for a scholarly man.

I find the tension unbearable. For Jack, there'll be the release of speaking the jokes to an audience. For me, there'll be no release. For me, it's like studying for an exam but not doing the exam.

Of the jokes we wrote that day, I remember only one. I remember it precisely.

It's the opening joke. Jack steps up to the microphone, the next Wednesday night, and removes it nervously from the stand. The audience doesn't recognise him. They don't applaud.

I recite the words with him, softly, as if it were holy writ, as if he were a Rabbi and I were an echoing member of his congregation. And while I recite, I count down to the agony/ecstasy of the punchline, the orgasm, the release.

Good evening, ladies and gentlemen, my name's Jack Harris, welcome to the Holloway Tavern – don't worry, I tell myself, of course there's no laughter, this isn't meant to be funny – *we've got a great evening's comedy lined up for you tonight* – relax, I tell myself again, that's not meant to be funny either – *before we begin, just a couple of announcements* – not meant to be funny – *there are Fire Exits* – still not meant to be funny – *over here and over there* – start getting tense now – *so if there's a fire* – tense, tenser, but not tensest, no, not yet – *stay in your seats* – the punchline has started, I want to be sick, but I can't be. I can't be the thing I most want to be, which is sick. For godsakes, get it over with.

But he doesn't get it over with. The end of the punchline never comes. Jack, in these exam conditions, loses his way. He can't remember where the joke is heading, nor where it's been.

I watch him die just as, twenty-three years later, I'll see him dead. Dead, he didn't look so lonely. Dead, he didn't have to share his afterlife with a pub full of people. Jack carries on walking from side to side. Time is suspended. He can't go forward to the next joke, not remembering what that is. And he can't go back to the end of the last joke. Even if he remembers it, the end will mean nothing now. It's detached from its body.

Every silence is made to be broken. Hence the dawn chorus, the all-clear signal, the heels in church, the giggle, the hip-hop from the car outside your bedroom.

'Bollocks!' shouts a man at the back.

'Are you buying or selling?' asks Jack.

It's no use my saying 'you had to be there'. I was and I don't know whether it's funny. But it has all of Funny's effects. There's laughter, there's clapping, someone goes 'Whoo!'

Simon Glazebrook (*Radio Times*, 25th–31st May 1996): 'Can you remember the first time you got a laugh on stage?'

Jack: 'Yes I can, thanks, Simon.'

Is it a Jewish joke, of merchant stock? Is it anti- or pro-Semitic to suggest this, since the joke worked so well? Jack doesn't know or care.

After that, Jack departs from our script, never to return.

He's discovered, or so he later claims, that spontaneity's the essence of humour, which is his way of saying he can't remember lines. Already, he's preparing himself for Fame's autocue.

All around me, people decide they like him. They never change their minds. They like him, in fact, more than the comedians he's supposedly there to serve. He's better-looking. He's better dressed. He has brevity. He's on our side. The comedians affect to be, but many are too ambitious or unfunny or bitter to be convincing. Some seem like teachers imparting a syllabus, drumming into us the Differences Between Men and Women or the Anal Effects of Indian Food. There's an orthdoxy to them which makes Jack exceptional. He's unorthodox – he has no act.

During the night, he develops a trick. The comedian walks off and Jack walks on, demanding we applaud the comedian yet again, which makes him look generous. Then he adds a bogus piece of information. 'Tony Mason!' he'll say. 'Tony was a miner till he found out the work was underground.'

It's the humour of the schoolboy after the teacher has left the room.

I could add: *which proves his whole life was leading up to this night*. But that's not the case. Why should Jack's life have a satisfying arc, any more than yours or mine? Is that something to which fame entitles him, a life that makes sense? Let his authorised biographer make sense of Jack's life. But let that not be me.

At the end of the night, Geoff hugs him. I hug him too. He knows he's been a success and is careful to deny it. 'I couldn't have done it without you,' he tells me. That's the opposite of the truth. It was only by departing from the written word that Jack succeeded.

Nevertheless, he says he won't go on again unless I'm there. That night, he appoints me his Official Heckler. He wants to go on that stage at the start of the night knowing he'll be heckled.

That's my job now: I'm his Bollocks Man. It's a definite promotion, from co-writer, bringing me tension *and* release. The release is obvious. The tension, too: all day, filing in the council office (I refuse to be promoted, despite being told I'm the best filer they've had), all day I'm whispering 'bollocks' to files, in myriad ways, hard 'bollocks' to make a file angry, soft 'bollocks' to make it cry.

That night, I say 'Bollocks!' loud and clear, in the middle of his first announcement. That, after all, was when the original was shouted.

But, afterwards, Jack gets upset. He tells me my heckle was too early and threw him off his stride. The next week, he gives me a pre-arranged signal. He cues me by tugging the hair on the crown of his head.

Three weeks into celebrity, Jack is dictating the moment at which he's prepared to be heckled.

Six weeks later, a TV producer is drawn to the Tavern – that's what we call it, we Bollocks Men, we call it 'the Tavern' or 'the Tav'. He comes to see Jack, drawn by the reference in *Time Out*: 'hosted by the sharp and funny Jack Harris'.

It's easy to spot this TV producer at the bar, after the show. He's too eager to laugh at what Jack's saying, then too intense even to smile. Jack looks cautious and cool. Even from the other side of the bar, it's clear what this man is buying (Jack) and selling (himself).

Three girls in their early twenties stare at Jack. I watch them watching him. Then their attention turns to me. They whisper to each other. One walks over.

'I've seen you here before,' she says.

'Yeah,' I say. I haven't had sex for years. But I remember how it starts. With Anna, at Cambridge, it starts when she asks me how to hire a 'long thin boat' (a punt) to take her down the River Cam. It starts with the girl, that's the thing. It's a girl's right to choose.

I don't find this girl attractive. But that doesn't alter her right to choose me. Shouldn't I give myself to whoever chooses? Why must there be love? Why, given my circumstances, do I hold myself in this so-high esteem? All this goes through my mind in the time it takes to say 'Yeah'.

'You're always at these shows, aren't you?'

'Yeah. That's right,' I say. There's something edgy about her. I think I could find that edginess arousing.

'Thought so. Don't you ever fucking heckle him again.'

She pours her beer over my head. Around me, the pub-goers take a step back. They know a lovers' tiff when they see one.

She marches over to Jack and the producer and tells them what she's done. The producer looks taken aback. But impressed. He can put Jack on television, yes. But it's girls like this who'll keep him there. Already, he has fans devoted enough to attack people on his behalf.

Jack gives her an autograph, then looks round the bar to locate her victim. She points at me.

Jack looks at me as if he's never seen me before. Of course he does. He's not going to spoil it for the girl by admitting our collusion and friendship.

Nevertheless, the way he blanks me is chilling.

The next night, a taxi pulls up outside the squat. The cabbie gets out and knocks at the door. We have no bell.

He delivers a package. Standing beneath a damp patch big as a cloud, I rip off the letter taped to it. The TV producer has invited Jack to present a programme of late-night highlights from the Edinburgh Festival Fringe. Jack wants to thank me for all my help. He hopes this present will get rid of bad memories of the night before.

Jack has sent me a crate of shampoo.

Sometimes – often – as I write this manuscript, I wonder if Jack liked me. Then I remember the shampoo. It's for dry hair. How did he know not to buy greasy? Or normal? He knew because he knew my hair and wasn't afraid to show it. He could have bought normal to avoid being 'personal'. But no. On the contrary. This was a gift from a friend to a friend. What value's a friend who's not personal?

* * *

I can date it precisely. Tuesday, November 2nd, 1982, the opening night of Channel 4. Tim has gone to Alan Mitchell's Islington flat to watch it, as we still don't have a television. In fact, we don't even have a living room any more. The ceiling collapsed, killing my hi-fi. The council's informed us the property's been condemned. Our lives here are coming to an end.

'Your hair smells nice,' says Charlotte, as she scrapes the remaining kidney beans and rice out of our bowls and into a black plastic rubbish sack. From under the sink comes the clackety-clack we know so well: a mouse, caught in one of our traps, is shuddering its way to death.

The smell of the beans, the noise of the death, the scraping, the 'nice', the arch of her back – something or everything makes me come up behind her and put my hands on her breasts. I don't, I promise you, turn either anti-clockwise.

'Wow,' says Charlotte. 'This is a surprise. I hope you're not in love with me.'

'No,' I say.

'OK then. Let's do it.'

As we clamber into Charlotte's overused bed, she tells me she's going to fuck my brains out, as a reward for my bravery in the kitchen.

I pray that Channel 4 is absorbing, as I'm not sure how long that will take and she wants Tim not to find out. This is our little secret.

In the event, it takes a very long time. Charlotte may want it to be quick and dirty but I want it to last forever, to make up for the years of drought. In such a case, the male tortoise will always defeat the female hare. The tortoise takes an age, just to come out of its hutch.

When it's over, she repeats that I'm not to fall in love with her or think of her or write her any poems. But it's no use. I'm an introvert. A woman can't have sex with an introvert without his thinking about her afterwards. Isn't that what a woman is meant to want?

She said she'd fuck my brains out but the opposite happens. My brains go in, taking her with them. I'm obsessed with her. I'm in love with her.

The last few weeks in the squat are intolerable. The walls are no more than membranes. I go out and buy a cassette player with headphones, to stifle the sounds from Charlotte's room. My cassette of choice is *Before The Flood* by Dylan and The Band. It's a live recording, drawn primarily from concerts in New York City, Seattle, Oakland and Los Angeles. The audience applause is a godsend, coming at the end of each song, where normally there'd be silence. I find security and a sense of community in listening to that applause. It's the sound of thousands of people not having sex.

Within a year, Charlotte's a researcher for a Labour MP and is married to a left-wing lawyer. Tim is working for a rare book dealer. Even I, brought low by my parents' sadness, qualify as a teacher.

Don't worry. It's not a proper school. I teach English as a Foreign Language at a school in Oxford Street, a school without playing fields or assembly or cups or uniforms or lunch. There's no bullying or truancy or Educational Sub-Normality, now called Special Needs. No one shoots indiscriminately in the classroom, then turns the gun on themselves. Language schools just don't arouse that kind of feeling. English as a Foreign Language: it's not even English, is it?

I move into a Hackney flat with Tim, just a few streets away from the squat. We have a TV and a telephone and a firm ceiling.

I have my Storage Unit and more than half a crate of shampoo. I lack for nothing.

Jack rings me. I haven't seen him for months. I assume, these days, that he's too busy. He tells me he's been asked to host a late-night chat show on Channel 4.

He asks what I've been doing. I don't even mention the teaching, not wanting to be defined by what I do in the day to earn money. Instead, I say with pride that I've had an article accepted by *Clothes Line*, the Nottingham-based Dylan fanzine, about mirror imagery in Dylan's work, entitled 'So Concise and So Clear'.

'What are they paying you?' asks Jack. I tell him I'd happily pay them.

'I want you to work for me,' says Jack. 'We need writers. You'd be good, Dave. You know the way I talk.'

'I'm not sure.' But I am. I remember Roger Steinman and Glenn Masters and the Bollocks and the TV producer's red glasses. That's just not me, is it? I'm not built for that kind of show.

'Come on, Dave. You don't want to spend the rest of your life on the sidelines.'

Oh yes. Yes please. That's exactly what I want.

'I'll do the fire exit gag and I'll get it right. What d'you say?'

'It's just not me, Jack.'

'Yes it is, course it is. Come on. This'll be the making of you. You got to do it. You were Dad's favourite.'

There we are then. I must do it for the money and for Jack and his dad, whom he's plucked out of nowhere, like a dead rabbit out of a hat.

'No thanks, Jack. I'm happy as I am.'

5

The Years Apart

A few years later, in the late Eighties, Tim is married and I'm living in a smaller Hackney flat on my own.

If you live in the city where you grew up, you see ghosts who inhabit the grown-up bodies of your school contemporaries. It often takes a while to recognise these ghosts, at which point you have the choice to approach them or not. I have a better memory for faces than most people, so that choice is usually mine.

One Saturday night, I see Nigel Hoffman in the Four Aces in Dalston, a club famous for reggae and, later, drum'n'bass. From a distance, he looks as short and Jewish and intense as ever, though older than his years. He looks wary and wise. His adolescent curls have unwound.

I haven't seen him for over fifteen years. I weigh up the pros and cons of approaching him.

Nigel Hoffman went to live on a kibbutz. Then he came home and studied economics. Last thing I heard, via his mother and mine, Nigel was an Economic Adviser to the Treasury. But he doesn't look like an Economic Adviser now. He has an artistic, bohemian aura. He's surrounded by friends in battered leather jackets. They keep glancing at him, as if he's special. These are all pros.

Con is that I don't know what I'm talking about. Nigel could be an Economic Adviser trying too hard to look 'interesting'. Con is that the loudness of the music could make for a fruitless encounter, as in:

ME: Hi! You're Nigel Hoffman!

HIM: Pardon!

ME: I'm Dave Lewin!

HIM: Sorry, I don't smoke.

I want to tell him that, a few years earlier, I'd turned down the chance to write for Jack's chat show. Nigel will appreciate that. He's a serious man with a ravenous intellect. He'll know I did the right thing.

There's a Third Way, which is neither contact nor avoidance. I'll move towards him, stopping a few feet short. I'll wait till he looks in my direction. Then I'll smile. He might recognise me, in which case he'll smile back. But if he doesn't, no harm is done. That's the great thing about the Third Way. I'm just a guy smiling in a club. He'll assume I'm loving the music, or off my head, or both.

I walk towards him. I stop. I look at him. I ready my smile. Then, as he turns his head, I cancel it. For he's not Nigel Hoffman. He's Bob Dylan.

It's Bob. I'd know him anywhere. Yes, there's a little of the Nigel about him. But it's absolutely Bob. I know he's in England. I saw him the previous night at Wembley Arena. Now, he's seen me.

I could talk to Bob Dylan. I'm thirty-one years old. By this point in my life, I've listened to him more than I've listened to my parents. There is only one thing to do. I look at him, evenly, unthreateningly, then I look away. I treat him with the grace he deserves. I do the right thing with this chance of a lifetime: not take it.

I fantasise, of course. What might Bob have said to me, when our eyes locked? Great artists know your secret thoughts. They see what you want to hide. He might have said: 'You got a lot of nerve to mistake me for Nigel Hoffman'. Or he might have said something infinitely tender, in that haunting nasal croak: 'Thank you for letting me be'.

Friendship is not what it was. It's bigger and better. It's universal. It's twenty-four hour, thanks to the mobile phone. You call a friend to say you're 'on a train'. You make friendly noise, the friendship equivalent of muzak. To a man like my father, such *friendzak* was unthinkable. The phone was an instrument for conveying news. My father, had he owned a mobile, would only have used it to say he was *under* a train.

Why didn't Jack ring me more, in the two decades between the shampoo and our reunion? Why didn't I ring Jack more?

I rang him at home, after the first show of his first series. The show ended at 11pm. I sat by the phone for some time before making the call, wondering if Jack and I had anything in common. Do people on television watch themselves on television? If so, we had both just seen him on television. We had that much in common.

I put the phone down before he could answer. Perhaps the programme was live, in which case, being in it, he couldn't possibly have seen it. Nor could he be home ten minutes after it was over. Perhaps he wasn't going home anyway.

I rang him, instead, the next morning. He was delighted to hear from me. I was delighted to tell him how funny he'd been. The imbalance was there, of course. Jack was a public person now, while I was living in a flat in Hackney and teaching English as a Foreign Language. But we still had more in common than not.

171

Put simply, Jack had been obscure far longer than he'd been famous. His past outweighed his present.

After that, I ring him on the Saturday morning following the first show of a series. I always say how much I enjoyed it. He is always pleased. Then in Series Eight, things change.

'Yeah?' says Jack. 'I wasn't sure.'

He's never looked for reassurance before. I'm pleased I can give it.

'Oh yes. Phil Collins was great.'

'What about Mike?'

The sugar rush of fame is over for Jack. Now, four years on, there's sourness in his arteries, paranoia, insecurity. For the first time, my praise is insufficient. In fact, it's aggravating. What do I mean by 'Phil Collins was great'? Do I mean that Mike was not?

What can I say about Mike? Sadly, owing to a problem with my video recorder – my problem, not my video recorder's, which was only obeying my incorrect orders – I've failed to record most of Jack's show. I haven't seen Mike. I don't know who Mike is. Jack, by now, talks about 'Mike' without giving a surname. Mike plus a surname would be a name-drop. Jack doesn't need to drop names. After eight series, he thinks himself the equal of his guests. You don't drop the names of your equals.

'He was great, Jack.'

There is no going back from this. This is the lie that begets all the others, like the first lie of an adulterer, the one where he says he's going to Paris on business. Now he must invent business. Now he must invent Paris, a Paris where his so-called business takes place, a Paris of false events in true places.

'You thought he was great? I thought he was hostile.'

Jack doesn't believe me. That only makes me more determined to convince him I'm telling the truth. I feel a fierce loyalty to my own falsehood. I will stand by it and defend it. Mike was great, be he Mike Douglas, Mike Caine, or Princess Mike of Kent.

'Oh yes,' I reply. 'He was hostile all right. But that made for great television.'

'Yeah? You think so? Well, that's cheered me up. How's Hackney Council?'

Here's the imbalance. I feel grateful to him for remembering that I work for Hackney Council. In the past, that ever-receding past before he was on television, I wouldn't have felt grateful. I'd have taken it as my right, to have my friend remember where I work. But now, I'm touched that his famous mind has room for such information.

I'm grateful and touched, though I haven't worked for the council in years. Now, bravely, I'll tell the truth. A truth that will somehow rub off on my Mike falsehoods, making them more believable.

'I'm not working for the Council, Jack. I'm teaching.'

'Course you are. Sorry. So you really thought the Mike thing was fine, yeah? You're not just saying that.'

'Absolutely. Mike's great.'

'Oh, it's "Mike" now, is it?'

'I'm just –'

'No, no. Go on.'

'What more can I say? The man's magnetic. No one sleeps when he's on.'

Jack takes this in. He breathes down the phone.

'But they sleep when I'm on.'

'That wasn't –'

'I know. Sorry, Dave. I'm a bit stressed. You wouldn't believe the pressure. How's your mum and dad?'

The question looks glib in print, which does him a disservice. Jack is still devoted to the notion of family.

Sally Mishcon (*Jewish Chronicle*, February 11th, 2000): 'Who would you like to interview that you haven't interviewed already?'

Jack: 'Robert De Niro. I think he and I have a lot in common, coming from that background which is all about family. There are scenes in *The Godfather* which really remind me of growing up in a close-knit Jewish family in Golders Green.'

Where do we start? My father, since we're talking of family, would start by asserting that Robert De Niro wasn't even in *The Godfather*. Let that pass, along with the assumption that De Niro shares a background with the character he plays; that Robert De Niro IS *The Godfather II*. It's Jack's supposed kinship with the Corleones that invites incredulity. Jack's looking at the past with blood-coloured spectacles. I too am from the Golders Green Mafia. I know how many people woke up to find a horse's head in their bed. The same number that woke up to find a bacon sandwich. Who knew a horse? Who had the DIY skills to cut its head off?

Yet it can't be denied. Jack was the most Italian of Jews. (He couldn't have been the most Jewish of Jews or he wouldn't have married a non-Jewish girl.) He had an Italian's love for his mother, based on love of her cooking and pride in her pride in him, as opposed to guilt.

He had nothing to say to his brother Marcus, yet he flew him and his wife and kids to Antigua for the Millennium. It's not as if he flew them there and stayed here. Jack and Rita and the baby flew there with them. Marcus insisted his family fly Economy, but Jack wouldn't have it. They all flew First. Is that not fraternal love of the highest order? Jack would rather ignore his brother at close quarters than ignore him at a distance.

His devotion to family extended to mine. When my father died, he saw the announcement in the *Jewish Chronicle*. Why did he even read the *Jewish Chronicle*, when he read so little and there are so many non-Jewish chronicles? He rang me, full of sorrow, and asked when the funeral was. I was touched. I was touched when Geoff Bergman rang, to ask the same question. Yet I didn't say to Geoff what I said to Jack. To Geoff, I said the funeral was at three on Friday. To Jack, I said: 'The funeral's at three on Friday, if that's OK for you.'

This is what fame does to people. Not to famous people, but to me. Jack, to his credit, leapt on it: 'What d'you mean, Dave? You going to change the time for me?' I felt grief-stricken. I missed my father, who would have answered the question precisely without adding anything, without being anxious to please, without being craven in the telephonic presence of Sir Fame. 'My funeral's at three on Friday,' he'd have said. (No – he'd have said 'three pm'.)

Jack came to the funeral at half-past two. He hugged me and stood by me while I hovered outside the chapel. He took a step sideways as people – the Rabbi, the Lightstones, my cousin and his wife – approached the chapel. He was keen not to upstage me. He refused the Rabbi's bumptious request for an autograph. When Maurice Lightstone told him 'You're on the television', Jack looked surprised, as if he'd never realised – so that's what the cameras were for!

He dealt beautifully with Arlene, my cousin's wife, a New Yorker who always gets her own way, as is etched on my cousin's face. She insisted they'd met before. Jack assured her they hadn't. She re-insisted. She told him she was always right about these things. Jack knew, as did I, that she'd simply seen him on American cable TV. But he denied himself the pleasure of admitting he was famous and, in doing so, kept her nice and frustrated.

Jack and I entered the chapel. I gestured to him to follow me down the aisle, to sit with me and my mother and sister. But no, he peeled off immediately. He took a seat at the back, that least famous of rows. What celebrity ever has 'back-row seats'? Please, he implied, with a shake of his head, seat me badly. Give me your worst seat. Stick me behind a pillar. Put me between two senile farters.

The rows fill up. Jack finds himself seated between the Goldmans and the Kreitmans. The pall-bearers bring in the coffin. Just before the Rabbi speaks, a mobile phone goes off. It's 1989. Mobile phones are not yet commonplace. They never will be, in this congregation, most of whom still answer the phone with a questioning, pre-digital 'Meadway 2183?'

Maurice Lightstone, who's sitting behind me, belatedly hears the mobile phone. 'Smoke alarm,' he says to his wife. (They know about them, in their old people's home.) 'Of course,' she replies. 'It's a crematorium.'

The mobile phone, I'm sure, is Jack's. I look over my shoulder. He's apologising, with his eyes, to the Goldmans and Kreitmans. He switches it off and looks hard at the Rabbi.

I can't help it. I look at him again, a few seconds later, as the Rabbi states the time and place of my father's death. Jack is sobbing. Bea Goldman, my mother's best friend, has her hand on his arm. That is why I will never know what the Rabbi said about my father or what my sister said about him or, surreally, what I said about him. I delivered my oration without taking it in. I simply transmitted.

I miss my father's funeral because I'm thinking about Jack's tears and their consequences. My predictions come true. Bea Goldman and my mother are full of praise for Jack's sensitivity. 'He's become a fine man' are my mother's words.

What I don't predict is the bouquet Jack sends my mother next day. A hand-written note apologises for the intrusion of the mobile phone which, in her funereal daze, my mother hadn't even noticed. The bouquet, she tells me, is marvellous. Such a fine-man's choice of flowers. And so enormous it conceals the torso and head of the man who delivers it.

I'm sure that Jack didn't order the bouquet. A girl at his management company did that. Nevertheless, she must have asked him how much he wanted to spend and what kind of bouquet he wanted; and Jack, knowing nothing of such things, must have said: 'Fuck it, just ring the florist and tell them to send her the shop'.

My mother puts the flowers in her biggest vase, which they topple and smash with the weight of their own generosity. But this is good. My mother has an urgent reason to leave the house. She and Bea Goldman go vase shopping, which takes her out of herself. The healing process, thanks to Jack, has begun.

After a couple of weeks, she stops talking about the flowers. But she still, to this day, talks about the vase, which now takes up most of her bedside table in her pyschiatric hospital ward; where it looks – if you'll pardon the expression – mad.

As for me, well. Jack sent me a note saying that my dad's funeral had made him cry, as it reminded him of his dad.

What exactly would I have written, had I been a writer for Jack?

To begin at the beginning: Jack walks on, the band plays, the audience goes wild, Jack looks surprised and flattered, says hello, thank you, whoa, yes, good evening, welcome, wow, you're hot tonight, thank you, then raises his hands and lowers them, to signal to the audience they should cease their wildness forth-with. None of this is written. It's a spoken tradition. It's TV lore.

'Well, it's been quite a week,' Jack says. That's script. Those words have been re-drafted and buffed, then typed on to an autocue, where they spool into existence then out again, fast as it takes to say them. Jack is desperate for script. He knows nothing of 'the week' with its tiresome topics and current affairs.

(Or, rather, he knows nothing if he isn't affected. He rings me in the winter of 2001, to say how sorry he was to hear my mother had been sectioned. When I ask him how he is, he says: 'Americans won't fly. We've lost so many guests. Nine-eleven's been a disaster.')

I used to watch his topical jokes with the sound down. I couldn't bear to hear him struggling with everyday sounds: *condoleezza*, say.

That would have been my tragedy and small fortune: to spend twenty years writing 'topical gags' for a man who only did them because American hosts do them. (*Iraq*, there's another one. Jack could only say it American-style – *eye-rak*.)

I could have been the right-hand man to a TV star. Is that, in fact, the story of my life? That my life is no life compared to the life I could have had?

It's a genre now, the no-life story. Typically, the author is Ken, a sixty-five-year-old retired quantity surveyor who sings in his local church choir in Birkenhead. Ken was in the same Quarry Bank Grammar School class as John Lennon. They sang Lonnie Donegan songs in the playground. They smoked Woodbines behind the bike sheds. (Why do bike sheds bother with fronts?) At a New Year's Eve Party in 1957, they discussed forming a band. Then – and here's the twist – it didn't happen. John formed a band with Paul and George and, eventually, Ringo. Ken was so near yet so far. Then he became so far yet so far. That's it. That's the non-story of Ken's no-life, as told in his memoir, *I Could Have Been a Beatle*.

But that's A Beatle. No one's interested in *I Could Have Been a Writer*. They want tantalising proximity to the red-hot glow of

178

fame. They want *I Could Have Been a Brother – The Story of Beverly Everly*.

I've tried to avoid lists in this memoir, because lists are
  1) Lists
But Jack did twenty-two series of chat shows. What else but lists can do justice to Jack's professional life, with its repetitions and lack of narrative development?

That's All We Have Time For is an unwritten book of lists, with the syntax varied in the hope that the reader won't notice.

Among the many great actresses Jack interviewed, the most memorable were.

Jack had a particular affinity with rock stars, who loved his anarchic humour. Some became friends, among them.

In the fourth show of the ninth series, his guests included.

And then he had a fascinating conversation with.

And then he interviewed.

And then he talked to.

And then he joked with.

And then he sparred with.

And then he had a chat with.

Then on came.

And then.

Phil Collins appeared on *The Jack Harris Show* no fewer than nine times, singing such great songs as.

Let him stand for all of Jack's 462 guests. Phil Collins was the third guest on the sixth show of the fourth series, transmitted Friday November 10th, 1989. (The other guests were   and
          .)

I watched it yesterday, on tape, in the living room of my cottage, on a VCR so old you expect it to have a handle.

Phil comes on. Jack stands. Applause. Smiles. Handshakes. Sitdowns. Jack asks him what he's been doing. Phil talks about his latest album *But Seriously*. He's very excited about it. Why wouldn't he be? Jack asks the kind of questions you or I might ask, were we showing interest in Phil's album, such as how long it took him to write the material and how it differs from his previous material. Jack's not so interested that you think him insincere nor so indifferent you think him rude.

Jack goes on to say that Phil is justly famous for being the only artist to appear at both the English and American Live Aid concerts. Has Phil ever thought of starting his own charity? To raise money for himself? He could call it Help the Collins.

Jack looks at the camera and talks directly to us. 'Hello. I'm Jack Harris. I want to talk to you about Phil Collins. Phil Collins needs help. Did you know that forty pounds is enough to feed an entire Phil Collins for one lunch, not including wine and service?' (Script. I would have helped write that.)

Phil laughs because Jack's amusing and Phil's a good sport. He's happy to be debunked by Jack. After all, before the debunking there was much bunking. Then Jack goes for the Pain Exclusive, reminding Phil that his album *Face Values* was written after a break-up. Was this album, similarly, the product of pain? If so, what? Jack looks concerned. Phil does or doesn't give him a PE. (In this case, he doesn't.)

Following more repartee from Jack, Phil is applauded all the way to the other side of the set, where he sings *Another Day In Paradise*.

That's the template. You can substitute any rock star with whom Jack had a particular affinity. Excepting the song, you can substitute any guest.

* * *

180

Remarkably, I've watched all the shows, even though I've no intention of writing the book. Jess goes out in the evenings and leaves me to it.

I watch Jack, on television, getting older. I admire the way he learns his craft. In Series One, he blinks too much. His head moves as he reads the autocue. By Series Two, his eyes are unblinking in his still head. He's found himself.

Who is 'himself' though? This is all anyone ever asks me about Jack (1983–2004): 'What's he really like?'

I hate this question. I don't even know what I'm really like. Everyone wants to hear that Jack is the same offscreen as on. How could he be?

Jack came to this cottage once, in the spring of 2004. Compare and contrast that Jack with Onscreen Jack. The differences are so prosaic, so banal, they deserve to be a list, a typical list, one that appears to be all-inclusive. Nothing has more bogus authority than a list.

Here's how Cottage Jack, as he walks into my living room, differs from Onscreen Jack:

1) He has no make-up
2) He has no band
3) He has no autocue
4) He has no guests
5) He doesn't know where to sit
6) He's not being paid
7) He's not in a box in the corner of the room
8) He can see me

I have a list too. Mine's secondary, of course. But here's how I, when Jack walks in the room, differ from the 'I' who watches him on TV:

1) I'm the same size as him
2) I can't switch him off

3) I can't make him more orange
4) I don't leave the room while he's talking
5) I don't masturbate

I suspect it happens more than we think. How often do we think it happens? We have no way of knowing. There are viewing figures only; everything else that ends in 'ing' goes unrecorded. I should point out that it happened only once, last night, a product of the loneliness of writing this, not talking about it and not having sex with Jess. It was nothing to do with the guests on the show, who included Elton John and Princess Anne.

A year after my dad's funeral, Caroline Bliss rings me to invite me to a party. I'm surprised. She's often in my thoughts but I never expect to be in hers.

I've recently read her name in the *Sunday Times* Top 100 Media People. I've read her guest column in the *Evening Standard*: 'It's the fourth day of our skiing holiday. Tamsin's in tears. Harry's limping. I don't know how much more I can take'. (Those are her stepchildren, by the way.)

Here in the London Borough of Hackney, we know how she feels. After I toss my *Standard* in the bin on Dalston Lane, it's dug out by Mr O'Fock. Mr O'Fock wants it for some arcane purpose. He's looking for a pillow, perhaps, or a (sleeveless) vest. Mr O'Fock – not his real name – is one of Hackney's Top 100 Losers. He'll surely read the column. He'll doubtless shout his reaction at a passer-by, who may well break into a run. Mr O'Fock's reaction will go something like this: 'Fock, that's a focker, when your skiing holiday's focked!'

I tell Caroline Bliss I'd be happy to come. She's far too excited. Then she says: 'And how's your friend Jack? I keep seeing him on the telly. How does he cope with the stress?'

She's never met Jack. How does she even know I know him?

Fifteen years before, he visited me in Cambridge, when she was there too. A leaf falls in Cambridge and fifteen years later, Caroline Bliss goes 'A-ha!'

She wants him at her party. She wants me to bring him. But she doesn't want to state it, brutally. She hopes that, prompted by her concern, I'll bring up the subject myself. I'm meant to say, 'Yes, he's stressed. He needs a party to relax him. Why don't I bring him to yours?'

Then Caroline Bliss can say, 'What? I hardly know him! Oh well. All right then.'

If hypocrisy's the tribute vice pays to virtue, hers is the tribute transparency pays to subtlety. But the woman is incapable of subtlety. She can only manage SUBTLETY!

I call Jack to invite him. He's free and he's happy to come. He says people often don't invite him to things because they assume he's busy. I give him the address of Max Woodward and Caroline Bliss's Islington house.

'How are you then, Ondiments? What's happening in your life?'

'Nothing,' I reply.

'Fair enough,' says Jack. 'Don't become a nowhere man, OK?'

There are twins in my class. Helga and Steffi are from Munich. As their teacher, what I appreciate about them is this: Helga wears her hair up while Steffi wears it down, despite 'amusing' requests from their classmates to swap hair and confuse me.

The twins' strict adherence to this rule leads the classmates to tease them for being 'Germanic', as does their dedication and focus. They don't mind. They have each other. As a teacher, I'm only too happy to see their bright (and distinguishable) faces.

Their party trick is to recite, in unison: *a rough-coated, dough-faced, thoughtful ploughman coughed and hiccoughed through the streets of Scarborough*. They have trouble with 'Scarborough', which means nothing to them, so I change the end to *through thoroughly clean streets*.

I make it a rule not to socialise with students. Speaking clearly all day makes me want to spend my leisure in silence. But I can't refuse their invitation to supper.

There I am, then, clutching my A-Z and bottle of Mateus Rosé, emerging from Streatham station on a cold November evening, which turns to night as I walk to my destination.

My heart is heavy from being in these streets. Helga (hair up) and Steffi (hair down) have rented a flat in an SW17 location that's either Tooting or Streatham, which is to say it's neither Tooting nor Streatham. Doubtless they were told, back in Germany, that the flat was in 'London'. But it's not, not to me. I'm a North Londoner who comes from a place, Golders Green, with a name. Sometimes, in remote parts of Turkey, I've wondered how and why the inhabitants of a house came to live in the middle of nowhere. But Helga and Steffi don't live in the middle of nowhere. I started in the middle of nowhere and have walked for twenty minutes. This must be the edge of nowhere. This, as an estate agent would say, must be within easy reach of Nowhere Borders. Jack's prophecy has come true. I'm a nowhere man.

I arrive at a terraced house in a road in the gutter of A–Z pages 108 and 109. I'm rough-coated, dough-faced and I want to go home. Instead, I ring the bell.

Helga and Steffi feed me the Squat Food I know so well. Their dish, So-Called Risotto, is one I've made many times. It's not risotto but rice with added stuff. The stuff, in their case, is bacon and tinned tomatoes and mushrooms. When that runs out, there's only rice and more rice, untainted by juice or flavours.

The girls, though, are irrepressible, laughing, filling my glass, telling me stories, comparing and contrasting our two cultures, as in: 'English men are more polite'. I barely interrupt. It's they, curiously, who interrupt themselves, breaking off in the middle of sentences to sing along to the Abba tape that's too loud to be background, too quiet to make us shut up and listen. Steffi, drunk and emboldened, tells me I am 'a nice man with a sad face'.

Eleven becomes midnight then twenty to one. There's no prospect of my getting home by public transport, other than an ambulance. A few minutes later, I'm lying on the sofa bed in the living room. Helga and Steffi have gone to bed.

It's too short to be a bed, too bed-shaped to be a sofa. The whole night is like that. Sofa/bed, Helga/Steffi, Tooting/Streatham, rice/risotto, Abba loud/Abba quiet. Everything is either/or or neither/nor.

I've fallen through a hole in the universe. I'm a thirty-four-year-old language teacher in a stranger's – no, two strangers' – flat. Where am I? Who am I?

I try to sleep. I'm falling, falling, when a weight lands on the edge of the sofa bed and makes me sit up. There's enough street light through the ill-fitting curtains for me to identify Steffi.

I assume, as her teacher, that she's come to discuss a problem. One of those problems that wakes you in the night, such as: can you split an infinitive in an emergency? But then she says 'Hello' in a sing-song way. I sense that she's in playful mood. She is, let's face it, naked.

With her right hand, she lifts my floppy cock. With her left hand, she cradles my testicles. These are neat, deliberate movements. I'm reminded of the Underbed Storage Unit instruction leaflet. Figure 1, lift floppy cock. Figure 2, cradle testicles.

'It's nice, yes?' asks Steffi, who's here for three months to learn English, remember. She's on holiday. She's here to have adventures, to grow. Figure 3, grip floppy cock lightly. Figure 4, raise and lower hand in piston motion until floppiness disappears.

The Germans will have a word for Figure 4. One of their composite word-structures, their Verbal Storage Units, with idea bolted onto idea in perfect and logical sequence. Something like *Handkochpistongeschaften*.

I know what I must do. (I should point out that, in those days, it was permissible to do it; this was before teacher/student sex became *verboten*.)

I must do it for many reasons. Not simply to end my latest sexual drought. Not because Steffi has completed Figure 5 to my extreme satisfaction; nor because she has progressed to Figure 6, *Aufkochcondomungefurlen*.

This is my opportunity to advance, from nowhere to sexual somewhere. To finally detach – this is an emergency – sex from love. This is my opportunity to show I understand that sex is a service which men perform, like fixing a car, like plumbing. When a woman takes her car to a garage for a service, she doesn't want the mechanic to say: 'I'm sorry. I can't touch your car. I just don't love Peugeots'.

Steffi wants sex. I feel no love for Steffi. That's the Tooting/Streatham in which I find myself. I mustn't let that lack of love keep me from Figure 6 to Figure 12, the ultimate figure, the one after which you doze.

We get there. The pleasure and pride are physical and mental and, dare I say it, cultural. This, after all, is a girl whose grandparents were, quite possibly, Nazis. I like to think, in my own small way, I've done something to lessen the possibility of another Holocaust.

Steffi leaves. I hear her talking to her sister as I drift off to sleep the sleep of the just. Minutes pass. Or hours. Who can tell? In my dream, I hear the sing-song 'Hello', that erotic call-sign. But it's not a dream. It's an intervention. I open my eyes and there she is, on the edge of my bed.

This is fantastic. This is what a man remembers just before he dies, not his war record or his allotment or his splitting of the atom or his reign as President or his forty-seven years with the Post Office. His erotic life flashes before him. No, not flashes. He watches it in real time, for as much real time as is left to him.

Steffi has come back for more. My cock, that sword of truth, is full of steel. Her hair, as she looks down at it, obscures her face. Steffi (hair down), Helga (hair up). It never fails. Except at bedtime, when girls with hair up let their hair down.

Steffi puts her right hand on my sword and her left hand on my testicles. Or does she? If girls let their hair down to go to bed, this could be Helga. And Steffi, my Steffi, my Figure 12, may have been Helga too.

Think, man, think. It must be the first one again, surely. No two people would say 'Hello' and touch your genitals in exactly the same way, unless they were twins, German twins, who adhered to a set of precise sexual instructions. Is that racism? Or experience? Where are those German Twin Sex Study results when you need them?

It was Helga and is Steffi. It was Steffi and is Helga. It was Helga and is Helga again. It was Steffi and is Steffi again. And if it's the same twin both times, why does the other twin not want me?

Cursed with anxiety, my sword subsides. She works harder. I

could simply ask her, which one are you? But that would demean us both.

It's a human right, to know who you're having sex with. I feel worse now than before that first 'Hello'. Then, I didn't know who I was. Now I don't know who anyone else is either.

(Jack, when I tell him the story at Caroline Bliss's party, loves this bit and wants to hear it again and again, like a child. He finds my tortured state hilarious. She knows who she is – why worry?)

I get out of bed. She stands. I stand behind her. She's puzzled. Why am I forming a queue? With uncharacteristic assertiveness, I make my intention plain. I want to mount her from behind. In that way, I might find anonymity, hers and mine. With our faces concealed from each other, she could be anyone and so could I.

She submits to my wish. I try to be a creature in a wildlife documentary. A mating lion. We've all seen them. They look so casual, so matter-of-fact, so slightly bored. They look, ironically, like they're having sex because there's nothing good on the telly.

I roar, silently. I rock my head from side to side. No stiffening occurs. I remember those Seventies sex manuals, with their Abba-looking men. Those manuals told you what to do, all right. That's not my problem. I need someone to tell me what to *think*.

We give up, Helga/Steffi and I. I tell her/her that I have to go. I leave immediately, even though it's very late at night/very early in the morning. I walk the twenty minutes back to Streatham station. The first train is not for another two hours, so I walk north, to the top of page 109, then halfway up page 93, arriving at Clapham Common underground in time to catch the first Tube to Tottenham Court Road. Now I'm just two hours early for work. I plough thoroughly through a Full English Breakfast. Why would anyone want to feel so English, or so Full?

At nine thirty, I enter the classroom. Guido, the class clown, asks if I need him to borrow me his razor. I don't correct his

English. I'm too tired. I look, fearlessly, at Helga and Steffi. I want to be a man about this, not a boy or a greatcoated student.

It's not enough to look a person in the eye, though. You must wear the right expression in your own. One twin I satisfied, one I disappointed. Since I don't know which is which, I must look at each with an expression that applies to either. But how do you look at someone with smug regret?

My story, which lasts three glasses of champagne, delights Jack like nothing else I've ever told him. He wants more and more detail, more and more angst from the man he now calls 'Twin Man'.

'You've done a famous thing, Twin Man.' A famous thing? What does he mean? It didn't make me feel famous.

It just made me feel more alone.

Jack goes off and says hi to a man from Duran Duran. Jack and this man are in the Famous Club. Any member can go up to any other member, unannounced. There's no need to introduce yourself. Your name is a given.

I, who've been living a Kentucky-Fried life, eat like there's no tomorrow and was no yesterday. This is the heyday of nouvelle cuisine, so the table's laid with a vast collection of tiny edibles. Only the rich can afford portions this small.

Max, a bony man in a cream suit, engages me in our traditional agonising conversation. He can never remember what I do. When I tell him, he says *of course!* as if it's been in all the papers. I always remember what he does, but I can't construe it. Does a merchant banker merchant a bank or bank a merchant? I ought to know. It's arrogant of me not to. But my lack of interest is genuine.

'Darling? Five minutes?' Caroline Bliss calls to Max.

'Five minutes, darling,' he replies. This is the way they converse. This is the ping-pong of their darling-darling.

Max seems so unnatural in the presence of his wife, overly coiffed, tense, too handsome. Handsome is not what women want, is it? Aren't handsome men what men want?

I spill some peanut sauce on my shirt and see a similar-sized stain, quite dry, at the same shirt-height, on the other side. The parallel stains make a wet and dry Rorschach. I'm not upset at the new stain. It's the old one that gets me. How can I have put on this shirt without noticing it? How did I get out of the house wearing that stain?

No woman would have let me out with a stain like that. I see Alice Jarman looking at me. Alice, a schoolfriend of our hostess, is a top-ranking civil servant, as if Caroline Bliss would know a bottom-ranking one.

Alice lives on her own. Could it work? Earlier in the evening, when there was only one stain, she told me she'd just been talking to a man who'd argued forcibly in favour of railway privatisation. Alice said she'd disagreed with him 'out of politeness'. She knew he would welcome debate.

No, it couldn't work. I feel low. But I'm about to feel much lower.

The insistent rapping of a spoon on a Conran Shop oak table shuts everyone up.

We all look at Caroline Bliss and Max, standing together on the table, gripping each other's hands. Caroline Bliss's four-inch heels make her tower over Max. How did she get on a table in those? She must have taken them off, then put them back on again.

Max's left leg is shaking. He adjusts it. He takes his hand away from his wife's, wipes it as discreetly as he can on the inside of his trouser pocket, then places it back in hers.

Jack looks puzzled. Like me, he's never seen two people standing on a table before.

Caroline Bliss thanks us all for coming. Max looks more and more vulnerable and brave, but silent. He becomes a kind of Prince Diana.

Caroline Bliss says how much it means to her and Max that they have such good friends who they know will always be loyal to them both. She tells us that she and Max are divorcing, after seven years of marriage. She tells us this is a painful time for both of them. She and Max wanted all of us, the people they love, to hear the news at the same moment.

They love each other very much and have enjoyed extraordinary happiness. They're profoundly sad but feel divorce is the only way forward. However, they will never stop caring about each other. No one else is involved.

In one minute, she announces, the music will start. It will give her and Max huge pleasure if we all dance till we drop. But, before that, will we raise our glasses in one last toast to them both.

Two hundred people raise their glasses and toast 'Caroline and Max'. Then, from the back of the room, Alice Jarman booms: 'Bravo!' Everyone claps.

Caroline Bliss's girlfriends, many of them in tears, queue up to embrace her. Jack sums up his feelings as Keith Richards plays the unimpeachable opening riff of *Brown Sugar*: 'She's a piece of work, isn't she? Great legs.'

This can't be denied. Caroline Bliss has fantastic legs. That could be why she chose to stand on the table.

I tell him I need some air and work my way through the throng, out of the room, down the corridor, along the galley kitchen and out of the back door, into the walled green handkerchief that passes for an Islington garden. I can't get out of there fast enough.

At Cambridge, I couldn't compete with Caroline Bliss's success.

Now I can't compete with her failure. The end of her marriage has just inspired applause and respect, admiration and awe, from top-ranking civil servants, bankers, barristers, fashion editors. Her failure is a huge success.

I'm delighted to see Tim walking towards me. I'm desperate for a laconic remark from Tim.

He takes out his pack of Gauloises Disque Bleu. We smoke. The cigarettes, pathetically warming in the November air, accentuate our sense of being outside. And being outsiders. A long time ago, in the recent past, stinking French fags could do that.

'This garden's absurd,' says Tim. 'I'm thinking of moving back to Suffolk. You could buy this house with five times the land for half the price. I don't know, you know. I'm thinking of opening a bookshop. My grandfather left me a few quid. He owned two houses in Eastbourne. I never knew that till now.'

It's the longest thing Tim's ever said to me. I feel overwhelmed. Suffolk. The very name sounds unsuccessful. There'll be more land and sky than people, more churches and footpaths than success.

'I'd like to come with you, Tim.'

'OK.'

Through the French windows, we see Jack and Caroline Bliss in conversation. Everyone else is jaggering about to *Satisfaction*, their taste in rock deep-frozen the day they left school. To be heard, Jack and Caroline Bliss have to put their mouths to each other's ears.

It's the start of a business relationship that will culminate in the publication of *My Next Guest*, a compilation of Jack's best interviews. If you've not seen the book, here's an extract:

JACK: Great suit!

STING: Thank you very much.

JACK: Where d'you get it? How much you pay for it? It's not *that* great. Can you take it back if you don't like it?

Honky Tonk Women kicks in. Caroline Bliss can't contain herself. She bumps and grinds and struts. She gives it everything. Full-on and fuller-on, her two modes. Jack takes her on. He goes for it, inadvertently knocking Alice Jarman to the floor with a whippy swing of his buttocks.

Caroline Bliss laughs. Jack scoops Alice up from the floor and puts her over his shoulder, while continuing to dance. Alice squeals with pleasure. Jack sees me through the window. He looks rich and happy and loud and proud in his blue tartan suit.

He indicates the dumpy little Alice on his shoulder and the long, leggy Caroline Bliss by his side. With mock-amazement, he mouths the word 'Twins!'

At Jack's wedding lunch, I'm placed next to Geoff and Ruth Bergman. Here we are, on Table Fifty-Seven, in a marquee in the grounds of Jack and Rita's Buckinghamshire house, on a beautiful June day in 1994. On the other side of me is an amiable couple, Terry and Jo. Terry introduces himself: 'Hello, I'm not famous'. I want to kiss him.

Jack, as a schoolboy, had three friends: Geoff Bergman, Nigel Hoffman (whom he didn't like) and me. Now, at his wedding, he has six hundred. I feel sorry for him. The poor man can't have as few as he'd want. How would it look? Photograph? Read? *More than five guests gathered in the grounds of* – it's unthinkable. Rita, his bride and former make-up artist, knows and understands that. She loves it, in fact. She's married it.

When Jack stands up to make his speech, I don't know where to look. Do I look at him, in flesh and blood, or do I look at his image on the video screen above Table One?

When the speech finishes, to roars and cheers, I turn to Terry. 'Congratulations. Really funny.'

'Thanks,' says Terry. 'But the best jokes were the Guv'nor's.'

Terry's the man I could have been. That's why, I assume, Jack slyly put us together. No. Maybe not. Jack and Rita will have delegated the *placement*, no?

Terry took the offer I couldn't but did refuse. For eleven years, he's been writing for 'the Guv'nor'. He and Jo live in Surrey and lead a quiet life, about which Terry is amusingly ironic. When I ask him what he does for fun, he says he does nothing in case he enjoys it, for who knows where that would end? But he's dissembling. This is a happy man.

When Terry and I say goodbye, he wishes me good luck with my bookshop. He thinks that, because I'm at the Guv'nor's wedding, I must own the shop.

I go off to say goodbye to Jack, who's in a huddle with Judy Taylor, formerly Judy the Fish. I think, no, I can't say goodbye to Jack, not now – he's working. A drunk Tam Vietnam lurches into me from behind. I stagger a little, then turn and apologise.

Ruth Bergman tracks me down. Do I want a lift to the station?

Jack and Rita give a summer party every year, on their wedding anniversary. The only place I feel comfortable is by the bouncy castle. Children, in my experience, never ask you what you do.

I stand there, pining for someone, anyone, who's not famous, will talk to me, and won't bounce. Seeing a dad whose face I don't recognise, I strike up a cheery conversation. I ask him his name and, somewhat reluctantly, he tells me he's Al Conroy. Hoping he won't respond in kind, I ask him what he does. 'What do I do? I'm Al fucking Conroy.' He walks away.

I didn't know then and I don't know now what Al fucking Conroy does. But, by God, I'll never ask him again. Do you ask Elvis fucking Presley what he does? Or J F for fucking K?

The year after that, I don't go to the party. Nor the year after that. The year after that, I don't get an invitation. Jack, I suspect, wants to save me the embarrassment. It's an act of kindness.

In the summer of 1999, Jack and Rita send me – and six hundred others – a huge envelope. Inside is an announcement.

Eric has arrived in our lives and will bring joy to us ever more it says, above a baby photo the size of half a cot.

Jack has, finally, started his family. A baby has arrived, a delicate way of saying that Eric's adopted.

Celebrities, of course, rarely conform to the reproductive template I learned as a boy: sex, cigarette, baby. Cursed by their Dysfunctional Celebrity Childhoods – the dead dad, the problems with authority – they often have difficulty conceiving, as if they're reluctant to manufacture childhoods for others. So it is for Rita and Jack. Rita, in her *Mail on Sunday* column (May 14th, 2000) simply confides that she and Jack had 'given up hope of conceiving naturally'. No blame is apportioned.

Mercifully, Jack and Rita don't adopt in a celebrity way. There are fashions in children, as in everything else. In the early Nineties, celebrities adopted Romanian orphans. Then, one day, some style guru dismissed Romania: 'Oh, please! No one goes *there* any more.' Sorry, baby Gheorghe. Bad luck, baby Nadia. Neither of you will ever be in *Hello!* magazine.

Baby Eric is, though. Rita shares this (*Hello!*, May 25th, 2000): 'Eric was adopted through Buckinghamshire County Council.

Buckinghamshire's our home and we wanted a baby who was born here.'

Over to Katy Parun in the *New Zealand Herald* (October 8th, 2000): 'Do you ever feel less of a father because your son's adopted?'

'The first time I saw my son, I've never felt love like it,' says Jack. 'The love my wife and I feel for Eric is as strong as love can be. You don't have to have a Caesarean to feel connected to your child. We're Eric's parents and always will be. That's it.'

It's certainly an endorsement of family life. But it's the endorsement of a man who's in New Zealand while his family's in Buckinghamshire. What's Jack doing at the Dunedin TV Festival? Apparently, 'New Zealand's a growing market for me'. True. It could hardly be a shrinking one.

Note, too, the Caesarean reference. Jack knows that, had Rita given birth, it would not have been *à la Romania*. He told me as much, when I rang him to congratulate. Adopting, he said, was better than having to 'push a tiger through a catflap'. I don't think that was a line of Terry's. That was Jack, making the best of things.

'You must come over and see us,' says Jack.

'Yes,' I say. But I doubt I will. I don't expect to see Jack again.

Biography's a form of adultery. Mine has been going on for three months now.

I come into this office, Bedroom Two of my cottage, and I think about Jack for hours. I think about Jack much, much more than I think about my girlfriend Jess. It's psychological, necrophiliac adultery.

To compound my guilt, there's the lying. This morning, when Jess asks me how it's going, I say as I always do: 'Fine'.

'Why won't you show me any of it, then?'

'I don't want to show you till it's finished.'

She's asking me about the progress of my authorised biography, *That's All We Have Time For*. I might as well say, 'I don't want to show you till it's started'.

I tell the truth about Jack and me. But I lie to the woman I love.

'Finish it, then,' says Jess. 'Get it over with. Then we can all move on.'

There are no full-time writers. I reckon I'm roughly a half-time writer. Sometimes, I just sit here and look out the window and watch the world pass by. (That sentence, by the way, can't be classed as writing. A monkey, having typed that sentence, would definitely throw it in the bin or delete it, were it using a PC. 'Watch the world pass by'? Come on. What kind of tired cliché is that? And 'tired cliché' is itself no better. 'Tired' as opposed to what? A wide-awake cliché, hot to be hackneyed, full of the joys of spring?)

I'm distracted by the street life in our village. The Yoxford street life is Charlene, Samantha and Leonie.

At five to four, every schoolday, they walk past my cottage, shouting. Charlene and Samantha eat crisps. Leonie never does.

They're ten, maybe eleven. They could be twelve. I'm not a parent so I can't tell.

What they shout, apart from each other's names, is:

1) Loser!
2) Double loser!
3) Whatever
4) Get a life

By the time you read this, these shouts will be quaint and

outmoded, shouts shouted only by losers. But now, in their heyday, they get to me, sticking in my mind like a Beatles hook.

The first time I heard Charlene, Samantha and Leonie, I thought they were shouting at me. I got up from my desk and leaned out the window. They were oblivious, of course. Charlene was shouting at Leonie while Samantha laughed. Charlene is the Queen. Samantha is her courtier. Leonie keeps her own counsel.

Charlene was shouting at Leonie about Parmesan. Leonie was having pasta with pesto and Parmesan for supper. The crisp-eating Charlene considered this 'weird'. She thought it was the food of a loser.

Since I became a half-time writer, I've learned a lot about Parmesan Leonie, who interests me more than the others. She's never been out with a boy. She's the least advanced sexually but the most intelligent. Charlene, I imagine, will make and/or marry money but Leonie never will. Her mother is a cello-teaching single parent who drives an unwashed car. Leonie, I'm sure, will grow up to have values, rather than things of value.

Why am I always not-writing when they walk past? Is it because I stop writing, moments before, in anticipation of their arrival? Or is it because they walk past at a time of day when no one can write, because blood sugar levels are low? Did Jane Austen, perforce, look out the window at three fifty-five?

Some American biographer will know. They'll know if it was a fully rebated sash-style window. As Charlene would say, without irony: *Oy, biographer, get a life*.

The difference is this: what Jane Austen wasn't writing, as she looked out her window, were books. Whereas, what I'm not writing is a non-book, designed for non-publication.

Jesus! They've just banged on my door, then skittered down the street, screaming and laughing. Charlene and Samantha, that is. Leonie walked behind them. She wouldn't do a thing like that.

Look, they're ten or eleven or twelve or thirteen. Didn't you do things like that when you were those ages? I did, I'm sure of it. I don't remember doing them but I must have done. Most likely, Jack did them and I was with him, just as Leonie is with Charlene and Samantha, who don't know me and didn't bang on my door because I'm a loser.

I'm aware that Jess has hardly figured in my story. She's not 'Jess' yet. She's a mere 'J', like the wife in a politician's autobiography:

> *At 6.15pm, Margaret calls me into her office and tells me of my forthcoming elevation to the Cabinet. I'm absolutely thrilled. It's the culmination of everything I've worked so hard to achieve. I return home to Chester Square, walking on air. I invite Norman, Peter, John, Ann and Leon to supper. J, who gave birth that morning to a charming baby girl, rustles up an excellent fish stew. I open a bottle of Bollinger. I propose a toast: 'The Ministry of Defence!'*

Of course, having said too little, I could now say too much. I could overwhelm you with our intimacy. I've written of the warmth she brings by cupping my testicles. Why not travel west from them to her milky thighs? Then north to the rounded orbs of her breasts?

No. I don't think so. Why porn-praise a woman anyway? Aren't you just praising yourself? Are you not saying, in essence, *my bird's got fantastic tits*? Why praise something over which she has no control? Praise her face, by all means. A woman has the face she deserves, does she not? But the tits?

Rita, Jack's wife, now that's different. Rita bought those breasts. She chose them. She went to a cosmetic surgery and, as it were,

199

browsed through swatches. Her breasts are evidence of her taste and, as such, fit subjects for praise. To Rita, you're entitled, nay, encouraged to say: 'Great breasts. Where did you get them? Were they in the sale?' But I digress.

Sometimes, when I read back what I've written, I can't understand why I've turned out like I have. The person who writes what I write has opinions, frank and firm. He, that is I, sounds like someone who's made his mark on the world, who's stood up to be counted; whereas, as we know, I've sat down to be discounted.

I can impose my will on a sentence. That's the thing. It's easy to make words, unlike people, do exactly what you want. You can order words around. You can boss punctuation and parts of speech.

Noun, preposition – hands up!

Verb, definite article, adjective, noun – face the bleeding wall!

Adverb – quickly!

Adjective – quick!

Capital letters, swearword, question mark – WHAT DID I FUCKING SAY?

I meet Jess in the summer of 2001, when Tim and I go to see a Cuban band at Snape Maltings, the concert hall near Aldeburgh. I find myself sitting next to a pale-skinned girl with reddish hair.

The band is led by a dapper trumpeter in his seventies, a man delighted to play the music he's played for fifty years. Within two numbers, Jess's companion, a girl with green-tinted hair, is dancing in the aisle. The band's singer, a youthful thirty-something, proud to be part of his nation's musical heritage, claps his hands together over his head as the trombonist solos. We all join in. Jess's friend slips and grabs Jess's shoulder to steady herself, causing Jess to lean against me sharply. Her first word to me is 'Sorry'.

As Tim and I take our seats after the interval, she gives me the slightest of smiles and it's all I can do not to say: 'Listen, I'm not gay. I'm only here because his wife has a migraine'. Instead, I ask her whether she's enjoying the concert. 'Yes,' she says.

I assume that's an end to it. Neither of us wants to volunteer more. More might not be what's wanted. Then, long after that moment's passed, she says: 'It's a bit boring, though, isn't it?'

We're lucky, here in rural England, to be able to watch such a gifted group of musicians. They're cultural ambassadors from a distant Communist country. By welcoming them, we're uniting nations. We're contributing to the well-being of the world. It's a magical and inspirational occasion. I would never say that this music is boring. I would only think it, over and over again, as each song merges into the next, or is it the previous? Cuba, please. Shut up.

I shouldn't bandy the word 'love', not in my forties, not when a description of the kind of woman I'd like to meet would read: Any. But you weren't there. You can't understand and I can't explain, which may be on account of my deficiencies as a writer or because it's (inexplicable) love. Anyway, I love her for saying that, here and now, as the second half's about to start.

At the end, we congratulate each other on surviving the evening, with encores we were powerless to stop with our four hands not-clapping. I say to her: 'If you're ever in Yoxford, you must come to the bookshop.'

I don't even say I work there. It's Tourist Information.

* * *

She doesn't come and doesn't come. She never comes. But she does, a week later, send me an invitation to a party at her parents' house.

The invitation, addressed to The Man Who Doesn't Like Cuban Music, is put through the letterbox of the bookshop. She came to the bookshop when it was shut. She avoided me, in case I didn't welcome her visit, even though I'd requested it. With her step forward came a step back.

The door opens and there are Jess's parents, Ginty and Johnny. The one high-cheekboned and pretty, the other square-jawed and tall, with strong, impressive, outdoor hands. But this is Suffolk. These are the upper-middle classes. It's Johnny who's pretty. He wears a white linen jacket and a cream silk shirt, while Ginty appears to have bought her clothes in a field.

'Ginty' is her early childhood mangling of her given name, Georgina. Three years after meeting her, I still find it hard to say, or write, or even think. It's such a brutal index of the distance I've travelled, from the Golders Green of Sylvia Harris and Bea Goldman to the Suffolk of Ginty. Why not go the whole hog and call yourself 'Gentile'?

'I'm a friend of Jess', I say, which makes it odd that, when Jess comes to greet me, I'm obliged to tell her my name.

I discover that Jess is a portrait painter. Her green-haired friend is Sharon Combes, a Young British Artist who's always on television saying 'fuck'. I tell Jess that I too know someone on television. (It always comes up. Within a minute or a day of meeting someone, certainly no more than a week, I've told the new person that I'm Jewish and I know Jack Harris.)

Jess says she never watches chat shows. She looks at me with her painter's eyes, the only eyes that are *trained* to undress you.

I ache to go to bed with her and now I have reasons. We have so much in common. She knows someone on television, I know someone on television. She met me at a concert, I met her at a concert. Let us not delay.

Johnny and Ginty live in the Great Glemham house Johnny inherited from his father. There's a walled garden which Ginty maintains, supremely. Ginty, who's never worked, works harder than most who do. Apart from bringing up Jess and her sister Caro, she's cooked and gardened and charity'd and committeed. She's driven food parcels through Ethiopia. She's un-crumbled the house. She's spent days up ladders, clearing out gutters and fixing roof tiles. (My mother would only be up a ladder if a fireman were carrying her down in his arms.)

Johnny, an Old Etonian who read English at Oxford, has the air of a seventy-year-old undergraduate. He's a bald man with invisible floppy hair, prone to monogrammed slippers and 'interesting' headgear he bought in Tangiers or Calcutta.

Inevitably, he's a poet. In the time I've known his daughter, I've had three birthdays. For all of them, he's given me a book of his poetry. I look on the bright side. I'd much rather be given these books than buy them and the poetry could be worse. Take these lines, chosen at random from my birthday before last:

> *Seeds of greatness, seeds of despair*
> *What fruit is there?*

They're a tad pompous, I grant you, but the second line is nicely ambiguous. Stress the 'is' and the sense is: will the seeds bear fruit at all? Stress the 'there' and the sense is, what kind of fruit will those seeds produce?

After Oxford, he joined his father's firm. He was a reluctant and inadequate estate agent till he was thirty-five, when he sold his share of the business to his brother, with the aim of living by his pen. It had to be a pen, not a typewriter.

Taking a lease on a disused chapel in Saxmundham, Johnny started a secondhand book business to supplement his poetic income of ten pee a year. Johnny's spent half his life in the place. Week in, week out, the stock changes; and yet, whenever I go in there, I always see the same *David Cassidy Annuals* and *Perry Mason Stories* and *Who's Who 1958*. Surely by now it should be *Who Was Who*. Or, simply, *Who*?

Johnny and Ginty have no money. If you drive past their house, you won't know this. From the road, they look rich. This is what I've learned in my Suffolk period – you can be land-rich but cash-poor.

Jess goes off to talk to Angus, a silver-haired judge who keeps looking at her bosom, which I still refuse to describe.

Jess's Uncle Norman comes up and says: 'You're a friend of my niece.' It's the perfect opening remark, establishing through the tone of his voice that he adores her too.

Norman calls over his boyfriend, Leo. Leo, a dentist in his fifties, turns out to live in Hendon. His parents knew Jack's parents. Leo is a Feigenbaum, one of the Hendon Feigenbaums. I feel elated. I feel at home, far from home.

Johnny cooks coq au vin, a staple of the ancienne cuisine he mastered in his twenties. I sit next to Jess. Because she and not her parents have invited me, I feel like a young person. There are so few people there, maybe fifteen or twenty. I feel chosen.

At the end of the night, I ask her if I can ring for a minicab.

She's surprised that I don't drive. 'I hate cars,' I say. This has always been true but its meaning has shifted over the years. In my teens, it meant that I felt myself too brainy and sensitive to drive. In my twenties, it implied laziness; in my thirties, poverty. But now, thankfully, it suggests I want to save the planet.

She asks me where I live and I tell her. I ask her where she lives. Can she give me a lift? She tells me she lives upstairs, because she doesn't earn much, she gets on with her parents and she's able to use one of the outbuildings as a studio.

She says, though, that she'd be happy to give me a lift upstairs. I'm shaky with happiness. I feel that my knees will give way.

There's no cupping of cheeks or gazing into each other's eyes. Perhaps because we're made for each other, the sex is devoid of love. It's devoid of everything except sex. It's pure sexy sex, as opposed to an expression of something else. Sorry, Vicar. Sorry, Rabbi. You don't know what you're missing.

Afterwards, I say 'Thank you!' It's my only mistake. Jess grabs my nose and twists it till it hurts. 'Don't say that again!' I have to have it explained to me that gratitude's not sexy.

I wake up shivering, in that hellish bed, so hard and concave it's more like a bath. I hoick myself out of there to comb the walls for a radiator. There's none. Cold's the way Johnny and Ginty like it. They wear nightdresses, woolly hats and socks. They get dressed to go to bed.

She wakes. The mood is too tender for sex, so we talk about it instead.

Jess tells me that Angus the judge was her mother's lover, in the early years of her marriage. Later, he became her father's.

In Jess's family, in Jess's world, gay's everywhere. The men absorb gayness with their mother's milk and father's whisky. Jess's father is gay, as was his father Walter, his grandfather John, and so on and so on, a gay family tree that goes back to Adam. (I mean, come on. Adam. Adam! The more you say it, the camper it sounds. Would a straight man wear a fig-leaf?)

Johnny loves Ginty, no question about it; he's lived with her since 1957. He loves women but it's men he likes. Ginty puts up with it. She doesn't complain. She drinks, though. She's of the pre-Why Me? generation for whom drink is the shrink.

Norman lives alone in a house in Ecclestone Street in Belgravia. Two weeks after I meet him, he gives a party there for two hundred people, safe in the knowledge they'll all go home at the end of the night. Even his current boyfriend, Leo. Apparently, he only has current boyfriends. Their currency always runs out.

The first thing I notice is a Christopher Wood pencil portrait of Winifred Nicholson. And this is the hall. This is merely where you take off your coat.

As Norman approaches, I shout: 'Christopher Wood! 1901–1930!' Jess, who's attracted to my mind and knowledge, who didn't go for me because of my *milky thighs* or *average cock*, is more delighted than embarrassed by the date-calling.

Norman and I start a conversation which has never stopped: twentieth-century British art (which he loves and owns and lends anonymously to exhibitions), the history of Germany between the Wars, food, Russia, Napoleon, Miles Davis, tennis, soccer.

We establish, in the hall, that Norman doesn't 'have a team'. Norman's a steely aesthete. He supports no one except the game, regarding the twenty-two players on the pitch no differently from paintings in the Louvre. There will be some of no interest, some which are minor, and the odd one that's sublime. In the Louvre, for what it's worth, he loves Rubens's *The Village Fete* (c 1635); on the pitch, it's Gianfranco Zola. (Now Zola's retired, Norman watches his old matches on video.)

Norman has always been crucial in Jess's life. It was he who arranged for her to spend a year in Paris, after she left school; he who found her a flat in London when she was at Camberwell Art School; he who got her her first commission, a portrait of Angus which hangs in the Inner Temple.

He's accomplished, that's what I admire. He can ride, shoot, drive too fast, sail. Only fools and fellow-millionaires play poker with him.

Back in the Seventies, while staying in a Rome hotel room with appalling art on the walls, Norman had an idea. Why not mass-produce appalling art for hotels?

He called the company Art Room. He set up his then-boyfriend, Tom, one of those art school graduates who can paint in any style but their own. Tom got cracking on his sub-Matisse and faux-Dufy prints, his French Bread on Check Tablecloths, his Alpine Dawns, his Wicker Baskets of International Fruit. Then he died of a brain tumour. But the business lived on. Norman hired more Toms. He installed a managing director to run the business, withdrawing from day-to-day involvement. He made money, lots of it, at a distance, not compromising his position as a Cork Street gallery owner with a passion for his artists.

But artists are subject to the fluctuations and vicissitudes of the art market, as well as their own. No one fluctuates like an artist, promising one minute, then drunk or spent or out of fashion the next.

Hotel rooms aren't like that, though. They're always the same. There's always the mini-bar and the shower gel and the complimentary mint and the TV operating guide. And the Fishing

Boats at Sunset, which you never get tired of because you don't even notice it's there.

As we walk down Ecclestone Street after the party, Jess keeps saying 'Pardon?' and laughing. I'm speaking too quietly. It's a new trait I've acquired from conversing with Norman, who speaks in a famously quiet voice. You have to lean in to hear him, which puts you in his thrall. There's no need for me to answer Norman in a voice as soft as his. But I do.

In the hall, when I'm leaving the party, Norman helps me on with my coat. I shake his hand. He tells me how nice it was to meet me again and I repay the compliment. Then he adds:

'It would be marvellous if you and Jess came to my house in France.'

I reply:

'Oh yes. That would be marvellous. Marvellous.'

'Are you free at Easter?'

'I think so. Yes.'

He opens the door.

'Easter it is then.'

This year, 2004, we went to Norman's house in Provence, in the olive groves above the River Saigne, for the third Easter running.

The Easter boyfriend is Bob Ridgeon, a plumber in his thirties. They met at a bus-stop in Bath, where Bob lives. Typically, Norman tells us nothing more. We can't believe that Norman travels by bus.

At first, I like Bob. We arrive at the house. No one's in. Jess, exhausted after the drive, goes off to have a nap. After a few minutes, Bob appears in the kitchen, in his shorts, fresh from his run. He's cheery. He introduces himself as 'the Bath plumber,' which suggests he doesn't take himself too seriously. But then I think how many times he's said this and I feel depressed.

'What would you like to drink, Dave? Red or white?' Why's Bob, who's known Norman a few weeks, offering me a drink, when I've known Norman for years? Surely, he should wait for me to ask him what he'd like to drink.

I've got status in this house. Norman calls me his 'book-taster'. At Les Oliviers, he only reads what I've read and presented for his delectation. Sometimes, he'll reject it with a gentle 'Not for me'. Other times, he's overjoyed to be introduced to an author or subject previously beyond his ken. It's lovely to see the silvery Norman, an expert on military history, tucking into a Nicholson Baker or a decent biography of Morrissey.

My aim on this trip is to read and play chess and tennis. In the time we've known each other, we've played seventy-eight chess games. Norman's won forty-four, I've won twenty-nine, with five drawn. As for tennis, I've won sixty-eight to his fifty-two. We score in games not sets, playing five games at a time. Norman is seventy-one, after all. He still wins plenty of games, though, because he has a second serve. That's how accomplished Norman is. My second serve is, like everyone else's, my first serve slower. But Norman's has its own integrity. It spins. It lands in.

But we hardly play chess or tennis. Bob, the garrulous plumber, never leaves us alone. In the pool, on that first day, before the salade niçoise and the tarte tatin, the unvarying lunch we love – 'we' being Norman and Jess and I – Bob talks to me as he swims alongside me. He punishes me for the basic breast-stroke that leaves my mouth in a speaking position.

'I hear you know Jack Harris, Dave. What's he really like?' I shrug. Bob doesn't notice. Maybe he thinks it's part of my stroke. So I have to say something which answers him politely but ends the conversation. I say: 'Complicated. Deep.' And then, as if cued by 'deep', I dive down to the bottom of the pool and wish I didn't have to come up.

Bob has a passion for cars, especially Norman's, which he's driven from London to Provence. He talks a lot about Norman's car, whereas Norman never mentions it. He has no need. He owns it, therefore the world knows it's beautiful and expensive. But Bob constantly picks up the keys, which hang on a modest nail in the kitchen, and plays with them in an uninhibited 'pocket billiards' style.

It's a Mercedes S Blah Blah Blah. (As you know, I know nothing about cars.) And guess what? According to Bob, it has 'fabulous roadholding'. That's right. The Mercedes S Blah Blah Blah is in constant contact with the road. Even at high speeds, it's not airborne. In fact, the entire Mercedes range comes without stewards or lavatories.

As well as the driving, Bob does the salad dressings.

I used to do the salad dressings at Les Oliviers. On the first day, seeing Bob with his hand on the balsamic, I'm about to say something – I don't know what – when Norman gives me one of his subtlest looks, a kind of eyeball implosion, in the manner of the great dead-now comic actor John Le Mesurier. I say nothing.

Bob's third and last passion is genealogy, which is to be encouraged, since it keeps him on the internet while Norman and I steal a few second serves.

On the third day, I suggest we go to Aix, in two cars, in case we want to go on from Aix on separate excursions. The key word is 'separate'. I don't want to go anywhere from Aix. I simply want to go to Aix and back not in the company of Bob.

Jess and I sit in our hire car, waiting for Norman and Bob to come out of the house. We wait a couple of minutes. I suggest to Jess this is long enough for a homosexual act. She's annoyed.

'Bob's probably looking for his sunglasses.'

'True. But, you know. Maybe he left them on Norman's person.'

She lectures me on the subject of Bob's non-sexual virtues. He's loyal, he's domesticated and he has his own interests. (In other words: driving, salad dressing, genealogy.)

'There's more to their relationship than sex,' she concludes.

Bob and Norman come out of the house. Bob is whistling. I don't say this proves an act has taken place but it's circumstantial evidence.

They head for the car. Norman doesn't speak. I sense he's not looking forward to being trapped with Bob. Sure enough, a bizarre thing happens. Bob whistles his way to the driving seat. But Norman ignores the front passenger door and sits in the back, as if the Merc SBBB were a roadholding minicab and Bob were its driver.

Jess turns on the ignition. She doesn't comment. But I feel I've scored a victory.

Norman turns his head to look at us. I catch his eye.

'History's a fascinating thing, Dave. Do you know, there've been Ridgeons in Bath since 1876.' We're standing outside the cathedral in Aix.

'When I get home, I'm going to have a DNA test. They're digging up skeletons all the time, you know, Dave, on archaeological digs. If I do the test, they can tell if I'm related to the skeletons. Some of them go back to the first century BC.'

Everyone's at it. Everyone's an autobiographer now. Everyone's searching for an ancestor whose existence anticipates and validates their own. Bob hopes to find a skeleton with the bent backbone and elongated neck of a plumber. The lunatics have taken over the afterlife.

The Cathedral of Saint-Sauveur in Aix contains elements of Roman, Early Christian, Romanesque, Gothic and Renaissance architectural styles. I know this from studying my guide book in the hope that Bob will drift away, which he does. He falls into conversation with a Scottish family. They're amused to discover that Bob, a plumber, comes from Bath.

Jess heads inside. Norman hangs back to have a quiet word with me. It's the closest he ever comes to acknowledging the difficulties of his private life.

'You're wondering why I sit in the back of the car. I'm getting headaches, you see. I find the back less headache-inducing.'

'Of course,' I say, as if everyone understands that the back of a car is less headache-inducing.

Why did Norman choose Bob? He's clearly not the right man for Norman. He's a good wrong man, though, as are all of Norman's boyfriends. Bob's opinions, which don't interest Norman, never interrupt his thoughts. Bob can't stimulate Norman intellectually but nor can he distract him. Norman doesn't want intimacy and in Bob he hasn't found it, as he knew he wouldn't. Sitting in the front would bring him no closer.

It's obvious, isn't it? Norman is the new Jack, now Jack has gone out of my life.

I feel as if I'm part of Norman's family. He has, of course, no children. But then again neither do I.

If you ask Jess how old she is, she'll tell you she's thirty-five in December. When I met her, she said 'thirty-two'. But now she's stopped saying how old she is, only how old she'll be in December.

She wants to have kids. I don't. I fear it. My father's dead, my sister's a stranger and my mother, when I was forty-five, finally succumbed to post-natal depression. She'd have had a happier life if she'd married someone else and, by definition, not had my sister and me.

If one of us wants kids and the other doesn't, what is the compromise?

6

The Beginning Of The End

It's Saturday morning. Jess and I have just come back from Provence. We've been living together (three days a week) for more than two years, which is a miracle. I've never lived with anyone for that long, apart from myself. I've never wanted to inflict my habits on anyone which, as Jess points out, means I've never wanted anyone else's habits inflicted on me. It's true that I find the habit of aloneness hard to break. Sometimes I turn the light off when I leave a room, forgetting she's there.

Jack is spending the morning in a Norwich bookshop, signing copies of his *Crack a Joke* book, the proceeds of which will go to children's charities. He's then having lunch with a Norfolk woman he's never met. She's paid two hundred pounds for the privilege, at a charity auction of promises.

After lunch, he's coming to us. We've spent the morning preparing for his visit, which we don't want him to think of as yet more charity.

I get up and I bump my head on the – shit! – beam as I go to the bathroom. The bumping of the head is not a habit. It's a sign. Jess says I do it if I'm worried about something. So she knows I'm nervous about Jack's visit. I can't deny it, though I find it ridiculous. Jack's just a man, a man I've known since I was six.

'What shall I wear?' asks Jess.

'How do you mean?' I reply.

'How do you mean, how do I mean?'

The day, not yet five minutes old, is in trouble.

'Wear what you normally wear,' I say.

'What do I normally wear?' she asks, plunging a verbal kitchen knife into the day's warm corpse.

'I don't know,' I say.

'I don't know either.'

If she's painting, Jess wears an old shirt and trousers or a boiler suit. Two days a week, she works at a garden centre, where she wears gardening clothes. Once a year, she spends an outrageous sum on a dress. 'Dress' isn't the right word. She loves a costume. The last dress she bought is like something worn by Elizabeth the First, only shorter.

The point is, Jess doesn't have any clothes that aren't fit for a jumble sale or a queen. So we drive, which means that she drives, to the fashion shops of Beccles and Halesworth. Their fashions are fit for a queen, but sadly it's Elizabeth the Second. So we end up in a surfing shop in Aldeburgh where she tries on a skirt and top that she's worried look 'too sexy'. 'You don't look sexy,' I assure her, which of course pisses her off.

We drive home to wait for Jack's arrival. 'What do you think we should do with him?'

'I don't know,' I say, as I keep saying. 'Drive him to the coast?'

'We've just driven to the coast. What's he like?'

'Don't ask me that. Everyone always asks me that and –'

'I mean, what's he like doing?'

As a boy, he liked climbing trees and doing card tricks. What does he like doing now? I don't know. He likes being famous. I could call him on his mobile and ask him. But it's too close to the Al fucking Conroy question. I feel I should know.

Finally, seven hours after we started worrying about it, Jack knocks at the door. He hugs me. He tells me I'm turning into my dad, but that's OK as my dad never went bald. I introduce him to Jess and he's courtly, shaking her hand and being careful not to burden her with any charisma.

'I didn't know what to get you,' he says. 'So I got you this.' He didn't have to get us anything, of course, since he's not staying overnight or even for a meal.

The gift is rectangular. 'Is it a box of used fivers?' I ask. It's the first of many unfunny things I'll say in the next few hours. Perversely, I'm the one who tries too hard, while Jess, who doesn't know him, is natural. Having invested so much tension in her clothes, she's wearing what she always wears (jeans and a blouse). Yet the investment has yielded a surprising return: she's relaxed.

Jess unwraps a DVD box set of *The Godfather* trilogy. She's delighted, since she's only seen the first of the films. I thank Jack wholeheartedly. Then something occurs to him, brought on by the smallness of my cottage, the smallness of my life.

'You've got a DVD player, haven't you?'

'Yes,' I say, because that's the answer he wants.

'No,' says Jess, overlapping. 'But we'll definitely get one now.'

'I'll buy you one,' says Jack, who won't be denied.

Jess drives us to the Co-op Electrical Shop in Leiston, where he chooses the cheapest, saying all DVD players are, in his view, much of a muchness. Jess is impressed. She expected him to show off his wealth. His refusal to waste money marks him out as a real person, earthed to everyday concerns. The saleswoman, too, is impressive. She has a lovely way of not reacting to Jack's fame, treating him as she would anyone else, with quiet courtesy. It's a Suffolk characteristic, this unyielding calm. Natives of other counties might gush.

So. That just leaves me. I see, by the toasters, an antique dealer

I know. I call: 'Hello, Martin!' Jess maintains that, in normal circumstances, I'd have ignored him. (I've never liked him, it's true. What fuels his self-importance? Why does his shop smell of dead birds?) Certainly, he merely returns my hello and makes no move towards me. I make a move, though, according to Jess. I take a pace sideways to position myself closer to my famous companion.

I don't believe her. Nobody takes a pace sideways. Perhaps I angle myself in Jack's direction. If so, I'm not drawing Martin's attention to the fact I know Jack. I'm drawing Jack's attention to the fact I know Martin. I'm saying to Jack, look, don't feel sorry for me, living in the country, not working for you. I'm all right. I'm popular. Everyone round here knows me.

We leave – 'Bye, Martin!' – and drive to the tea-shop in Westleton. En route, Jess stops at a rickety table outside a bungalow. The table's covered in home-grown vegetables, their prices marked on a piece of cardboard. Jess bags us a couple of beetroots and some spring greens. She gets out her purse.

'This I must see,' says Jack, following her to the table. I watch them from the car.

Jess drops a series of coins into a Tupperware box, which lies open on the table with the day's takings in it.

'You put your money in that?'

Jess nods. She helps herself to some change.

'What's to stop you stealing the money?'

'Nothing.'

Jack can't believe it. We grew up in a North London suburb. And here I am, in a place so rural, folk leave money on a table outside their house.

'Hold on,' says Jack, 'I get it! There's closed-circuit TV in the oak tree! Some man in a tower in Ipswich is watching us! If you nick the box, he radios two men concealed in that hedge.'

Jess smiles but, to her credit, doesn't laugh. 'That's a beech tree.' How does she manage to say these things? She's always so *herself*.

They get back in the car and, after tea, Jess drives us to Dunwich beach.

In the boot of the car are a pair of beach towels and swimming costumes, on permanent alert. Swimming always enhances our mood. We do it at every opportunity.

Jess suggests we do it now. I'm embarrassed. I know Jack won't want to swim in the North Sea in May. We don't have a costume for him anyway. It's early evening already. We better be getting him back to our cottage, outside which his driver will be waiting.

'Do you fancy a dip?' she asks him.

'Sure,' he replies. 'But I don't have a costume.'

'You can borrow Dave's.' She turns to me. 'You can swim in your pants, can't you?'

'I can swim in mine,' counters Jack.

'OK. You swim in your pants then Dave can lend you a pair of his pants to go home in. There won't be enough time to dry your pants before you have to leave.'

How many more times is she going to say 'pants'? Please, I silently beg her, don't bother him with pants. This is a famous man who knows nothing of pants, whose pants are bought by others, washed by others, ironed by others and – who knows? – worn in by others.

Yet Jack goes swimming, happily, in his much-talked-about pants.

'Ohmygod! It's freezing!' he says. It's what everyone says. He's not giving us any unique marine *shtick*, which we'll be expected to remember forever. He's accepted, after the Tupperware routine, that nothing special is required of him. He doesn't have to try. Being with us is enough.

My mood duly alters. My heart soars. Here we are, the woman I love and the man I've known the longest. The sea, that great leveller, is freezing us all. We're connected.

Back at the cottage in the early evening, each of us drinking a glass of whisky that feels truly earned, Jack asks Jess about her work. What does she do? What's she up to at the moment?

No more than you ask what a famous person does, does a famous person ask what you do. And look – it's a chat show host putting the question, with the same intonation, the same facial expressions, he uses when asking Phil Collins what he's up to. He's chatting, in private, for free. It's as if an Olympic athlete were to sprint out of our lavatory.

Jess tells him she's a portrait painter but he won't have heard of her.

'You must paint my portrait,' says Jack.

'Don't you want to see my work first?'

'No. Dave's a man of taste. He wouldn't live with a painter who wasn't fantastic.'

This is so all-embracingly charming, we don't know what to say. And he means it.

'Can you come to my house? I'd love you to paint my portrait in my house. I'll get my people to fix it up. How long will it take?'

'The sittings normally take a couple of weeks. About four hours a day.'

'OK. The series ends next week . . . blah blah blah . . . end of May?'

Jess nods. That's only a few weeks away. The urgency's unusual. There are no twenty-four hour portrait painters, driving a van with a phone number and NO PORTRAIT TOO SMALL. No one calls in the night to say, quick, come round, you've got to paint me now – my face is falling!

'OK. That'll happen,' says Jack. 'Sorry. I have to go.'

I understand now why I banged my head on that beam this morning: I didn't want Jess to like him. Or, rather, I wanted her to like him less than she likes me. I wanted her to feel that his values were skewed, that his pursuit of fame and wealth made him a lesser human being than me, who's got no fame or wealth and hasn't even pursued them.

But I was wrong. He's a generous man who makes things happen. I'm happy she likes him.

We walk to his car. From the middle of my living room to the kerb – it's no distance at all. There's no time to say anything. He kisses Jess on both cheeks then he and I hug.

I want to be generous to him too. So I tell him. Keep my pants.

A fee of six thousand pounds is agreed. Jess lowers the back seats of Johnny and Ginty's old car, fits in her easel and the tools of her trade and drives off to Buckinghamshire.

She spends the days in Jack's house, then retires to a nearby bed and breakfast, despite Jack and Rita offering her a guest bedroom, an offer she knows to refuse.

It's strange, as I sit on my own in the cottage with our *Godfathers*. I've been to Jack's house four or five times, for wedding and anniversary parties; yet I've never been in his house. Everything's always happened outside, in marquees and Portaloos.

Jess and I phone each other every night but she's unforthcoming. When I ask her the unforgivable question – what are Jack and Rita really like? – she says she doesn't want to get involved. She's there to do a job.

But when she comes home, it's immediately evident that the

job has affected her. The first thing she tells me is that Jack and Rita's hall is the size of my ground floor. It's 'like a reception without a receptionist'. She and I must buy a place together. We can't live in this tiny cottage any more.

'Did Jack put you up to this?'

'Nobody put me up to this. It's what I feel. I've earned nine thousand pounds in the last two weeks and –'

'I thought it was six.'

'Well, it wasn't. He gave me nine.'

It's a body-blow, this nine. It may be generous, but it only serves to reduce my earnings further in Jess's eyes.

'Are you planning on spending the rest of your life working in a bookshop?'

'I'm not planning anything.'

Within two days, we're looking at four-bedroom houses and wondering how we can afford them if we sell my cottage and Norman gives us an interest-free loan of, say, thirty thousand pounds.

We see a three-bedroom house we like, on the road from Westleton to Middleton. We could just about afford to buy it. But we couldn't live in it. No. Not without removing all traces of the current owners' taste, knocking the front and back rooms into one and building an extension to the kitchen so it's no longer 'galley-style'. Then there's the roof. We don't even know what's wrong with the roof. But we know a surveyor will tell us.

The estate agent drives off, leaving us outside looking in.

'We're always fifty grand short, aren't we?' Jess says. 'Neither of us is ever going to earn any money.'

'I don't know about that,' I reply. 'I mean, you've just earned nine thousand.'

'It's hopeless, isn't it?' She unlocks the car door but doesn't get in the car.

'Why can't you drive? It means I can never leave you, doesn't it? You can't go anywhere without me.'

'That's not true. There are buses. Not here, maybe. But, you know, one can always walk.'

'Oh. You'd walk home now, would you?'

I ponder this. If Jess left me here, the walk to my cottage would take about an hour, if I went along the roads, via Middleton. There might be footpaths that would shorten my journey. But I don't have a map.

It takes time to think this. In that time, Jess is lost to me. It's no different from my break-up with Anna, the Italian, twenty-five years earlier. The girl (then) or woman (now) says something which I analyse and to which I belatedly respond. But I don't argue with that something. They must like me, I reason, for my non-argumentative qualities.

'Yes.'

'OK. You walk then. You do that.'

Jess gets in her car, slams the door, turns on the ignition and drives off.

I duly walk home. It takes three and three-quarter hours. But that's because I don't want to arrive. I know I'll find a message from Jess, either written or left on the answerphone. I can't face reading/hearing it.

In the pub in Theberton, I wonder how to make one drink last an hour. I don't like bitter. So I buy a pint of that.

I drain my glass, finally, with the last of a hundred sips, then I walk to the bar, in search of crisps to prolong my stay further.

'What flavour would you like?' asks the barman.

'You're asking the wrong question,' I reply with baffling bitterness. 'Ask me what I wouldn't like.' Salt and vinegar, crinkle-cut, does the job nicely. I get home at half-past three.

The message, in fact, is on the 1571 answering service. It was

223

received today, a voice tells me, at 11.57. 11.57, I note, is an anagram of 1571. I hear Jess's voice and press the button that saves the message till later. I can't listen to it, not now, not after that anagram thought, with its facetious and defensive detachment.

I wait. I listen.

She's at her parents and will get in touch when she's ready. If she needs any more of her stuff, she's got a key and will get it while I'm at work. I play the message again and again, poring over it in true singer-songwriter fashion, a process as morbid and unproductive as reading chicken bones.

You know she's a painter who loves gardening and swimming. She's natural and direct. *Oh yes,* you think, *I know the type. No nonsense. Cheery. Healthy glow. Good at sex. Comes from growing up with animals, you know.*

I'm sorry but you don't know anything. When I love her, which isn't all the time, since I'm incapable of that – when I love her, I don't know where I end and she begins. I don't love a 'type'. To hell with you.

What chance do you have when I get it so wrong? I write that she's *natural and direct.* Yet look at the way she gets twisted out of shape by her friend Sharon, the Young British Artist who swears on the telly. (You know the type.) For fifteen years, Sharon has mined one seam – Men Watching Sport. Photographs and video installations of Men Watching Sport. They're in galleries all over the world. She owns a house in Hampstead.

When I attack Sharon, Jess defends Sharon. When I defend her, Jess attacks. There's nothing direct about it. Nor is there in her feelings about her own work. She never set out to be a portrait painter. Norman got her the commission to paint the judge and that was it. She wanted to be more like Sharon. She hates the fact that 'portrait painter' is as cutting-edge as 'bell ringer'. She loves it when she's doing it, though. She hates it when she's not. She calls it 'the staring profession'. Clients pay six thousand pounds to be stared at for a fortnight. Then they expect to look 'good'.

Let's go back to the day she left me, knowing we'll reunite.

I've been living alone for no more than an hour when the phone rings.

'Twin Man! It's Jack! What are you doing on Friday night? Let's meet up in London. I've got your pants.'

I pause only to think about money. I hate money now. It made Jess leave me. As a consequence, I can't think about anything else.

I won't be able to get a cheap day return because the last train to Darsham, my local station, leaves London at half-past eight, which is far too early. The last train to Ipswich, however, leaves London at half-past eleven. So. A single from Darsham to Ipswich and a return from Ipswich to London. How much is that? Plus the late-night taxi –

'Twinno? Still there?'

I apologise. I explain that I'm not feeling good. I tell him my news.

'Shit. I'm sorry to hear that,' Jack says. 'Come on then. You need to be taken out of yourself.'

The night begins at Jack's flat, in a purpose-built block in Covent Garden. The directions are labyrinthine. I find myself in a top-floor bolt-hole that overlooks (fire-escapes, ventilation shafts, backs of restaurants) but is overlooked only by pigeons. I study them as Jack pours the champagne. They're not what they were. They've changed since I lived in London. Is it an emigrant's nostalgia or have they put on weight? They don't fly as high as they used to.

Jack's flat is all man: a black leather sofa, a glass-topped low table, an outsize chrome fridge, a jukebox (the curse of the Eighties celebrity). There are TVs in the bedroom, the living room and the kitchen. All the walls are the same colour. I'm sure that Jack, when he's not in the flat, couldn't tell you what that colour is.

'How are you?' he says, handing me my glass and settling back in the sofa. I drink, to delay my answer. Since he became a celebrity, I've never told Jack how I am. I don't want to bore him, not now he's a famous entertainer whom, instinctively, I want to entertain in return. How I am is not entertaining.

'Tell me,' says Jack, looking up at me. So I tell him. I tell him for twenty minutes, maybe half an hour, standing or wandering while he nods and listens and twiddles with his central strand of hair, which has moved off-centre now he's got a bald patch. It's a shock for me to look down on pink pate, the size of a tennis ball. I've never seen it on television, where Jack is all front.

I give him the Pain Exclusive: my life is going nowhere, my girlfriend has gone, I've got nothing and feel like no one. How I am, it transpires, *is* entertaining. Jack's presence makes it so. I exaggerate. I put in details, like the salt and vinegar crisps, that have him nodding with approval, as if I were pitching my Pain for his yay or nay.

I ask him the inevitable question: what did Jess say about me?

'She said you were going nowhere but you were lovely.'

This has the salty tang of a truth accurately remembered. I'm glad he feels he knows me well enough to say it. And there's hope, there must be. She thinks me lovely.

226

'So how are you then, Jack?'

Jack shakes his head, gets up from the sofa and tells me the evening is not about him. He fetches a take-away menu from the kitchen. There's a stack behind the open, empty breadbin.

'Do you like Thai?' he asks and of course I do.

He holds the menu away from his face and points at an item. 'What's that say?'

I put on my reading glasses. 'Gaang Gy – chicken curry with coconut.' I offer him the glasses. He puts them on and nods his agreement. I tell him he should get a pair.

'Don't worry. Rita's booked me an appointment. He does the Queen's eyes, Elton's, everyone. Six-month waiting list. Costs a fortune.'

'Great,' I say. I can go to a chemist and, for a few pounds, buy a pair of glasses. But Jack has to wait six months for the vision the Queen enjoys.

'Have whatever you want,' he says. 'Rita mentioned the place in her column. They haven't charged me since.' It seems that things in his life either cost a fortune or are free.

Half an hour later, we walk down Long Acre to the restaurant; a two-minute journey that takes a quarter of an hour. For every shout, Jack has a shout in reply, often followed by a conversation. 'Hello, Jack!' shout the office workers outside the pub. 'Hey, Jack, love the bald patch!' shouts a girl, from the first-floor window of a graphic design company. 'Give us a smile, Jack!' shouts a taxi driver, stuck at a pedestrian crossing.

I feel spring-heeled, as if I'm on God's camera. 'Reflected glory' is not the right phrase. It feels more like glory. I talk louder and seem, to me, more interesting. When Jack regrets his riposte – 'Thank you!' – to the bald patch shout, I come up with: 'I'm trying to look more like my bottom'. I know it will work. I'm confident.

But Jack ignores me. He's too busy extending his hand to meet the hand of a well-wisher. Jack hasn't noticed, as I have, that the well-wisher is raising his hand to hail the taxi. No matter. Jack shakes the hailing hand anyway and wishes the man good luck, as the taxi drives past.

After ten minutes banter with the Thai restaurateur, who laughs at everything Jack says, we emerge from the restaurant. But we don't retrace our steps. We cross the street. We return to the flat via the wrong side, so Jack can work both sides of the street.

Jack has no complaint about invasions of his privacy. On the contrary, he's only too keen to invade the privacy of others – a Japanese couple consulting a map, a woman in a wheelchair whom Jack accuses of ogling his crotch. We came out to fetch our take-away. What could be more banal? Yet every moment is charged, exciting.

Midway through the meal, a leather-jacketed man arrives. Jack asks if I recognise him. I don't. It's Little Jeremy, the son of Jack's girlfriend Eileen; now Jeremy, a man with an indoor pallor and a grin.

Jack asks if Jeremy's got the scripts. Jeremy opens his briefcase and gets out the scripts. Bafflingly, they're no bigger than an inch square, folded like origami. They can't contain more than haikus. Jack opens up the first script and scans the white powdered text. Now I understand.

Jeremy, I learn, as Jack karate-chops the powder into lines, got in touch with Jack a few years earlier to see if Jack could help him get work in showbusiness.

Jack tells me that Jeremy has written a script. But now he's no longer talking in code. Jeremy has written a script, a script script. Jeremy asks if now is a good time for Jack to read it. Jack says he'd love to but he has to take care of some business. He suggests that Jeremy reads his script, out loud, to me. I'm a great wordsman. I've written for magazines. (A reference, I assume, to the Bob Dylan fanzine and the school magazine.) They call me, Jack says, 'The Prof'.

During this exchange, Jack rolls up a note, snorts a line, then passes the note to me. It's a fifty-pound note. I've never seen one before. Perhaps it's only minted for snorting. I bow my head. I abase myself. For the first time in my life, I take cocaine.

I look at Jeremy, with his blue eyes and black hair and his mouth hanging slightly open, like a fish fishing for plankton. I remember him, in his school uniform, coming into the kitchen for a glass of water while his mother shouted abuse at Jack. I feel my skull turning into sculpted glass, with two exquisitely tubular nostrils. I see myself, with perfect clarity, as a man who has no woman or children, no Little Jeremy. This is a gain, not a deprivation. Without children, a man has no obligation to set a moral example. Spared the hypocrisy of parenthood, I can say what I know to be true: cocaine's fantastic. If I speak ill of it at any point, it can only be because, at the time of writing, I'm not on cocaine.

Jack takes his mobile into the bedroom and turns on the TV. Jeremy starts to read his script, *The Woman*, about a single mother who takes revenge on the men who've wronged her. These men all have names beginning with V: Victor, Vince, Van, Vernon, Vaughan. I like the situation. Not the situation in the film, the situation in the living room: this young man desperate for my approval, speaking the lines too loudly. The dialogue never rises above the level of the tautologous 'I'll drill a hole in your arse!' But, then again, it never sinks below it either. The constant mania's curiously impressive. I particularly like the stage direction: 'She cuts off his head and makes him eat it.'

'What do you think?' says Jeremy. I tell him straight. Why hide it? I'm right and I know it.

'You have third-act problems,' I say, a phrase culled from a film magazine article I've read or, as far as Jeremy knows, written.

'Right,' says Jeremy. 'What are they then?'

'Your third act's the same as your second act. Which is the same as your first.' He looks crushed. But I don't care. The crusher doesn't care.

'The proactive heroine is good,' I say. 'The energy's good. The names give unity. Some of the violence is original.'

'Yeah? You think so? Can you show it to your contacts in the industry?'

'Leave it with me. But don't hold your breath. They're busy people.'

'Thanks,' says Jeremy.

'No problem,' I say.

Jack comes out of the bedroom with a pack of cards and does a trick for Jeremy. I sense he does a trick for every visit. I watch as Jeremy picks the six of diamonds, looks at it, then puts it back. A minute later, he's invited to check the card face down under the vase (which has no flowers). Jeremy removes this card and says: 'Wow! Fantastic!'

But the card is the eight of hearts. It's the eight of hearts. Cocaine's not hallucinogenic, is it? Why does Jeremy think the trick's fantastic? Because both cards are red? The sycophancy scares me.

Jeremy leaves. Jack and I sniff and cluck our way through the first hour of a detective drama called *Docherty*. In Jack's world, all roads lead to Jack; Docherty's played by his friend Clive Duncan, formerly the ranting Scots stand-up, Tam Vietnam.

The drama perfectly meets my mood. Docherty is hard-drinking, moody, alone. There's a paedophilic serial killer on the loose in Glasgow. That bores him. His ex-wife doesn't understand him. His girlfriend, an aristocratic garden designer, can't make him heal. These are the things that fascinate Docherty. Colleagues sprint down corridors and scramble up walls; but Docherty's narcissism is like a rock attached to his leg. Only when his daughter becomes a target for the killer does Docherty look into a mirror, with serious intent. Docherty's a wonderful father. And he knows it. No nasty little serial killer is going to harm Docherty's hard-won self-image.

I tell Jack I have to go or I'll miss the last train.

'You can't go,' says Jack. 'I've got people coming. Then we'll go to my club. You got to be taken out of yourself.'

Yes. He's right. That's why I'm here. He's looking after me. Jack, who makes things happen, has only to say 'people' for the buzzer to ring again.

The people, whose names I don't catch in the flurry of their arrival, are two women in their twenties. I know better than to ask what they do. They have the big voices and raucous laughs of actresses or singers I should recognise. Within seconds, they're calling me *darlin'*. They're probably soap stars. I must be careful not to mention any soaps, in case they're in them. I'd better not mention *Docherty* either. Gorgeous and black, they're prime casting for lower-ranking policewomen.

Jack builds me up. I'm 'the Prof'. I live in the country. I know a lot about books. 'That's nice, darlin,' say the girls. An hour of champagne and cocaine later, the process of taking me out of myself is almost complete.

'Been on holiday?' asks one of the girls. It's what I don't say that counts. I don't say I've been on holiday to Provence with my girlfriend, who's now left me.

Instead I say, 'Yeah, I've been on holiday to Provence, to a friend's house, which was great.' Like a client talking to a hairdresser, I feel superficial and good. I snort the last of the script. We've reached The End.

'So. Are we going to the club?' I ask. The girls look to Jack. 'Later,' he says. I shudder as, one after the other, the girls land on the sofa, on either side of me.

'I hear you like to party with twins,' says one.

'Yeah,' says the other.

'My treat,' says Jack, with a look that says: this will take you out of yourself.

'Once you've had black, you'll never go back,' says the one, while the other licks my right earlobe. But it's no good. I can still hear myself think.

I do go back. To a south London flat, fourteen years earlier. Jack is repeating the twin opportunity of a lifetime; and therefore, like a Time Lord, is repeating the lifetime. He's treating me to it, just as he treated me to Gaang Gy, by placing an order over the phone, presumably on his mobile, in the bedroom, while Jeremy recited his script.

These girls are take-aways, from the fantasy restaurant, where take-aways deliver themselves and remove their own lids and are ready, after you've consumed them, to be consumed again, on repayment.

'Do you want to see my lovely black titties?' says the girl with the access to my vacant ear, articulating one of my many concerns. Jack and I grew up in a heavily Jewish London suburb. We had no black neighbours. The only black people I called by their first names were 'Jimi' and 'Aretha' (which, incidentally, annoyed Jack, who found it pretentious). How should I feel about the blackness of the titties? I wish I could phone Charlotte the MP. She'd know what I should think. She had plenty of sex with black people. She didn't pay them, though. Is Jack's 'treat' nothing more than exploitation, a hateful allusion to our slave-owning past?

My legs quiver, as she stands and takes off her dress. But my mind holds firm. Her underwear is of photoshoot quality. Jess would never wear underwear like that. She'd be embarrassed to spend so much money. The underwear is proof that this young black woman earns far more than me. Prostitution has empowered her. Surely, it's she who's exploiting me.

What if she's a student selling her body to pay for her education? What if she's, as I was, a student of English at Cambridge, burdened with loans where I was freed by a grant? My duty, as a concerned citizen, would be to have sex with her and recommend her to others.

The girl on my left stops licking my ear, for fear it will shrink.

Think, man, think! The rightness of any sexual act derives from mutual consent. Their consent hasn't been freely given, not like Helga's and Steffi's. It's been bought. That demeans us all. Especially me. However second-rate my sexual encounters, I've always been able to pride myself on the woman's consent. Consent flatters any man. To obtain it is an achievement. 'I had great consent last night' is, in my view, not a nonsense.

'Cheer up, darlin', says the girl in the underwear.

'I'll open some more champagne,' says Jack, moving into the kitchen, sensing his presence in the room inhibits me.

When he's gone, I say: 'I've got a girlfriend.'

It isn't true but it feels true.

'That's all right, darlin, I've got a girlfriend too,' says the underwear girl.

'Yeah. I'm her girlfriend,' says the other.

'But you're twins,' I say.

'Yeah,' says underwear.

'Whatever,' says other.

Why don't I just get on with it? Of course they're not twins. Why can't I suspend my disbelief? Jack is treating me to a fantasy.

They're fantasy twins, as twinned as six of diamonds and eight of hearts.

Jack stands in the doorway of the kitchen. I look at him.

He gestures to me to join him. He shuts the door.

'You're not happy, are you? I'm sorry. It was meant to make you happy.'

'No, no. Don't be sorry. It's very generous of you.'

'I made a mistake. It's too soon after Jess, isn't it? She's a great woman, Jess.'

Neither of us knows what to say.

'Would it help you if I took them off your hands?'

'Yeah.'

'OK,' says Jack, gravely. 'I'll see you at my club in an hour.'

'Thanks, Jack. Thanks.'

An hour later, I wait in the reception of Jack's club in Soho, watching the celebrity parade. Clive Duncan enters. An hour ago, he was *Docherty*. Now he's here. I find this alarming, his transition from television's time to ours.

Jack arrives, with all the glazed bonhomie of a freshly double-fucked man. We enter the club room, where he hugs Clive who expresses surprise at his bald patch.

'It's deliberate,' says Jack, 'I'm trying to look more like my bottom.' Clive gives a huge throaty laugh. Jack, to his credit, touches me lightly on the arm, in acknowledgment. He introduces me to Clive, who shakes my hand and smiles queasily at my forehead as if it contained eyes.

Clive and Jack talk and drink, while I stand there and make no difference. Clive has just been asked by Comic Relief to make a fund-raising film about the food shortages in Swaziland. Jack says he has just been asked to make a similar film in Lesotho. Clive tells Jack that the famine is worse in Swaziland. Jack isn't sure. 'Definitely,' says Clive, with the menace that made him Tam Vietnam. 'The girl told me. It's worse there than anywhere. They desperately need me.'

'You're the charitocracy,' I say, embarrassed by their conversation, keen to say something on which they can agree. But Clive, in his celebrity bubble, doesn't hear me.

'We're the charitocracy,' repeats Jack, like a simultaneous translator. This Clive hears.

'Charitocracy! I like that!'

Then in walks a man with a shaven head. Within a few minutes, we're in a cab, on our way to Buckinghamshire.

The shaven man's name is Kevin Osborne. I've never heard of him. His show's on Channel 5, which I can't get on my Suffolk TV. Osborne, apparently, has replaced the chat show with the do show. Osborne is the master of ceremonies, hilariously gay. People do things like weigh their penises, while the audience votes to predict who has the heaviest. Jack is in a rage. He asked Cher and Peter Ustinov how much their breasts weighed. But he didn't get them to weigh them. He seems both jealous of Osborne and proud of the tribute.

Jack, paranoid, grips my arm, as if I'm thinking of fleeing the moving car. He tells me he's far more famous than Kevin Osborne. An old mate of Clive's works on the *News of the World*. He's told Clive how much the paper would pay for incriminating photos of celebrities. For Jack and Clive, apparently, they'd pay seventy thousand pounds. For Kevin, nothing. Not even for photos of him with a woman.

I'm confused. Doesn't that simply tell us that Kevin has nothing to hide? The world knows what Kevin is. A lion is not 'incriminated' by a photo of him chewing the neck off a wildebeest. Like Kevin, the lion is already 'out'.

'That's TV Jack who did those things tonight,' says Jack, loosening his grip but still maintaining a hand on my arm.

'It's me, isn't it? But it's not.'

He leaves this hanging.

'I love my wife. She's a rock. She's told me she'd cut it off if she found me with another woman.'

'You weren't with another woman. There were two.'

This, intended to lighten the atmosphere, is treated as an insight, an argument, an intelligent remark.

'That's right.'

He looks at me, hungry for more. I'm The Prof. I'm the *consiglieri*. I can provide an intellectual framework. I can give him dignity. It's the least I can do, after all he's provided and is continuing to provide. My free ride continues. London's behind us now. I can see a field.

'Betrayal implies a qualitatively similar experience,' I say. 'A man betrays a marriage by treating another woman as his wife. Making love to two women isn't something you do with your wife.'

'That's so right. That's so right,' says Jack, with such conviction that he confers on it a kind of (late-night) sense.

The car stops. The field I saw was Jack's. Jack and Rita's. I reach for my wallet.

'No, no. Come on. This is on the show.'

'Thank you,' I say to Jack and the driver.

We get out. We slam the doors. The driver drives off.

'I live in Suffolk,' I say, which makes Jack laugh out loud.

'Seriously, Jack. I have to be in the bookshop at ten.'

'What time do you have to set off then?'

'Well. I mean. It's four in the morning. I have to set off round about now.'

'I'll call them at ten and tell them you're sick.'

With that, he unlocks a black box next to his twenty-foot gates and taps in a four-digit number. The gates open and we walk in.

It's Saturday. My return ticket to Ipswich is no longer valid. But it doesn't matter. Jack has taken me away from my problems. My life is in his hands.

7

The Middle Of The End

I wake at twelve in a bedroom in the guest wing. On the wall above my head is a print of a lake at sunset. Since Rita is Scots, it could be a loch. Either way, the shimmering wine-dark water is redolent only of the Great Indoors – hotel room art, in the style of Norman's company.

My curtains are ruched. My carpet is pastel blue. Soft white guest slippers and talcum powder are provided for my feet. Everything has been designed for my comfort, in a perfect but glacial everything-has-been-designed-for-your-comfort way. On my bedside table is a bowl of pot-pourri. After last night, it looks like antique cocaine, swollen and brown through hundreds of years of gaining value.

Jack knocks and enters. He tells me he rang the bookshop and told some spinster-ish woman I was sick. I feel a complicity I haven't felt since we were teenagers. Jack's made me naughty. As ever, my naughtiness is less than his. A bookshop day, missed – what's that compared to Jack having his *it* cut off?

'I'll see you in the gym.'

I get dressed and walk through the house to the gym. The house, a farmhouse of no great distinction, is now mostly wings: there's an exercise wing, a guest wing and a children's play wing.

Finally, there's a wing full of computers and desks, a pool table, magazines but not books, photos of Jack and Rita, mantelpieces with small golden angels who turn to be television awards. It's a wing without portfolio, a wing wing.

When I get there, Jack is on an exercise bike. He puts me on the neighbouring bike then projects a DVD on to a screen that covers the wall in front of us. Jack and I cycle our way through *The Godfather*. There's a rightness about this. We need to suffer, after last night's excesses. We gaze at the lurid magnificence of the Corleones. We're so virtuous compared to them, this murderous family that never takes any exercise.

Rita calls. Jack knows it's Rita because the call comes through on a wall-mounted pink phone. Jack freezes Pacino's brooding face. Rita is calling to make sure that Eric's birthday present has arrived. Rita, it transpires, is with Eric and the nanny in the West End, letting Eric choose some presents for himself.

Jack's voice, which is barely audible, agrees with everything Rita says, then explains that I'm here, staying in their house. He gives her a pen portrait of me, stressing my intelligence, then dials an internal number to instruct some unknown person to go into town and buy a 'shitload of wrapping paper'.

Jack asks me if I've had enough exercise, reminding me that with exercise, 'it's the thought that counts'. I'm delighted to hear him say this. I'd feared that cocaine and a fitness regime had destroyed his humour.

A few minutes later, we're floating in the swimming pool, spreadeagled like starfish, gazing up at a patch of gloriously blue June English sky which Jack, it seems to me, owns.

'This is fantastic,' I tell Jack.

'Yeah,' says Jack, not pretending it isn't.

'What do you want to do then, Dave? There's still time. You're six months younger than me. What's your fantasy?'

I tell him I've always wanted to write a radio play about the relationship between Matisse and Picasso.

I'm glad he cannot see my embarrassed face. This is not a good enough fantasy. It's not male enough, not successful enough. When did Hugh Hefner dream of writing a radio play?

Jack, though, is keen to help.

'You can do it by the pool. I'll lend you a laptop. First we'll wrap the present.'

He leads me to the Big Room in the children's wing, where we wrap Eric's fifth birthday present, which is a piano. An hour later, daft mission accomplished, Jack sets me up by the swimming pool, as promised, and leaves me to write.

I make some notes. They're better notes, I'm sure, than the notes I used to make on this project. With no prospect of any more cakes, there is nothing to do but write the thing. Jess created here. Now it's my turn. I must ask to see her portrait of Jack. But I'm not ready for it yet.

Jack comes out and gives me a straw hat, then films me 'writing'. He shows me how to use his digital video camera, claiming it's so easy that the box said Can Be Used By Jews. He's right. I film, successfully, Rita, Eric and the nanny heading for us in their swimsuits. Jack confides in me, in the last moments before they reach us. He saw me from his bedroom window, a few minutes earlier. I looked so happy that he rang the bookshop and told them I wouldn't be coming to work for a week. I tell him that he can't have done it and he tells me that he did. He told them I'd had a nervous collapse. Well, why not? It's almost true. My girlfriend's left me. Why wouldn't I have a nervous collapse?

Rita, in her sarong and shades, extends her hand and asks me what I'm writing. I explain. She introduces me to Eric and his nanny, a Chinese woman called May. Eric and May jump in the pool. Eric tries to mount a lilo. Jack films. Rita takes off her sarong and settles in her sunlounger.

As I talk to her about Picasso and Matisse, I try not to think of Picasso and Matisse as the names of her naked (new) breasts. Picasso and Matisse implies an ill-matched pair, instead of two bouncing twins. (Why so many breasts in my story? Why so many twins?) Her breasts are, however briefly, the most famous in Britain. Only two days earlier, in the shop in Yoxford, I've seen them mentioned on the front page of the *Sun*. RITA'S HOOTERS: SEE PAGES FOUR AND FIVE. But, heroically, I don't look at pages four and five. I prefer to imagine them, in a life-size photo, precisely filling both pages.

'Did you and Jack have a nice time last night?' She takes off her sunglasses, which makes her question more like a policeman's.

'Very good,' I say. 'We had a Thai meal then we watched TV then we went to Jack's club.' I give a detail which validates the truth of the whole, telling her how strange it was to see Clive Duncan on television, then an hour later in the club.

'Lovely Clive,' Rita replies, as if I've omitted part of his name. 'Did you know we come from the same part of Glasgow?' I shake my head. I look into her warrior's eyes. There's nothing she can do about their ferocity, immune to all surgery. Nor would she want to.

We turn our heads, cued by a muffled, childish roar. Eric has managed to straddle the lilo, face down. Rita tells me he's very athletic. She asks if Jack has given me a tour of the house. He hasn't, of course. It's more hers than his, anyone can see that.

We head for the house, Rita now mercifully topful. 'I hear you went to Cambridge,' she says. 'Yes,' I reply. 'Long time ago.' But the length of time's irrelevant. She's delighted that Jack has a friend who went to Cambridge and works in a bookshop: 'It's so important for him to have old friends who aren't in the business. Who don't want anything from him, you know?' I nod. What do I want from Jack?

As we enter the house, she stops at a blown-up photo on the wall by the back door. 'That's me as a girl.'

I look at three girls aged fourteen or so, in front of a terraced house. They're in the classic Charlene-Samantha-Leonie formation. There's a leader with her tongue sticking out, a follower whose tongue sticks out less far and a chubby bespectacled girl, wearing hotpants to overcome her shyness, which they only accentuate. This is the Before Rita, as opposed to the rich, new-breasted After Rita by my side, the Glaswegian girl who grew up in a terraced house, became a make-up artist and now has no neighbours.

'Which one are you?' I ask. Rita laughs and touches me on the shoulder. 'I can tell we're going to be friends.'

And we *are* friends. Jack, Rita and I. That night and the next morning, over drinks and dinner and breakfast, we spend a lot of time in each other's company. Eric and the nanny eat separately from us and Janet the cook, a tense thin woman, has the servant's gift of making you forget she's there. It pains her when Rita, at the end of dinner, thanks her loudly on behalf of the three of us for another excellent meal. Rita and Jack bang their wine glasses with a spoon. I follow suit, less vigorously, for fear my glass will break. (A few meals later, of course, I'm attacking my glass like Keith Moon. As in any family or school, the rituals cease to be strange.)

Jack is subdued but not unhappy. He reminds me of the way he was when he lived with Eileen. He carries himself like the mature father of the family. Now he really is mature, the manner suits him better.

He defers to Rita constantly. He looks out for her, refilling her glass before it's empty. In return, she's his champion. At breakfast, she tells me his current projects, now his latest series is over: the charity film, the car commercial, the American film. (*Movie. I must say movie*.) She talks to me as if I were in the business. She sells him to me, which is unnerving. I'm happy, though, to keep on saying that's terrific/fantastic. The sun is shining and the butter and bread and strawberry jam and grapefruit and eggs and coffee are organic and delicious. Everything's organic, in fact, except the terrifics and fantastics, which come out of my mouth in an artificial spray.

The movie excites Rita most. She's read the script and it's perfect for Jack. *Shoe Shop* is a romantic comedy about a movie star who comes to London to make a movie and falls in love with a girl who works in a shoe shop in Clapham, where he's gone to visit his English cousin. Jack is to play the talk show host who asks the star what he's been doing in London when he's not been filming. The star replies that he's been looking for 'great shoes'. Jack asks if he's found any. The star says yes and mentions the shop in Clapham. And the girl who works there. We see the girl's reaction as she watches TV with her flatmates. Rita goes on to tell me the rest of the story, which you don't need to know because you already know it. It ends with a chase to an airport and the star not boarding his plane. It upsets me how, as she describes it, my heart leaps with joy.

Shoe Shop, she concludes, will be a major breakthrough for Jack, whose show is not widely known in America. Jack says: 'That's right.'

'Come on then,' she says. 'Time to give Eric his present. What did you think of it?' she asks me.

'I think it's fantastic,' I say.

'He's very musical,' she says.

We gather outside the Big Room. Rita tells Eric his present is inside. Eric nods. Rita unlocks the door and Eric runs round the room at high speed, roaring, ignoring the piano, till May orders him to stop and open his present. The present has to be pointed out to him. I sympathise. It's somehow too big to see. It's so big it seems like a fixture, something that came with the room.

Eric rips off the wrapping paper in the vicinity of middle C and plays a black note, fortissimo, before rushing into the arms of May. Jack tells him he's going to have lessons, so he can write hits that will be played all over the world. Eric nods, as he knows he must, without listening.

'We've already started him on the drums,' says Rita. I want to say he looks more like a drummer than a pianist. But I decide against it.

We stand there, like actors wondering who has the next line. I conclude it must be me. I apologise to Eric for not having bought him a present. I explain that I didn't know till yesterday that today was his birthday. This is of no interest to him and, being a child, he doesn't pretend that it is. So, for reasons I can't explain, I go over to him and say: 'This is what my grandpa always gave me for my birthday.' Then I pinch him on both cheeks.

'Don't touch my son!' shouts Rita. My stomach heaves. She looks like she wants to kill me. But it's Eric, not Rita, who attacks me, leaping up and pinching my cheeks in revenge. For a second, he actually hangs from my cheeks, which is hilarious. I cry out in pain over the laughter, then I fall to my knees, then I'm on my back and he's straddling my chest, still gripping my cheeks, and Rita is saying 'He's so strong! He's so strong!' and I'm the clown prince of the family.

May drags him off me then pursues him as he runs out of the

room. Rita apologises. It was a mother's reflex reaction. There are so many weird people in the world. But, she adds hastily, I'm not one of them. A new silence descends.

'Let's show him the commercial,' Jack says.

The commercial is for a Japanese four-wheel-drive big car thing, built for crossing deserts but bought for driving to school.

Jack and Rita draw up outside the school gates. They get out of the car. A lone Eric rushes out of the school and asks if he can bring a friend home for tea. (This is the first time I've heard him speak. His voice sounds dubbed.)

Rita and Jack nod. Eric turns and shouts 'It's OK!' A dozen kids run out of the school and into the car thing, which accommodates them all with ease. A smiling voice tells us that when you buy this big thing, everyone's your friend.

Rita and Jack ask me what I think. I'm not sure who to praise first. I tell them they have a talented actor on their hands.

Rita and Jack agree. They're happy for him to do more acting jobs. But schoolwork comes first, says Rita. And his privacy, says Jack. His privacy and his normality, says Rita.

Jack tells me the commercial has been very good for the brand.

'Yes. It looks a nice car,' I say, unconvincingly. 'Very spacious,' I add, proving beyond reasonable doubt that I understood the story.

'I'm not talking about the car,' says Jack.

'The brand is us,' says Rita.

'That's right,' says Jack. 'My dad sold a brand. I am a brand. That's the difference.'

It's his Underbed Storage Unit voice, hard and proud, making you believe in progress.

* * *

Two hours later, I look down at the garden. It's being transformed for Eric's party, which is due to start at four. Inevitably, there's a bouncy castle and a table covered in celery and carrots and cucumbers and dips, which the children will probably disdain. Less predictably, there's Twenty Four Carat Diamond, a Neil Diamond tribute band, and llamas.

As for the kiddies' running track, such a satisfying pristine white grid when seen from this first floor window, it's not quite what it seems. There'll be three-legged and egg and spoon and running and sack races, but Rita's decreed there'll be no winners – in case, I suspect, Eric should lose.

Jack unlocks the bottom drawer of his desk and pulls out a carrier bag.

'Why's there a camera crew?'

'It's just a few shots of me and Eric. Parenting shots. I'm making a film for the government. They specially asked for me.'

It's the 'specially' that does it. This is the tone of the Jack who gripped my arm in the back of the car, wanting me to know he's still wanted, though I'd never expressed any doubt. You ask for Kevin Osborne. You specially ask for Jack.

'Listen. If you ever need any money. Please. Petty cash. Help yourself.' He shows me where he keeps the key. Then out of the bag, he takes not money but a Jeremy-style nasal script.

Seeing my expression, he tells me not to worry. (How did I know that Rita wouldn't approve?) Rita is busy organising the party. There's no chance she'll come up here.

'I never do drugs in the house,' says Jack. He snorts, then shakes his head like a wet dog. 'The house is sacred. It's a family house. I just do it here. In the wing.'

He gestures to me. I put my snout in his trough.

'Same with sex.' He pauses then does his snort'n'shake. 'No sex in the house. With anyone. Specially not my wife.'

247

I feel a sorrow stronger than cocaine, which famously brings on indifference.

'You're lucky, Dave. You're not married. You don't know what it's like to have no sex with your wife.'

'That's sad, Jack.' I sense he doesn't want to say more. So I change the subject.

'What's this film then?'

'Department of Health. It's an anti-drugs film.'

I nod. I'm a guest in his house. There are limits to what a guest does. A guest, as here, snorts cocaine. But a guest doesn't snort with derision. Isn't that right?

'I was expelled from school for drugs,' says Jack, in a way that suggests he's said it many times. Then he remembers: 'You were there. You know.'

'Now look at me. I've got a wife, I've got a kid, I've got a beautiful house. I've done twenty-two series. I'm an example of what you can achieve if you get off drugs.'

Jack, who's given it a lot of thought, tells me why the film is good for the brand. Confessing to drug use gives him credibility among the young. Forswearing drugs in favour of family life increases his appeal to an older demographic and corporate sponsors. Best of all, he's announced that he's giving his fee to an anti-drugs charity, which appeals to everyone in the world.

'I can't do enough for charity. It makes people love me and remember me. It's money in the bank.'

I'm not even tempted to snort at this. I find it refreshing. He, a famous person, is not claiming that he cares. Look, he's saying, I'm a self-centred man. Better that, surely, than bogus self-righteousness.

I know what's coming. When he looks at me, suddenly paranoid, and asks if he's 'full of bullshit', I'm ready. A *consiglieri* is always ready.

'Course not. Your film's not anti *this* drug.' I help myself to more. 'This drug's high quality. And you can afford it. Your film is anti poor people's drugs. You're talking to the man on the sink estate in Glasgow who sells his kids' trainers to buy his gear. How are you going to get through to him? By going out there into that garden and giving the performance of your life. This is a performance-enhancing drug. This drug will make your anti-drug film *better*.'

'Oh yes!' says Jack, though I can't tell if he's responding to me or this drug.

Alone now, carroting a dip, I watch Jack and Rita walk through the party, hand in hand. Eric rushes up, and drags them off to see a llama.

This is no more real than the car commercial. Jack and Rita don't collect Eric from school, any more than they walk hand in hand through their garden. Eric never rushes up to them to drag them off to see a llama. It's all for the sake of the film.

Jack's superb, though. He's more himself than ever. He's himself, enhanced.

The llama, who's not a performer, doesn't like Eric running up to it so fast. The director asks Eric to walk slowly, which doesn't come naturally to Eric.

After they've done it three or four times, Eric runs off to the lavatory.

Jack looks anxiously round the garden, searching for a woman called Sophie, who's apparently the new Head of Everything in Jack's world. (Forgive my vagueness. If you work in television, you'll know who Sophie is – or was, in the Summer of 2004. If you don't, you won't be interested.) He can't see her among the guests, most of whom are adults, with the swagger of Heads of Everything.

Eric returns, in tears, bent double.

'I cor my wee-ree imma zi!'

Jack doesn't understand. Nor does Rita. Nor do I.

'I cor my wee-ree imma zi!'

May's the only one who understands. She runs towards him.

Eric, the adopted son of a Jewish man and a Scots woman, speaks in the accent of his nanny from Hong Kong. She puts her arms around him.

He's hot and exhausted. The llama awaits. To make matters worse, the poor little chap has caught his willy in his zip.

Two hours later, the garden is empty. Twenty adult guests are gathered in the house having drinks before dinner. I watch a news-reader talking to a newspaper editor, presumably about news. Does a newsreader read the news?

They stop talking. Each takes a step sideways as Rita approaches, to welcome her into their midst.

Jack, meanwhile, gestures to me to follow him out of the room. He'd like to give me the chance to borrow some clothes. By now I've been wearing the same clothes for three days.

In fact, as we know, I've worn the same clothes for nearly thirty years. Rita has doubtless had a word with Jack. She doesn't want my denim suit and blue work shirt at her dinner table. I tell Jack I understand. He thanks me.

'What about this?' he asks, handing me a cyclamen pink shirt from his wardrobe.

'It's just not right for me, is it?'

'That's the beauty of it.' So saying, he sets off for the trouser end of his wardrobe. His trousers are a walk from his shirts.

I put on the cyclamen shirt, because it's wrong for me and

I'm here to be taken out of myself. I'm here to become more cyclamen.

At the supper, I let no one down. I pass unnoticed. I eat my salmon slowly. It's easy, when no one's talking to you, to eat your food too quickly, leaving you with nothing to do.

By midnight, I'm hanging my wrong shirt and trousers in my guest bedroom wardrobe. I'll wear them tomorrow. That's better etiquette than giving them back and putting on my old clothes again.

I get into bed. I realise I haven't thought about Jess all day. I can't sleep for thinking about her.

I get up early on Monday morning, hoping to make myself breakfast before Janet the cook arrives. As a guest, I can't face giving her orders. I regard her as above me, in the hierarchy of the house.

We arrive in the kitchen at the same time. She asks if I want breakfast. I say no. She asks me again, doubting my sincerity. 'Don't be polite,' she says. I relent. She offers me fruit and muesli and juice and eggs and croissants. I say 'yes thank you' to everything, because blanket gratitude is not the same as an order.

I sit by the pool, as before. What were Matisse and Picasso really like? That's the question, soon followed by another – why did Janet give me three eggs, when I really wanted none? I agonise on the nature of generosity, in the poolside changing-room lavatory.

When I emerge, I hear, then see, Rita running out of the house, screaming Eric's name. Jack runs out after her. I walk briskly towards Jack.

It's just after ten. Eric's not at school today because it's half-term. At ten, the piano teacher arrived to give him his first lesson. Rita couldn't find him anywhere. Then she discovered his bed hadn't been slept in. May is not here either. Her bed hasn't been slept in. Her car is gone.

'That fucking witch has kidnapped my son!' screams Rita.

'It's OK!' says Jack, 'I'll call the police!' He gets out his mobile.

'Have you tried calling May?' I ask.

'She's not going to answer the fucking phone! She's a kidnapper!'

'She might,' says Jack. 'She'll want to fix a price. What's her number?'

'You don't know her number! She's your kid's fucking nanny! You're useless!'

Rita grabs the phone, dials the number and screams at May. Jack grabs the phone from her and, in a businesslike voice, asks May how much she wants. It's clear to me that Jack is playing a part. He elongates the *a* of want. 'How much do you *waant*?' he asks. He's imagining that he's in an American drama, which is upsetting to see, as the drama is genuine and English.

The *waant* is followed by a long pause then a series of quiet yesses. Finally, he says: 'Stay there. We're coming.'

He tells Rita that May and Eric are at May's sister's flat in High Wycombe.

'Why?' she asks.

'Why? She's a kidnapper! You don't ask a kidnapper *why*. What am I, her shrink?'

'Stay here. What's the address?' she asks.

'I don't know. I thought you'd know.'

'Give me the phone!'

'No! You'll shout at her! That's dangerous!'

'Shout at her? I'll snap her head off and give it to the dog!'

'She doesn't have a dog,' says Jack, calmly. 'You're not going if you're like this. You'll make a scene. There'll be headlines. That's bad for the brand.'

Rita, amazingly, agrees. Then gets back on the attack.

'Why do you want to go on your own, Jack? Are you sleeping with her?'

'I could go with him,' I say.

Rita and Jack look at me.

'Thank you,' says Rita. 'I trust you.'

Half-an-hour later, I'm on a rug in High Wycombe, in the flat above the Chinese restaurant run by May's sister and her husband. Eric is sitting on top of me, again, pinching my cheeks, again. I struggle to hear what's being said. Eric has no interest. The spoken word holds no fascination for him.

Jack tells May what she's done is unforgiveable. She's taken Eric away from his house for a night without telling his parents. They were worried sick. What kind of nanny does a thing like that? Haven't Rita and Jack always looked after her and paid her well and bought a car for her to use?

May explains. She thought it was wrong to make a film at Eric's birthday party. She thought it was wrong that, after the party, Eric didn't see his parents. She brought him here to her sister's flat where it's warm and cosy and he would get love and attention.

Jack asks how long May was intending to keep him here. 'Till you rang me,' says May. 'My phone is always on.'

'Correction,' says Jack. 'That's our phone. We pay for that phone.'

'Why didn't you ring me till ten this morning? Why so long before you notice he's gone? Didn't you go to his bedroom last night to say goodnight? Didn't you go to his bedroom this morning to say good morning? What kind of –'

Jack cuts her off. He says he's terminating her employment and asks her to give him the car keys and the phone. May quietly does as he asks.

Keen to advance my relationship with Eric, I roll over and sniff the floorboards beyond the edge of the rug. Eric follows suit.

'Pror crackers!' he shouts. 'Yum-yum!'

Jack tells Eric they're going home now and he must say goodbye to May. He gets to his feet. May hugs him and sobs.

Jack takes out his cheque book and looks for a surface to write on. He opts, showily, for the mantelpiece.

He holds up the cheque, tantalising May, and says it's on condition she keeps the affair to herself. She appears not to understand.

'You mustn't sell your story to a paper,' says Jack, thrusting the cheque at her. I want, very much, to know the amount. But the cheque has its back to me.

'I'd never do a thing like that,' says May, with dignity. 'I'd never do anything that might hurt Eric.' Jack crumples the cheque into a ball. It looks like he might throw it on the fireplace but he stuffs it in his pocket.

Outside the flat, Jack hands me May's car keys.

'Would you mind driving her car back?'

'I can't drive, Jack.'

'What are you talking about?'

'You know this. I failed my test when I was eighteen and I haven't taken it since.'

'Listen, Dave. I understand. You've been busy.'

The badinage has a comforting, familiar rhythm. Like Russian dolls, we've had our bigger selves discarded and discarded, till we're down to our teenage versions.

But it can't last, not with Eric shoulder-charging a lamp-post, not with me in my cyclamen shirt, not with all this grown-up weirdness, which I know now will only get weirder. How much

254

was the offer May nobly refused? Ten grand? Twenty? For saying nothing. I'd say nothing, if Jack gave me money.

The restaurateur comes out to shake Jack's hand and give him a free spring roll. Jack declines on the grounds that he never eats anything that looks like a cigar. The restaurateur laughs and asks him for an autograph.

Does the restaurateur know that Jack's just fired his sister-in-law? Would it make a difference? What if Rita had just snapped her head off and given it to a dog? Would he still ask for an autograph? Why not? A famous person is a famous person and dogs have to eat.

'We're back to normal. We can be happy again,' says Rita at lunch to Jack and Eric and me. I nod and smile. Eric asks yet again when May will be back.

Jack and Rita take it in turns to praise me. Sometimes, they overlap. I was the one who suggested calling May. I was the one who volunteered to accompany Jack. I was the one who kept Eric occupied while the deed was done. None of it could have happened without me.

After lunch, Janet's despatched to May's flat by minicab to bring the car home. Jack goes off for a meeting in London with the Head of Everything.

Once more, then, I'm by the pool, working on my play. But now I have company. Eric thrashes around in the water. His mother, inches away, watches his every thrash, apologising to me for the disturbance.

Eric's had enough. They get out of the pool. Rita towels him down. He's unusually quiet, exhausted from his adventure, which was probably too exciting to allow for sleep. Rita puts his head in her new bosom, ruffles his hair and tells him he needs a nap.

They walk into the house, hand in hand. I watch them. Rita, a big curvaceous woman, has no idea that she looks at her best from behind. From behind, she appeals to the imagination. You can look at her free bottom – free as in sashaying, free as in costing no money – you can look it and imagine her without those scary eyes.

When she comes back, I know there'll be no more writing.

'I'm sorry you had to get involved,' she begins.

'It's all right,' I say. 'I was glad to be of service.'

'Do you think I'm a bad mother?' she asks.

I recall a nightmare I had when I was ten. The bell rings. I open our front door. Hitler's on the doorstep. He asks me if I'm Jewish. I cannot tell a lie yet I cannot tell the truth. (My mother is proud of my nightmare. I don't drown or fall from a building, as other nightmare boys do. I have a philosophical and moral dilemma. My nightmare is about Higher Things.)

'No,' I say to Rita. But Rita knows I'm lying, just as Hitler knows I'm Jewish. For Christ's sake, he's in Golders Green. What does he expect?

'You think I don't spend enough time with him.'

'I don't know. I'm not a parent.'

'Why didn't you and Jess have kids?'

The name is a shock, though why should it be? Jess was here for two weeks, painting Jack every day.

'It's complicated.' I look down at the pool.

'I know. Jack and I had so many problems trying to conceive.' I can't look at her. I know, from her column in the *Daily Mail*, that Rita has started Misconception, a charity for women who can't conceive, to fund research and create a network of support groups. But Jack has now told me he and she don't have sex. Was that the problem? It would be sad if, after funding all that research, Misconception discovered that sexual intercourse was the leading cause of conception. I can't look at her, I just can't look at her.

'You're very shy, aren't you? It's nice. Jack's not shy at all. I saw you looking at me the other day. You were trying not to look at me. But I know you were. Most men just stare. They're very crude. You can look, you know. It's all right. They're beautiful and I'm proud of them.'

I look at them. I'm happy to. Rather that than the eyes.

'You must be truthful with me, David. Jack really values you. He tells you things, I'm sure. If he tells you anything, or does anything, that you think I should know . . . tell me. That will help me. And Jack. You'll be helping both of us.'

I nod.

'You can't take your eyes off them, can you?'

I arc my head upwards towards the sun, as if I were going to do that anyway, and remark on the beauty of the day.

'Maybe you should take Eric away,' I say. 'Just the two of you. For a few days. Bonding in the sunshine.'

'That's such a good idea,' she says. 'We need time together where I can just focus on him.'

Within the hour, she's booked a flight to New York for the two of them, leaving in three days' time. They can be together constantly and shop.

It's my idea and one of my worst. Why's she flying to New York to be a mother to her son when they live in the same house?

Eric returns to us after his nap. He's dive-bombing a rhododendron as Jack's car pulls up in the drive.

'You should wear bright colours more often,' says Rita. 'It makes you more attractive. You wish I weren't married, don't you? I can see it in your eyes. You're too shy to say it yourself.'

By telling me I'm shy, of course, she makes me shyer than I already am. She's using my shyness as a weapon against me. Something repressed, she's implying, is more powerful than something revealed. Those crude men, staring openly at her, have only superficial lust. My shyness is a guarantee of true desire, heart and loins, the lot.

'I've been sacked!' says Jack. 'Sophie sacked me. That's it. I'm off the telly. No more shows.'

His phone rings. He tells his mother he's fine. He shows great concern for her welfare and doesn't burden her with his bad news. I admire his style.

Geoff Bergman has lung cancer. They've given him six months. ('They' being National Health doctors – Geoff abhors private medicine, even supposing it could save his life.) 'They've given me six months so I've taken it,' is the way he told it to me, in an email. I haven't seen him. I can't face him. I can't deal with my own sorrow. This, I admit, is a fat lot of use to Geoff.

Thirty years of heavy smoking, beginning before the school dance – to calm his worries about his height – have done for the great man.

On the afternoon of Jack's sacking, Geoff's cancer is the thing to which Jack constantly returns. There's always someone worse off than you and, in Jack's case, it's Geoff. He's due to see Geoff the following morning. Rita insists he does so, with me. Jack mustn't hide. He mustn't cancel appointments. 'We must carry on as normal,' she says. Rita's fixated on normal. It never occurs to her that she has abnormal norms. Why should it? This is her world and she's determined to control it.

Jack withdraws into himself. He can't keep repeating that he hasn't got cancer. Rita goes into warrior mode. After a dozen phone-rebuffs, she finally gets through to Sophie. I expect banshee wails. But no. Rita's voice is soft and she calls Sophie 'love'. All she asks is that Sophie doesn't release the news to the press for a few days, as Jack's just heard his mother has cancer. I put my hand on Jack's shoulder, shocked at the cruelty of this double-blow. He whispers: 'It's OK. She's making it up.'

We're meeting Geoff in an Oxfordshire village called Hook Norton. Why we're going to Hook Norton is a mystery Jack won't explain.

His mood as he drives me there is mature, my least favourite of his moods. If Jack's moods are a house, mature is the hall. It's boring. You know he's only passing through. But, more and more, he feels obliged to linger there.

Maturely, he can see the merits in Sophie's decision. Jack, who was the scourge of the establishment, is now the establishment himself. Sophie is new and wants to make changes. Shows can't go on forever. (I told you it was boring.) Mercifully, she's given him a few days to ponder his next move.

He stops at the church and spends a long time consulting a set of instructions. He does a U-turn, then turns left up a lane without a name, which explains why he missed it. He parks near a pair of red-brick nineteenth-century cottages. The left hand one, Rose Cottage, turns out to be our destination.

Outside the cottage are a dozen comedians, wearing light summer suits and trainers or deck shoes, apart from the former Judy the Fish, who's in a cream linen dress with multi-coloured plimsolls.

I hang back as Jack greets them, with serial hugs. They're his people, his generation. I recognise them all from the Holloway Tavern. And now here they are, twenty years on, some who sell out West End theatres, some with the seen-the-devil eyes of alcoholics, and one or two whose performing nights still end with an increasingly ominous: 'Time, gentlemen, please!'

Tony Mason, a quiz show host, announces that Sophie has

cancelled his series. Jack leads the chorus of Sophie-abuse, without revealing his own demise.

Clive Duncan arrives and gets out of his car with his passengers, Geoff and Ruth Bergman. Everyone cheers and claps and stamps their feet. Geoff is delighted but bemused. He's no idea why he's there.

From nowhere, three photographers appear. I stand with Jack as Clive addresses us all.

Clive says everyone, apart from the photographers, is here because they love Geoff and owe him everything. He gave them a chance when they were unknowns. He did their fillings at three in the morning, before they could afford to go private. (Laugh.)

Clive unlocks the boot of his car and gets out a framed list of names. Sixty-seven people have donated to a fund to buy Rose Cottage for Geoff. Geoff can breathe the country air. He can sniff the flowers and get well soon.

'It's all yours, Geoff!' concludes Clive, as Judy steps forward, curtseys, and gives Geoff the keys to the cottage. Under the applause, Clive's phone rings.

Clive conveys apologies from Kevin Osborne, who sends 'big love and respect' but can't be there because he's filming. Jack's face tightens.

'Don't worry,' I say, 'he's probably having his passport photo taken.'

Jack shouts: 'Yeah – he's having his passport photo taken!' This goes down brilliantly. Everyone fears Kevin, who's only twenty-nine.

Prompted by the interjection, Clive adds that we ought to give special thanks to Jack, whose whole idea this was. There's yet more applause, which Jack quickly silences with his two-hand movement, just as he does at the start of his chat show. Or did.

Geoff, whose voice is understandably weak, holds Ruth's hand

and tells us he doesn't know what to say. Judy starts crying. Geoff says again that he doesn't know what to say. Tony Mason, next to Judy, cries too.

Suddenly, Geoff knows what to say: 'Listen. I've already got lung cancer. Please. I don't recognise any of you without a cigarette. For godsake, start smoking.'

Everyone lights up, except Jack. They smoke for Geoff.

The three photographers, whom Jack calls the 'Oxfordshire paparazzi', aren't sure what to do. They don't want photos of celebrities smoking, not these days. Smoking suggests villainy or sleaze or, let's face it, cancer. Then they see Jack without a cigarette and take a barrage of shots of him outside the cottage he and his pals have bought for their dying friend.

Geoff is surrounded by those famous pals. I know I can't approach. Then he sees me. I'm Jewish, I'm from Golders Green, I'm not famous. No one, except his wife, has more in common with him.

He comes over to me and embraces me and asks me what I'm doing there. It's a simple question. I want to give him a simple answer, because he's dying and I don't want to tax him. I tell him, in false cavalier mode, that I went out with Jack last Friday night and the night hasn't ended.

'That doesn't sound like you,' says Geoff. 'You're the quiet man.'

I tell him how lovely the cottage looks and hope he'll be happy there.

'Yes,' says Geoff. 'It's a wonderful thought.' Then he breaks down and weeps into my shoulder.

'You understand, don't you? You understand everything.'

I nod, hoping he'll tell me what it is I understand.

'I like noise, Dave. I like buildings full of people. I like traffic. Don't make me die in the country.'

* * *

Back in the car, thinking I may never see him again, I say to Jack how wonderful it was to see such warmth and affection.

'That's right,' says Jack. 'People love me. I'm going to be all right.'

'What are you doing here?' Two hours later, Geoff's question bites deeper. 'Here' is the Finchley Road. Jack is taking me on another secret mission. Secret, that is, from me.

It's Tuesday afternoon. I'm missing the bookshop. My job, I know, does not fulfil my potential. But that's good as well as bad. My job saves me the trouble of fulfilling that potential. And it keeps me from asking soul-searching questions like 'What am I doing here?' I'm doing my job here. If it's Tuesday afternoon, I have no choice but to be here in the bookshop.

As we head for Golders Green, I have a premonition. We're returning to Jack's old stamping-ground.

'We're going to see your dad, aren't we?'

'My dad died thirty years ago, Dave.'

'Yes, I know. But –'

He opens the glove compartment of the Jag and tells me to find Corringham Road in the A–Z.

'When you're famous, you need secrets. Otherwise your whole life belongs to the public.'

I don't believe him. Jack just loves having secrets. Secrets have become his fetish.

When I was a child, I had no idea how old grown-ups were. There were young grown-ups, like Eileen, and old grown-ups like my grandmother. But the ones who were neither could have been thirty or sixty.

When the mystery man in Corringham Road answers the door, I'm not shocked by how old he is. I'm shocked by how young he must have been when I last saw him. He's in his eighties now, his cardigan and spittle years. When I last saw him, in his pomp, he was roughly the age I am now.

'Good afternoon, sir,' says Jack.

'Have you come about my son?' he asks, which is a very bad start.

'No, sir,' says Jack. 'We've come to pay our respects.'

'I'm expecting my son back at any moment. He went out for something, you see.'

What am I doing here?

Jack takes the initiative. The Cromp follows Jack into his own house. I follow The Cromp, which involves a lot of stopping, as he moves with painful slowness. I hope to find a nurse on the premises but there's no one. The living room, a symphony in browns, clean and neat, with fresh flowers, suggests he has a local daughter, since there's a photo of a daughter-looking woman with her children on the London Eye.

'Can we make you some tea, sir?' asks Jack.

'Tea?' asks The Cromp, startled, which Jack takes to be a yes.

There's a photo too of his son, Ned, with a woman, some chickens and a pig in enough shit to make it happy. In the background is an obviously American car. You can bet Ned tinkers with it to save buying another. The Big-Nosed Freak is now bald on top but has long frizzy grey hair at the back and sides, split-ending at his shoulders. His idiot grin is intact. The woman looks weary from underfunding. She's a Mother Earth figure who knows exactly what she has to look forward to: Grandmother Earth, then Earth.

I go into the kitchen, fearing that Jack doesn't know how to make tea. I send him back into the living room, so he can say whatever it is he's come to say to The Cromp.

263

'My name's Jack Harris, sir. You expelled me. Do you recognise me?'

'Eh?'

'Do you recognise me, sir? Do you have a television?'

'Television? There's a television there. Doesn't work, I'm afraid.'

Jack turns on the television, which works perfectly.

'That is marvellous,' says The Cromp, looking at a big woolly bird on a children's programme.

'I've done twenty-two series of *The Jack Harris Show*,' says Jack, who won't be denied. 'You must have seen it. Don't tell me you don't know who I am.'

'Is it a wildlife programme?' asks The Cromp. Jack turns off the television.

'Come on. We'll take you out for tea,' says Jack, which annoys me, as I've just brought in the tea.

'He doesn't want to go out,' I say.

'Look, he doesn't know what day it is. Out, in, in, out. What difference? Let's take him for a drive.'

Yes. The Cromp doesn't know what day it is. Yet Jack expects to be recognised, as if chat show host recognition were the last faculty to be lost.

Some minutes later, under the impression that we're taking him to see his son, The Cromp shuffles out of the house. We guide him down his drive to his front gate, then across the pavement to Jack's car. It's more akin to a kidnapping than anything May did to Eric.

En route to the gate, to fill in the time, I tell him that my name is David Lewin and that I too went to his school. He smiles. But of course he could be smiling at something that happened in 1934.

We lower him into the back seat, then take our positions in the front.

Without looking round, Jack says: 'When you expelled me, I told you that one day I'd make you sniff my Jag.'

'He's an old man, Jack.'

To me, Jack says: 'So what? He can still sniff, can't he?'

Then, to the rear-view mirror, he shouts:

'Breathe in, sir! You can do that, can't you, sir? Breathe in my Jag. Get some Jag aroma down you.'

I look over my shoulder at The Cromp. He's staring at me. He's agitated. His head quivers. The old man is struggling to deliver himself of some kind of mental baby.

'David Lewin,' says The Cromp. 'The George Crabtree Prize for English Literature.'

'OK, that's it,' says Jack. 'Out!'

He gets out and opens The Cromp's door.

'Are we there?' asks The Cromp.

An hour later, Jack and I are still in the Jag in Corringham Road, going nowhere. Jack needs to talk and talk and talk. The incident's convinced him his life has been a failure. I take the opposite view. I, who won the George Crabtree Prize and an Exhibition in English Literature to Corpus Christi College Cambridge, am sitting in Jack's Jag; he's not sitting in mine. The low-grades, the failures, the expellees, the misfits . . . they're the ones who make it to the top. School league tables have it upside down.

But Jack, cruelly, is now convinced that mine is the life he should have led. That afternoon he spent with me and Jess convinced him. My book-lined cottage, my roadside vegetables, my sea, my freedom from the pressures of success: he wants what I've got.

Doesn't he understand how desperately I want what he's got?

Doesn't he know what I'd give for fifty thousand pounds? Look, I'd say to Jess, I've got fifty thousand pounds. Let's buy that house, or another house if that house has gone by now, which it probably has. Let's do it.

'I must go back to studying. It's not too late. What should I study? Tell me.'

'Shakespeare and Bob Dylan.' I don't want to make it easy for him.

His mobile rings. Rita wants his news. How was Geoff Bergman? Where are we now?

We are, apparently, stuck in traffic, on our way from Oxfordshire to the West End, where Jack has 'a seven o'clock' at his club with Terry, his writer. They'll be working on Jack's next after-dinner speech.

Rita hasn't stopped. She's already fixed up meetings with Jane This and Peter That to talk about 'forging relationships', her euphemism for Jack's future television career after his sacking's made public.

'I've got to go, babe. We're moving,' says Jack. It's a lie which he makes come true, pulling out and heading for Hampstead Garden Suburb. We're going, he tells me, to the best bookshop in Hampstead. I'm supposed to know what that is.

We're now, genuinely, stuck in traffic, on the hill down to Hampstead Station from Whitestone Pond.

'I'm shooting *Shoe Shop* next week,' says Jack. 'That's the future for me. Acting.'

'The chat show's finished. That's what Sophie said and she's right. Guests in love with themselves. Come on, Dave, tell me the truth. I need my old friends to tell me the truth. My show was just noise, wasn't it?'

I slide my hands under my thighs. I literally sit on my hands. Then, for added measure, I make them into fists.

I must not and will not tell Jack the truth. Stars have said to him how important it is to have old friends who tell you the truth. It makes him feel starry to say it. But he doesn't believe it.

'It was a great show, Jack. Didn't matter who the celebrities were. You were always great. People watched the show to see you. She's mad to cancel it.'

Jack takes this in.

'Maybe that's true. Anyway. She did. If Clive can act, I can. Don't you think so?'

'Pull up anywhere here,' I say.

Earlier that day, outside Rose Cottage, Clive shook my hand, prompted by Jack saying, 'Clive, this is my friend Dave.' Jack didn't remember he'd introduced us only a few days before, in his club. No matter. Clive didn't remember either. 'Nice to meet you, Don,' he said, looking at the place on my forehead.

Jack went off to talk to Judy, leaving Clive no choice but to make conversation with Don. 'Are you in the business, Don?' he asked.

'No,' I said. There was no reason for me not to say 'It's Dave' or 'I'm Dave' or simply 'Dave', but I didn't want to make him feel bad or wrong. Worse, far worse, I didn't and don't feel my identity's so fixed that I couldn't be Don. I could, perhaps, be happier as Don, not having fulfilled my potential as Dave.

Jack, who's fulfilled his Jack-potential, can only be Jack. He has many moods and throws many shapes but his core of Jackness is inescapable. Does anyone believe that Jack can be anything other than Jack? (In the credits for his movie, it will surely say: Jack Harris – Himself.) Jack thinks of Clive as *Docherty* and imagines he too could one day be a *Surname* not his own. But Clive, for all his burliness and menace, is an actor-ish kind of man, a striker of theatrical poses. One can imagine him in a cravat, arriving backstage for his panto.

Jack parks on a double yellow line. We go into the supermarket-sized bookshop. Jack asks me what Shakespeare he should read first. I say *Macbeth*, then regret it. He might think I'm thinking his wife is Lady Macbeth. (As it happens, I am.) So I say: 'Maybe *Midsummer Night's Dream* might be better. It's a comedy.'

'What are you saying? I'm not deep enough for a tragedy?'

'No, no. I didn't mean that. The fact is, every play he wrote is worth reading.'

That's all Jack needs. He marches up to the nearest assistant and asks where the Shakespeare is. The assistant leads Jack and me to the back of the store.

I know, from fourteen years' experience, how much like seagulls or football hooligans we bookshop assistants are. We know when something's happening to one of our number, however far away. We have bookshop radar.

Within a minute, every assistant knows that Jack Harris is buying every Shakespeare in the shop. Everything Shakespeare Must Go! Those that aren't boxing Shakespeares up are carrying Shakespeares out. Those that aren't boxing or carrying are watching or watching and phoning and/or texting.

The assistants giggle and flirt with each other as they put the boxes in the boot of the Jag and then, when the boot is full – for the Jag isn't built to accommodate ten little kidsworth of Shakespeare – they put the Shakespeares in the back. And, yes, I see one girl sniff.

'That was brilliant,' says Jack, as he drives us away, handing me a parking ticket to put in the glove compartment with the others.

Was it brilliant? I can see he's given pleasure. But now the orgy's over, what are we supposed to feel? We have Antonys and

Cleopatras and Romeos and Juliets. We have Shrews and Merchants and Wives and Tempests. We have Labours and Errors and Measures and Nights, Twelfths and Midsummers. We have at least Ten or Twelve Gentlemen of Verona. So what?

At five to seven, as we enter the club, he asks me to do him a favour. Could I sign myself in as Terry? We get to reception. Jack banters with the girls as he signs his name, writes his time of arrival then passes me the pen.

Why does he want me to be Terry? It can only be that his meeting with Terry is fictitious, a cover for a meeting of a different kind. When he told Rita he had a seven o'clock with Terry, this is what he had in mind: arriving here with me, using me as his cover, entering the club with me then going off with her. Why should I let myself be exploited in this way? Isn't this what Rita meant when she asked me to be truthful?

I sign 'Terry' then decide to stand up for myself. 'What's my surname?' I ask Jack.

The girls laugh. They love it. Here's Jack and his friend in the cyclamen shirt, putting on a little show for them, making them laugh, satirising the notion of a showbiz club where members go to drink and forget, including their own names. I feel attractive and amusing, which annoys me. I wanted to feel angry.

We move through to the bar, we being they, Jack and Terry, whose name I never complete.

I say to Jack, 'You've got an assignation.'

'Yes,' says Jack. 'If Rita came looking for me, the girls could point to our names. We were here when we said we'd be here.'

Two minutes later, when we're back on the pavement, Jack tells me his assignation is, in fact, elsewhere. He'll meet me back here around nine, for dinner.

'Why don't you buy yourself a shirt, Dave?' He reaches for his wallet. He gives me a fifty-pound note.

I look pained but Jack insists. 'Go on. You can't wear mine all the time. Try Marks.' He gets into a taxi and then he's gone. Try Marks. Our teenage catchphrase. To our parents, Marks & Spencer was the source of all things good, a kind of retail synagogue.

I walk up Dean Street. If I turn left at the top, I can go to Marks & Spencer; turn right and I can go home, via Tottenham Court Road, Liverpool Street, Ipswich and Darsham. Tim could pick me up from the station.

What am I doing here, on the evening of Day Five of my night out with Jack? I barely saw him for twenty years yet now, though I'm alone in the open air, I'm his captive. I have to know where Jack has gone and who's waiting for him there. I am an Attendant Lord. His life is my life now.

I walk into Marks & Spencer and look at the shirts. I buy one. I have no free will.

The chef at Jack's club, more interested in fashion than taste, has confected my starter from now-sounding foodstuffs. It's called something like Corn-Fed Fennel and Hake Tsunami. I can't eat it, not because it's bad but because I've lost my appetite.

Jack has just told me that his assignation, at a hotel in Paddington, was with Caroline Bliss. He and Caroline Bliss have been seeing each other for fourteen years, since I brought him to her divorce party. But their relationship now is different from what it was then.

They meet, occasionally, for an hour. It must never be more than that. There's no sex. She gives him advice. She'll tell him, for example, to watch Channel 4 News or buy property in Croatia.

He tries his best to do what she advises. Tonight, she's told him to stick to television and forget about acting. But, in this case, he's going to ignore her.

The sex they do have – he pauses as the waitress refills his glass – the sex they do have is no sex, not penetrative sex. Last time, for example, she put on a pair of leather gloves – there is no need for me to know this or you to hear it, but why should you be spared when I wasn't? – last time, she put on leather gloves and stroked his cock while he watched Channel 4 News. Then she asked him questions about the news. Such as: 'What was proposed at the conference on climate change?' Jack, apparently, got the answers wrong, as he'd taken his eyes off the screen. So, as a punishment, she didn't do that again tonight.

Tonight, she was inspired by a gay conductor friend – not a man on a bus, of course, but a maestro with a knighthood. This friend, who worships her, sent her an exercise DVD, made by some Playboy model, which demonstrates how to lose weight by pole dancing. So tonight she pole danced, while Jack, presumably gloveless, stroked himself.

I feel myself shrink to nothing. You could pop me in my wine glass. Jack and Caroline Bliss are the two most charismatic people I know. Their union is gigantic. It blots out everything.

She wanted to be Prime Minister by thirty. She didn't succeed. But her sexual activity is above and beyond Prime Ministerial. Caroline Bliss has Presidential sex. They clinton each other, she and Jack. There's no other verb for it.

I don't want to believe it. I lash out, as shrinking men will.

'What do you mean, pole danced?'

'She pole danced.'

'What pole? They don't have poles in hotel rooms.'

'You can get them to put one up. Well, *you* can't. It's a celeb thing.'

271

'Was it screwed to the carpet? Fixed to the ceiling? How do they put it up and take it down without leaving marks? Where do they find a pole that's the same height as the room? Do they ring up a pole shop or something?'

'Dave. Don't fixate on the pole.'

What's more important than the pole, he says, is that she's married and he's married and that's not going to change. He's not in the business of stealing other men's women.

I was sorry for him when he told me he had no sex with his wife. But now I don't feel sorry. Jack has gone beyond sex. Ordinary people have sex. He wants what ordinary people can't have.

We arrive home at midnight. We carry the boxes in. I hand *Julius Caesar* to Jack for bedtime reading. He apologises. He can't read anything at the moment. He'll start on *Julius Caesar* when he gets his glasses.

'Hello, my lovely boys,' says Rita, entering the kitchen. She stands next to her husband. They hold each other's hand, just as they did when they walked through the garden for the anti-drugs film. *Movie.*

'How was your meeting, babe?'

'Very good. Terry was buzzing.'

She turns to me.

'What did you do while Jack was with Terry?'

'I went to Marks & Spencer and bought a shirt.'

'That's so sweet!'

She gives me the look I know well, the look Jack's mother used to give me when she saw me playing with Jack, aged six. I'm glad he's with you. You're nice.

* * *

I've always been inhibited by the greatness of my characters. I've read everything they wrote. I've read everything they said that was recorded by others. But none of that can save me. It's a play, not a historical record. I have to set scenes and put words in their mouths. At some point, Matisse has to say: 'More absinthe, Pablo?'

On Wednesday, Day Six, I break through. Instead of inventing dialogue for real people to say, I'll invent dialogue for invented people to say. I can dramatise the relationship between Picasso and Matisse by creating characters who embody their essence. Matisse was a refined and cerebral man, a lawyer turned painter. His colours were revolutionary but his art was serene. Picasso was a masculine man who played to the gallery. His art was often violent and confrontational. He knew the power of ugliness. Everything about Picasso makes me think of 'bull'. He was a bull-necked, bullfight-loving, bullshitting bull in a china shop.

Sitting by the pool, thinking how far I've travelled from the Hackney squat, I imagine two men in their twenties, sharing a run-down house in the East End. One's a law student, the other's a poker player. How should they go about re-decorating their house? What effect are they trying to achieve? The play starts in the paint shop in Dalston, where Matt and Bull have gone to choose their weapons.

This is as far as I get before Jack tells me he's going out for the day. He and Rita have a meeting in the afternoon. But first, he's going to call in and see his mother. I know what that means: it means he's not going to call in and see his mother, any more than he's going to 'read' a 'script' or 'meet' 'Terry'. I ask him what 'call in and see his mother' means. He says it means he's going to call in and see his mother. He asks how my mother is.

Eight hours later, my jeans, which are Jack's jeans and will have cost the price of trousers, are green from wrestling on the grass

273

with Eric while Janet, who's looking after him, tells me the story of her life.

She's divorced from a restaurateur, who's re-married and fathered a child, which he never did with her. How do I ask her if she's having an affair with Jack? Eric, irritated that he doesn't have my full attention, gets off my chest and pulls on my hand to drag me away from Janet. I get up slowly as, unprompted, Janet tells me I probably think she's having an affair with Jack, which she isn't. (Is she meant to say this with Eric there? He's not listening, that's for sure.)

Jack tells her things, though. Often he gets lonely, late at night, and talks to her long after she's due to go home. He tells her about this woman he sees. Nothing happens, so it's all right for him to tell Janet and for Janet to tell me. They just watch television. I can't help myself. I say: 'Yeah. Channel 4 News.'

Eric, who's seen a stray cat and wants to pursue it, drags harder on my hand. He's already experiencing the thrill of the chase, even though it hasn't started. After two days apart from his nanny, his Chinese accent is fading. He pulls my hand and shouts at me:

'Come on, Dad!'

Something stops me from correcting him. Perhaps it's the same impulse that stopped me from correcting Clive Duncan when he called me 'Don'. Eric is a young celebrity. It's hard to tell him he's wrong.

An hour later, I sit between Jack and Rita on a sofa, drinking champagne and eating olives.

'Will you tell him or will I?' asks Rita.

'I will,' says Jack. But they both tell me. I get dizzy from turning my head.

'We're going to do a show together,' says Jack.

'Husband and wife show.'

'Husband and wife show. But it's not a chat show.'

'It's not a chat show. There's no desk.'

'There's no desk,' says Jack. 'There's a sofa.' He says 'sofa' as if no one has ever said the word before, as if Sofa is a new-found land.

'It's just Rita and me and the guest between us and the idea is . . . it's not a chat show or a do-show.'

'It's not a chat show or a do-show.'

'It's a be-show!'

'A be-show!'

'It's just people being together. It's natural. Telly's never natural. You want to talk about your mother, you talk about your mother. You want to eat an olive, you eat an olive.'

Jack looks at me with such intensity that I eat an olive.

'What do you think?' asks Rita.

'Yeah, what do you think?' asks Jack. 'We're going to be on television five afternoons a week. That's a lot of being. But we can do it. We can be it. Then we'll take it to America.'

'Shut up, darling. We want to know what David thinks.'

I think, as I eat my olive, of a previous olive. Geoff Bergman and I are waiting for our main courses in KV, the kosher vegetarian restaurant. Jack hands round a bowl of olives. He tells us he wants a KV in every town in England. KV, he tells us, will soon lose its kosher connotation. It will sound no more Jewish than 'Big Mac' sounds Scottish.

'KV will be like Hoover,' says Jack. 'It'll be a successful sound.'

I believed him then and I believe him now. I believed him when he said Underbed Storage Unit over and over again. Jack, a master of repetition, said Underbed Storage Unit so often, you believed other people were saying it as often as he.

I say: 'People will want to come on your show for the olives.'

275

Jack laughs and pounds the armrest of the sofa with his fist. Rita claps.

Here I am, sitting between them on their sofa, like the first guest on their new show. I've said something amusing. They've reacted, in pounding/clapping harmony, like a perfect couple, united in their reaction but expressing it in distinct, individual ways. I'm proof that their show works. Now they're thinking about the film stars and presidents and singers who will sit in my place and eat olives and talk and laugh and feel pain and be.

Rita stands and asks Jack if she can borrow me before supper. Within two minutes, I'm sitting at her desk in the den wing and she's leaning over me as I look at her screen but it's all right, this is not sexual, this is editorial. Rita wants me to read the copy for her weekly column, which must be emailed tonight before she and Eric fly to New York in the morning.

There they all are, the key words: birthday, llamas, anti-drugs, Lesotho, *Shoe Shop*, New York, shopping, my little boy, comedians, cancer, Rose Cottage.

Rita tells me she's still very insecure about her writing. She, like Jack, was expelled from school at sixteen. (She abortion, he drugs.) She's so glad to have a man who went to Cambridge in the house, to tell her where she's going wrong. What would I write differently?

What I would write is irrelevant. The I of the copy is Rita. The readers want Rita. So, for the next half-hour, I'm Rita. It's not difficult. By now, I'm used to it. Already this week, I've been Don and Terry and Eric's Dad.

'The llamas are the indubitable highlight of the party.' It's the only sentence I change. That 'indubitable' is too insecure, the word of a woman who's trying too hard to sound intelligent. Rita is clever. She must be. Look how far she's got. She's no need to prove she's intelligent too.

I change it to: 'The llamas are the highlight of the party.' Rita thanks me. She doesn't know what she'd do without me.

We have a light supper of chicken and asparagus and New Zealand Pinot Noir. The chicken is the finest I've ever tasted. And so it should be. It's a local organic chicken that's allowed to range freely, says Rita, who speaks of it in the present tense, since we're currently ranging it freely in our mouths. 'Everything is done for the chickens,' she tells me. 'All they have to do is be happy.' I go with Rita's flow. I let the chicken make me as happy as the chicken was itself.

Reeling with bonhomie, we sit back down on the sofa, in our be-show configuration, Rita to the left of me, Jack to the right. Perhaps they have sides of this sofa, as they have sides of their bed.

Rita tells me that Jack and she have had an inspired idea.

'It was Eric's idea,' says Jack. Rita agrees that it was Eric's idea. Referring to me, her wee boy asked her: 'Does that man live with us now?'

'And we thought, that's a lovely idea.'

'We did,' says Jack.

Rita reaches across me to hold the hand of Jack, an extraordinary, unnatural movement. As her forearm rests on my knees, my cock stirs briefly, like a cat opening one eye. But there's nothing for it here. The forearm signifies captive friendship.

'Eric wants you here when he gets back,' says Jack. 'And so do I.'

'And so do I,' says Rita.

'But –'

'Don't say a word,' says Jack. 'What are they paying you at the bookshop?'

'   ,' I reply. (I can't reveal the figure. It's too embarrassing, for a graduate, in his forties, not suffering from mental illness.)

'We'll match it,' says Jack. 'Plus you've got free board and lodging. You can sell your cottage and invest the proceeds. And there's these. Take them.'

'It was the nanny's,' says Rita. 'We want you to have it.'

'It's a gift,' says Jack.

I take the keys to my new car, just as Geoff Bergman took the keys to his new cottage. The similarity doesn't end there. When he sits in his cottage, the cottage goes nowhere. The same will be true of my car.

'Now you've got a car, you'll learn,' says Jack.

'I'm overwhelmed,' I say.

'Don't be,' says Rita.

'Don't be,' says Jack.

'What do you want me to do?'

What they want me to do is what I've been doing. Jack wants me to whisper in his ear (charitocracy/he's having his passport photo taken). He wants me to be his companion. Rita wants me to be his companion too, for obvious reasons. And she wants me to help her with her column, just as Jack wants me to help him with his after-dinner speeches, following him from dinner to dinner, which Terry is increasingly reluctant to do, now he has kids.

When they're making their show, I won't be needed, not on the set, though it would be nice if I were there every night, when they'd finished. This means that I would have plenty of time to be in their house, writing my plays and being nice to Eric. (And Janet who, it turns out, likes me too.) Jack and Rita are thinking of getting a Labrador, which they may ask me to walk. They want me to help them choose it. They want to make sure that even the Labrador likes me.

'Basically, your job is to be our friend,' says Rita.

'Yeah,' says Jack. 'You've done it for free. Now do it for a living. Why not?'

We all go quiet as I search for the reasons why not. I have no wife or children. I have no dog or cat to which I must return. No human or animal is waiting for me, their nose pressed against the window.

'What do I do about clothes?'

They look at each other, baffled.

'You go back home and get them, Dave.'

'Of course,' I say. I'd forgotten I could do that. I can go home whenever I like.

'How do I do that, though?' I ask. 'I mean, how do I get the gates to open? Don't you have to punch in a number?'

They love this. They think it's sweet and funny. Jack loves it so much that he finds a biro and writes the number on the back of my hand.

'So. Come on. You going to do it or not?'

'Don't pressurise him. He needs time to think,' says Rita, in the soft voice she used when telling Sophie that Jack's mum had cancer. Her soft voice is different from Norman's. His derives from a natural authority. Rita's had to fight for and win her authority. That's why her soft voice is much, much louder than his.

'I have go to bed now. The car's coming at five. I hope you say yes.'

She presents her cheek to me and I kiss it. Then she kisses Jack and leaves.

Jack waits till he hears her footsteps on the stairs.

'How long's it take you to get to your mother from Suffolk?'

'About three and a half hours,' I say.

'Forty minutes from here. Minicab. I'll pay. You won't have to stay for an hour and a half to make your journey worthwhile. "Hello, mum. Still depressed? *Mazel tov.* See you Friday. Bye." That's it.'

We sit there silently as I think about this. I can't argue with a word of it. It's brutally perceptive.

'Thanks, Jack. I'll think about it.'

'We got a whole Shakespeare library now. Borrow anything you want.'

'Thanks, Jack.'

'Listen,' he says, in his confessional voice, which I've now come to dread. He'll say something like 'I had sex with your mother', and then it will be my duty to explain why that was a good thing to do.

'After the meeting, I bought Dylan's *Greatest Hits.*'

He shouldn't call him 'Dylan'. Only those who love Bob are allowed to call him 'Dylan'. Or 'Bob'.

'Which *Greatest Hits*? *Greatest Hits Volume 2*? *Greatest Hits Volume 3*? Or the one just called *Greatest Hits*?'

'I don't know. It's got *Lay Lady Lay* on it.'

'Right. That's Volume 2 then.'

'Yeah. I love that song. He's a great poet.'

'He's not a great poet. It's a song, Jack. You said it yourself. Dylan writes lyrics for songs. It's a fundamental category mistake to call him a poet. If Dylan wanted to be a poet, believe me, he'd be a poet.'

I stop, many sentences short of my full rant, which can be found in my article 'Skipping Reels of Rhyme?' in the March 1994 edition of *Clothes Line*. I expect him to get angry with me. Not a bit of it. He's meek.

'Sorry. He's a songwriter. Listen, don't worry. I won't sing it round the house. Dylan has to sing it.'

'Bob Dylan.'

'Bob, Dylan, Bob Dylan, whatever. I won't even hum.'

A door slams upstairs. He shakes his head.

'You've got to do it, Dave. Don't leave me alone with my wife.'

8

The End

There'll be no more bills, I think as I wake up. Presumably, this will be my room. The guest wing will cease to be a guest wing. It will be the friend wing, the me wing. But I won't pay for my lighting and heating. If there's a damp patch, it won't be my damp patch. Someone else will sort it out, as instructed by Rita.

This is my destiny. I was always destined to be with Jack. I resisted it once, when he was first famous. This is my second chance. Jack wants me to swap my low beams for his high ceilings. Only a fool would say no. He wants to take care of me, in return for my taking care of him, which is a good and fair contract, one my father wouldn't wish me to re-negotiate.

I'm needed. I'm needed by Jack and Rita and Eric and Janet and our future Labrador. What does a man want more than to be needed? They've made my decision for me.

I put on Jack's orange shirt with the double cuffs. I roll the sleeves up. Now I've customised it. Now it looks like mine. All I have to do now is call my old friend Tim, and give him four weeks' notice of my quitting the bookshop.

Jack's in the kitchen, talking to Janet. Rita and Eric are long gone. 'I'll do it,' I tell Jack. He hugs me. Janet, who knows what

I mean, kisses me on both cheeks, while Jack calls Rita who, with romantic comedy timing, is at the gate about to board her plane.

'Start now, yeah?' says Jack and of course I agree. I don't want to bother him about the bookshop.

'Right,' says Jack and within five minutes we're side by side on those exercise bikes, cycling nowhere to *The Godfather II*.

'That's De Niro at his greatest,' says Jack, stopping the bike. 'OK, get your laptop. Let's go poolside.'

I dismount, to get my laptop and go poolside.

'Hold on,' says Jack. 'Let's do a couple of lines of script before we start.'

'No thanks, Jack.' I think of the peppermint tea in the book-shop. That's what I normally have at this time, five minutes after I get to the shop.

'Do some coke with me, Dave. That's an order.'

'I can't,' I say. 'I'm working.'

My grandparents came from Lithuania and Poland to make a new life in England. My maternal grandfather was a furrier in Whitechapel. My father was a barrister in Lincoln's Inn.

'You were always a good boy, weren't you?' says Jack, chopping out a line on his treadmill.

My grandfather, had he been born when I was, would not have pursued a career in now-controversial fur. My grandfather and father fitted into society as they found it. I find, in this society, that I'm a paid friend.

I do the coke then get my laptop. We go poolside.

'Make it bigger,' says Jack, looking at the first page of my play. This is not what I expected. I thought Jack would want me to make notes on his new show with Rita. But no. He wants, it seems, to give me his opinion on my play, as soon as the words are big enough for him to read.

'Bigger!' We settle on a twenty-four point typesize, which makes the play look like something toddlers would enjoy.

'Who's Matt and Bull?' asks Jack. I explain.

'Why d'you make things difficult, Dave? Everyone's heard of Matisse and Picasso. I did twenty-two series and every guest was someone people had heard of. D'you want this play to be a success or don't you?'

The answer, of course, is yes and no. Which is to say, this play is an exercise in solving a riddle to my own satisfaction. If I do that, I succeed, in my own terms, regardless of what the world thinks. How do I say that, but shorter?

'You want to get this play on the radio, Dave?'

'Yes,' I say.

'I can't hear you.'

'Yes!' I say.

'OK,' says Jack. 'Let's read it.' I explain that it's not ready to read. It's work in progress.

'We'll read it in progress then,' says Jack. 'Which one am I, Matisse or Picasso?'

Which one is he? It had never occurred to me that he was either. But here we are, by his pool. He's an actor, or wants to be, and I've written the play on his land.

'You're Picasso, Jack. Bull.'

The opening lines of the play are:

BULL: (angrily) I want my house to be a colour that will scare people away!

MATT: May I point out, respectfully, that the house is as much mine as yours?

These lines make no sense if they're spoken by 'Matisse' and 'Picasso'. But it's too late to stop Jack now.

'Ah want my arse to be a collar zat will scare pipple aweh!' shouts Jack.

It's a shock to be this close to him when he's acting. There's no mistaking the (angrily). I can see and hear Jack's anger. I could hold it in my hand. I could toss it in the air and serve it into the forehand court. This is not Jack angry. I've seen that. This is Jack the actor acting 'acting angry'.

What can I say? He's a man who makes things happen. Don't I want things to happen? In a year's time, I could be sitting in a radio studio, watching this play, with Jack at the microphone and some journalists outside, waiting to find out what attracted him to the part.

'Come on,' says Jack. 'It's your line.'

How do I follow his line? 'Picasso', apparently, speaks English with a heavy French accent. Logically, 'Matisse' will speak in a similar way.

There's a voice in my head and the voice says, fuck, this is your play, say it how you want to say it. But Jack is staring at me. I must do it. I change the voice to *ferk*.

'May ah point out, respec-foo-lee, zat ze owse is as merch mahn az yoors?'

'What the fuck was that?' asks Jack. 'What are you, fucking Inspector Clouseau? I can't work with you if you're going to act like that.'

I want to go home. But this is my home now. I miss my old life, which surely can't have ended overnight, because Jack and Rita say so and I agree. Yet that is what has happened.

Jack's mobile rings. I long for Jess. I excuse myself and head for the house. I want to see her portrait of Jack.

Why has he never shown me the portrait? Is it bad? Surely not. A bad portrait, as Jess always told me, is a portrait your client doesn't like. Jack paid nine thousand pounds for his portrait, having agreed to pay six. It must be very good.

I look from room to room, from wing to wing. No portrait. I find myself, finally, in Jack and Rita's bedroom, staring at their vast bed. They sleep separately in the same bed.

The portrait is not in their bedroom. That leaves the en suite bathroom. But it's not in the bathroom either. I come out of the bathroom, back into their bedroom. Then I notice a door in the opposite wall. Of course. There are His and Her bathrooms. His seat is never warm from Her bottom. His mirror reflects only Him.

The portrait is above Jack's bath. That must have been Jack's decision. Jess would never have recommended that. Condensation will get under the glass. The whole thing will eventually warp.

Jess's portrait of Jack is very good indeed. She's painted him in his office, in his swivel chair, wearing a suit and T-shirt and trainers, hands and forearms on the arms of the seat, legs splayed, heels on the ground, toes up. She's caught his mischief and his cockiness and his edginess. She's even got his restlessness – the chair, somehow, looks recently swivelled. Behind him are shelves stacked with tapes, awards and framed front covers of the *Radio Times*, the products of his success.

Yes, the portrait of Jack is terrific. But Jack's not alone. Two men look out at us. The other man stands behind Jack, to one side, a respectful few inches away. Jack grins but this man's unsmiling. He wears a dark unfashionable suit and tie and his hands are by his side. He's the same age as Jack but he looks older, less flamboyant, less successful. He could be some kind of manservant. He's certainly a lesser character, proud but awed to be in Jack's presence.

Awe is appropriate. The man is Jack's father, Danny, who's been dead for thirty years.

*   *   *

I make the journey from Jack's bathroom to the back door. A big house gives you time to think.

I keep coming back to the same thought: I have to run away. 'Running away' is what children do. But it's appropriate, somehow, for a man who can't drive.

I want to run away to Jess. I've never felt so close to her. Jess and I are equals. We have people in our lives in whose shadows we live. There's Jack. There's Norman. There's Sharon.

Jack would have said he wanted to be painted with his father. Jess, having established his father was dead, would not have laughed in his face. She'd have asked, pleasantly, for photos of his father. That's the kind of thing we do. We don't say, 'I'm not going to paint you with your father. That's mad.' Who are we to say what's mad?

No, it's not the madness I hate him for. I can understand the madness. It's the money.

He said he'd pay Jess six thousand pounds to paint him. But she didn't. She painted him and his dad. For nine thousand. Why? Why not twelve? She painted twice as many people, did she not? Did Jack get a reduction for buying in bulk? Is Danny half his size?

I'm out the back door now and heading for the pool. My certainties are disappearing. The further I move away from that bathroom, the more I can see it from Jack's point of view. Why should he pay twice as much for a portrait of two people? Suppose the painting were of Jack alone. There'd still be something in that Dad-shaped hole, a something included in the original price. Presumably, it would be more background – more shelves and more awards. That's as time-consuming to paint as Dad, though surely less rewarding for Jess, whose subject is the human form. In that sense, by adding Dad, Jack was doing Jess a favour.

Portraiture is not subject to strict arithmetical laws. Is a Last Supper worth thirteen times as much as a Crucifixion?

He's not by the pool when I get back. He's gone indoors. Clive Duncan has just called him to say that Kevin Osborne is to be Jack's replacement. Kevin's do-show will be at ten-thirty on Friday night, in the slot vacated by Jack.

Jack is in his gym. He's angrier than I've ever seen him. He's angrier than Picasso.

Taxi Driver plays, with the mute button on, so I can hear Jack ranting, in between snorts on the treadmill. Jack and I are alone in the house. Janet has left a day's worth of food in the fridge, with written instructions on the kitchen table, such as 'Put on oven gloves before taking casserole out of oven'.

I don't tell Jack I'm leaving. Of course not. I can't hurt him now. I'm his organic chicken. My job is to be happy. And make him happy. In return he'll look after me and I'll sacrifice my life.

'So he's young. So he's gay. So fucking what?'

Jack's rant contains many unanswerable questions like this. I nod and look at the ground. I behave remarkably like a chicken.

Then comes a question which, unfortunately, I'm obliged to answer.

'I can be young. I can be gay. I can do anything. I'm not spending the rest of my life on a sofa with my wife. You think I don't get enough of that at home?' (That's not the question.) 'I'll make him young and gay. What do you think?'

At first, I don't understand. It sounds like he wants to make Kevin Osborne young and gay. Like the failing magician he is, he wants to turn someone into something they already are.

In fact, he's referring to the talk show host in *Shoe Shop*. He wants to make that character young and gay.

'Don't they want you to be yourself?' I say it as quietly as I can, in the hope that will make him less angry. He merely gets louder, to compensate.

'I'm a fucking actor! I'm going to fucking act a young gay man! You think I can't do that?'

A giant Robert De Niro is on the wall, talking mutely to himself in a mirror. The De Neroid intonations in Jack's voice are unmistakeable and embarrassing.

'You know what a real actor would do? He'd have gay sex. That's the way you play a gay man. By being one.'

'Where you going to find a gay man, Jack?'

'Same place I found the twins,' he answers.

'I'll get them round too,' he says. 'That'll make it more, you know, normal.' He's already losing his nerve.

'Listen. When I say gay sex, it might just be, you know, a Channel 4 news job. It's a great idea though, isn't it?'

'Of course,' I say. 'It's a question of intensity. Take the top fifty tennis players in the world. What's the difference between number fifty and number one? It's not the backhand. It's not the return. It's the intensity. Number one has the intensity.'

'You make everything understandable, Dave. You were always so fucking intelligent.'

Jack's going to be gay to play a gay. Mercifully, he hasn't been cast as a serial killer.

'Will you film it for me?'

'I don't understand,' I say, though of course I understand. I don't *want* to understand.

'I can't watch you having sex, Jack.'

'I'm not asking you to watch me. I'm asking you to *film* me. I want to see myself on film. Being gay. I want to know I can make it believable.'

'I've never filmed anyone before.'

'Course not. That's great. I don't want a fat sweaty porn guy. I want a friend. You're the only one.'

Does he mean I'm his only friend? Or does he mean I'm the only friend who's guaranteed to be available? Or does he mean I'm the only one he can trust, a kind of sex-filming Jeeves? All these meanings carry the same message, which he's not too shy to state:

'I need you, Dave.'

Jack arranges for the twins and a gay male companion to come to the house at nine. Then he goes off for a read-through of *Shoe Shop*.

By the time he returns, I've made my plan.

My plan is characterised by goodness and intelligence, the qualities Jack's always prized in me. It involves, I grant you, his destruction. But that's for his own good and the good of his family. I'm not condemning him. He's condemned himself. His life, at this point, is a condemned building that needs to be knocked down, in order to be rebuilt.

He has coke and hookers and delusions of grandeur. He wants to be filmed having sex. He is, let's face it, a showbusiness personality. He's no longer Jack. It's Jack who must be rebuilt.

He's condemned to spending the rest of his life on a sofa with his wife. Listen to the way he says 'wife'. It isn't right. It's not right that he and she should be a brand. They're not a loving couple. The hypocrisy's grotesque. They're an Underbed Storage Unit; they make a promise they can't fulfil.

He said so himself. (Forgive me for using that phrase; it's a barrister's trick I learned from my dad, implying Jack's responsible for everything that follows.) He said so himself – the *News of the World* will pay seventy thousand for incriminating photos.

Ten minutes later, I put on the oven gloves and take the casserole out of the oven. Fish stew. I eat it direct from the casserole, alone, like a sad bachelor.

Look, this is not my knife and fork, this is not my casserole, my kitchen or my home. That's why I wear oven gloves throughout the meal. I'm keeping my distance.

To goodness and intelligence, we must add friendship. What I will do, I will do as a friend. It's the friendship equivalent of tough love. I'm giving Jack tough friendship.

The photos will force Jack and Rita to re-evaluate their marriage. Re-evaluate could be a euphemism for 'end'. Yet that's not as bleak as it sounds. Look at Caroline Bliss and her first husband, Max. They've discovered that, without each other, they can be themselves. What's more, they get on better now than when they were married. Divorce unlocked the door to a harmonious relationship.

Equally, the photos could strengthen the marriage. After the recriminations, the confessions, the treatments and therapies, the lost contracts and Pain Exclusives, the photos could end in a front-page, hand-in-hand reunion. Jack and Rita could re-swear their marriage vows. Their bed could get smaller.

Either way, Eric will be happier because his parents will be happier. I don't forget the boy.

Let's talk about fame, love and charity now. We all know which is the greatest. I want fifty thousand pounds. That's all I've ever wanted since Jess abandoned me on the road at Westleton. She said so herself: 'We're always fifty grand short.'

Not a penny of that will come out of Jack's pocket. The newspaper will give me that money. Nor will I keep a penny more than that fifty thousand. I'm doing this for Jess and me. I'm not doing it out of greed.

The remaining twenty thousand will go to charity. It will go to relieve famine in Lesotho.

'What kind of material?' asks the woman on the line, from the office of the *News of the World*.

'Photos of him with prostitutes,' I say, though the photos have yet to be taken.

'What do you mean, "with"?'

'Engaged in sexual acts with,' I reply fluently. I can tell she can tell I'm intelligent. I want very much to sound superior to the people who usually make these calls.

'How did you get these photos?'

'They're actually digital camera images. But I'm sure you can downgrade them.' Damn. I meant to say 'download'. That may not be the right word either.

'How did you get them?'

'I took them. I filmed them. I was there. I'm a personal friend of Jack. Have been for years. I can't tell you my name. I can't sell you the material unless you guarantee not to mention my name.'

I fear I've been too pompous about my name. I've somehow implied that, were my name to be used, it might damage British interests overseas.

'Can you hold?' she says and, miraculously, I hear a tinny version of Neil Diamond's *I Am I Said*.

She tells me that, depending on the quality of the material, they might pay up to fifty thousand. No, I tell her, it's seventy, Clive

293

Duncan said his friend said it was seventy. And now, with the mention of Clive Duncan's friend, I'm no longer a person of superior intelligence. I'm a blabbermouth, spouting irrelevancies.

'We wouldn't go over fifty,' she says.

'Seventy,' I say.

'Fifty,' she says.

'Listen. I'm giving twenty of it to Comic Relief. You're stealing food from the mouths of African babies. Is that what you want?'

'I'm sorry,' she says. 'Try another paper.'

'One of the prostitutes is a man,' I say. Immediately, I know I've said something relevant. It buys me time. I get another verse of Neil.

'We'll go up to sixty.'

Sixty it is then. I'll reduce my cut to forty. I promised the babies twenty and I won't let them down.

'Thank you,' I say. 'You've helped a lot of people. Bless you.'

I arrange to bring the material to them tomorrow, Friday, the day that Sophie will announce to the world that Jack's been sacked in favour of a young gay man.

The phone in Jack's kitchen is wet with my sweat. It feels like the phone of a fat sweaty porn guy. Memo to self: wipe phone.

I enter the gym at nine-thirty, as arranged with Jack. He and his guests have been there for half-an-hour. He's had time to explain my presence.

'Hello, darlin', how's your girlfriend?' asks the ear-licking hooker. I'm touched she remembers.

'Fine, thank you.'

'Nice camera, darlin',' says the other.

'Thank you,' I say. Then, to prove how relaxed I am: 'Nice titties.'

'Thank you, darlin'.' She turns to the young gay man. 'This is Joe. This is David. He's sweet.'

I'm proud of myself. Here we are, the hookers and I, gassing like fishwives. We have a camaraderie based on equality. We're all here because of money. I'm here because I'm in Jack's employ and will be till I walk out of the gates in the morning, while Jack's still asleep. (I won't have breakfast. It wouldn't be right.) I glance at the biro'd number on the back of my hand. Five oh four nine. That'll unlock the gates to freedom.

Jack puts on a pair of shades and runs his hands through his hair. 'Come on then, Dave. Let's get started. You're the director. How do you want us?'

I look through the viewfinder thing.

I'm making a charity porn film with consenting adults. It contains no illegal acts. It will benefit many people. It's a good and intelligent thing to do.

I don't take the camera away from my face for the next hour. Like the oven gloves, it allows me to feel that I'm there and not there, doing it and not doing it.

Often, I simply shut my eye. (With the other, I focus on the sexless exercise bike.) Jack doesn't know this, of course, and constantly asks 'How do I look?' He expects, and I give, the answer 'Great!' That's all he wants to hear. He doesn't want direction. He's not that kind of actor.

When the pink phone rings, at midnight, I'm not filming at all. I'm sitting on the treadmill with the camera on my lap. But there's nothing to fear. Jack can't see me. A woman's bottom covers his head.

I hastily look through the camera again, as Jack gets up to answer the phone, in that hateful low-volume 'intimate' voice. It's late afternoon in New York. Eric, we gather, is sleeping, exhausted from the flight. Rita is keen to know what Jack is up to.

The gay man is yet to be in the film. For the last hour, he's sat in a corner, bored, drinking wine. The phone call's his cue to get up and walk around. As he does so, he knocks his wine glass over.

Rita, evidently, hears this, since Jack tells her no, he's not alone, he's entertaining the producers of *Shoe Shop*. The girls, who I like more and more, shout 'Hi!' They're nice people. They want to help.

'Yes, Dave's here,' says Jack. Yes, Dave's here, nice Dave, Hebrew Classes Dave.

'What do you mean, what have we been doing?'

Robert De Jack loses his temper.

'You want to know what we've been doing? I'll tell you what we've been doing. Andrea sat on my face. And Dave filmed it. Does that answer your question?'

Jack hurls the receiver against the wall. It's his worst acting yet. Who does that in real life?

'OK, that's it,' says Jack. 'Forget it.'

The girls start putting their clothes on. The gay man reaches for his jacket, the only thing he's taken off. Jack, ignoring me, heads for the door.

'Hold on,' I say. 'I haven't said "Cut!"'

They all look at me. They don't expect me to be assertive.

'Come on, Jack. You can do this. You know you can do this. Intensity.'

He stops. He walks around, nodding his head intensely, acknowledging my faith in him. He turns to Joe the gay man, who's dark, with curly hair.

'Are you Jewish?' he asks. Only I know why. Only I understand that it wouldn't be right for him to have sex with a Jewish man. It's something, obscurely, to do with wanting to make our mothers proud.

'Do you want me to be Jewish?' he replies, which makes Jack think he is Jewish.

'Just answer the question,' says Jack.

'No,' says the gay man.

Jack turns to me. 'It's no good. I just can't do it.'

I take charge, as I sense he wants me to.

'It's easy. Shut your eyes. Then you won't know what's happening.'

'Yes I will. I'll feel it.'

'Shut your eyes. I'll toss a coin. Heads, I'll put a woman on you. Tails, a man. You'll never know.'

'OK. So it could be either, yeah? That's good. That's intense. That's acting, all right.'

'Eyes shut?'

Jack nods.

I toss a coin. It lands on the ground. I don't look at it. I go up to the man and whisper in his ear.

The gay man does as I ask. I zoom in on Jack's face, having discovered the zoom thing.

'OK, that's a cut,' I say. (I realise I should have said, 'That's a wrap.')

Jack opens his eyes, uncertain if he's just been gay.

Andrea says to the gay man: 'Long way to come for that, eh, Joe!' Luckily, Jack doesn't hear.

At three in the morning, still in that gym, Jack is gripping my arm.

'Tell me the truth, Dave. I can't act, can I? I'm not a comedian, I'm not an actor, I'm not a father, I'm not a husband. What am I?'

'Let's sleep on it, shall we?'

'OK. Tomorrow we'll live. What was that Latin word you taught me? Begins with V. Let's live.'

'*Vivamus.*'

'That's it. Rita has this carpenter. You'll love him. He's got a ponytail and everything. He can do a *Vivamus* sign. We'll put it above the front door. Will you sort that for me? I'll get the spelling wrong.'

'OK,' I say, trying not to look at him. I can't bear these tender flourishes, like the ponytail and the spelling. I can't bear to like him, not now. Please don't make me like you, Jack.

'Good night,' I say.

'What the fuck are you doing here, Dave? Why aren't you married to Jess? She's a diamond.'

'She doesn't want me.'

'Make her want you then. You're so lucky, Dave. You're ordinary. She's nice, you're nice. Just drive round and get her.'

I can't sleep. I've got to get the camera to the woman from the *News of the World*. I've got to make sure it's all right.

It's those shades. That's what's keeping me awake. He put on his shades before I started filming. He never took them off.

What if she says her readers won't know it's Jack? I have my arguments ready – Stevie Wonder and Ray Charles. But my arguments aren't convincing, even to me. In the gay sequence, he's wearing shades *and* his eyes are shut.

I get up and I put on Jack's clothes, for the last time.

I'm off now. But first, I'm going to tell him the truth.

I find him sprawled on his back on an exercise mat in the gym, still in the shades. I don't look at him. I've looked at him enough.

'Are you listening, Jack? I'm going now. I've had enough. You're a self-centred monster. Always have been. You don't care about me. You don't care about anyone. Everything's about you. How dare you pay me to be your friend? What do you think I am? You can pay a dog to love you. I'm off.'

I stop. I want a reaction. I deserve a reaction.

'Are you just going to lie there?'

I look him straight in the shades. He's dead.

That number, five oh four nine, allows me to open the gates to let in the ambulance. Jack is taken to Wycombe Hospital, where he's pronounced dead at five twenty-two am.

The cause of death is a heart attack. The Term is 'ischaemic heart disease'. Jack dies of the same heart disease that killed his father. His father died at forty-seven. Jack dies at forty-nine. Jack would have liked that.

I tell the hospital that Mrs Harris is staying at the Mercer Hotel, New York, New York. Then, for a couple of hours, I stay alone in the house. I can't bring myself to leave. I have breakfast after all, though I can't finish my piece of toast.

The phrase is: 'He could have gone at any time.' But he didn't. No one ever does. They always go at a particular time. I try to feel the correct things – sadness, bereavement, the soul's departure, the setting-in-stone of his noblest qualities. But the particular time haunts me. The gay thing haunts me. Norman, the man I most admire, is gay. Gayness is something you are, not something you do. You cannot be gay for a minute, with your eyes shut, because you're frustrated or mad or want to show you can do anything. And I was there. I made him do it.

I'm in no hurry to go anywhere. No newspaper will publish my material, not now. You don't hit a man when he's dead. My mission, to destroy Jack, has been accomplished by Jack. In death, as in life, he's ahead of me.

Why did I set out to harm him, though? He was my friend. He wanted to give me a home. Ashamed, I hurl the camera into the kitchen bin. Then I take it out and put it in a Tesco bag, the better to conceal it. Then I put it back in the bin, take it out again and bury it in the garden, like a dead pet.

I take off Jack's orange shirt and put it in the washing machine. I put his trousers on a hanger in his wardrobe. I look at all his trousers, his empty trousers. I try to cry. But 'empty trousers', my attempt at a poetic thought, makes me want to giggle. No one ever says 'Pass me my empty trousers and I'll fill them.'

In my denims, I go to his desk and take out the carrier bag of 'petty cash'. It isn't theft. It's what he would have wanted. I go back to the trousers and take the key to the nanny's car – my car – out of the pocket. Then I walk out of the house, as the buzzer rings, yet again. It's been ringing, on and off, for the last hour.

I walk down the drive. It's just after seven thirty. There are thirty or forty people on the other side of the big black gates that so impressed my mother. Many have cameras. I should identify with them, having recently been a cameraman myself. But no. I identify with Jack. I'll protect him. I'll say nothing. I'll protect the man I was trying to destroy, just a few hours earlier. Whose side am I on?

It's hard to say nothing. So many people are shouting at me, mostly women. They're shouting variants of: 'What can you tell us?' 'Tell what you can happen you tell us happen what can what did he what can when?' they shout.

I stare at a tall stick-thin woman with a microphone and earthquake-proof hair. There's something of the Caroline Bliss about her. There's no wastage, in her body or expression. She shouts the question I fear the most.

'Who are you?'

I do what I've seen Prime Ministers do, from the earliest days of my television-watching. They come out of their house in Downing Street and everyone shouts. They smile and say nothing and get in the nearest car.

I smile at her. I say nothing. I get in the nearest car, which is mine. I slam the door. I can't drive, though, and even if I could, I wouldn't open the gates for fear those people would come in.

So I act as if I've forgotten something, not that I can act. I slap my forehead with my palm. How many of the people beyond the gates will think I've forgotten something? If they notice at all, they'll think there's a fly on my forehead.

As I get out the car, there's no more noise. They've given up on me. I'm no one, with nothing to say.

I walk back up the drive and, avoiding the house, go through the garden, past the swimming pool and climb an apple tree at the back of the tennis court. Its branches extend over the wall, to the world outside.

Climbing the tree, like burying the camera, is wonderful and absorbing. There's a rightness to it. Jack was such a good climber.

The drop is no more than eight feet or so. I slide down, scraping the knees of my trousers against the wall.

A few feet away, a photographer is trying to find a foothold. 'Give us a leg up, mate,' he says, assuming I'm one of his kind. 'What's in the bag?'

'It's a bag of his rubbish,' I say.

'Nice one! Get a few hundred words out of that! Come on then.'

I tell him I'm sorry. I can't help him. I'm a family friend.

I walk down the road and, a few minutes later, find the last phone box in England. In it are business cards for hookers and minicabs. Within half an hour, I'm on my way to Suffolk. Jack and his carrier bag are treating me to the hundred pound fare.

The driver and I wordlessly come to a gentlemen's agreement. We won't talk, acknowledging that, if we did, we'd have to do it for over three hours. He switches on the *Today* programme on Radio 4. It's eight twenty-two and on the line is Melinda Spears, the cultural commentator.

'He was funny, he was rebellious, he was anarchic,' says Melinda. 'He was an anti-showbiz figure who got absorbed, as it were, into the establishment.'

'Are you all right, sir?' asks the driver, breaking our agreement.

I can't explain to him why I'm crying. I'm not sure myself. I'm not crying for Jack, clearly, because he's not in any pain. I think I'm crying because Jack was a man in a house with me and now it's as if I never knew him. He belongs to everyone and no one now. Anyone can fill Jack's empty trousers with their cultural comment.

'Would you like me to open your window?' asks the driver sweetly, as if that will help. I thank him.

'I understand you went out with him when you were teenagers,' says the woman from *Today*.

'Yes. He did wonderful card tricks,' says Melinda. 'I'll miss those card tricks,' she adds, as if Jack were round her place last night, doing tricks. Then she's gone, to wait by the phone, for someone else to seek her reaction.

At eight twenty-five, on comes Sophie, Head of Everything, to pay her nervous tribute. She knows what's coming.

'Weren't you about to announce that his show had been cancelled?'

Jack, that genius, has died the day he was due to be fired. (I'm not saying he was a genius; just that he had a genius's timing.) Sophie, the witch, fired a dead man. You can't do that, even if you do it when the dead man is alive.

'No, no, we were simply in discussion about different ways to use Jack's talents.'

I cackle at her discomfort. I slap my thigh. The driver shuts my window, annoyed that I'm now so well.

I get home around noon. I don't know what to do. I go to the bookshop, even though Jack told them I'd be absent all week.

Tim, Rose and Lydia are overwhelmed to see me. It's the only time Rose ever touches me. They thought I was dead or missing. Tim was on the point of contacting my mother.

The previous Saturday, some guy had rung up to say I wouldn't be in. And that was the last they'd heard of me.

Jack never made the subsequent call to say I'd be off for a week, with my nervous collapse.

I tell them I've been staying with Jack Harris. This doesn't account for my absence. Not really. There's no reason you need to be with a friend in the days before he has a heart attack, out of the blue.

But it's a bookshop. As I've explained, not much happens. And now I've made it the centre of the universe. I was with Jack, the TV star who's (famously) just died. They grant me, retrospectively, compassionate leave.

Lydia, for the only time, finds me exciting. 'I'm sorry about your loss,' she says.

When I get home there is, as I hoped, a message from Jess.

It's the first time she's called me since the roadside abandonment. Two weeks have passed.

I go round to her parents' house to see her. This time, I pay the minicab driver with my own money.

I tell her everything, except for the sex and the camera. I tell her about the cocaine and the nanny and the party and the breasts and the portrait and the paid friendship. She loves, especially, the cocaine and the breasts. The breasts make her laugh out loud.

She understands everything I tell her. 'That house made us mad,' she says. She embraces me.

'I've done you a terrible wrong,' she says.

We go to bed and, next morning, thank Jack for bringing us back together.

Jack's funeral is for members of the family. I don't quite qualify.

The day of the funeral, Janet drives my car from Jack and Rita's house to my cottage. Eric comes with her. Rita thinks this is better for him than attending the funeral, which could traumatise him.

Rita's arranged for a chauffeured car to pick them up from my cottage. It will take them to a seaside hotel in Aldeburgh, where they'll spend the afternoon and night, having fun, before being driven back home.

I come back from the bookshop at lunchtime, to greet them. Eric rushes past me into the cottage and up the stairs. A few seconds later, we hear a wail. He's hit his head on a beam. How does he do that? He's a five-year-old boy, about two foot shorter than the height of the beam. He must have jumped up and headed it, in a game of imaginary soccer.

A day after the funeral, I get a call from Caroline Bliss.

Jess and I decide we'll postpone buying a house together till the book is completed. The upheaval would be too distracting.

The rest you know.

9

What Now

That's it. That's the book I wanted to write. That's the truth about Jack. And me. And Jack and me. That's the story Caroline Bliss and Rita don't want me to tell you, the story I've been paid not to write.

What now?

I print this, I photocopy it, I stuff it into padded envelopes. I address them to my friends, as intended.

They open their envelopes. They find the manuscript. At first, they think it's my authorised biography. Then they find it's something else.

This is weird upon weird. They never asked me to send them the authorised manuscript, let alone its bastard offspring. What are they meant to do with it?

In a panic, they realise. They're meant to read it. It lies there on the kitchen table. It's there when they leave for work in the morning and it's there when they come back at night.

If they don't read it, they can't contact me ever again, not after I've gone to such trouble. If they read it and hate it, they won't want to contact me. If they read it and like it, they'll still avoid me. What can you say to a person about the story of their life? You can't say: 'I really enjoyed your life. Mind you, I found your life a bit long.'

No. It's absurd. I can't send out an unsolicited manuscript. I can't delude myself it's a gift when I know it will punish the recipients and the donor alike.

But what about the truth, you say? The truth will out. The truth must out.

This is the vanity of (unauthorised) biographers – to think they're human torches of truth when they're journalists with more space.

Consider this headline: THE TRUTH ABOUT ELVIS – SEE PAGE 5. We turn to page 5. What do we find? Cheeseburgers and white panties. You know. The white panties of truth. We never find: ELVIS WAS A GOOD SINGER – By the Woman Who Knew Him Best.

Jack was a forceful and exciting person. Through no grand design beyond making his mark, he became a much-loved popular entertainer. Will you remember that truth? Or will you recall that he died without knowing if he'd had a gay blow job?

Then there's me. The winner of the George Crabtree Prize? Or a man who makes porn films and buries them in the garden?

I don't think about death as I did when I was young. When Danny Harris died, I felt pious. Not any more. It's a lower-case thing now, death. It's the fourth thing I look for in the morning, after the front page, the sports page and the arts reviews.

Since Jack died, I've read obituaries of Alan Amiss, 41, Europhile Theatre Director (who lived with my school chum Magnus Thornton, the Norwich House Manager); Maurice Lightstone, 89, Geoff Bergman's father-in-law, the Dynamic Music Publisher I feared would see me eat my Yom Kippur meal; and Shulamid Spears, Melinda Spears's 76-year-old mother, A Talented Sculptor and Naturist. (The 'talented' applies to her sculpting. You don't need talent to be a Naturist. That's the point.)

Ten days ago, at six on a Friday morning, the phone rings. It can only be the Grim Reaper. Who else is up? Or a ten-year-old ringing numbers at random which, by coincidence, is the Reaper's working method too.

'Hello? It's Bob Ridgeon.' The man's voice is urgent. I've no idea who he is. Bob's name, without his salad dressings and running shorts, means nothing to me.

'Hello?'

It sounds like the man's calling from a car.

'Who's speaking?'

'Bob. Norman's Bob. Is Jess there?'

I hand Jess the phone.

Norman isn't dead. He's lying in the back of the car, with a headache. Thirty minutes earlier, at his London house, Norman had a fit. Luckily, Bob was there. (So. Bob stays the night now.) Bob's driving Norman to hospital.

Jess wants to drive to the hospital too. It's a three-hour journey. I persuade her to wait for further news.

The next news, at eight-thirty, is that the consultant has decided Norman needs a brain scan.

Twenty-seven hours later, on the Saturday morning, we're on the A12, driving to Norman's house. The CT scan has revealed a tumour in the parietal lobe. On Monday, Norman will go back into hospital for a biopsy. A week after that, he'll know.

But Norman knows already, which is why Jess pulls over into a layby, twice, and cries till she can drive again.

On Friday night, Jess and Norman had a two-hour phone call. Norman told Jess he will die of a brain tumour. It's poetic justice.

Tom, the hotel room artist, died of a brain tumour. Norman got rich through Tom's labours. Tom, who was the love of Norman's life, sacrificed his own life for Norman. Now Norman will repay him in kind.

Norman, who never indulges in this kind of talk, is making up for it now. He has little time left to say the things he wants to say.

I think of The Phrase: he went the same way as Tom. And The Term: parietal lobe.

I sit in the drawing room with Norman, Jess and Bob, looking at an Eduardo Paolozzi collage that Norman bought at the Whitechapel Gallery in 1956. He keeps telling Bob he should go back to Bath, that he's already sacrificed – that word again – enough time on Norman.

But Bob won't go. He offers to make tea.

Norman tells Bob to stuff his tea up his arse. He'd like to be alone with us. I've never seen Norman confront Bob before and try not to enjoy it. Bob apologises to us for Norman's behaviour and goes upstairs.

Norman tells us how glad he is that Jess and I have made the journey. It may be the last time we see him. He repeats all this over and over.

Jess tells him he's not going to die and he should stop talking about it. Norman obeys. But he can't talk about anything else. I can see that it pains him to be silent, so I ask what music he wants at his funeral. Jess rushes out in tears.

But Norman loves the question. Death's like an old mate he and I like but Jess can't stand.

He finds a pen but has trouble writing. He remembers that Tom had this trouble too. He writes down Mozart Requiem, then shortens the others to 'R'. Brahms R, Faure R, Verdi R. I tease him: 'This is like Death's Greatest Hits.'

'You're right. What's a suitable, suitable Morrissey?'

(He remembers Tom's repetitions too.)

'*Every Day Is Like Sunday.*'

'Yes.' He writes it down. 'That conjures up heaven. Heaven.'

Jess comes back with a tray of coffee, in lieu of Bob's arse-stuffed tea.

'I'm so sorry, Jessie,' says Norman. He advances towards her, forcing her to put the tray down hurriedly, so he can throw his arms around her.

Norman hugs her and says nothing. Then he hugs me.

'I don't want to lose you,' I say, each word demarcated by a breath.

'It's all right, it's all right,' says Norman.

'Sharon's aunt had a tumour just like yours,' says Jess. 'They spotted it early. She made a complete recovery.'

'You're going to be fine,' I echo.

But I don't believe it. Norman's going to die. He said so. What Norman says goes. That's how it is in Jess's family.

He lets me go, the better to address us both.

He speaks in his softest tone, looking at neither Jess nor me.

'I'm leaving you this house.'

Everyone is quiet. Nobody moves.

'The house and its contents. I know how much you'd appreciate them.'

Yes. Oh yes. Oh yes please. Thank you. This house and its contents.

I must stay calm.

I don't want Norman to die. But when he does – *if* he does – I will live in this house. With its contents.

I'm excited. Is that acceptable? Is that appropriate?

Yes.

It's the presence of the coffee that reminds me of Jack. The coffee is uncanny. Drink the coffee! That's what Jack told me. I will think of this house and its contents as Dead Man's Coffee.

This house is a three-and-a-half-million-pound cup of coffee. And the contents – the Christopher Wood and Matthew Smith and Richard Hamilton and Eduardo Paolozzi – they are the cream, the sugar and the saucer.

'We don't want your house,' says Jess. 'We want you to live.'

'Yes!'

That's me, agreeing with Jess. Too quickly.

Norman shakes his head. He looks frustrated and tired and old.

I want to help.

'But if we can't have you and the house,' I say, 'we'll take the house.'

'Thank you,' says Norman. Jess stares at me as if I'm the devil.

When Norman first met me, he confided to Jess: 'I like your friend. He's not concerned with money.'

This is my reward for being unconcerned with money: money.

I could never live in Norman's house. It's too big. It's too overtly concerned with money. But we could sell it. Oh yes. We could sell it and buy a (biggish) house in Suffolk, with Norman's Contents on the walls. I reckon that would leave us with just under three million pounds. We could live happily off that for the rest of our lives. Happiness, in financial terms, means living off your interest and leaving your capital untouched. The per annum interest from three million is – but let's not talk about money.

Jess will paint in the studio we'll build at the bottom of our new garden. (Our *land*.) I'll read, I'll think, I'll listen to music,

I'll walk and swim and play tennis and pursue my Dylan studies. I might write some not-for-profit poetry. We'll travel.

But, first, I'll send my advance back to Caroline Bliss. What can she do? She can't make me write the book if I've given the money back. Her anger will be ferocious. I find the prospect exciting. Sexy, even.

And of course I'll bury this memoir. I won't feel the need to tell the world the truth about Jack and me.

If Norman dies and leaves us that house, I won't feel the need to do anything.

Jess has been distant from me ever since, as if I can will a man's death. We're more and more estranged.

I don't want Norman to die. I never did and I don't now. But if the man has a malignant tumour, death will save him from further suffering. And if that saves me from further suffering, so be it.

I'm prepared. I'm ready. Art Dealer of Exquisite Taste. That's what the papers will say.

Please understand. If I hadn't known Jack, with his twenty-foot gates, or Norman, with his houses in Belgravia and Provence, I wouldn't feel what I feel tonight. It's the proximity that gets you. I'm not a money-grubber. But, if Norman dies, I'll accept my fate. I'm a money-acceptor.

Tonight's the night, you see. Jess is downstairs, waiting for Norman to ring and tell her the result of his scan. I'm upstairs, in the bedroom, ironing. It's a solitary activity that appeals to certain males, a kind of indoor fishing. I don't iron to get away from Jess, though. Jess is not my Bob.

On Saturday mornings, when I also iron, Jess collects our box of organic vegetables from Darsham. We care about what we eat. And we're environmentally-friendly. Jess drives there, so you could argue that the carbon emissions cancel the cosmic good we do by buying the vegetables. But I said we were friendly to the environment. I never said we were married to the bloody thing.

I am, as you can tell, feeling bumptious.

While I iron, I listen to a Dutch station that plays nothing but Old Man Rock. The DJs announce the tracks *after* they've played them, which means my pleasure's prolonged. I have a lusty sing-along to *Woodshtock*. Then, when it ends, I have a lusty announcealong to *Croshby, Shtills, Nesh and Young*. (In English, the stresses are even. In Dutch, the stress falls on the *Croshby*.)

There's no need to wonder how pathetic this is. I know perfectly well. But I'm on my own. I'm not inflicting my pathos on a living soul, apart from Jess, who's on a different floor and sought out my pathos anyway. She came back to me after Jack's funeral because she couldn't bear to hurt me. That's what she told me.

The iron hisses. The radio plays. I'm in my reverie. Consequently, I don't hear the phone ring or, two minutes later, Jess come up the stairs.

I know as soon as I look at her.

I think I'm going to faint. I put one hand on the iron and the other on the board. She tries to hug me but I can't take my hands off them.

And then, within a minute, I'm on the phone to Norman, and he's saying it all again to me. Luckily, the tumour's benign.

Happily, the tumour's in a good position and can be removed without complications.

The consultant has said there's no reason he shouldn't last another twenty years. That's The Phrase, then. Near-Death, too, comes with a Phrase.

As for The Term, I can't quite make it out. Not because he's speaking softly but because it's a Latin-sounding Term I don't recognise. It sounds like 'Men-In-Tuna'. Apparently, that's the kind of tumour Norman has.

I could ask him to spell it. But I don't. All that matters is, the tumour's benign.

The more he says Men-In-Tuna, the more excluded I feel. Inevitably, it sounds very gay. Just as Jack and I, in default mode, could always go exclusively Jewish, throwing in a *naches* or *meshuggenah* to distance everyone else, so Norman's tumour is a tumour I could never get. I'll never be a man in tuna. I'm too straight to get down with those fish.

Then Norman says how wonderful Bob has been.

I know what's coming. I brace myself. It comes all right. But the bracing doesn't help.

Bob is giving up plumbing. Bob is selling his car. Bob is going to drive Norman's car, as Norman is banned for two years following his epileptic fit.

Bob is – wait for it – Bob is doing a course in Art Appreciation at Thames College.

Bob is moving into Ecclestone Street to look after Norman.

Bob, on his first night in his new official residence, will slam down his electric toothbrush on the bathroom marble, like a pub bastard asserting his empty glass on the bar. Then he'll enter the master bedroom, in his monogrammed dressing gown. He'll look at Norman and think, *there's no reason why he shouldn't last another twenty years.*

Perhaps I'll do a course in Plumbing Appreciation. Why not? Why shouldn't I be able to Appreciate Plumbing as much as any other man? Why should I always have to say: 'Yeah, erm, it doesn't seem to be leaking now. Great.'

My voice becomes as soft as Norman's.

'I'm so happy for you, Norman.'

'Thank you, David. You and Jess have been marvellous. You must come and see us again soon.'

'I'd like that.'

I thought death would take Norman from me forever. But it's life that's taken him from me. Life with Bob.

'You were relying on it, weren't you?'

'What?'

Jess doesn't dignify this with a response.

It must be about five in the morning. I don't even know if I'm awake.

'You've got to stand on your own two feet, Dave.'

I hate the use of my first name. It makes me feel we don't know each other and never will. It makes me feel the bed is a thousand miles wide. And of course it reminds me of Bob.

'When I came upstairs, you were ironing my tights. There's no need to iron tights. Why didn't you do the sheets?'

I don't argue. It's all true.

'Would you sit in the front of a car with Bob?' I ask.

'If the back and the boot were full.'

She laughs. It's not sex but it makes me feel we have a future.

At eleven, Sarah from Caroline Bliss's office calls for a chat. How am I? How am I doing? How is the book coming along? Am I enjoying it? Am I still excited? They're still excited, very excited. But worried too. Why haven't I been in touch with Rita to interview her about Jack?

I explain that I'm still working on Jack's life before Rita. Then I start blathering. I say anything I can think of. I say I've been finding it hard to work, as my girlfriend's uncle has just not died.

Sarah, who makes a hundred phone calls a day, says 'oh no' and 'no problem'. But she says them just a fraction before they're due, as in:

'It was terrible. We all thought he was going to die of a –'

'Oh no!'

'– brain tumour.'

This suits me well. She responds to my sound, which is urgent, not my sense, which is threadbare.

Caroline Bliss wants to fix up a time to come and see me. I promise to look in my diary and call Sarah back. That, at least, will give me time to go out and buy a diary.

But it's Sarah who calls me back. She suggests a date, a week from today. Caroline Bliss is going to get on a train and visit me in Suffolk, where she'll buy me lunch. In exchange, she wants me to show her the first thirty thousand words of *That's All We Have Time For*.

Sarah says that's a rough figure. She wants to see the first few chapters, that's all.

At lunchtime, Jess says she's going to London. She wants to be with Norman. I understand. She thinks this will help me anyway, as she won't be around to distract me while I work all hours to finish the first few chapters.

* * *

315

It's three forty-five. I look out the window. Parmesan Leonie walks past, without her friends Charlene and Samantha. She carries a book, in a familiar bag. I designed that bag, with Tim. Each side looks like the front cover of a book called The Yoxford Bookshop. It's not Picasso nor Matisse but it works.

I'll stop not-writing. What am I not-writing anyway? My book is over and it's far too late for *That's All We Have Time For*.

I'll go to the bookshop, where I was happy.

I don't want to have the dark heart of a middle-aged man. I want to be like Jess. Younger, more optimistic. She believed Norman would live. Night after night, she lay awake and thought of Sharon's aunt, the one who survived a similar brain tumour.

As I hover outside the bookshop, the name of Sharon's aunt's tumour comes back to me. Of course. That's The Term: meningioma.

I hover because I'm nervous. I haven't been back to the bookshop since I left it, four months ago. I hover because Lydia, she of the belly button, is squatting with her back to me, down at Local Interest. I don't want to enter while it's possible for her to think I'm looking at the taut 'y' of her thong.

Lydia stands up. I walk into the bookshop.

Rose smiles and says 'Hello, stranger!' I'm glad.

Lydia smiles too. Not directly at me. But I know it's in my honour.

Tim is absent, with the accountant. No matter. I still feel happy. My life hasn't been wasted. From this bookshop, for fourteen years, I dispersed enlightenment in all directions. West to Peasenhall and Sibton Green, east to Westleton and Dunwich, north to Wenhaston and Blythburgh, south to Kelsale and Saxmundham. Who knows where it went from there? This is not the Suffolk of the eighteenth century, most easily approached by boat. This is the Suffolk of email, where a book I recommended to the Person from Peasenhall was electronically touted that very morning to her friend in New Zealand.

My heart feels bookshop-warm. Norman has found a man to look after him. At seventy-one, he's admitted he has to share his life. He's surrendered his privacy and opened himself up to love. I'm happy for him.

I think of my supreme moment, as witnessed by Tim and Rose. Though it happened as long ago as Christmas 1995, they speak of it to this day.

A woman came in and walked up to the counter. She had a puzzled expression. She couldn't speak. She was struggling to remember something. 'Erm,' she said.

I replied: *'The Name of the Rose.'*

'Yes!' she said. 'That's amazing! How did you know?'

Like all magicians, I couldn't tell her. It's years of looking at faces and bodies and clothes, even shoes. You know what books people have read and what they're likely to read. And then, if you're very good, you become a Special One. You know what books they're trying to remember.

'Would you like some tea?' says Rose.

'That would be nice, thank you.'

'We've got some peppermint tea, haven't we?' Rose asks Lydia, sweetly recalling what I like. Lydia nods and goes to the back room.

'So. Have you read any good books lately?'

'No. I've been writing one, though.'

This is nice. This is light and fast and funny and touching.

Rose knows all about my book. It's not a secret any more.

'I heard your chap on the radio last night. They played a bit from an interview he did with an actress. I can't remember her name. But he was quite amusing.'

'Thank you,' I reply, for Jack is mine now, I field his compliments, his posthumous life is in my hands.

'How's everything here?'

'Fine.' She nods towards the back room. 'Madam's leaving at Christmas. Going to live with her boyfriend in York. We're too sleepy! Have you read this? It's terrific.'

She hands me Roy Jenkins's biography of Winston Churchill. I look at Lydia through the open door of the back room. If she's leaving, Tim will need someone. Why couldn't I have my old job back?

'How's the violin going?'

Rose doesn't answer. She's busy selling a *Harry Potter* to Leonie's friends, Charlene and Samantha.

Charlene, the loud one, asks if Rose can gift-wrap the book. Rose apologises. It's not a service we – sorry, they – provide. Samantha asks if their friend can bring it back if she's got it already. Charlene adds that she's probably got it as she reads a lot of books. From this, I infer they're buying the book for Leonie. It's probably her birthday.

Rose assures them that the book can be exchanged on production of the receipt. Charlene and Samantha leave the shop. Lydia comes in from the back room with the tea. There are no customers now, only Lydia, Rose and I.

I put the Roy Jenkins book back on the shelf, in the manner of a man who still works there. Those who don't have the powers of booksellers – let's call them 'muggles' – can't do what I do. They angle a book into a gap. They tilt the book backwards and, leading with the bottom edge, gingerly wedge and lower. I use a straight left. I slam it in the gap. Bam. The books on either side don't feel a thing.

I quit this bookshop to write a book about Jack. Then I quit that to write a book about Jack and me. And now, with the windfall unfallen, with the windfall stuck up a tree, I've no idea what I'm doing with my life.

Rose remarks to Lydia how wonderful it is that Harry Potter's inspired a generation of children to pick up books and read. Lydia feels no need to add anything. The remark is a given, a sentiment with which we all agree.

I can't stop myself. When it comes out, it comes out with such venom that I shock even myself.

'Christ, I'm so sick of that four-eyed little fuck.'

Rose's lip trembles. She believes to her core that a person should be good. She works for Amnesty International, she gardens for the hospice and now, I hear, she's started going to church.

She's a childless woman. (As a man, my childlessness can't compare.) She has maternal feelings which need an outlet. They find one in Harry and the children who love him.

She bursts into tears.

'Apologise!'

I'm jealous of Harry. That's the truth. The twenty-foot gates . . . the house in Belgravia . . . Harry.

'Apologise!'

She's right.

'I'm sorry,' I say. 'I didn't mean to upset you.'

'Apologise to him!'

Yes. I owe Harry an apology. I owe him more than that. We all do, we booksellers, current and ex. How much of my wages, in the years I worked here, did the four-eyed boy wonder pay?

I want to placate her. I do. But it doesn't come out right.

'He's a fucking fictional character! Should I call him on his fucking fictional mobile?'

'You're banned from the shop.'

That I won't accept. I worked here when this bookshop opened. I was here years before Rose.

'You can't ban me. I'm a customer.'

Rose is confused.

'Buy something then,' says Lydia with a smirk.

Right. I will. Watch me.

I stride to Children's, my cheeks hot. With one hand, I grab three Potter hardbacks. Don't try. It's another of my powers.

I take them to the till and present them to Rose. I'd like to flutter a handful of notes in the air and let them fall where they may. But I only have a pound coin and cards.

Rose swipes my card. We wait, silent as two graves, for the machine to gurgle its assent.

She tears the slip. She hands it to me. I sign it. She puts the books in a bag. I say, 'Don't bother.' And I storm out the shop without them.

That's right. I leave without my purchases.

If you take three books from a shop without buying them, you're a worthy biographical subject. Why did you steal them? What happens next? What did your parents do to you to turn you into a thief?

But if you buy three books from a shop without taking them, no one cares. You're a Nowhere Man.

It's Sunday. At twelve, when there's a knock on the door, the cottage being too small to warrant a bell, I think it's Jess, back from Norman's house. She has a key but she chooses to knock, so I can open the door, see her smiling face and throw my arms round her.

It's the girls: Charlene, Samantha and Leonie. For once, Leonie is the leader. Charlene and Samantha hang back. While she talks, they look around for something better to do, knowing there's nothing.

Leonie gives a speech she must have given many times. She forces herself, overcoming her shyness with diction clear to the point of exaggeration. One thing's in her favour – she has a clipboard to grasp, which solves the problem of what to do with her hands.

She's playing her cello in a Stringathon to raise money for Oxfam. Would I like to sponsor her? She goes on, I think, to tell me how many hours of music she intends to play. Maybe she tells me who else is involved. She probably recommends an amount, based on what others are giving. I don't know. I can't concentrate on what she's saying, only on who she is.

She's so intelligent and complex. I want to talk to her and know what she thinks. I want to recommend books for her to read and cities for her to explore. Paris, Dublin, Seville. What worries her? How can I help? These feelings overwhelm me, not with their sentimentality but their precision. I can sum them up, with clarity: I want to be her father.

'Wait there,' I tell her.

I run upstairs and fetch Jack's carrier bag, which I keep under the bed. I raid it for causes he'd think worthwhile. Last week, he treated Tim and me to seats for *Hamlet* at the Theatre Royal, Norwich, plus petrol and midnight curry. And now he'll sponsor Leonie, in memory of his unmade trip to Lesotho.

I run back downstairs and offer Leonie the carrier bag. In my excitement, I fail to explain its contents. She looks inside. Charlene and Samantha look too. 'Fucking hell!' says Charlene, then puts her hand over her mouth as Samantha squawks with laughter.

Leonie, flustered, has to depart from her speech. She tells me she's not asking for money. The money comes later, after the event. I tell her to take the money, count it and, after the Stringathon, work out retrospectively how much I've sponsored her per hour. I'll then sign for that amount.

But it's her turn not to listen to me. Charlene and Samantha shout at her to take the bag. She gives them the clipboard and takes it from me. As they run off, giggling, I shout after Leonie, as any father would, to keep the bag safe. I add: 'Happy Birthday for last week!'

She doesn't hear me. They don't turn round. I hear Charlene say: 'He's a fucking nutter!'

I feel elated. Jack would have been proud. I made my mark. The girls won't forget their encounter with me. It's fame of a kind, a local kind. I'm The Fucking Nutter of Yoxford.

The phone rings. I fear bad news. Lately, the phone has been no friend.

I answer by stating my name, just as my father did.

Jess asks what's wrong. That's fair enough. She's not obliged to offer up a nicety first, a hello, a hi, an it's me. What's intimacy if not rudeness? I say 'Nothing', which I know she'll know is a lie, so I leave no gap before: 'Where are you?'

She says she's at her parents'. Knowing that will bother me, since she's supposed to be here, she leaves no gap either: 'How's the book going?'

'Good,' I say.

'Every time I looked at it, it was about you. You and sex and Bob Dylan and stuff.'

I feel violated. How dare she look at my work without my permission?

'I said you couldn't look at it till it's finished.'

'That's not what you've been paid to write, is it?'

I feel myself subsiding, as if I'm made of melting wax.

'It's never going to happen, is it?'

That 'it' is more than the book. It is everything. Everything is

322

never going to happen. The observation doesn't hurt me. I feel known. If anything, what she says brings her closer to me.

'I'm five months pregnant. You don't want kids so I'm not going to force you to have one.'

'That's not true,' I say with conviction. But how can I describe the evidence? I can't tell her I want a girl called Leonie. You're meant to want kids in general. It's unborn kids you're meant to want.

'I'm having the baby at Ipswich. Then I'm going to live with Norman and Bob. They're doing up the basement. Bob's putting in a new bathroom. We'll be fine. Why didn't you notice? You're so wrapped up in yourself.'

'Are you happy about it?'

'Yes and no. Why didn't you go up to Bob Dylan? I don't understand. You love him. He's there. Why not go up and say, "You're Bob Dylan".'

'He knows that.'

I eat lunch on my own, with the Roberts radio parked on the table next to the cheese. I should get a cat, if this is to be my life. The cat would sit on the table, where the radio is, exuding warmth. But I mustn't be sentimental. I don't like cats and never did. Radios don't shit.

I feel closer to Jess than anyone else. When I hear the knock at the door I think, as I did at the last knock and will at the next: it's bound to be her.

She's a cello teacher. She's a single mother. She drives an unwashed car. To these things that I know about Leonie's mother, I can now add another. She's in the Yoxford String Quartet with Rose. A leaflet came through my door yesterday, advertising one of their concerts.

Her unwashed car, which is parked outside my cottage, has been washed. Maybe she's paid Leonie to wash it. Isn't that what you do with girls aged twelve or thirteen, to inculcate the value of hard work and earned income? I'm sure Leonie prefers it washed. That's one less thing for Charlene and Samantha to tease her about.

'Did you give this bag to my daughter?' she asks. Unlike her daughter, she's not shy. A single mother, I imagine, can't afford to be.

'Yes,' I say.

'Are you aware of its contents?' she asks. Her diction's hostile, where Leonie's was compelling. She knows she's morally superior to me. Classical musicians, in my experience, always do. It doesn't help that the radio is broadcasting Part Three of *The Monkees Story*. She won't appreciate the security I find in the pop songs of my youth. I could show her my CD of Glenn Gould playing *The Goldberg Variations*. But I wouldn't give her the satisfaction. Let her suffer the crass chord changes of *Daydream Believer*.

'I could take you to the police,' she says. I'm not sure what she means, which is worse than knowing. I'm obliged to imagine the crime she thinks I've committed. I feel paternal towards her daughter. I'd want to hurt any man who had sexual feelings for her. Is that in itself a criminal offence? I wouldn't want to admit it to a policeman.

'What's this?' she says, producing from the carrier bag a Little Jeremy script.

'That's not mine,' I say. 'That belongs to a friend of mine. I didn't know that was in there. He's dead now,' I add, as if, like Lydia, she'll be sorry for my loss.

'Are you in the habit of giving young girls drugs?' she asks.

'Certainly not!' I say. But the how-dare-you-madam tone is unconvincing.

If I lived with Jess and we had a kid, none of this would have happened. I have to be ordinary, as soon as I can.

'I'm sorry,' I say. 'It was an accident.'

She thrusts the bag at me, making sure there's no contact between my hands and hers.

'What about the starving people?' I ask.

She spits it back. 'You care about the "starving people", do you? If you ever come within fifty feet of my daughter, I'll call the police. Understand?'

I try to picture fifty feet. Is it the distance between two lamp posts? What is fifty feet, in yards or metres? What's fifty feet in feet?

I'm a good person who's made a mistake. How can I make her see? I'll refer her to the good person we have in common.

'Ask Rose about me. She'll vouch for me. We were colleagues for fourteen years.'

'Don't you worry,' she says as she gets in her car, 'I know what you called Harry Potter.'

I kneel on the floor with my chin on the rug and put the bag under the bed. I stare at the Underbed. What will happen if I lie down there, clutching the bag, for good? How long before someone discovers me? My next appointment is lunch with Caroline Bliss, in two days' time. If I don't turn up, she won't come looking. She'll merely get her secretary to call me. Two days after that, around ten on Thursday night, Tim will knock, en route for our drink in the pub and our weekly smoke. Yes. It will be Tim, who has a key, who will find me. 'He lay there for more than four days before he was discovered.' That's what they'll say on Friday's early evening regional news.

More than four days. That's actually quite good. Some people don't get found for a week.

It's Jess that keeps me from the Underbed, with her 'yes and no'. Jess doesn't want me to disappear. She didn't say she was happy to have the baby without me. She said she was happy, yes and no. Her door is only half-closed.

I call Tim and tell him Jess is pregnant, omitting the yes and no. Tim's delighted. He says I'll be a loving and anxious father. I ask him if I can have my old job back, when Lydia leaves at Christmas.

'It's out of the question. You've moved on. And Rose and you are poison. And I can't pay you a dad wage. So forget it.'

Tim has been gentle with me for more than thirty years. Now he's had enough.

I go back upstairs and empty the contents of the bag on to the bed: three thousand, seven hundred and fifteen pounds, that are not going to charity.

I'm due to meet her at the Lighthouse restaurant in Aldeburgh at one. It's a twenty-five minute drive from my cottage. But I can't drive. I set off at eleven, not knowing how I'll get there. When I walk down the street, an acquaintance may be getting into their car to go to Aldeburgh. A van on its way to Aldeburgh may be making a delivery at one of our shops. A bus might appear. I want to get to Aldeburgh by fate. That's all I have now. Fate. I don't have thirty thousand words. I don't have an excuse. No dog has ever eaten that much homework.

I walk to the A12 and stick out my thumb. I'm wearing my suit, my one suit, which I wore for my father's funeral and Jack and Rita's wedding. There's nothing to be gained by looking dishevelled. Why throw yourself on the mercy of a woman who has none?

Why does no driver stop for me? Do I need to be holding an ALDEBURGH sign? No. I'm a hitch-hiking middle-aged man. I hold enough signs as it is. I see them – LONER – reflected in the faces – LOSER – of the drivers that pass. I HAVE ROPE.

I walk back to the cottage and call for a minicab, reducing the contents to three thousand seven hundred.

Caroline Bliss wants to know everything. How long is the fish grilled? What kind of leaves are in the green salad? Is the salad already dressed and, if so, what oil is used? Soon she will ask how the water is stilled.

After all that, what? She orders a piece of cod and a salad, a lunch fit for a cat. Caroline Bliss is on a new diet. She explains it to me but I can't understand it. She can't combine food with other food. Something like that. She can only have food. She got this diet from the wife of the Chancellor of the Exchequer.

I, by contrast, order oysters followed by steak. Like Leonie with her clipboard, I want something to do with my hands. The oysters will give me something to cling on to, each one a huge worry bead. The steak and the chips and the vegetables will add quantity. In the next half-hour, I expect to be sick. I want to have lots to bring up. I don't want to vomit gastric juices, like I did when I travelled overland to India and saved money by not eating.

What happens at a business lunch? I assume that now we've ordered the lunch, she will begin the business. But no. She wants to know about me. How am I? Where am I living? Am I in a relationship?

'I'm in a relationship. But it's difficult. What about you?'

She wants to hear more about me. Who is the other person in my difficult relationship? What does she want from me?

I tell her far more than I want to, in the hope that she'll tell me more than she wants to, further delaying the business.

My plan goes well. She's split up with Alan Mitchell, who's involved with his Parliamentary Private Secretary. She's 'fallen in love' with a younger man, Emilio, a Brazilian PhD student who used to live with Melinda Spears.

'Yes,' I say, 'I met him researching the book.' Why did I have to say 'book'? I French-kiss an oyster to kill off the subject. But it's too late. The business has started.

'Listen,' she says. 'About the book.'

This is my moment. I must tell her I refuse to write *That's All I Have Time For*. It goes against my beliefs and values and instincts. It shatters my integrity. I want my baby's father to be a *man*.

'People want to read about love,' she says. It's the second time she's mentioned that word.

'Yes,' I say.

I can't tell if she looks older or younger. The split from her husband has aged her, but the union with Emilio has rejuvenated her. Her hair is now surprisingly, girlishly long and blonde. The too-young hair invites you to look for the mutton in her lamb.

I finish my last oyster. The waitress removes my plate. Let her bring my steak soon, so I can eat the chips with my fingers.

She tells me that the latest publishing phenomenon is the *wife story*. A wife story, apparently, is the life story of a man, written by his wife. There are two wife stories in the bestseller list. One is about a dead actor written by his widow. The other is about a comedian.

'Your book could be even more special,' she says, as the waitress puts my steak in front of me, like a plate of Fate.

'This is what we want you to do,' says Caroline Bliss.

What she wants me to do is stop writing my book, the one I've not started.

'Jack and I were lovers. Don't worry. Rita knows all about it.'

Rita, it transpires, mentioned Caroline Bliss to Janet. Janet went quiet, remembering everything Jack had told her. Suspicion was aroused in Rita's new breast. She confronted Caroline Bliss.

But this is a woman whose divorce was a triumph. Out of her adultery, Caroline Bliss has wrought a strong friendship with Rita. Jack, as potent dead as alive, has brought the two women together. Caroline Bliss has helped Rita confront her anger. At the same time, she knows with greater certainty that she – Rita – truly loved Jack and loves Jack still. Only true love could survive such humiliation. She and Rita have been over and over it, time and time again. Since that confrontation, they've had lunch every week.

The last lunch turned into a business lunch. Caroline Bliss proposed that the two of them should write a book about Jack. A book about a man who was loved by, and loved, two women. A wife story and a mistress story in one.

Caroline Bliss tells me this has never been done before. She thinks the book trade will be very excited by this 'unique proposition'.

'I think we'd look great together,' she says. 'I can see us on the box.'

Now I understand. Caroline Bliss is the new Jack. It is she who will fill his empty trousers. Caroline Bliss and Rita want to share a sofa. They want to *be* together, on television, the one skinny and posh, the other curvaceous and working-class. Who will say no?

Wicked Bread and Butter Puddings with a Shot of Scotch arrive on the table. I have no memory of ordering them.

'We'll put the book back by three months, if that's OK with you. Coffee?'

She thinks I can keep up. She thinks an old donkey like me can keep pace with a racehorse.

'I don't quite –'

'We want you to write it. We don't have time. It'll be in our names but you'll write it. Rita adores you. Obviously you'll have to share royalties with us. Let's not get bogged down with that. Will you do it? Do you like the idea?'

'Will there be pole dancing?'

'I don't understand.'

'Hotel poles.'

She looks blank. Then the two words, such strangers to each other, meet and make sense. She's amused.

'Gosh! He told you that, did he? No. No poles. I'm happy to be sexy but we don't want details. It's a love story.'

We come out of the restaurant at about three. We've been talking about the new book for more than an hour. I've agreed with her about everything.

I've got away with it. I went in that restaurant to be destroyed and I've come out with champagne on my breath.

But there's no satisfaction. I've done nothing. Fate, as owned by Caroline Bliss, did it all.

'You're OK to drive, I hope,' she says.

'Yes,' I reply. It's the answer she wants me to give so I give it. I can't start disagreeing now.

'Can you give me a lift to the station?'

I nod.

'You're a star. Where are you parked?'

I gesture towards the sea front. We walk along, side by side. I adjust to her fierce pace. Her great legs are not just for show.

'Jack always spoke very fondly of you,' she says, as if Jack and she were senior to Jack and me, which may be the case.

'Which way now?' she asks, as we reach a T-junction. Her body is angled north, towards Thorpeness.

'This way,' I say, with a vague wave, like a TV weatherman indicating the whole of the east. She sees a line of car parking bays and, naturally, heads for it. I follow. A woman comes out of the hotel opposite. She gets in a blue car and drives away.

'We don't really want the childhood, that's boring. Start with Jack meeting me. We met at a party I gave when I was with Max.'

'Hey! That's my car!' I shout.

Caroline Bliss goes into action. She gets her mobile out of her bag and thrusts it at me.

What am I meant to do with it?

'My car doesn't have a phone,' I say.

'The police, you clot!'

I dial a three-figure number, making out it's 999. The Time, a mature male voice tells me, is sponsored. The word makes me think of Leonie. For every hour of Time, presumably, the sponsors send a pound to charity.

'Police!' I shout.

I tell the pretend police my car's been stolen. Caroline Bliss has already found out the name of the road. 'Opposite the White Lion Hotel,' she adds. I pass on her information to Constable Not-There.

'It's a blue car. Registration number . . .' I give the number of a nearby parked car.

'Is there anything else you need to know?' I ask.

'You haven't given him the make,' she says.

What is a good-sounding make? What car would Caroline Bliss believe I drive? What's that Italian one? Begins with 'F'?

'It's a Fiat,' I say.

'Fiat what?' prompts Caroline Bliss.

I feel so tired. Acting exhausts, when you can't do it, as Jack couldn't, as I can't. Then there's the Speaking Clock, which does nothing but tell me that time is passing and death is getting ever nearer.

I want to be in charge. Just once.

'Listen,' I say to the Speaking Clock, ignoring the Fiat What question. 'It's three twelve and thirty seconds. If you haven't found my car by this time tomorrow, I'll want to know why. No one steals my car and gets away with it, d'you understand? OK. Bye.'

This is meant to impress and excite her but she simply says: 'You didn't give them a contact number.'

She calls her secretary and asks her to get us a taxi, though her secretary's in London and I'm right here, with all my local knowledge. Caroline Bliss looks at me with benevolence.

'God, you're so sweet and hopeless.'

No, I won't have that. Not any more. I want Jess's unborn child to be proud of me. I want to look after it and care for it. I don't want it to be born in the shadow of Norman, as I've lived in the shadow of Jack.

'Listen. You can't just change the book like that. I've already written forty thousand words. Now I have to start all over again. You've got to pay me for the four months I've wasted writing the book you told me to write.'

Caroline Bliss is dumbfounded. This is not what she expected.

'I'll call you when I get back to the office.'

At six thirty, she calls to say that she has, with difficulty, persuaded her boss that the company should make me an additional payment of ten thousand pounds.

This is my moment. The worm has turned. I must hurry before it turns back.

Fiat Tango, Fiat Quango, Fiat Honcho, Fiat Jumbo, Fiat Panto. Yes, that's it. Fiat Punto. The car Jack gave me is a Fiat Punto.

It is six fifty-two in the morning. The sun is rising over Yoxford as I get into the car.

'Drive round and get her.' His last words.

Clutch, brake, accelerator. That's it, isn't it?

I'm behind the wheel. What a crass metaphor that is, for a man trying to take control of his life. No matter. A crass metaphor is what Jack would have wanted.

I put my left foot down on the clutch. My left leg trembles, in the style of early Elvis. I take my foot off and put it back again. I turn the key in the ignition. I put my right foot on the accelerator. Brmm.

I raise my left foot and lower my right. That's what you do, isn't it? The car aches to go, like a dog on a lead. I go.

It holds the road, it holds the road! The engine roars and I change into second gear. I'm in control now. I look in the rearview mirror. There's a car behind me. Why so close? Why me? I resolve not to look again. I try to speed up but the car is useless. Jack and Rita have given me a weak car. It lacks performance or high-speed injection or something. Petrol.

I stop at the junction. I reach for the handbrake. It's already on. I've driven several hundred yards with the handbrake on. I didn't know that was possible.

Driving is easy. I've already done some. It's turning that's hard. South, where Jess lives, is to my right. I could go left and left and left. That, too, adds up to right. In his life, a man need never turn right, as long as he has the time. The woman in the car behind me honks her horn.

I look to the right, then to the left, then right again. Nothing helps. The turning is on a bend. I can't see enough of the road in either direction. The trick, I'm sure, is to do it fast. I launch into the middle of the highway, then turn the wheel, this way and that, at roulette speed, with much roaring and screeching, most of it from my mouth. I swerve. I almost mount the pavement. I would, wouldn't I? That's where I belong. It starts to rain. I press a button. My window opens. I try another. My seat moves back.

As the woman overtakes, she stares at me. Let her. Let the rain come through the window and get blown in my face. I'm telling myself a love story. Caroline Bliss is right, as always. Love stories are what we want. Here I am, at the end of my story, willing it to be about love.

When I pull up in the drive of her parents' house, when I stagger out the car, she'll throw her arms round my bleeding stump. Her eyes will fill with disbelief and pity. And love.

The dual carriageway ends, just before the Aldeburgh turn-off. Now there's a line of cars behind me. I refuse to speed up. This journey's not the race to the airport at the end of *Shoe Shop*. (Jack's part, incidentally, was taken by Kevin Osborne.) I must get to Jess before the baby is born. I have months.

Still searching for the windscreen wipers, I turn on the winkers. (Danger lights? Safety lights?) It couldn't be better. Those winkers will tell the other drivers that I have a problem. They'll think I'm overheating or running out of fuel. They'll feel sorry, never guessing that my problem is, I can't drive.

'Drive round and get her.' A man undertakes Herculean tasks

to prove his love for a woman. He swims rivers, climbs mountains, conquers the Beast. What greater Beast can a man conquer than his own inadequacy?

Turning right off the A12 at high speed, to avoid oncoming traffic, I mount the grass verge and bounce back down on to the road. No one sees. No one complains. No one dies. Had I been driving in Golders Green, I could have wiped out a Phil Cohen. In Hackney, it could have been Mr O'Fock, as he rifled a corner bin. That's the joy of rural England. There are fewer people, with more space between them.

At last, I find the windscreen wipers, just before it stops raining. I travel at twenty miles an hour, in second gear, till I reach Johnny and Ginty's house in Great Glemham. Nobody stares at me. Nobody's interested. This is the ordinariness that I crave. This is what Jack saw in me: the potential to be ordinary. I want to fulfil my potential.

I arrive at seven twenty-five.

Jess sees me from her bedroom window. She comes out of the house in her nightdress and dressing gown and wellington boots. It's too wet for slippers. I look at her and think: that's two people.

I get out the car. 'I drove round to see you,' I say.

'You're mad. You could have killed yourself.'

I construe this for signs of love. Of course I find one. She's angry that I could have killed myself, not that I could have killed others.

She walks round the car, inspecting it for damage.

Then she looks me in the eye.

'God. This is so unlike you,' she says. I smile. It's a compliment, no question.

* * *

So far, I've written fifty thousand words of *Our Jack*, subtitled: *Jack Harris – by the Women Who Loved Him*. There are two photos on the front cover. One is of Jack and Rita on their wedding day. The other is of Caroline Bliss, sitting alone on a bench in Hyde Park.

I meet the women twice a week, in a hotel in Covent Garden. They're nice to me. They fuss if my cappuccino's not right. Rita, last week, rang room service to complain about my ham and mozzarella and rocket ciabatta, which she (not I) decreed was under-hammed.

I'm undemanding and malleable and discreet. It's their story, I keep reminding myself, not Jack's or mine. This manuscript, the one you're reading now, is our story. I can refer to it whenever I'm hungry for (what I consider the) truth.

I'm earning a dad's wage. That's what matters.

I interview them, sometimes separately, sometimes together. I then transcribe the material and put it in chronological order. I often pad it out with lightweight historical allusions, such as *on the day Mrs Thatcher came to power*. Though my name is nowhere in the book, my knowledge of Jack is everywhere. I add telling details, such as Jack's attempt to get Neil Diamond to shake hands with his mother. Sometimes, I throw in a scene from his childhood, pretending he described it to Rita in pillow talk. *I always hated authority. One time the teacher told me to tuck my football shirt in my shorts.*

I never forget it's a love story, though. The women, in their different ways, are romantic heroines.

The man Rita loved and fought for was unfaithful then died. Now she is telling her story, along with his mistress. That makes her brave and generous, a woman with more love than bitterness in her heart.

Caroline Bliss is powerful and sexy, with a softness and lone-liness you don't at first suspect. She suffers. She's the woman who waits, waits on the bench for the man who may never come. (In the photo, of course, she's not waiting for anyone. It was taken long after his death. It's a photo of a woman publicising a book.)

The narrative voice changes from page (RITA HARRIS:) to page (CAROLINE BLISS:). Last week I came up with the idea of joint-narrative sections. They loved that idea.

RITA HARRIS AND CAROLINE BLISS: *Jack had his favourites among his guests. He really liked Phil Collins.*

And

RITA HARRIS AND CAROLINE BLISS: *Jack was always very tense the night before a show. Sex was the only thing that could relax him.*

Caroline Bliss, commissioner, author and subject of the book, is also in charge of the marketing. There's a Sarah, Sarah Hamilton, who's the marketing director. But I fear she'll find she's only pouring the milk.

Caroline Bliss says the line about sex will be perfect for the poster. It's sexy but not detailed; precisely what she ordered in the restaurant.

When *Our Jack* comes out, in June, I'll have written two books about Jack in a year. I hope not to write any more.

Now I'm an impending father, I have to give up cocaine. Norman and I tooted the script in a private, two-man party, one night in the dead days between Christmas and New Year's Eve. Remarkably, he'd never taken the stuff. After one line, he said nervously:

'I think I'm too old for this. Must I have more?'

I told him, yes, he had to have more. He thought hard before replying: 'Good'.

Jess and I got married in January. Norman offered to pay but I insisted (I insisted that Jack paid). The carrier bag was officially emptied.

We got married in Woodbridge Registry Office. I was so happy, I kissed Bob. To give him pleasure, we hired a Rolls-Royce Phantom, which he drove to the reception on Southwold Pier. He even wore a chauffeur's uniform, paying for it with his own money, though I (Jack) would have happily rented it for him. 'My pleasure, Dave. That's a hundred and fifty quid well spent!' he told me, in needless detail.

I could have worn that uniform myself; a week before the wedding, I passed my test.

Jess gave me a driving lesson, the day I drove to see her. She made me turn off the A12 and pull up in a parking place. Then she told me to lie on the back seat, while she bounced up and down on top of me. There was no need. As I later discovered, that doesn't form part of the test.

My mother died the day I passed, so I never had to tell her. I did tell her about the wedding, though. (She never met Jess. Jess offered many times but I always said no.)

I said, with slow, shy-Leonie diction:

'Mum, I'm getting married.'

There was a long pause before she replied. But then there was a long pause before she said anything, from that psychiatric hospital bed.

'Don't let her hurt you,' she said. Is that depression speaking, or maternal love?

We didn't buy the house in Westleton. We felt we should get away from Suffolk. Jess had to distance herself from her parents. I had to leave Yoxford. Deserved or not, I'd acquired an aura of weirdness. One Saturday afternoon, walking home, I saw Graham, who runs the post office, coming towards me. I waved. Not only did Graham ignore me, he crossed the road and looked in the butcher's window till I was safely inside my cottage. He knows I know he's a vegetarian.

Here we are then, Jess and I, in a maisonette in South London, the finest we could afford. We're in Tooting, a few streets from Helga and Steffi's flat, though I couldn't say in which direction.

Long-term, the prospects are good. Jess is going to give life drawing classes in Norman's house. Kevin Osborne, who's now part of Norman's circle, has already signed up.

Osborne – his friends call him Osborne not Kevin – is the funniest person I've ever met. He's like a funny bomb that can be detonated at any moment, by anything from a pair of unusually-shaped ears to an outbreak of avian flu. It's fantastic and exhausting. In his company, I probably say no more than five things an hour. But, for some reason, he loves them all, clapping his hands and laughing and booming *that's right!* in his Belfast accent.

He's already been asked, at thirty, to write his autobiography. He'd love it if I wrote it with him. He says I'd be perfect. I'm nice. I'm an experienced ghost. And he wouldn't fancy me in a million years, so it will never end in tears.

Jess goes into hospital tomorrow to have the baby induced, which means that we know the baby's birthday – February 26th, 2005 – before we know his or her gender or weight.

We know one more thing. The baby's father is Jack. The baby's father is Jack.

We've always known that. By 'we', I mean you the reader and I the writer. Anyone who's written or read this far has known it since 'pregnant'. I was officially told on the day of the driving lesson. Why haven't I written it down till now? Perhaps because the more I write, the more I think of my life as a fiction. Fiction, my father thought, was whodunnit and who-slept-with-whom. That's why I've held back the information. For the sake of the ending. For the last-page thrill. Whodunnit and who-slept-with-whom? The answer, to both, is Jack.

The baby was conceived after a lunch at a restaurant in Buckinghamshire to celebrate the completion of the portrait. The incident took place on some grass. Jess doesn't know the address of the grass. But it wasn't on Jack and Rita's land.

After the lunch and before the conception, Jack told Jess he was infertile, which may well have been true, until it wasn't. It's a phenomenon: a couple adopts because they can't have children then they find, miraculously, that they can conceive after all. In Jack's case, it was simply a matter of altering the couple.

Jack died. She decided she'd never tell me about the sex. There was no need. Jack was gone. She did say she'd done me 'a terrible wrong', but she knew I'd take that as a reference to her abandonment of me, on that road in Westleton.

Then I was commissioned to write his biography. She was distressed. Jack was not gone. On the contrary, he was the work to which I went every day. He was my office, shop and factory.

Against that, she was delighted for me, for us. I'd broken free of the bookshop. I was earning good money. I was no longer stuck. When Jack talked about me, that's what he said – I was a man who was stuck because I was 'too intelligent'.

Then, within days of my 'starting' the book, she found she was pregnant. She thought about abortion. I'd always said I didn't want children. How much less would I want Jack's? She ached to confess everything to me but I was preoccupied and remote. Why couldn't I see how unhappy she was? (Some of this stuff, Jess admits, is soupy and melodramatic. She hates the idea of presenting herself as a sufferer. I love her for that.)

Then she read some of the book. Why would she give up a baby for me, a man determined never to make anything of himself? She'd rather be on her own with her baby, than have me drag her down.

Jess and Johnny and Ginty and Norman – please, not Bob – decided that a move to Norman's house would give the baby a good start in life. At any rate, a good address.

Jess made that yes-and-no phone call. She says that as she dialled my number, she intended to tell me who the father was. She can't explain why she didn't. I know, though, from my own experience. Secrecy has its own momentum.

Jess sometimes takes my hand for no reason and I know why: she's wanting me not to feel bad about Jack, our baby's co-author.

She had sex with him because she was lonely and he was lonely and he kept telling her how beautiful she was. She found him monstrously egocentric, then suddenly tender. The tenderness was all the more beguiling, given how surprising it was. He often made her feel mad, as when he told her he wanted his dad in the portrait. Sometimes the madness made her feel capable of anything, like sex on the grass after lunch. She thought she had an aversion to sleeping with married men. She thought she couldn't have sex so soon after lunch but she'd only had a salad, as the cocaine had suppressed her appetite.

She told him it wouldn't happen again. She felt she was using him to get away from me. He was a 'portal'.

* * *

341

Don't assume I hate Jack. On the contrary. He thought Jess was wonderful, with which I agree. I salute him as a man who made things happen. He's responsible for most of the things that are happening to me.

I wanted, I admit, to be free of him. Those feelings no longer apply. I'll never be free of him. He's family now. What other word is there? He's the father of our baby. I want to think only good of him.

He looked after me. He took me in when I was low. He felt sorry for me, sorry Jess had left me, sorry she'd had sex with another man who, admittedly, was him.

Goodbye, Jack. You died without knowing you'd fathered a child. You'll never hold your baby. I will.

Goodbye, Jack. I'll see you tomorrow, somewhere in the baby's face.

Two things recur, as I study the London A–Z to plan my route to the hospital. (I'm an intensely nervous driver. I'm going to keep the BABY ON BOARD sign till the child leaves home.)

First, Melinda Spears thought Jack and I would make the perfect man, which augurs well if the baby's a boy.

Second, there's Johnny's couplet:
Seeds of greatness, seeds of despair
What fruit is there?
We shall find out.

At what age do you tell your child their father is not their father? At what age do you tell them their father is a famous dead chat show host? How old do *you* have to be to cope with telling them this?

Johnny and Ginty and Norman (Bob doesn't know) will guard the family secret. We want our child to hear it from us.

That's why this memoir is going in a drawer. The information must be locked up until it's time to release it.

Only Jess has read it, apart from me. She likes it. She finds it truthful. She hopes that, in fifteen or twenty years' time, our child will read it too.

Jack's ashes are next to his father's, in the Garden of Rest at Golders Green Crematorium. His father is immortalised by an azalea. Jack is a philadelphus.

One day, I'll go there with my son or daughter. I might even say a few words. By that time, some liberal Rabbi may have come up with a Prayer for the Real Father of My Child.

If not, I suggest:

Good evening, Ladies and Gentlemen, my name's Jack Harris, welcome to the Holloway Tavern. We've got a great evening's comedy lined up for you tonight. Before we begin, just a couple of announcements. There are Fire Exits over here and over there. So, if there's a fire, stay in your seats and the Fire will leave through the Exits.

www.vintage-books.co.uk